THE FESTIVE AND THE FURIOUS

THE FESTIVE AND THE FURIOUS

BOOK 1

HEIDE GOODY

IAIN GRANT

1

CHARLOTTE

"Frapper!"
"Jizzock!"
"Cheggs!"
"Scurd!"

Charlotte was auditioning some new swear words. Scurd had a good, snarling mouth-feel. She tried it some more.

"Scurd, scurd, scurd," she sang in a high and happy voice as she navigated a junction.

Charlotte's problem was that she had a lot of powerful emotions, and her brain had not found a proper or safe outlet for those emotions. She recognised perfectly well that she had a problem and was working on it.

That's why she tried to work on her swearing before she got to work.

The problem was, the reason why people used the swear words they did was that they were *good* swear words. Scurd kind of felt good but it was the artificial methadone of the swearing word.

"Sorry, scurd," she said. "Sometimes only a fuck will do."

Hedgelord Garden Centre was out on the A31, just past the double roundabout with the big supermarket, on a plot of land that, if it wasn't a garden centre, would just be the corner of yet another field. It was a ten minute drive from Charlotte's home on the edge of town. Her mum's house was a ten minute drive in another direction. Their church (or at least what had been their church before the unfortunate incident with the candlestick and the pigeon) was a ten minute drive in yet another direction. Rajput's curry house was ten minutes in a fourth direction.

If the rest of the world ended tomorrow – be it the End of Days or a zombie apocalypse – Charlotte's world could shrink to that ten minute radius and she would barely notice.

If it was a zombie uprising, she'd be coming to Hedgelord first. For survival gear, post-apocalyptic farming supplies and handheld weaponry it would be her one-stop shop. She'd already thought about it, several times. No actual firearms were available on site, but she'd heard that Luka, who worked in the outdoor plant section, had connections with gangster types and could lay his hands on guns if required. For the purposes of zombie-squishing she would have to rely on the nice solid baseball bat she kept in her car boot, and which she used as another part of her self-devised therapy on an almost daily basis.

She allowed herself four more lusty and enthusiastic 'fucks' before she tried to stop for the day.

The huge car park was nearly empty first thing in the

morning and she parked in a space close to the entrance. The weather was wet and mild for the first of December. It was not yet Christmas in the outside world.

"Fuck," she finished before stepping out of the car. If she was good then that would be her last expletive of the day.

She swiped her smart watch and opened the Curse Count app.

The counter read:

Fuck: 0
  Shit: 0
  Bitch: 0
  Dickhead: 0
  Asshole: 0
  Damn: 0
  Hell: 0

THERE REALLY WAS an app for everything.

Beyond the green wire mesh fencing separating the car park from the outdoor section of the shop she saw Gallagher piloting an orange wheelbarrow down one of the paths. Literally piloting it. The scrawny tattooed man sat in the barrow, a plastic plant pot on his head, a length of bamboo cane between his knees as a joystick. He angled left, and white-bearded Luka, providing the forward locomotion and (Charlotte thought she could hear) the airplane sound effects, steered the barrow down a side path.

For a round chap who must be nearly sixty, Luka could

push a barrow at a fair lick. He was European – Swedish, Russian, something like that – and Charlotte didn't know if the gangster rumours about him were true or just lazy racism.

The barrow jet fighter disappeared along a canyon of potted fir trees and on towards the maze of display sheds and garden offices.

"Fuck me," she whispered in disbelief.

Her smart watch vibrated.

"Oh, no, that doesn't count! Fuck!"

It vibrated again.

Two 'fucks' and she'd not even got inside.

Clamping her mouth shut, Charlotte went indoors and straight to the Pagoda Tea Rooms, which was inside the huge central shop, not a pagoda in sight. She put a cup under the coffee machine and pressed the cappuccino button.

"Charlotte, are you in charge of elves?" called Sophie from the cash register.

"That depends," said Charlotte.

"I don't mean real elves. I'm not saying you're in charge of real elves."

"Good," said Charlotte, bringing her drink to the till. "But it still depends."

Sophie had a lined face but the wide bright eyes of a china doll, made all the wider and brighter by heavily made-up lashes. The overall effect was one of almost constant bewilderment and surprise.

"Am I in charge of the elves globally? Yes," said Charlotte. "Elves come under seasonal promotions and therefore are under my purview. But as for hiring, firing and general capering, Daffyd deals with that. And he works for me."

Sophie nodded as though she understood. She held a poster with the bold red heading of WANTED ELVES. Charlotte wished Daffyd had put a colon in that because it just looked like it was a police request for assistance with finding fugitives.

"I hear they're hiring again," said Sophie. "After that *unfortunate business with Alejandro.*" She mouthed the last words.

"Please don't whisper it," said Charlotte. "It makes it sound like he's been put on a register. His work visa had run out."

"Right you are. I'll speak to Daffyd."

"You're thinking of applying for elf duties?"

"Well, you're never too old," said Sophie with a smile.

As far as elfing was concerned, Charlotte suspected you very much could be. "Or you could focus your energies somewhere else, perhaps?"

"No," said Sophie. "With my poor Douglas at death's door, I really need to take my mind off things."

"Oh, I'm sorry to hear that," said Charlotte as Sophie waved away her attempts to pay for the coffee.

"And when you say in charge of the elves globally...?" said Sophie.

"I do just mean here," Charlotte clarified.

"Right you are."

Tom Eccles appeared next to Charlotte before she could move away from the till.

"Your bauble coach and horses is blocking my loading bay," he said.

"That sounds like code," she said, having no idea what he was on about.

"Your bauble coach and horses. My loading bay. I have a big consignment of farmhouse kitchen jams coming in this morning, and if your coach and horses is still there when it arrives there will be..." His mouth twitched.

"A jam?" said Charlotte.

"Hell to pay. I was going to say, 'hell to pay'. I just didn't know if it offended your religious sensibilities."

"Christians can say hell, Tom. We're quite fond of the word." Her watch buzzed. Hell was okay though. Perfectly fine. 'Hell' and 'Bloody' were the watered down methadone against the crack-cocaine profanities she needed to shake.

Tom Eccles was the retail manager at Hedgelord Garden Centre. Charlotte was marketing and seasonal promotions. In the massively unclear staffing structure at Hedgelord they were possibly of the same rank. At this time of year, if it had tinsel or it or went "Ho ho ho" it was her domain; if it hadn't or didn't, it was his.

"I know nothing about a bauble coach and horses," she said.

"Cameron wants to talk about it," said Tom.

Charlotte groaned. "Didn't even get to drink my bloody coffee."

2

CHARLOTTE

Cameron Clasp's office was on the first floor of the shop building. It was, it appeared, the sole reason Hedgelord had any sort of upper floor. The office occupied a square turret or pavilion on top of Hedgelord, giving Cameron a panoramic window view of his entire kingdom. Charlotte entered his office to find him gazing out between Venetian blinds at the plant section.

He was wearing a blue blazer, cream trousers, and a colourful cravat under a white shirt. She liked to think of this as his 'little sailboat captain' outfit. She had wondered if he owned a little captain's hat somewhere. He had the complexion and mildly startled hair of a man who spent a lot of time out in the elements, probably with a glass of something expensive in his hand.

"Good morning, Cameron."

He glanced round at her. "Merry Christmas, Cameron."

"I'm Charlotte."

"I'm Cameron. And you say Merry Christmas. First of December, no? Your work starts here."

Charlotte felt a compulsion to correct him. The work for Hedgelord Garden Centre's Christmas celebrations – the grottos, the decorations, the reindeer, the café Christmas menu, the stock choices, the press coverage, the food hall seasonal items, the charity sponsorships, the primary school events – it had all started long ago. In fact, it would only be two weeks until she attended the Xmas Expo trade show for next year's events. She did not correct him. Correcting him contained the hope of changing him and that was something she had given up long ago.

"It's like you say," she said.

"Must be your favourite time of year."

"I'm quite glad when it's all over," she said.

"Oh, I thought you were one of them."

"One of...? Oh, that. I do value that aspect of things. But I'm a God is for life not just for Christmas sort of woman."

"Of course, of course," he said, bowing his head in an overly earnest manner. "Never got the hang of it myself. But must be lovely. The angels, the shepherds, the..." He waved a hand meaninglessly in the air and then gestured at her takeout coffee cup. "...The gingerbread lattes."

"All of that," she agreed. "Symbolically important."

"And this year we're going to pound Bloomers into the fucking ground, aren't we?" he said, and pointed out of the window to the side.

Bloomers was another garden centre of similar square footage and appealing to the exact same customer base. It was less than half a mile away, the buildings visible from

Cameron's office. Cameron had put a white cardboard picture frame on the window so that, from his desk, he could see Bloomers through it. Someone had written the word 'Twats' on the frame and put some gold star stickers around it. Charlotte had never asked if Cameron had done that himself or told an underling to do it. Whoever it was had put in some effort.

"Pounding the competition very much the intention," said Charlotte. "We have superior grottos this year. Our social media videos are already cued up."

"Reindeers?"

"Arriving day after tomorrow. Gallagher will be looking after them."

"I thought I saw him flying a wheelbarrow through the Christmas trees."

"Yes. But he has a way with animals. And Nick Bellingham is coming in today."

"Nick Bellingham?"

"The local resident with the massively decorated house. Guinness book of records. That man. We're going to make sure he goes away with Hedgelord lights. Get ourselves in the papers."

"Brilliant."

"Cameron?"

"Yes?"

"Tom says there's a bauble coach and horses in the loading bay."

"Ah, yes. Thought I'd give you a hand. Thought we'd have a winter princess display at the entrance. It's a splendid, illuminated coach and horses, very striking. If we get a gorgeous young actress to do some meeting and greeting in a fancy frock then so much the better."

"The entrance is already decorated. We've got Bruin the Bear. The animatronic polar bear we bought two years ago. Very popular."

"No. No. It's winter princesses this year. Kids will love it. Polar bear? What were you thinking? People see a polar bear and they think ice caps melting. They think dead baby seals."

"Do they?"

"They think fuck me, that thing's going to eat my face off. And 'Bruin'?"

"Bruin?"

"Latin. *Bruin*. Means fucking 'brown'. Oh, it's a car crash image-wise. What do they teach in schools these days? No, winter princesses is the way forward. Your little elves can set it up before lunch, yes?"

"Message received and understood," said Charlotte. If she had given full vent to her feelings it would have been "Message fucking received and fucking understood," but she was going to have a good day and kept it in.

She fixed a smile onto her face and went to speak with Tom about moving the polar bear.

Charlotte went round to the loading bay to check out the bauble coach and horses. Tom was there, shouting orders at someone who was trying to unload a lorry.

"Look at this thing!" said Tom. "It's slap bang in the middle of everywhere. We can't even get a pallet truck through."

"Yeah, I'm just catching up with events myself," said Charlotte. "I need someone to get rid of the polar bear at the entrance. Any chance you could get Luka and Gallagher to do it? If we get that out of the way, the coach can go in its place."

Tom sighed. "Getting that pair to do anything other than what they feel like doing is a challenge at the best of times. When you say you want it getting rid of...?"

"In the skip. Its animatronics broke last year so we might as well just sling it."

Charlotte ignored Tom's continued huffing. She suspected he was slightly scared of the two plant area men in the way that some educated types were always scared of the honest working classes. Tom much preferred it when he could leave them well alone.

Charlotte concentrated on the bauble coach in front of her. Apparently this was now her star attraction. It was eye-catching, definitely. The coach on its own was around the size of a Smart car, and it was constructed entirely from translucent twirly rods, intended to resemble wrought iron. The rods had LED lights built into them, for maximum impact after dark, so Charlotte needed to risk assess whether crashes in the car park from blinded drivers were likely to increase.

The horses were made from a similar material. Their improbably bouffant manes splayed high above the ground, making them much taller than the coach. In fact, the horses took up loads more room than the coach itself. The front ones were in a dramatic rearing pose, wide mouths chomping at bits that had yet to be fixed in place. Why on earth were there six horses? Charlotte examined the harnesses and wondered if it might be possible to split them up. Surely a coach only needed two horses? She could put the other four somewhere else. There was a very real danger that this display was just too big to go by the entrance.

"You reckon we could separate these horses?" she said to Tom.

"Probably not," he said. "It looks as if they are all wired together."

"Well, see what Luka and Gallagher can come up with." Charlotte walked away. "Fuck," she whispered. She thought she'd got away with it, but her wrist buzzed as another expletive was added to her tally.

3

GALLAGHER

Gallagher made a hard right into Terracotta Canyon, fighting the G-forces of his wheelbarrow fighter as they then twisted left into Birdbath Alley.

"Coming into land at base," puffed Luka behind him.

"Aw, really?"

"Or engine one will suffer catastrophic failure," said Luka, wheezing.

Gallagher nodded sadly and pushed his bamboo joystick forward and touched down, the barrow's rear legs scraping into the gravel.

Luka let go and stepped unsteadily away. "Textbook landing."

"Thanks, mate," said Gallagher. He swivelled in the barrow to face Luka.

The big guy was gulping in huge breaths. He slipped off the sheepskin jacket he wore over his green overalls and wiped his sweaty pink forehead with the back of his hand. "It is my exercise for the day."

"Appreciate it." Gallagher, still sitting with knees raised in the barrow, looked at the world about him. The rows upon rows of plants and pots and stupid garden ornaments. "But what's the point?"

Luka threw out a hand. "You are not cheered up by Wheelbarrow Top Gun?"

"I can't live in a wheelbarrow, mate," said Gallagher.

Luka nodded. He understood this as a truly profound statement. "It would be hard. No roof."

"If it rains, I'd turn it over and hide under it."

"No toilet."

"I've got a wheelbarrow. Always on the move. Crap and go."

Luka frowned. "You want to live in a wheelbarrow?"

Gallagher slipped his plant pot crash helmet off and tossed it away over the nearest shed. "I'm fucking thirty-nine, mate."

"You think wheelbarrow living is a young man's game?"

Gallagher huffed and watched his breath mist in the air. "Thirty-nine. I'd like to live somewhere that isn't an utter shithole. I'd like to be able to earn a living where every last penny doesn't go on rent and heating and bloody council tax."

"Do not pay tax," said Luka.

Gallagher felt the familiar swirling queasiness in his stomach that Wheelbarrow Top Gun had alleviated for a few minutes. The queasiness wasn't just bills and the fact he was paying rent on a damp plaster box above a Chinese takeaway which had black mould in the bedroom with more oomph and ambition than he did. The queasiness wasn't just the lack of money and the credit cards, seven of them, that he was only partially managing to ignore. The queasiness wasn't just the fact he hadn't touched a woman in what felt like months, and when he looked at the gaunt spectre of Death in the mirror every morning he couldn't imagine a woman wanting to touch him ever again. The queasiness was no single one of those things. It was all of them, along with the powerlessness, the shame, the despair.

"I'm drowning, mate," he said. "I'd fucking kill myself if I had the guts."

"Hey, hey," said Luka. He bent over and gripped Gallagher's shoulders with those powerful fatherly fingers. "Do not talk that way. You have so much to live for."

"Like what?"

Luka's hands stayed where they were, as did the half-smile. Only Luka's eyes twitched as he searched for an answer. Whatever that answer was, it was too slow in coming.

"Fuck," Gallagher gasped miserably.

There was the crunch of footsteps on gravel. Tom Eccles, the retail manager, rounded the fibreglass deer and tree trunk birdbath at the end of the row.

"Ah, this is where you two are," he said.

Luka stood upright. "This is where we are."

Tom had been in the same year as Gallagher at school, but the years had treated them differently. Tom didn't look like a dried-up husk of a man. He didn't look like anything. He had a schoolboy's haircut and an unfinished schoolboy's face – like God hadn't decided what kind of a man he was going to be yet.

Gallagher was prepared to bet that Tom didn't live in a foul box of an apartment which stank of cooking fat and prawn crackers. He was prepared to bet that Tom didn't share his bedroom with an aggressively expanding patch of black mould. And he didn't have half a dozen credit card companies fighting each other to get their knives into him.

"What is this?" said Tom, gesturing at Gallagher's ride.

"It's a wheelbarrow," said Gallagher. "The Maxi-Barrow 2000. Forty-nine ninety-nine."

Tom frowned and looked at Luka.

"It is a wheelbarrow," said Luka.

"I meant..." He did circling motions to indicate the situation.

"Team building," said Luka. "Morale boost."

"I assume you have actual work to do."

"We do all the work."

"Those pallets of compost are still by the landscape gardening office. You said you would move them."

"The pallet trolley is broken. I am fixing it this afternoon."

Luka had a gift. He said things with such simplicity that it was hard to refute them. Tom could have asked why they weren't moving the compost by hand, a bag at a time. Tom could ask why the repairs needed to wait until the afternoon. But Luka had given an answer and Tom's mouth just worked silently and his coward's gaze was unable to lock onto them.

"I've got something I need you to do," said Tom.

Luka took out a tiny spiral-bound notepad and a pencil

from the single pocket over his chest. The notepad had a picture of a pink unicorn on the front. He licked a dirty thumb and flicked through the pad. He paused as he read something he'd written and then flicked on. He looked at Tom. "Go."

"The polar bear at the entrance to the shop needs to go," said Tom.

"Polar bear?"

"The big polar bear that welcomes grotto customers. The model."

Luka stuck out his bottom lip and shook his head. "Which polar bear?"

"It's the only polar bear we've got, Luka. It's..." He put his hand up like claws. "Polar bear."

"Go where?" said Luka.

"It needs breaking down and binning. You can do that. Take it apart. Put it in the skip. And then we can get Charlotte's bauble coach and horses out of the loading bay."

Luka put pencil to paper and wrote slowly. "Polar bear."

Luka finished and smiled at Tom. Luka's smile was part of his gift. His smile was warm and told you everything was okay. It put a seal on everything he said.

"You'll get onto it immediately," said Tom.

"I have written it down," said Luka.

Tom waited and looked at them. If he expected them to leap into action, he was mistaken. "I am your line manager," he said eventually. "You know that, right?"

Gallagher looked at Luka. Luka looked at Gallagher. They then both looked at Tom. Tom broke first. He backed away, irritated. He waved a finger at the wheelbarrow again, never quite managing to directly point at Gallagher.

"This... This is not..." His boy's face twitched again. "Okay?" he said and disappeared.

Gallagher listened to the receding crunch of feet on gravel. "Is he really our line manager?"

Luka was looking at his girly notepad. "Polar bear," he intoned.

4

ANIKA

Anika Chowdhry crossed the dual carriageway by the roundabout and then walked across Hedgelord car park.

Anika hadn't really meant to come to the garden centre. Surely, no one under the age of thirty ever deliberately went to a garden centre. Going to garden centres was in her mind, part of that large blob of activities which indicated your life was over and you were now merely ticking off the days until death. Other activities in the same category included going on cruises, taking up bird-watching, and being really passionate about how the cutlery drawer was organised.

Anika was nineteen and knew that life after thirty was either about having children and waiting for death, or just waiting for death. She had yet to see any evidence to the contrary. And she had no plans to have any children. If her own parents were anything to go by then the Chowdhrys should never be allowed to have children.

What had started as a simple conversation about her life choices and university course had escalated into a full-blown row. Her mum had actually used the words, "Don't throw your life away" and then followed it up with the classic "While you're under my roof, you'll do what I say!" (while her doormat of a dad just stood there, unable to take sides, take the *right* side). Anika had to get out from under said roof and she stormed off at top speed.

It was one of those towns where you didn't have to walk far before you ran out of town. Twenty minutes of walking, earbuds in, listening to Nothing But Thieves at full volume, she realised she would have to go home at some point. Especially if she was serious about not going back to uni. And going home to that angry house probably meant going back with some sort of peace offering.

She hit upon the idea of Christmas decorations. The Chowdhry Christmas effort involved a tired little plastic tree and a several strings of foil decorations that were older than Anika. New decorations would be a good peace offering, but the strings of fairy lights in the supermarket were way too expensive, so now here she was, entering the elder-zone that was the local garden centre.

She was immediately blasted with a sense of wonder, embarrassment and irritation. Wonder because this place had gone completely overboard with Christmas decorations in the first section. Row upon row of icicle-style lights hung down from a dark ceiling. It was like seeing stars in a midnight sky. It was like catching the first sight of winter snow in the air. Below there was a stand of nearly life-size deer, executed in fuzzy white plastic, like creatures composed of pure frost. And then, off to the side, was a whole display table full of little pottery buildings, lit from within: houses, post offices, churches, pubs, all with snowy roofs; together creating a completely saccharine sweet but nonetheless wondrous Christmas town.

The whole scene was a direct punch to the feels, a transportation back to childhood Christmases. And then the embarrassment and irritation hit. It was embarrassing that she could be so easily pulled into this child-like wonder, and it was irritating that her anger with her parents could be so simply dashed aside by some cheap decorations and low lighting. More peeved than ever, she picked up a box of the icicle fairy lights.

"Fifteen quid? Jesus Christ!"

She only had to glance at the little pottery houses in the Christmas village to know they were going to be too expensive. But even so she was shocked at the price. Thirty pounds for a pottery thatched cottage.

"Fuck me," she whispered.

She spent enough time worrying about the impossibility of her ever getting her own place and getting on the property ladder. Turned out she couldn't even afford getting on the model property ladder.

This Christmas decoration plan was a bad idea. She didn't have money. Even at uni, every penny she was spending either came from loans or the bank of mum and dad. It seemed clear that if she was going to be serious about quitting the bloody awful computing degree and navigating her parents moodiness, then she needed a decent financial alternative.

There was some crashing and grunting further into the shop. She left the low-lit Christmas decoration onslaught and went through to find two men by the entrance to the shop proper, engaged in battle with a polar bear. This she had not expected.

The older one, white-bearded and barrel chested, had the huge display tilted over at an angle, holding the bear in place by its neck. He was doing this so that the younger junkie-looking one with tattoo sleeves running up both arms could work on its upraised paw. Around them, a snowy backdrop and surrounding lights had been pulled down. For all the world it looked like the two men were wrestling the bear: one had it in a headlock so that the other could pin down its arm.

"Are you stealing this bear?" said Anika.

The younger one scowled at her. "Who would steal a bear?"

The older one said, in some Russian-ish accent, "The bear has to go. Surplus to requirements."

Anika still didn't get it. "Is this a climate change protest?"

"A what?" said the tattooed one, grunting as he tried to twist the bear's arm.

"You know, icecaps melting, bears starving to death."

"Do we look like Extinction Rebellion?"

She looked at their overalls and their shoes. As far as she could work out, most of the Extinction Rebellion and Just Stop Oil crowd were retired middle class people looking for something to do while they waited for death. The old guy might be Extinction Rebellion. Maybe he was a retired engineer or car salesman. The younger one looked like he'd be more at home lobbing bottles at the opposition fans on a football terrace.

"You're not Extinction Rebellion," she said.

"She is a clever girl," said the old one.

"What do you want?" said the younger one.

"Looking for Christmas decorations." She pointed at the lights that they had pulled down from the display but not yet turned off. "What's happening to them?"

"Skip," said the older one. "You want them?"

"Yes. Absolutely." She stepped up onto the display area, treading over a polystyrene ice-block. She unplugged the lights and spooled them quickly around her arm. "For free?" she said, checking.

"Free. Going in skip otherwise," said the older one.

"Thank you! When they ask me at the till..."

The old guy said, "Tell them, Luka said you could have them." He let go of the bear to put a hand on his chest. "Luka." He pointed at his colleague. "Gallagher."

Gallagher was wobbling too much under the weight of the bear to offer any gestures or words.

Anika backed away with her loot and hurried off before they changed their minds.

This was excellent! She'd scored some decent decorations at zero cost. That meant money saved. So the moment she saw a little café beyond a posh little food hall she decided she would be able to treat herself to a drink. A café gave her a reason to stay out of the house for at least another hour.

5

ANIKA

The cafe was self-serve apart from the hot plate area, where breakfasts were being served up to a small queue of pensioner types. Anika ignored that and went to the hot drinks machine and pressed for hot chocolate.

She took it to the till.

"You want squirty cream on that?" asked the cashier, an older woman with big eyes and bigger lashes.

"Cream sounds good."

The woman moved around to the counter bit and topped up Anika's mug with cream.

Back at the till the woman, whose nametag read *Sophie*, said, "What do you think the key qualities of an elf are?"

This was not the kind of question Anika expected to be asked. "Sorry?"

The woman, Sophie, showed her a job advertisement poster she had at the side of her till. "They're hiring again because *they had to get rid of Alejandro.*" She whispered the last bit conspiratorially.

"Alejandro?"

"*Couldn't work here anymore.*"

Anika frowned. "Sorry? Was one of the elves a paedophile?"

"That's what Charlotte said. How odd." The woman tapped the advert. "They need a CV if you want to apply."

Anika laughed briefly at the idea of a CV for an elf job, but then she looked at the poster properly and saw it said exactly that. "An elf CV. That's why you're asking about elf qualities. You want to know what skills they're looking for?"

"I've given it some thought," said Sophie. "I think that singing must be a part of it. You always hear lots of singing coming from the grotto. They'll need to be tech savvy, because they do that thing where they make the Santa photos appear inside snow globes and things like that. They probably have to have good knees with all that capering they do."

"I see." Anika thought perhaps these represented some areas where Sophie herself had concerns. Was she afraid of singing and technology? Did she suffer from knee pain? She was afraid to ask. "I bet they show you how to do the photo stuff, so I wouldn't worry too much about that."

Sophie looked uncertain. "Well yes. Sometimes, though, there are people who need showing things like that *a lot* of times. Apparently." She looked up and smiled. "Ah, here's someone who might know. This lady, Charlotte is in charge of elves. Globally."

Anika looked at the woman who approached the tills.

She was attractive in an angular, uptight kind of a way, but her face was dark with the kind of severity that reminded Anika of her own mother.

"Another coffee?" said Sophie.

"You counting?" said Charlotte.

"There's such a thing as too much."

"Like a legal limit? We've not even properly started the day and everything is ... not going well."

"Oh dear," said Sophie. "Charlotte, this young lady and I have elf questions."

Charlotte's gaze slid across Anika, barely noticing her. "Let's see. Yes, the elves are magical creatures. No, they're not Santa's slaves. No, Santa is not their captive. Yes, they're all happy and get paid holidays. Aren't you a little old to believe in elves?" she asked Anika.

"We meant about the job," said Sophie. "You know – that business where the elves get the Santa photos inside the snow globes? Is that really complicated? Is there training?"

Charlotte nodded in tired understanding. "This about the elf vacancy? The tech side is easy, you just have to not be a complete idiot."

"Right. So does that mean there's training?" Sophie asked again.

"There's training. Look, to be perfectly honest with you, we just need someone who will work hard and do a whole bunch of different things. Daffyd will explain what those are, but I wish I had a spare elf right now, things are getting away from me a bit today."

"Oh dear. I'd help, but I'm still on shift here," said Sophie.

"We'd be thrilled to see your application though," said Charlotte, picking up her drink.

Sophie beamed.

As Charlotte turned to leave, Anika blurted out. "I could do it!"

Charlotte turned back and stared. Sophie stared too.

Anika mustered a more coherent sentence. "Why not sign me up as an elf? I could come and help you right now."

Sophie looked shocked. "But have you even made a CV?"

"I'm here. That shows initiative and willingness. I'm finished with my uni studies for the term so I'm, you know, partially educated. You could give me a whirl."

Charlotte looked at her and then unclipped a radio from her belt. "Daffyd? Can you come to the café? I want you to check out an potential elf for me."

Anika did a little fist pump. Free decorations and maybe a new job. Oh, the smug look she'd be giving her parents when she got home...

6

GALLAGHER

The polar bear was proving to be more of a challenge that Gallagher expected.

It *was* eight feet tall and its innards full of some animatronic gubbins that made it twist its head and limbs when it was switched on, but it should have been easier to carry and dismantle.

It was now laid on the display stand, staring up at the ceiling. The penguin models, which had been gathered around its feet like joyful followers, now stood around his fallen body like frantic mourners, questioning the heavens as to who could have killed their big bear friend.

Gallagher regarded its face. "Why's it look so miserable?"

Luka shrugged.

"No seriously. If Baloo the bear can smile all the time, surely a polar bear can too?" Gallagher kicked the white stand. "Someone, somewhere in the world has the job of designing anima-fucking-tronic polar bears, and they decided this one should look miserable. What a waste."

"You would like a job like that?"

"Mate, I'm not even trusted with the woodchipper because I don't have my certificate."

"Certificate is easy. We should print you one."

Gallagher scowled because the certificate wasn't really the point.

"I helped put this together," said Luka, patting the polar bear's big chest.

"And now we're taking it apart," said Gallagher. "Circle of life."

Luka nodded. "I killed a polar bear once."

Gallagher looked aside at him. "No, you didn't."

"Bare hands."

"No, you fucking didn't."

Luka gave him a sincere nod. "I did."

Gallagher scratched his tattooed neck. "This is some Cold War Eastern European bullshit. You think because you've got that accent and I believe your stories about communist crap and the Brotherhood of Gangsters or whatever—"

"I killed a polar bear," Luka insisted. "Edinburgh Zoo. Nineteen ninety-seven."

"Edinburgh Zoo?"

"Papers covered it up."

Gallagher snorted. "Whatever."

Luka slapped Gallagher's shoulder with the back of his hand. "You think you can mock? What would you do when faced with a polar bear?"

"I would let it kill me. I'd stick my head in its mouth. And you didn't fight a polar bear."

Luka's expression was one of sad disapproval. "You have no idea. Situation like that? Adrenaline kicks in."

"Nah, pretty sure that didn't happen. You got drunk up in Edinburgh didn't you? Got in a fight with a haggis or something."

Luka slammed a hand hard into the fallen polar bear's midriff as though delivering a killing blow. "No! Listen to what I am telling you. The will to survive makes you act when faced with genuine danger. Actual polar bear would make you shit your pants!"

"So that's what you mean by 'act'? Shitting my pants?"

Luka rolled his eyes with impatience. "You shit your pants and *then* you find out whether you a fight or flight kinda person. Is an important thing to know about yourself. Me, I am a fight person."

Gallagher shook his head. "This another one of your bullshit personality tests? You're worse than those magazines for teenage girls. I was stupid enough to buy into that one where you said you don't really know a person 'til you see them blind drunk."

"We learn true nature of a person with the outer layers removed," nodded Luka, his smile wide. "I was right, wasn't I?"

"Fucked if I know. I spent the night on the compost heap. I was in no fit state to learn deep truths."

"So, you going to do this or not?"

"Eh? Do what?" Gallagher wondered if he was expected to go to Edinburgh and break into the zoo.

"We use this polar bear as tool for you to confront your fears. See what you are made of. We move this and then you give me an hour to prepare."

"I think we've established we can't move it."

"We use pallet truck."

"I thought that was broken."

"Maybe I've fixed it," said Luka. "We move it. I set up challenge. Give me an hour."

"Fine." Gallagher had stashed half a joint in one of the display gazebos. If he left Luka alone, Gallagher could have a smoke and maybe Luka would shut up about polar bears.

7

ANIKA

Anika soon found herself in the bizarre situation where she was being interviewed by two people at a table in the corner of the café.

Charlotte introduced a man called Daffyd. He was entirely bald and, because of this, at first glance he looked like an overgrown baby. However, his eyes were mirthless and stern. He scrutinised Anika in silence for longer than seemed polite.

"Right then." he said eventually. "Name."

"Anika Chowdhry."

"Age."

"Nineteen."

"Address."

"Collerthorne Avenue. You know, in town. Just down from St Stephen's church. The one with the big nativity scene outside."

"I know the one," said Charlotte in an oddly cold voice.

"Well, Miss Chowdhry, tell us what you'd have put on a CV if you'd been through the *correct* process," said Daffyd.

Anika felt that was a little harsh, when she'd just been trying to help with what sounded like an emergency, but she tried to rise to the occasion. "I'd have put my GCSEs and A Levels down. I got two As and B on my A Levels."

"Oh, a Smartypants," said Daffyd.

"And I'd have said that I'm currently enrolled at Nottingham Uni, but I'm having a bit of a re-think. Although I think you'd probably be more interested in when I helped out at the youth theatre group."

"Oh, good! Acting experience of any sort is a good thing," said Daffyd, making tiny marks on a piece of paper.

"Er yes," said Anika. She had actually worked on painting the set because her best friend had dragged her along for company, but it wasn't a lie if it didn't pass her lips, was it?

"Any other experience?" Daffyd asked.

"Um, no. Not really. I am a quick learner though."

Daffyd pursed his lips.

Charlotte leaned forward. "Anika, our mission statement is written on that wall over there. Please read it for us."

Anika read it aloud. "Hedgelord is dedicated to being the best garden centre possible, providing customers with the products, services and ideas they need to extend our loving community into their homes."

"Now what does that mean to you?" asked Charlotte.

Anika paused to digest the sentiment behind the words. She hesitated slightly and watched Charlotte for a reaction. "I think that the key word is 'community'. I guess it means that colleagues look out for each other as well as helping customers."

She knew she'd hit the mark, as a smile touched Charlotte's face for the first time since she'd set eyes on her.

"Very good. Give us a moment, would you, Anika?" said Charlotte.

Anika stood up and wandered to the window overlooking the outside plant area. She could see a paddock area fenced off in the middle, with a sign declaring the Hedgelord reindeer would be moving in very shortly. She wondered if the elves would get to interact with the reindeer, but decided no, they probably wouldn't. It crossed her mind that she had no idea what an elf would actually do. She should have asked.

She was called back to their table a few minutes later.

"Great news, Anika, we'd like to take you on as an elf," said Charlotte. "Daffyd will sort out the paperwork, and get you onto elf induction in the coming days."

"Elf induction?"

"The toughest training course outside of the Royal Marine Commandos," said Daffyd.

"In the meantime, if you can start immediately, I need you to tackle the display space near the entrance. I've got to find room for a bauble princess coach and a team of horses, heaven help us."

Daffyd pushed some paper across the table. "Fill these in please. I'll also need your size details for your elf outfit. You will want to accessorise and customise your outfit."

"Will I?"

"You most certainly will. If you need ideas, check out

our socials and see what the other elves do. Some of it's about basic layering." Daffyd patted his body and enunciated his words very clearly as if he was talking to someone who knew nothing about how to get dressed. "You'll want a colourful t-shirt or jumper to go under your dungarees. Maybe thermal undies if you're on outside duties. There's a pointy hat to wear, which you can decorate. Entry level stuff is badges and brooches. No slogans, obviously, and always go for festive colours. You can add baubles and tinsel to any part of your outfit. Fairy lights work nicely too. You need to sparkle, Anika, can you do that?"

"I can definitely do that," said Anika, wondering how she was going to manage customising an outfit when she hadn't even worked out how to tell her parents what she was doing.

"Oh! You'll need an elf name too. Very important," said Daffyd.

"An elf name."

"You know, something fun for the kiddies. Something like Sparkles, Snowflake or Snusk."

"Bless you," said Anika.

"No Snusk is a Norwegian word, means snow or something," said Daffyd. He frowned. "I think it was snow."

"I'll have a think, thank you," said Anika.

"I'll leave the paperwork here for you to fill in," said Daffyd. "Drop it off at Customer Services when you're done, and we'll clock you in so that you can go and sort the entrance display."

"Don't I need my outfit before I can start work?"

Charlotte gave her a penetrating look. "You don't need to

be dressed as an elf to move some pots and bags of compost out of the way."

"Right," said Anika.

Charlotte and Daffyd left her to it. Anika bent over her paperwork. Form-filling was like schoolwork. She could do that with ease.

The woman from the till, Sophie, eyes were wide in interrogation, appeared. "Well?"

"Er, yeah. I'm going to be an elf."

Sophie sighed. "I used to be young too, you know. Things come so much more easily to young people, don't they?"

"You're going to apply though, aren't you?" Anika asked.

"Making a CV seems like a lot of work. You know, computer work."

Anika saw a glimmer of possibility in the shape of someone who clearly hated technology. "How are you with decorating costumes? Apparently it's all part of the elf thing."

"Oh that's right up my street. Sewing, crafting, Christmas! I love anything like that. I used to make things for my Douglas, though there doesn't seem much point these days."

"I can see a way that we can help one another," said Anika. "How about I do your CV for you if you help me customise my elf stuff?"

Sophie's eyes grew even wider. "Oh. Yes please! I need to know your favourite colour pom poms, and how do you feel about sequins next to the skin?"

8

GALLAGHER

Gallagher flicked the switch to open and close the roof over the plant area. It was supposed to allow customers to browse the plant area under cover, while allowing rain to water the plants at other times, but it was a rare and hardy customer who braved the plant area in early December. If anyone had asked him, he was testing the mechanism; but the truth was he enjoyed turning the outside into the inside and then back again.

That enjoyment might have been enhanced by the joint he'd quietly enjoyed while waiting for Luka.

"Come with me," said Luka, appearing at his side. "To the skips."

"The skips?"

"We must not be seen."

Gallagher followed. The plant area was their place, but it was definitely not private. Customers might appear, even in December, and they both knew that Cameron, the old boss man, had a direct view from his office. The skips, however, were in the lawless gated wasteland existing between the building and the car park. They were screened off from casual scrutiny because waste disposal was never pretty.

"You will like this," said Luka. "You will like this very much."

However, whatever polar bear fighting experience Luka had planned was forestalled by the appearance of Tom Eccles. "There's still a big bauble coach in my loading bay," he said.

Gallagher looked at Luka.

"It is code," said Luka. "He is constipated."

"I'm not constipated," said Tom. "I asked you to get rid of the bear so you could then put the coach and horses in the entrance."

Luka solemnly took out his little pink unicorn notepad, licked his finger and flicked through the pages.

"Polar bear," he read. "No mention of big bauble coach."

"Do it. Do it now. Please," said Tom. "Charlotte wants everything to look nice. I've got a consignment of jam waiting to unload. And we've got an important customer coming in at any moment."

"Who?" said Gallagher.

"Nick Bellingham," said Luka. "World-record holder for most Christmas lights on a house. Minor celebrity."

"Right," said Tom. "So, if you wouldn't mind..." He swept his arms round to direct them back to the main building.

"But the bear..." said Gallagher.

"You can dismantle the bear later," said Tom.

"Yes. Later," said Luka.

9

ANIKA

Anika had clocked in. Actually clocked in. On her first job, ever. It felt like a power move, starting the clock on her earning potential. She felt good about it until she went to the entrance display space and realised she didn't have a true clue what she was meant to be doing.

The entrance space that had recently contained a bear was now empty. Princess coach and horses the manager woman Charlotte had said. That was fine, but if she needed to shift more stuff out of the way then she wasn't really sure where she was to put it. There were several boxes of artificial Christmas trees, bags of decorative pinecones, and some stacked terracotta plant pots. With no direction on what exactly what she was to do, she began hauling the pots, one by one, right out the front of the shop and hoped she wasn't putting them in a place people would trip over them.

"Oi, oi! Horse coming through!" cried a voice.

It was the two polar bear wrestlers, this time with a rearing white horse between them.

The younger one – Gallagher, that was his name – stopped with the horse's head over his shoulder and looked at Anika.

"What are you doing?" He glanced at the pots, several in and several out of the entrance area. "Are you stealing pots? Like very, very slowly."

"I work here now," she said.

"Really?"

"I'm an elf."

"Where's your elf hat?"

"I haven't got it yet. I'm meant to be clearing things so we can put a coach and horse display in here." She led the way through and came to the spot where the display needed to be. Gallagher looked at it contemplatively.

"What is occurring?" said the other man, Luka, from the rear end of the horse.

"We've got a new elf and not enough space for six horses and a carriage," said Gallagher.

Huffing, Luka dropped the back end of the horse and looked round at Anika.

"She is right. Not enough room for six horses. Maybe two?"

"What even are Christmas horses?" said Anika.

"Well. I am but a lowly plantsman," said Gallagher, "so I am not paid to know things. But I think the sequence of events went something like this." He looked to the sky as he sorted through events in his mind. "We had a polar bear on display here by the entrance and it did the job of looking massive and festive, then Cameron, the owner, decided a new display was needed, so he bought a winter princess coach and horses. Apparently that is a thing."

"Like *Frozen*," said Anika.

"It's a beautiful film," said Luka.

"And," continued Gallagher, "there's a customer we have to brown-nose every year because he gets in the paper. And we need all this doing before he arrives." He contemplated the space around them, "In the meantime, my colleague turned the rejected polar bear into a killing machine to test whether I'm a fight-or-flight guy, and I'm going to get a chance to sacrifice myself to its chainsaw claws as soon as this is done."

"It ... it's what?" said Anika.

"I'm at peace with death, to be honest."

"Buddy..." said Luka.

"No, it's all right. I think I'm just going to consolidate all my debts into one massive, messy, 'suicide by bear'."

"Buddy—"

"No, really. You've done a real good job of trying to cheer me up but—"

"Buddy, we need less of the chitter-chatter and more of the horse moving."

"Oh."

They angled the rearing beast round into one corner of the display area.

"We're going to fit two in here, max," said Gallagher.

"Two horses here then," said Luka. "The rest outside."

Anika tidied up around it some more while the men went and fetch the other rearing horse.

"Facing each other? Or both facing out?" said Luka.

"It's either going to look like they're fighting each other or about to trample the customers," said Gallagher. "We need to make it look festive."

"Well, dur, we give them antlers," said Anika, splaying her fingers around her head as mock antlers.

"Fuck me," said Gallagher with a smile. "Could do."

They both stepped around, casting a critical eye over the horses. They were made from some sort of tough white plastic, like a wireframe model.

Anika reached over for the one of the boxes containing fake Christmas trees. "Fake tree branch antlers. Pretend they're reindeer."

"Reindeer don't have manes," said Gallagher, patting the horse's extravagant neck hair.

"Check you out, the reindeer expert."

"If we give them big enough antlers, nobody will notice the manes," said Anika.

They worked together to transform the horses with extravagant antlers made from fake tree greenery.

"This doesn't look entirely shit," said Gallagher eventually, which was apparently a high compliment. "What's your name anyway?"

"I don't know," said Anika. "I still need to pick one."

"You do not know your actual name?" said Luka.

"Oh. Oh, my actual name is Anika. I thought you meant... I need to come up with an elf name."

"It is nice to meet you, Anika," said Luka. He said it with both a very sincere tone and with a roguish twinkle in his eye. Anika could well believe many a grey-haired lady would be swept off her feet by that kind of charm. "What is an elf name?"

"Apparently they all have names like Sparkles or Snowball or something. Someone called me Smartypants earlier. I'm wondering if that would suit."

Gallagher looked aside her. "Yeah, I reckon that seems about right."

"Uh – thanks?" she said.

Gallagher stepped back from the display and clapped his hands together in satisfaction. "Right, let's bring the coach and other horses round and work out where to put them. Then who wants to see me get fucked up by an animatronic bear?"

Anika shrugged. "Yeah, all right."

10

CHARLOTTE

Nick Bellingham came into Hedgelord during the early afternoon. Charlotte was tipped off by Karen on the tills when she saw his car pull up into one of the disabled bays.

Charlotte hurried to the entrance, glancing sideways at the animals which had replaced the polar bear display. For some reason, the bear had been replaced by two prancing horses with great fans of fir tree branches round their heads. They looked like Rio Carnival dancers, except with tree branch headdresses instead of feather ones. And they were horses. Quite angry looking horses. Charlotte couldn't tell if the overall effect was festive or not. It was too bloody weird for any assessment to be made.

Forcing herself to put it out of her mind, Charlotte focused on the customer coming in. She hung back slightly until record-breaking Christmas decoration fan Nick Bellingham was inside the building, then walked forward pretending she had just stepped out from the Customer Service desk.

"Good morning Mr Bellingham. Welcome to Hedgelord."

"Hello! Glad to hear you've got the Christmas tunes playing," he said, taking his hand off his wheelchair control to point at the speaker above. "It's the season of full immersion." He waggled his head so that his light-up reindeer antlers bobbled on his head.

Charlotte had trained herself not to listen to the ambient music during the festive season. When she heard those well-loved Christmas tunes for the first time in months, it brought a smile to her face, but by the twentieth loop round, they had definitely lost their charm. Beyond that it was like some sort of low level torture.

She forced a smile onto her face. "I know! Don't we all wish it could be Christmas every day, eh?"

"Very much! I've pimped my ride." Nick had decorated his motorised wheelchair with fairy lights and holly wreaths.

"Very nice," said Charlotte.

"We're early in the season. I'll break out the big guns in the fortnight before the big day," he said.

"Big guns?"

"Full Santa sleigh with reindeer."

Charlotte tried to picture it and failed. "That's going to be ... big?"

"I'm a big guy," he grinned, patting his belly.

"You really love Christmas, don't you? Now can I show you our range? I think you will be impressed."

"Ready to be impressed."

They went through the entrance into the main retail space past the rearing Christmas horses.

"Bold," said Nick. "Sort of a twist on the Welsh tradition of the Mari Lwyd?" he suggested.

"Ye-es?" said Charlotte, who had no idea what he meant.

"At least you've steered clear of the winter princess theme," said Nick. "It's everywhere, as if we're all tweeny girls." He rolled his eyes.

"You're right of course," said Charlotte, "but those tweens are a demographic that drives a lot of Christmas buying."

Nick nodded in acknowledgement. "I'm sure you know better than me. Not a fan myself."

Charlotte smiled. "Now I know your primary interest is the larger displays, but I wanted to show you this range of tree decorations we have in from a small artisan maker. We really want to support our local talent, so Angela Twinkle's Victoriana range is very special. Exclusive to Hedgelord, I believe."

"Erm, I don't think so. I'm pretty sure I saw those in Bloomers," said Nick.

Charlotte froze.

There were a great many factors making up the special magic of Hedgelord. She herself had written the vision and mission statements which were displayed at various points around the store. She'd erected them early one morning and everyone had assumed they'd come from Cameron Clasp, but she'd simply seen a gap and filled it. She liked to think she had cultivated a caring community amongst her colleagues.

In terms of the goods that they sold, there were only so

many manufacturers in the world, so Hedgelord kept their leading position by seeking out specialists and 'artisans' where they could. If Hedgelord offered a quality range that was unavailable elsewhere then they could justify their relatively high prices. If Bloomers were selling those same exclusive artisan goods she had worked so hard to source, then something had gone badly wrong.

Charlotte forced a smile onto her face and swallowed her anger. She would look into this later. "Bloomers? Really? Good for them. A quality artist like Angela will always attract attention, and Hedgelord are proud to say that they helped to give her a leg up. All part of our programme to give back to the local community."

As Charlotte said this, she could see Luka and Gallagher and the new elf, Anika, through the window, shunting the bauble coach towards the entrance. It was mounted on a single massive pallet, and it looked as though they were using two pallet trucks in tandem to move it.

"Would you excuse me for one moment, Nick?" Charlotte asked. "I just need to speak with someone. Take a look at our new range of lights, perhaps?"

She jogged around to the entrance and held up a hand to stop Luka and Gallagher. "Listen, will you do me a favour? Don't put the coach by the entrance until that car's gone? We've got a really important customer and apparently he hates the winter princess thing. We'll just keep the horses there on their own and leave the coach round the corner for a bit."

"Okay," shrugged Luka.

"Time to go deal with the bear," said Gallagher.

As the three of them left, Charlotte rushed back inside to catch up with Nick.

"I might need a few basic lights sets if you can do them at a good price," said Nick. "Bloomers have said they'll set me up a computer program to control multiple sets on a special timer."

"Oh, we've got light timers," she said.

"No, this one's special. LumaGrid synchronised light controller. Put out your grid of lights on your roof or dangling from the front of the house and they can also spell out words and messages. 'Slogan for the day' sort of thing. I'll probably have it right at the front, it should be a big draw. Got to get it up by the weekend."

"Oh, one of those. I saw them at the Christmas expo last year. It's not in the shops."

Nick jerked a thumb behind him. "Jack at Bloomers said he's got one and they're going to provide it for me. You know Jack?"

Charlotte clenched her jaw with annoyance. "Jack Hartigan? Yes. I know him. Great guy."

"Isn't he?" Nick grinned.

Charlotte made a decision, perhaps not taking enough time to think on it. She chose to lie. "The words and messages controller. The Lumalight controller—"

"LumaGrid," said Nick.

"Yes, that. I didn't want to say because we were keeping it hush hush. We've got a VIP offering, but it's not out in the shop for the general public."

"Oh? You've got it. Oh, well, then! Can you show me?"

"VIP offering," she reminded him. "I can show you very

soon. I'll set up a demo." Charlotte racked her brains, wondering where she would get such a thing. Bloomers could not be permitted to get there ahead of her.

"Well it will need to be in the next couple of days, otherwise I'll just go with Bloomers. Need to get those lights up, I've normally done it all by now."

"Message received and understood. I'll give you a call later today if I can," said Charlotte. "Now on with the tour."

"Before we do," said Nick and pointed at the insane horse display, "there used to be a polar bear on display there. You had it there for a couple of years."

"Bruin the bear," she nodded.

"Bruin. That's right. Great name. I really liked that bear. What happened to it?"

"We retired him," she said airily.

"Retired?"

"We have to keep things fresh."

"So he's still around somewhere?" Nick asked.

Charlotte abruptly understood. "Oh. Oh – you're interested?"

"He would be lovely out front, on that massive space I have on the lawn. Polar bear, with a penguin entourage. Think I might have some penguins in storage. He had such a wonderfully mournful expression on his face, don't you think?"

Charlotte realised that it would quite possibly be in the skip by now. But could it be rescued?

"I will secure that for you, certainly," she said. "It's an excellent choice."

Nick raised his hands, framing the sight in his mind's eye. "Is it programmable, so that I can have it sing?"

"Programmable, no," said Charlotte. "It comes with built-in Christmas songs though."

What the fuck? she screamed in her own mind. *What did you say that for?* It was as though her mind, happy with one utter lie about the Luma-thingy lights they really didn't have, decided to go for broke with talk of singing bears.

"Christmas songs," he said, nodding thoughtfully. "I like it. How much would you want for it?"

Charlotte blew out. "Can you put a price on something like Bruin? I tell you what, you go with Hedgelord for your Christmas decoration needs and we will give you Bruin for nothing. Gratis. Free of charge."

"That's mighty kind of you, Charlotte," he said.

"And we'll have it delivered to your door," she said. "A fine handsome bear for your front lawn."

"Singing Christmas songs?"

"Singing Christmas songs," she said.

11

GALLAGHER

Luka led Gallagher and Anika into the section of wasteland that held the garden centre skips. "Here we have it!" he said as he shut the huge gate behind them.

Gallagher stared at the monstrosity in front of him and found himself entirely robbed of speech.

"Oh, my God," giggled Anika. "You guys are nuts."

"The fuck is that?" Gallagher managed to say eventually.

Luka patted his chest. "I am now designer of realistic polar bear. I gave myself that job because I can dream big, see? You want to tell me now what you would do when faced with a polar bear?"

"You've made it properly dangerous, you lunatic!" said Gallagher. "I can see the chainsaws it's got for arms. And what's that inside?"

The bear looked like something out of a particularly incoherent nightmare. As though someone had had a fever dream about a cyborg polar bear and then executed it in the least beautiful way possible.

Luka grinned. "Is shredder mounted on top of robot lawnmower, so it can move around. You think I am a good designer?" He started up a series of two-stroke engines with practised ease.

"Fuck," said Anika.

"Game on, my friend," said Luka. "Step back, elf girl. It would be terrible to lose a limb on your first day here."

"You are shitting me," said Gallagher, but his words were lost in the roar from the two chainsaws.

Luka had something on his phone that he tapped to steer his creation. It lurched forward.

Gallagher nipped out of the way, hoping the thing would topple over before it could advance towards him, but it moved smoothly, whipping loose stones from the ground underneath.

"So just to be clear, I might get chainsawed, shredded or mown? Possibly all three?"

Luka nodded. "You wished for death by polar bear, no?"

Gallagher saw his grin and knew it was for the thing he'd created. For the moment, he was blind to the mortal danger he'd introduced and was simply a kid with a cool toy, never mind that it was a killer polar bear.

It whirred louder and sped up, swivelling towards Gallagher.

"Fuck! How is it doing that? I thought lawnmowers were supposed to avoid obstacles?" he yelled.

"Firmware hack, my friend. Since capitalist tractor companies tried to prevent my people servicing their own vehicles, we have made it our business to take control of machinery. Lawnmower behaviour is now reversed and will actively chase the obstacle. You are the obstacle."

Gallagher had no time to query whatever the tractor scandal might have been, as the polar bear was now aggressively tracking him. Had Luka done something to its face too? It looked properly vicious. He picked up a broom and held it out. The polar bear swiped sideways and chopped off the brush end with one of its chainsaw arms.

"Fuck!" Gallagher wailed. "I don't want to die!"

"You said you did!" laughed Luka.

The demon bear swiped again.

"Hah!" yelled Luka. "Go Ivan, yes!"

"Ivan?" shouted Anika over the noise of the bear.

"I call him Ivan because he is terrible!"

"He's too good if anything!" shouted Gallagher, ducking once more.

"You know of course that 'terrible' in the context of Ivan IV really means 'bloody scary'," Anika shouted. "It's a common misconception."

"Fucking History A level isn't going to help me here!" Gallagher tried to make a rational assessment of his situation, but his mind was just a white noise of screeching terror. "Has he got an off switch?"

"No," said Luka.

"You definitely made your point! I choose flight, all right?"

"We just getting warmed up. What if this was genuine polar bear, eh? You could not choose off switch. Engage in the activity, Gallagher. Come on!"

Gallagher regarded the stump of broom handle in his hand. If he had karate moves, he'd knock the bear over with a super concentrated blow to the exact point on its head. He had no moves, only wishes. He backed away from the polar bear and his foot hit something that had been dumped against the fence. A quick glance told him it was a split bag of gravel that he should have bagged up and sold as a special in Bargain Corner, but he hadn't got round to it. Gravel.

He grabbed a handful and threw it at the lawnmower base of the polar bear. It made a rattling sound but seemed unaffected.

"Fucking stop, will you!" he yelled. He grabbed the bag and upended it, dumping the contents into a defensive semi-circle. The lawnmower rattled more violently as it tried to mount the gravel obstruction, then it stalled completely.

For good measure, Gallagher swung the empty bag at one of the chainsaw arms. The heavy duty plastic snagged in the teeth of the chainsaw and brought it to an abrupt halt.

"Ha-ha!" he roared, victoriously.

The other chainsaw and the shredder continued to grind noisily, but the polar bear was now stationary.

Gallagher was determined this experience was not going to be repeated. Now that the bear wasn't rolling towards him like a fucking terminator, he was able to look at it more analytically. He stepped round and grabbed the chainsaw arm that was still running. He took hold of its handles and brought the blade up so that he could use it on the polar bear.

"Right, let's fucking fix you," he grinned viciously.

12

CHARLOTTE

Charlotte waved to Nick as he cruised out through the door, Karen from tills behind him, wheeling a trolley full of lights to load into his car.

"We'll drop the polar bear round in the morning, yeah?" Charlotte called after him.

Nick nodded in acknowledgement.

Charlotte looked over to the horses arranged near to the entrance. Crazy horses or crazy carnival dancers – they remained a shocking enigma. "Fuck," she murmured. "But better than a tweeny princess carriage. Possibly."

At least wild dancing horses was something Bloomers almost certainly didn't have.

"Time to reclaim a bear," she said and made her way towards the rear of the store, out across the plant section and towards the waste area. She was thinking maybe, if she was lucky, the bear wouldn't even be in the skip, but perhaps just resting jauntily against it. That would be handy. That would be generally reflective of the half-arsed laziness of Luka and Gallagher.

She was still thinking this when she heard the sound of buzzing chainsaws and heard Gallagher yelling, "Who's the king of the jungle now, motherfucker!"

She came to the gate and saw Gallagher standing over the fallen bear, using a chainsaw, bizarrely attached to Bruins own paw, to cut off the polar bear's head.

Cackling maniacally, Gallagher turned off the chainsaw and hurled the head into the skip.

"Man – one! Bear – nil!" he crowed, staggering about as though punch drunk, sweat glistening on his tattooed arms.

The new elf, Anika, spontaneously burst into applause and Luka gently joined in.

Gallagher grasped Luka's shoulders. "Jesus wept! I cannot believe you actually did that."

"See! It was a success. You responded well," said Luka.

Charlotte, staring dumbfounded, finally found her voice. "What the actual—?" She bit down on the bile and rising fury, and the swear words queuing up to come out of her mouth.

Luka gestured genially for her to come. "It's okay. Bear is dead now."

"The bear was always dead, Mr Sibersky," she whispered.

The bear was headless. The bear that had cost just shy of a thousand quid two years ago and which they'd replaced with crazy dancing horses was headless, its chest violently stoved in, and with heavy duty machinery embedded in its arms, legs and throat.

"But is now dealt with," said Luka. "Job done."

"Job done?" she said. "You've destroyed it. You've left a hideous bauble coach ordered on the whim of a madman on display by the side of the shop, while what I can only describe as the two most horrifying horse things I've ever seen are looming over our artfully arranged Christmas wares inside."

"I thought they looked quite festive," offered Anika.

Charlotte silenced her with a laser-focused glare. "Meanwhile," she continued in a viciously controlled voice that she knew would get out of control soon enough, "our most valued Christmas customer is thinking of taking all his custom to those shitbags—" her watch app buzzed "—those people over at Bloomers. Jack fucking Hartigan." Another buzz. "All because Jack has managed to secure some lights that no one at all is meant to have yet!" She swung round so that each of them could see the wild unhappiness on her face. "But the one thing – the one thing! – that he thought might swing it back for us would be if we sold him that bear – *that bear!*" She stabbed a finger at ravaged, fallen, Bruin.

She spotted a length of metal, a broken piece from an old greenhouse frame, by the side of one of the skips. "You need to go now," she said.

The three idiots just stood there.

"Go now," she repeated, softly. She didn't add "or I can't be held accountable for your broken mangled corpses", but imagined at least one or two of them heard it.

They trudged out, Gallagher steering Anika by the elbow just as the young woman looked ready to say something stupid – like an apology or to ask if Charlotte was okay.

Charlotte watched them go, then watched them go even

further. She gazed down at the bear. She looked at his matted, dirty fur and the pieces of machinery poking through the spaces where his big gentle paws had once been. A beautiful, charming piece of Christmassiness, ruined in the blink of an eye.

Charlotte picked up the length of metal and felt the anger course through her.

She smashed it down on his chest – one, two, three blows – and bellowed her utter fury.

"Stupid motherfuckers! Fucking fuck-faced fuckers!"

Her watch was buzzing repeatedly now, but it was just the background track to a berserker's rage. She walloped and stabbed and gouged.

"It's fucking you or the fucking coach!" she bellowed. "Fucking shitting princesses! *Fuuuck!*"

13

GALLAGHER

"Have I lost my job on my first day?" said Anika as the three of them walked over to the shed area.

Gallagher gave her a quizzical look. "No. Why'd you think that?"

"Because we…" She pointed back the way they'd come, and the sounds of howling misery drifting over from the skip area.

"We were doing what we were told," said Luka.

"You made a giant fighting robot polar bear," said Anika.

"We were broadly doing what we were told," he said.

"So, I've still got a job?"

"Oh, yeah," said Gallagher confidently. "You did nothing wrong. And Charlotte's all about second chances. Big ol' Christian type is our Charlotte."

"Charlotte—?" She gestured once more towards the distant sounds of rage.

They were far enough away that Gallagher could no

longer hear the specific swear words, but they were definitely there. "Big ol' Christian," he said. "I heard she's banned from every church in town on account of her anger issues. The last one, St Stephen's, because of that thing with the pigeon and the candlestick."

"I heard that too," nodded Luka. He stroked his chin. "I will need to retrieve chainsaws and fix them to go back on display."

"Your concern for merchandise over your mate is noted," said Gallagher.

Luka started to roll a cigarette. "You shit your pants?"

Gallagher swivelled his hips and plucked at his underwear to check for unexpected leakage. "As luck would have it, no."

"And do you wish to commit death by polar bear now?"

"I do not."

Luka spread his hands as if to suggest that all was well. "Come then. It is time for cup of tea. Maybe we fortify yours with some *Śliwowica* as you are feeling delicate."

Gallagher straightened a little. The weird plum hooch was something Luka broke out only very occasionally. It was as close as he was going to get to an apology. "All right then."

"And you," Luka said to Anika. "You have learned valuable lessons today, I think."

"Have I?" she said doubtfully.

"Who can say? But you got free Christmas lights, did you not? Tomorrow is a new day."

"Elf training with that guy, Daffyd."

"Utter psycho," said Gallagher.

"Really? He seemed quite nice."

"Huh. You'll see."

Fifteen minutes later, Gallagher and Luka were sitting on the steps of one of their favourite sheds, travel mugs of plum-scented tea in their hands. It was four o'clock, but midwinter was nearly upon them and the sun had just about set. The sky was a reddish grey.

"I like this new elf girl," said Luka.

"Bit young for you, mate," said Gallagher.

Luka sucked his teeth at Gallagher. "I said like, I didn't say I wanted to build a cottage with her. She is nice. I like nice people."

"As nice as Alejandro?"

Luka shrugged. "Who could be as nice as Alejandro? Shame they sent him away like that."

"I mean but, yeah, he was a..." He did a mime of someone looking on a computer and moving a mouse. "Click, click. Wahey!"

"I do not know this idiom," said Luka.

"Inappropriate images on his laptop," Gallagher whispered.

"No. His work visa ran out."

"Oh," said Gallagher. "Sophie in the café gave me totally the wrong idea."

"Look sharp," said Luka and pointed.

Charlotte walked down the gravel path towards them. She had a metal strut from a dismantled greenhouse hanging limply in one hand. Half of her blouse was untucked and bits of her hair hung untidily around her face. She looked like she had gone ten rounds with the polar bear machine too. She looked at them with bleary eyes and took a deep breath.

"Gentlemen," she said, in a firm but well-controlled voice, "tomorrow morning I would like you to devote your energy to rebuilding Bruin the bear exactly as he was."

Gallagher opened his mouth to question that, but she was ahead of him.

"*Exactly* as he was. Every hair, every tooth, every claw. You will do it quickly, you will do it professionally, and then I may even ask you to help me deliver it to Mr Bellingham's front door."

"Right you are, Miss Charlotte," said Luka. "Can I interest you in a cup of tea?"

She wavered, literally wobbling on the spot, and for a moment it seemed she might say yes.

"No. Thank you. I have work to do." She nodded as though confirming the fact to herself, then walked away. "Oh!" she called out. "And the bear will sing Christmas songs!"

"I'm sure it will," Luka called after her.

When she was gone, Gallagher scratched his thin neck thoughtfully.

"Are we going to make it sing?"

Luka shrugged. "Who can say? That is a problem for future Luka and future Gallagher."

14

CHARLOTTE

Cameron Clasp stopped Charlotte as she passed through the shop. He was holding an odd, quilted package in his hands with an electronic control sewn into it. Hedgelord's owner looked her up and down.

"Good afternoon, Charlotte."

"Merry Christmas, Cameron," she said. She nodded at the folded quilted bundle. "What's that?"

"Ball warmer," he said. "Bloody important this time of year."

"Er ... right?"

"Everything go okay with the customer?"

Charlotte nodded slowly. "He was thinking of going with Bloomers for some aspects of—"

"Bastards."

"—but I won him round. We have some schmoozing to do."

Cameron's face pulled into a pained grimace. "Oh, dear.

Well, I can step up to the plate if need be. I didn't win that public speaking prize at Mizelhurst for nothing, you know."

She tapped her chest. "I will be doing the schmoozing. A charm offensive. It will feature a wonderful, all-singing, all-dancing bear."

Cameron shrugged and pulled another face. "Metaphor's lost on me, Charlotte. As long as it's our products and our names in the local paper. And us getting a mention in the Guinness Book of Records. I think I know someone who knows Norris McWhirter. I can give him a call."

"I think Norris McWhirter is dead."

"Is he? Blast. Well, I will leave it in your hands." He held up the quilted ball-warmer. "Got to put these bad boys to the test. Going to give Kirby Bletherington the pounding of his life."

She frowned.

"Squash," he said, as though she was mentally deficient. "Warm balls bounce better. Normally, I'd be teeing off with Patty Fufu this time of day, but you have to mix things up, don't you?" He sauntered off.

As the tills began to shut down for the afternoon, Charlotte sought out cashier Karen. "Karen, you know what I notice about you?"

"That I'm already running late to pick the kids up from school club?" said the tired looking woman.

"You have a very ... everywoman kind of look about you. Mumsy."

"Mumsy?"

Charlotte nodded. "You blend in seamlessly with a crowd."

"Is that so?"

"I might have a special job for you tomorrow. A shopping mission to a nearby establishment."

"Do I have to come in early?"

"No."

"Cos I can't. School club don't open their doors until eight."

"No. It should be fine."

"Christina runs the club with an iron fist. If you're there early and only so much as looking at the door, she'll giving you such a glare and make your children last in line for the cereal."

"No. Normal time."

"Because those Frosties go quick. You don't want to be the mum whose children were forced to have Shreddies when there were Frosties and Coco Pops on the table."

"No. Normal time," said Charlotte. "And dress normal. Low key."

"I can try."

Charlotte gestured at her trousers and top. "This is fine. Like this."

"Right."

Charlotte nodded, as much to herself as to Karen. Yes, this would all work. Bear fixed. Computer-controlled lights purchased. Nick Bellingham happy. Newspaper publicity secured. Christmas saved.

She still felt good about it when she went out to her car. The situation was salvageable.

She headed along the A31, went straight round the double roundabout by the big supermarket and drove into town. There had been a lot of stresses that day and she reckoned she deserved a takeaway from the Rajput, even though it was not the weekend.

It was not even six o'clock and, bar the chain pub, the town centre was dead. Retail was dead. All the shops that weren't boarded up were nail bars, Turkish barbers, vape stores or charity shops. Charlotte was a big believer in charity shops – at least the ones which supported proper decent charities (she had a list in her head) – but a town could not survive on charity shops alone. Hedgelord was truly one of the remaining bastions of friendly retail left in the area.

The large outdoor nativity scene was up outside St Stephen's church on the corner and, as the lights changed to red, she stopped beside it. They had some decent spotlights on the stable-shaped display area. The painted wooden Mary and Joseph positively glowed in the light.

She'd never admit as much to her non-Christian friends and colleagues, but just the sight of that nativity scene – the blessed parents, the wise men, the adoring shepherds, the attendant donkey – was a warming moment of connection with God above. Despite all the commercialism and fripperies, Christmas was an anchoring point in the Christian calendar. It was a reminder that, yes, Jesus had been here on Earth with the rest of humanity. God's feet had touched this soil, had known what it was like to be one of us, and reminded her that he was ever-present.

She wound down her window to see the scene without the glass between them. That wise man was still wrapped in the silky cloak she'd stitched for him. It still looked good.

The fact that there was still a piece of her connected to this church was both comforting and bitterly hurtful.

There was movement on the church steps. Reverend Ralph Roberston stepped into the light. He looked at Charlotte, stony-faced, and folded his arms.

Charlotte gestured viciously at the traffic lights ahead. "I'm waiting for the fucking lights, Ralph. I'm just passing."

"They're green, Charlotte," he said coldly.

There was a horn toot behind him and she looked. He was right.

"For fuck's sake," she said and accelerated. "I made that nativity – you fucking hear me?" she shouted.

Her watched buzzed. She took her eyes off the road to glance at the counter.

72 fucks, 18 shits, 2 arseholes, 1 damn and 5 hells.

Charlotte exhaled miserably. Life was tough when you gave a fuck.

15

GALLAGHER

The windows on Gallagher's crappy hatchback kept fogging up as he sat waiting outside Luka's house. He had the engine running and the blowers on full, but they did little to shift the morning condensation on the windscreen. Gallagher could see his own misted breath was adding to the problem. He tried not breathing for a while, but that was only a temporary measure at best.

The passenger door opened and Luka got in. The little car rocked as the big guy settled in.

"Took your time," said Gallagher.

"We will not be late."

"I'm not your bloody taxi, mate."

Luka patted Gallagher's knee with his big hand. "I value your generosity. You should not leave the engine running when stationary. You must think of the planet."

"I need to clear the windows. This car does not like

stopping and starting. You turn it off, it won't start again without a rest."

"This is not good," said Luka, taking off his scarf and wiping the windscreen with it. "You should get it fixed."

Gallagher put his car into gear, then pointed at the one parked on the driveway next to them. "Yeah. How are *your* repairs going?"

"It is hard to get parts. Nineteen seventy-eight Ford Capri Mark three. Classic car."

"Death trap."

"Three litre V6 engine. As driven by Bodie and Doyle in TV classic, *The Professionals*."

"Before my time, mate."

"Voiced by Petr Oliva and Alois Švehlík in superior Czechoslovakian version I saw as teenager."

"You may have mentioned..."

As they headed out of town, towards the supermarket by the double roundabout, Luka took his morning joint out of an overall pocket and lit it. He took a deep pull and passed it to Gallagher. Gallagher drew and held it as long as he could. The smoke was both chill and warm in his lungs.

"You know, I should become a taxi driver," he said after exhaling.

"You want to charge me for morning lifts?" said Luka, taking the joint back.

"I'm saying maybe I need to get a little Uber side hustle. Money's still too tight to mention."

"You mention it a lot, my friend." Luka said. "Allowing people into your car. It is the violation of a sacred personal space."

Gallagher looked at the grease smears Luka's scarf had left behind on the windscreen.

There was the buzz of a phone. Luka fished around and dug it out. "Yeah?" he said. "Sonia! Sonia. *Ja. Ja.* I know. I know." There was chatter on the line and Luka nodded along. "I know. I do. I can." He looked sideways at Gallagher. "I have a friend with a car."

Gallagher did a double take at him. "You what?" he whispered.

"And I will split the money with him," said Luka, which shut Gallagher up for a moment. "He is trustworthy. Pliable." There was more back and forth of an indecipherable sort before Luka provided a petering string of goodbyes and hung up. He put the phone away and looked ahead down the road.

"Well?" said Gallagher when it was clear no information was forthcoming.

"All is good," said Luka.

"Who. Was. That?"

Luka sniffed and took a drag. "That was Sonia Patterson. I owe Sonia a favour; a favour that pays. I promised I would take a package from Canon's Ashby to another friend in Clopton Howes."

"That's an eighty mile round trip."

"And she will pay a hundred and fifty pounds. Seventy-five each."

Seventy-five quid was good. That was more than a day's wages for a couple of hours' work.

"What does she want transporting?"

Luka cocked an eyebrow at Gallagher, his eyes flickering between the joint and Gallagher with meaning.

"Shit," said Gallagher.

"Quite good shit, I think you'd agree."

Gallagher was thinking on it as he swung into the Hedgelord Garden Centre car park.

It was not yet eight o'clock. Most staff hadn't arrived by that point. But Anika was waiting by the front door. She was stepping from one foot to the other, as though she could shake off the cold by minimising contact with the ground.

Gallagher pulled into a parking spot. The engine sputtered and died. Badly parked or not, the old girl wouldn't start again for some time.

The new elf girl Anika wandered over as they got out. Luka took another drag on the stubby joint and put it casually behind his back.

"Is there a way for me to get in?" she said.

"You need a swipe key," said Gallagher. "You a proper employee now?"

"I'm a Christmas elf."

Gallagher looked at Luka. "Do elves count as actual employees?"

Luka shrugged and exhaled through his nose.

"You smoking weed?" said Anika.

"Are you a cop?" said Luka.

"Can I have some?"

Luka pulled a considering face and brought the joint round to regard it. "You have smoked before?"

"I'm a uni student. Of course I have."

"I thought you were an elf," said Gallagher.

"I'm taking a sabbatical."

16

CHARLOTTE

"What are we doing again?" asked Karen Woodbine.

"Look, do you want to help or not?" said Charlotte, taking the third exit on the roundabout towards the rightly loathed Bloomers.

"Well, no, not really. You just pointed at me and said, 'You, you look mumsy. You'll do. Come with me'."

"I'm sure I said it much nicer than that," said Charlotte, but, thinking about it, wasn't sure that she had. "But it's good to get off the tills for a bit, right?"

Karen paused in the act of eating her frazzles. It was nine a.m. and the woman was eating frazzles for breakfast and getting crumbs on Charlotte's interior. Charlotte tried to keep her irritation on the inside.

"As long as I get paid and I'm finished in time to pick up Ron and Hermione."

Charlotte looked at her sideways. "Ron? And Hermione?"

Karen put a hand. "Don't. Just don't. You've got questions, ask my ex."

"Ron and Hermione but no... No Harry?"

"If we'd had three, maybe we'd have the full set. But he got the snip just before we split up." Karen must have seen the confused look on Charlotte's face. "Do you have kids? Ever been married?"

"No. Not yet. I don't have time for that. Too busy. Maybe one day."

"Well, if you want some advice, first up: that body is only going to be an attractive proposition for so long. Nobody wants to see a turkey on the shelf after Christmas."

"Er, right."

"And secondly: don't bother. Most of the men out there are a waste of space. It's like having an extra child in your house."

"Thanks for the tip," said Charlotte.

She turned into the Bloomers car park. She could almost imagine a frisson of hostile energy pass through her as she crossed over the boundary. Bloomers: home to the empire of evil, Satan's lair, the Death Star of garden centres. Hedgelord – the Hedgelord that Charlotte strived to build and nurture every day – was community focused, a green space, a vibrant heart for a town that sometimes felt like it had no heart at all. Bloomers – ugh! – a money grasping enterprise that try to foist shoddy plants, overpriced café food, and all manner of tat onto the paying public.

So similar but worlds apart. Charlotte didn't want to stay long in case she was tainted by the place.

She pulled up in a parking spot a considerable distance from the front door.

"So, what are we doing again?" said Karen.

"This," said Charlotte and took the printed sheet off the dashboard and passed it to Karen, who read it out, slowly.

"'*LumaGrid synchronised light controller.*' Four hundred quid? Bloody hell. You want to pay four hundred quid for lights?"

"That's just the controller. The lights are separate. Our beloved customer, Mr Bellingham, wants one for his house. We do not stock them. No one stocks them—"

Karen flicked the edge of the paper. "Except Bloomers."

"Right. And we're not having our beloved customer tell the local press that his lights were provided by bloody Bloomers. He's going to get them from *us*. Even if that means *we* get them from Bloomers."

Karen screwed up her empty frazzles and looked for somewhere to put them. She stuffed them in Charlotte's cupholder. Charlotte's face twisted but she kept the expletives on the inside.

"So, why aren't you going in there?" said Karen.

"Me? Go in there and buy something? Are you fu— flaming mad? That's enemy territory. That's the other side of the wall. That's East Berlin circa nineteen eighty-five. I can't go in and buy them. You're my undercover agent."

"Mumsy, you said."

Charlotte didn't know what she was complaining about. It was both accurate and not unkind. Karen Woodbine did look mumsy. Dyed blonde hair unevenly pulled back from a face made dull and rubbery by years of cares and woes. A body that was neither toned nor flabby but a sad little compromise of the two. She looked exactly like a woman who had to work an eight hour shift before going home to cook fish fingers and beans for her little terrors before settling down for a night of ironing, *Love Island,* and cheap wine. Charlotte had no idea if that was precisely true, but it felt true.

"You're helping me out. It's a very noble and Christian thing to do."

Karen blew out her lips dismissively.

"A Christian loves everyone unconditionally and will do anything for anyone. You should try it. It's very freeing."

"I'm saying why don't you just go in and cover up your work uniform?"

"I'm a known woman," said Charlotte. "My opposite number, Jack Hartigan, has my photo on his wall."

"Oh, I know Jack. He's quite fit, isn't it?"

"What?"

"He's got that smile and that faraway look in his eye. And that *voice!*"

Charlotte scowled. "His forehead's too big and his eyes are both too close together and too far apart. He is my nemesis. I fucking hate him." Her smart watch buzzed, profanity detected.

"I thought you loved everyone unconditionally," said Karen.

"I do! I do. Love the sinner but hate the sin. I love him unconditionally but I despise everything he stands for."

"Which is?"

Charlotte flung out her hand at the shop front. "That! Now, get out there."

She opened her purse as Karen stepped out. "Now you're going to have to put this on two cards." She passed Karen cards from her wallet. "Three hundred on that one. The rest on that."

"What's the pin number?"

"I'll call you when you get to the till."

"Why?"

"Security."

Karen hesitated before closing the car door. "There's people I know in there too, you know."

"Work there?"

"Sort of."

"Are they your nemesis? Nemesises?"

Karen tilted her head. "Family. Hard to say."

She shut the door and walked across the rainy car park to the Bloomers entrance. Charlotte watched her go in. She saw the screwed up frazzle packet. Lips pressed tight, she opened her phone and turned off the Curse Count app.

"For fuck's sake!" she spat. "Fucking take your shitty rubbish with you, woman. Fucking hell!"

Swearing didn't count if she was alone.

She snatched the packet out of the cup holder and somehow managed to fling crumbs about. Swearing, she got out, went to the boot, found one of her neatly stored carrier bags, put the packet inside, then got back in and spent five minutes picking up the spilled crumbs.

"Raised in a sodding farmyard some people. For fuck's sake."

When she was done, she contemplated where to put the carrier bag, deciding she wouldn't be happy until it was all in a bin, so got out and walked to a bin across the car park, disposed of it all and went back to her car.

17

CHARLOTTE

A further five minutes passed.

Charlotte thought about words and how to pronounce them. "Nemesises. Nemeses. Nemeesis."

Fifteen minutes passed.

She remembered to turn her Curse Count app back on, doing a few safety 'fucks' before doing so.

Twenty minutes passed. How long did it take one pre-menopausal woman to find a massive high end light controller? She sat for a further minute and made charitable silent prayers on behalf of all clueless breeders.

Then she phoned Karen.

"I'm in lights," whispered Karen.

"I should hope so," Charlotte whispered back. "Why are you whispering?"

"I'm being secretive."

"We don't need to whisper," said Charlotte, forcing

herself to adopt a normal voice. "Have they got the LumaGrid?"

"I'm looking. There's lots of lights."

"I know there's lots of lights. They're a soulless corporation, pushing the commercial side of Christmas."

"They've got more lights than us."

Charlotte laughed dismissively. "We have the largest light collection this side of Milton Keynes, Karen. I don't think so. Have they got the LumaGrid?"

The was rustling. *"AstraBeam Projection System?"*

"No. LumaGrid synchronised light controller."

More rustling. *"They've got a ... a PixelPulse Smart Lighting."*

"Does it say LumaGrid synchronised light controller on it?"

"No."

"Then it's not that." Charlotte cupped her hand over the phone and mouthed a few expletives. "Just keep looking," she said. "If you loiter too long, you'll draw suspicion."

"I'm just browsing."

"Oh, they'll have their beady CCTV eyes on you ri—" A sharp tap on the car window made Charlotte jump and drop her phone. "Jesus fucking Christ!"

A smiley face looked in through the window. Flustered, Charlotte picked up her phone.

"You all right?" came Karen's voice.

"Jack fucking Hartigan," said Charlotte and killed the call.

She opened the door. He had to awkwardly step back to allow her to do.

"Charlotte! It is you!" he said, beaming. "I thought I saw you by the bins and it is you. I haven't seen you since..."

"Xmas eXpo in Hull," she said.

"Last year. Of course. You going this year?"

"I wouldn't miss it," she said defensively. Xmas eXpo was the biggest Christmas trade event in the country. It was so big and so much in demand that each Christmas's trade show was held before Christmas two years earlier. To suggest she was not going to go was insulting to her whole Christmassy ethos. "Are you going?" she asked.

"I am," he nodded. "I'm taking my girlfriend, Kathryn, for a night in Paris the day before, but I'll be back in time, no worries." He gave Charlotte a mock quizzical frown. "And you've come to Bloomers today?"

Charlotte, for reasons she had not thought through for more than a microsecond, looked in bewilderment at the shop. "Is it? I hadn't... So it is."

"You coming in then?" he said. "Treat you to a Yuletide hot chocolate in the Lighthouse Café?"

"What? No. Do you even have a lighthouse in there?"

He smiled magnanimously. He did have a nice smile, but he used it too much. He was a right smug git was Jack Hartigan.

"Actually, I've come to have words with you about poaching our customers," she said, latching onto an acceptable half-truth.

"Poaching?"

"You know what I mean."

He nodded. "You mean Mr Bellingham—"

"He lets me call him Nick."

"He did come here, looking for some decorations because, and I'm only quoting here, Hedgelord were unable to meet his needs."

"Poaching," said Charlotte.

"Friendly competition." He gave her a scrutinising look. "This is about getting in the papers, isn't it? Record breaking lights."

She stopped herself nodding in agreement. "This is about doing the decent thing."

He frowned. "Are you saying that Mr Bellingham can't shop where he wishes?"

"No, I'm—"

"Not suggesting that members of the differently-abled community should settle for limited choices."

"They prefer the term disabled," she said.

"I don't think they do."

"I think they do. I've read the literature."

"You like reading literature about differently-abled people?"

"Disabled people, yes."

"Got a disability porn thing going on there?" He frowned at himself. "I didn't mean like that. I meant in a sort of disability tourist kind of thing, I..."

Charlotte's phone was ringing. It was Karen. She answered.

"*We got cut off before,*" said Karen. "*I still can't find the LumaGrid, I've asked an assistant to check the stock for me.*"

"You did? Erm, listen I might need to call you back in a few minutes, because would you believe I accidentally came and parked in Bloomers. Hahaha!"

"*What are you on about?*" Karen asked.

"And now, would you believe, I am talking to Jack Hartigan, who represents my role on the dark side."

Karen huffed loudly down the phone. "*Fine. Call me when you're done flirting or whatever.*"

As Charlotte ended the call, Jack Hartigan's phone rang.

He raised his eyebrows at Charlotte as he turned away to answer. "Well aren't we just the busiest people, eh?"

A few moments later he turned back and eyed Charlotte. "The LumaGrid? She wants that one specifically? Oh what a shame, we had a valued customer who was so excited by them that he bought the remainder of our stock. He was talking about getting some of his neighbours involved in his famous Christmas lighting display, so he wanted to secure several units. We can't get more until there's another shipment. Won't be this side of Christmas. See if she might like a PixelPulse, maybe? It won't do the slogan of the day, but a lot of the other functionality is there." He ended the call.

Charlotte made sure that her poker face was intact, even though her mind was screaming to unleash a tirade of heartfelt profanities. "Busy. Yes. Tell me about it."

"Oh, I probably don't need to. I think Mrs Woodbine works at Hedgelord, doesn't she? She can fill you in. We know Mrs Woodbine. You might as well wait around and give her a lift back to work, save her legs. Mind you she won't be carrying any purchases by the sounds of it."

"Oh – Karen?" said Charlotte, pretending to be uncertain. "Yes, I know her. She's probably just popped in to see family. I know she has a personal interest in lighting."

He gave her the full wattage of his broadest smile. "So many do, don't they? Listen, I'll leave you to gather your thoughts. I hope it's not too painful to learn that our offering just happened to be better this year. Lovely seeing you, Charlotte. Best wishes to Cameron."

As he walked off, Charlotte kept the smile on her face in case he turned around, but tried out her ventriloquism skills. Could she say 'fucker' without moving her lips?

"Hucker. You are such a hucker. You 'ake 'e hucking sick!"

The good thing about her poor ventriloquism skills was the app didn't recognise the swear words, so she got a freebie. That was worth remembering.

It wasn't long before Karen appeared back at the car. "You'll never guess what?" she said as she climbed in.

"Mr Bellingham bought up their entire stock of LumaGrid controllers?"

Karen was still poised with her mouth open, ready to continue. "That was a really good guess."

Charlotte shoved her seatbelt on. "Jack Hartigan came over to give me a running commentary on how lame we are. God I hate him!"

Karen smirked as she settled into her seat.

"What?" said Charlotte. "Why on earth are you smirking?"

"You have strong feelings for him don't you?"

Charlotte crunched her car into gear with a vicious shove. "You do know this isn't the playground, don't you? The rules of teen magazine pop psychology don't apply here. If I say I hate him it's because I hate him."

"Whatever you say, boss."

18

GALLAGHER

Gallagher sat with Luka in one of the larger summer houses. It wasn't where they normally spent time, but they didn't normally have a massive polar bear to put back together.

"Remind me," said Luka. "Why am I doing this?"

Gallagher paused in the act of carrying the polar bear's head up a step ladder and huffed. Maybe the weed was starting to affect Luka's memory. "Charlotte sold it to the customer we're trying to brown-nose. So now we have to fix it."

"But I did not break it. You broke it."

"You mean I defended myself against the cyborg monstrosity you made."

"You had a choice, my friend."

Gallagher wasn't going to argue. The day had barely started and he was already tired. "You gonna help or what?"

"I am ensuring that you are working safely at height,"

said Luka swinging his mug of tea to show how he was helping from his chair.

Gallagher wasn't going to point out he was only on the first step of the step ladder. "Well, I think it'll be good if we can give this thing another lease of life."

"I thought you hated it? You chopped its fucking head off."

"This is a different kind of closure though. Better."

Luka chuckled darkly. "We did not have closure in my day. Closure."

Gallagher fastened the head back into place on the body with white cable ties. He'd drilled holes in both pieces and was using the cable ties to create a plasticky sewn-on head look. He had almost gone right round, and it didn't look too bad. A strategically placed scarf would cover up the unavoidable Frankenstein scar.

"You do know it's not on straight?" Luka said.

Gallagher couldn't tell from where he was, right on top of the thing. He stepped down and walked back. "Oh yeah. It looks as if it's glancing over its shoulder, sort of coy."

Luka shrugged. "They're buying it as seconds. It will be fine." He slurped his tea, stroked his grey beard and looked out the open door. "Look lively, the king of the elves is on his way in here."

Gallagher rolled his eyes.

"Hello Daffyd," said Luka as the man entered.

Daffyd was followed by new elf Anika, Sophie from the café, and a handsome young man in an elf costume who Gallagher had never seen before. Anika gave Gallagher a little wave.

"You two lucky people have been selected to star in a small production of mine!" said Daffyd.

He stretched his face around that weird elastic smile he had. Gallagher thought that sometimes he looked as if he was half-man, half-rubber-puppet. The bald head and smooth baby face added to the effect, but his eyes were too unsettling for the rest of his face. They looked like small flinty stones.

"You do know that you don't have to talk like that in here, don't you?" said Gallagher.

"Like what?"

"Like 'oh, boy, have I got a surprise for you!'" He clapped his hands in pretend excitement and nearly fell off the stepladder. "We're not punters, we work here too."

"I'm sure I don't know what you mean?" sniffed Daffyd. "We have here a genuine opportunity to shine like the individual Christmas miracles that we all are."

Gallagher didn't dare glance across at Luka, who had little patience with Daffyd's flowery style. "Right. Good. How exactly can we help you, Daffyd?"

"Although I'm delivering a very busy induction programme today—" he gestured to the three people with him "—we are recording a range of tunes for a bespoke project and find ourselves in need of a baritone—"

"—Get the fucking elf to explain," said Luka. "I think she speaks English."

Daffyd put a hand to his mouth in a pantomime of hurt.

Anika stepped forward "Daffyd wants help with a voice for the polar bear."

"Voice? You want my voice?" Luka descended into a rich bass voice as he said this.

"I can do voices," said Gallagher, grasping the polar bear's wonky head. He affected a strangled falsetto. *"Aargh, someone cut my fucking head off and put it back wrong. Please help!"*

Anika nodded. "It is looking over its own shoulder, isn't it? No, it's supposed to sing Christmas songs."

"We've recorded the other elves singing," said Daffyd, "but they've all got high, tinny voices. I need some baritone."

Luka jutted a finger at the handsome young man. "What about him? He looks like a crooner. Like that, er, Mickey Bubbles, eh. Why not get him to sing?"

The handsome young man took a deep breath but Daffyd held up a restraining hand. "Gillespie here may have lounge singer looks, but we've discovered his singing voices is like ... like... What was it I said?"

"Like horses drowning in cement," said Sophie helpfully.

"That."

Luka shook his head. "Well, you find singers elsewhere. We are not paid enough to humiliate ourselves like that."

"Not even a little rumpa-pum-pum?" asked Anika.

"Rumpa-pum-pum!" sang Gallagher.

"Rumpa-pum-pum!" Luka added.

"Perfect! Yes, that. Do it again!" said Anika, pressing buttons on her phone.

Luka clamped his mouth closed.

"You know what?" Gallagher said. "I reckon we could do a bit of rumpa-pum-pum if we had some of that nice cake from the cafe."

"What about good old Christmas spirit?" said Daffyd.

"Vodka or schnapps?" said Luka.

"Cake or GTFO," agreed Gallagher.

Luka raised his eyebrows and nodded in agreement. "Cake. That's our price."

"I can get some now," said Sophie and began to sidle off.

Daffyd looked at her, giving the smallest of nods and a dismissive flick of his fingers.

"Good doing business with you, gents," he said. "Right. Miss Chowdhry, you seem to have a rapport with these gentlemen. You can do the recording, and then—" he did some vigorous jazz hands "—it's induction time! With me, Gillespie!"

Gallagher watched Daffyd and the fully dressed elf go.

"You know, I think Daffyd'd make a really good cult leader," said Gallagher, watching them depart.

"Maybe it is safer he is just an elf," agreed Luka.

19

CHARLOTTE

Charlotte drove back into the Hedgelord car park. God in heaven, it felt good to be back on home turf.

"I'll let you out here so you can get back on the tills," she said to Karen, pulling up in a space near to the entrance.

Karen climbed out and then leaned back inside. "I need to give you the bank cards back. Hold on, I'll just dig them out." She rootled in her enormous bag. Charlotte could clearly see that she had at least one pair of shoes in there. Half-eaten packets of biscuits and open packets of wipes churned past as she turned over the contents. "Almost there, I think. Ooh, that's mouldy!" She put a dusty green satsuma onto the seat of Charlotte's car and it gently puffed spores of mould onto everything around it.

Charlotte watched with growing frustration.

Eventually Karen found the cards and threw them onto

the seat. She picked up the satsuma, leaving the fallout as an imprint on the seat. "See you back inside!"

Charlotte was about to reverse and park her car correctly when someone tooted their horn from behind. She looked in the mirror. "Oh no!"

She'd pulled into the disabled parking space just to drop Karen off, and now another car had pulled up behind, blocking her in. She glanced round. Yep, it was him. It was Nick Bellingham at the wheel. He was gesticulating and mouthing something at her. She shrank down and tried to hide.

She hated people who used parking spaces they were not entitled to. But not her! This wasn't the kind of thing she did. This was so unfair.

Her phone rang. NICK BELLINGHAM – VALUED CUSTOMER came up on the caller ID.

"Hello?" she said, hearing the wobble in her own voice.

"I thought you ought to know, there's a car in one of the disabled spots that doesn't have a blue badge."

"Really? Oh, dear," she managed to say.

"Maybe you want to get your security team to move it?"

"Er. Yes, of course," said Charlotte, shimmying further down below the level of the dashboard. "I will see to that immediately."

She ended the call and thought for a second, scrunched against the passenger seat which had a strong smell of mouldy satsuma.

"This is fucking ridiculous," she muttered. Her watch buzzed. "That was totally appropriate for the situation," she hissed at the watch.

She put a call through to Tom Eccles. He picked up on the fifth ring.

"Charlotte."

"Hi Tom, I wonder if you could get someone to pop and give me a hand with something?"

There was a pause. *"I have my team and you have yours. Why don't you get someone from the grotto?"*

"Well, for one thing it's very time critical and they are all mid-flow. Daffyd is inducting the new staff today."

"That's not a reason to poach my people."

"For another I need someone who can drive. It's a car thing."

"A car thing? What?"

"Just get them to come round to the disabled parking, will you? As soon as possible."

"Oh. Another self-entitled prick with a massive car deciding to park in the disabled spots? Scumbags. We have a company that tows them away. I've got the number..." There was rustling on the line.

"No," she said, trying to keep her voice under control. "Just send someone."

Sophie had brought cake to the summer house: a whole rich Christmas cake, dark and glistening with fruit.

Anika consulted her notes about the songs they were recording for the bear. "I've got a list of parts I need from you. I record them on my phone and apparently Daffyd can mix it all together."

Gallagher carved off some generous slabs of cake and handed one to Luka. "Righto. We'll take your lead."

"Let's start with the rumpa-pum-pum, shall we?" said Anika. She started recording and counted them in.

Before they could sing, the door opened and the other manager guy, Tom Eccles, all but staggered in. "Here you are!" he said, flustered.

Luka looked about the chair he sat in. "Yes. Here we are. This is definitely us, Tom."

Tom gestured away. "Charlotte wants someone to help her out in the car park."

"That's nice," said Gallagher.

Tom gave them a pointed look. Anika thought it took Gallagher a very long time to get his meaning.

"Oh, you want one of us to go? Do we do car parks? We're plants."

"You move about as much as plants," said Tom. He couldn't do sarcasm properly, Anika realised. From him it sounded like miserable whining.

"And yet we are vital for the eco-system," said Luka and bit deeply into his cake, spilling royal icing crumbs down his front.

"Can either of you go?" said Tom.

"Are you asking us or telling us?" said Luka.

Gallagher tutted. "Yes. I can go." He put down his piece of cake, untouched, and stood up.

Tom looked about the space, especially at Luka reclining in his chair. "You do know those pallets of compost are *still* by the landscape gardening office? You said you would move them."

"It is on the list," said Luka, tapping his overall pocket. "But right now I must do special recording and the build-a-bear activity."

Tom's face twitched like he wanted to say something clever, then he left, slamming the door behind him. He immediately re-opened it.

"Sorry. Very loud," he said and closed it again.

Luka looked at Anika. "Right, young lady. Let us do the rum-pum-fucking-pums, eh?"

20

CHARLOTTE

Squatting in her car, still hiding from Nick Bellingham, Charlotte peered to see if help was coming. Gallagher from the plants section appeared. Charlotte saw him walk past the driver's window and glance inside.

She snaked a hand round to press the button to wind the window down. "Gallagher! It's me!" she whispered.

"Yes, I can see," he said, a half-smile on his face.

"Now listen carefully," she said, "I need you to be discreet and do exactly as I say. We need to make this situation go away."

"I didn't even know you were disabled."

"I'm not."

"Cos there's a lot of hidden disability these days. It's not all wheelchairs and gammy legs."

"I'm not disabled. That's the problem."

"Okay. Weird attitude," he said.

"We need to make this all go away. First of all, put your hands on your hips and make a massive show of telling me off."

"I'm being discreet but also making a massive show?"

"Discreet is the overall motif," said Charlotte, her head twisting at an uncomfortable angle so that she could make eye contact. "I don't want *him* to see that it's me in this car."

"Oh, the important customer whose spot you've nicked. Gotcha." He straightened up and made his face stern. Then he put one hand on his hip and wagged a finger. "You know that it's very wrong to park here, don't you? I've half a mind to report you to the parking police who will put you in parking jail. Do not pass Go. Do not collect two hundred pounds. Is it even against the law? No fucking idea. I don't think it matters what I actually say, does it? Nobody's listening, but still I need to look as if I mean it. You're a bad, bad woman and I want you to sit in the corner and think about what you've done."

"It wasn't that I was going to stop here," said Charlotte.

"You don't have to explain yourself to me." Gallagher rearranged his features again. "There's no use pleading for mercy. We have a zero tolerance approach to this at Hedgelord. Do you know what's going to happen now?"

"No?" said Charlotte.

"Oh. Well, I was sort of expecting you to tell me." said Gallagher.

"Yes, yes of course. Sorry, your method acting was very convincing there. Now I need you to approach Nick Bellingham who's at the wheel of the car behind. Explain that you're going to impound this car while you call the police or something. Basically, I need you to get him out of the way and move this car somewhere so I can sneak out of it without him seeing. Can you do that?"

"Leave it with me. You'll need to move off the driver's seat, mind."

Charlotte worked on that while Gallagher went over to talk to Nick Bellingham. She found the electronic button which would recline the passenger seat and dropped it back as far as she could. After that, she tried to slither on her belly like a snake into the back of the car. It seemed like a thing that ought to be possible, but the gearstick and handbrake conspired to make it very uncomfortable. She also had to leave her shoes behind in the footwell as she was certain the heels would damage the upholstery.

A few minutes later she had succeeded in getting into the back and Gallagher let himself in and sat in the driver's seat.

"Right, he's out the way for a minute and I can move your car. Any preference on where?"

"No, just somewhere out of sight," said Charlotte.

Gallagher reversed and started to turn the car. "I'll go round to unloading. We can go in the back way."

Charlotte grunted her agreement. She would be glad to get back on her feet.

"Shit," he spat. "There's something stuck under the brake pedal."

She remembered her shoes. "Oh hey, Gallagher! I left my—"

A loud bang accompanied Charlotte being slammed into the back of the driver's seat.

By the time Gallagher and Charlotte had made it out of

the car, Gallagher carrying her strappy heels, there was a small semicircle of people surrounding them and the car they'd backed into.

"Oh, bugger," said Gallagher.

It wasn't much of an impact, but it had smashed rear lights on both the cars.

"We'll need to find the owner," said Charlotte.

Gallagher gave her a look. "It's my car. My actual car. You're insured, right?"

"You were driving," she said and immediately retracted. "I'm sorry. Yes. I am. Fuck."

Her watch buzzed.

Charlotte looked round. Nick Bellingham had pulled up not far ahead and was looking out of his window at them with a most serious and quizzical look in his face.

"Can I have my shoes, please?" Charlotte asked Gallagher as she stood, barefoot, on the damp tarmac.

21

ANIKA

After an hour's work with Luka, Anika was able to catch up with the other elves for the induction.

Daffyd paced up and down in front of the three new elves in the currently empty grotto. The man walked with dainty little footsteps, as though his ankles were tied together, and he stared at each of them as he passed.

"Day one of basic elf orientation and Gillespie has come in his elf costume," he noted.

Anika pulled at her hoodie. She'd told her mum and dad she was off out today, visiting a friend. She'd made no mention of a job, least of all, a job as an elf.

"I didn't know..." she said. "Were we meant to...?"

Sophie, standing next to her, was wearing the same Hedgelord uniform she'd been wearing when Anika had seen her in the café.

Daffyd puffed himself up. "Gillespie presumes that if he dresses as an elf then he will become an elf. Clothes maketh the man. Charles Dickens. Does wearing the elf accoutrements make you an elf? But I ask you—" he dashed in at surprisingly speed until his face was up against Gillespie's "—what is an elf, Gillespie?" he whispered. "*What is an elf?*"

"It's one of Santa's helpers?" said Gillespie, recoiling from the shorter man.

Daffyd smiled indulgently. "One of Santa's helpers. One of *Santa's* helpers. Santa. I remember when he was called Father Christmas. But the Americanisation of our sacred rituals continues apace." He was suddenly in front of Sophie. "What is an elf?" he demanded.

Flustered, she waved her hands. "Oh. Oh. Just a happy little person? A jolly, um, sprite."

"Sprite." He nodded sagely. "Happy. Jolly."

Anika was ready for him when he sprang in front of her.

"Tell me, Little Miss University. What is an elf?"

She looked him square in his beady eyes. "I am."

"What?"

"I am an elf," she said, with as much confidence as she could summon.

He backed away, wagging a finger at her.

"You're all correct," he said. "And you're all wrong. An elf! Young and old. Tiny, but human sized. Carefree, but hard at work all year round." He bounced from side to side as he went through his contradictions. "An elf is all of these things and none of them." He stood proud as though to attention. "I was an elf for many years. Trained under Mikko Mäkelä, twelve time Lapland champion elf. I myself was a recipient of the UK Elfie award 1997 to 1999."

"Erm, well done," said Sophie.

"You become an elf by doing an elf," said Daffyd.

"Doing an elf?" said Anika.

Gillespie cupped his hands, clasping the buttocks of an imaginary lover. "Doing an elf?"

Daffyd ignored him. "You do elf things until you become an elf. And if you work hard enough, you will become the new elves in our grotto and get to work with the big man himself."

Sophie put up a hand. "Is this position to replace Alejandro?"

"It is," said Daffyd.

"But there's three of us. Only one of him."

"He was one hell of an elf!" Daffyd growled.

"He was," said Sophie admittedly.

"Second best elf I ever trained."

"Oh, who was the best?" said Anika.

Daffyd's eyes took on a dark, faraway look. "Nathan Carson," he whispered. "Cracker jokes tripped off his tongue. Babies stopped crying at the sight of his smile. A voice like an angel. A foul Judas betrayer of an elf! I'll not have his name spoken here!"

Anika made a mental note to forget the name at once.

"We have a lot of learning to do," said Daffyd, "along with the practicalities of being an employee at Hedgelord."

"Elf and safety training," grinned Gillespie. He was a handsome man – Luka was right, he did have the look of a young Mickey Bubbles, her mum's favourite Christmas crooner – but even a handsome smile didn't cover up a bad joke.

Daffyd's face, which seemed to flicker through all manner of emotions, become cold and funereal. "Health and Safety is no joke, my son. Have you ever had to cradle an elf after he's taken a broken bauble to the eye? I don't think so. You think Karen on tills, who's our health and safety officer, thinks everyday dangers are funny? Reindeer bites. Tinsel chafing. Back strain from lifting fat children. Your throats will be hoarse from singing. You will suffer from caperer's knee. You have a lot to learn."

"We're not afraid of hard work," said Anika.

Daffyd plucked a plush-covered snowball out of a large bin. "You will be. You will be. This way, elf-friends."

Daffyd led them through to the crowd control gate at the grotto entrance that stopped people just walking in. The entrance was sandwiched between concrete bird baths and bags of coloured gravel. The grotto itself was a series of interconnected sheds on the edge of the plant area near to the shop itself.

"Here we have the check-in," said Daffyd, patting a wooden bird feeding station that was being used like a lectern. "An elf will use the tablet to confirm each family's booking and let them in. If there are available slots, which will only happen early on in the season, then you can take payments from walk-in customers."

"That's a tablet computer," asked Sophie. "Where's the till?"

"Also on the tablet," said Daffyd.

Sophie looked horrified. Anika hoped Daffyd would not ask Sophie to be a check-in elf. After spending time helping Sophie with her CV, Anika realised that Sophie considered mastery of any computer skill a triumph, and talked about it as 'hacking'. Sophie had sat and embellished Anika's elf hat with pom poms while Anika hacked Microsoft Word.

"Now the first room here is the sleigh ride to the North Pole," said Daffyd. "Come inside and sit on the sleigh. I'll show you how to work the lights and the moving wall in a minute."

The room was laid out so that the customers would sit on wooden benches, arranged in a train formation. Daffyd turned on some machinery which projected a film onto the front wall, while the side walls were decorated like a stage set. Huge tinselly boards formed the curved edges of the sleigh, and beyond that were painted fir trees and snowmen dotted onto a cartoonish winter landscape.

"Are you all sitting comfortably?" Daffyd called. "Let's travel to Lapland shall we?"

He hit a button, and the painted walls began to move. They scrolled backwards, giving the impression the sleigh was moving forward. The screen at the front lit up and showed a similar landscape extending into the distance, with reindeer galloping ahead of them, pulling the sleigh, guided by a figure in a pointy hat.

"Oh my! This is quite magical," said Sophie.

Anika had to agree with her. It was corny and super-fake, but she found herself wanting to suspend her disbelief and just go along with it, because it was so very delightful.

The figure at the head of the sleigh turned around and addressed them. Of course it was Daffyd, who also stood to the side, looking smug as they all watched his filmed introduction to the grotto.

"Once we arrive at the North Pole, you will spend time in Mrs Claus's kitchen, making reindeer food. She will no doubt sing lots of jolly Christmas songs with you." Film Daffyd smiled widely.

Real life Daffyd stopped the film and turned off the moving wall. Anika felt a small jolt of disappointment to be back in the world of work.

"So, this film lasts around ten minutes, and tells the customers about what's in the rest of the grotto. We send a group through every fifteen minutes, so there are a few minutes' worth of flexibility in the schedule. Why is that important? Because while we want to keep to schedule, turnaround is dependent on the next room being empty. You will need to get the hang of either whisking them through as soon as possible to make up time, or filling time until the next room is empty."

"How do we fill time?" asked Gillespie.

"You are elves. Pay attention at the back. Elves! What sort of things might you do?"

Daffyd picked up some of the plushie snowballs and juggled them, all the while wearing an expression of impatience.

"We juggle?" Sophie asked. "I'm not sure I can—"

"Juggling is something you could learn if you wanted to," snapped Daffyd. "It's up there with British Sign Language as a skill that a top-notch elf might have. What else might you do with these snowballs? Think hard."

The three of them looked at each other. Anika was drawing a blank.

"No? Seriously? You don't know what to do with snowballs?"

"I mean, we could throw them," said Anika. "But you said that health and safety was really important."

"Snowball fiiiiight!" yelled Daffyd and suddenly snowballs rained down on the three trainee elves. Somehow he had access to more and more snowballs, and they just kept coming. They didn't hurt because they were featherweight fake snowballs, but the shock of them all pelting through the air took a moment to recover from. Anika bent to the floor and gathered her own armful of ammunition. She roared and sent them flying back at Daffyd.

"Good! Good! Keep up that energy! Elves are naughty and lively. Combine it with capering. Knees high!"

Anika hadn't come across the word capering before she came here, but she had the notion it involved footwork, a bit like Irish dancing. She tried that while she threw more snowballs.

"Knees higher! Hup! Hup! Hup!"

Snowballs flew and all three of the trainee elves huffed with effort as they tried to get their knees as high as they could.

The lights turned fully up and Daffyd yelled at them all. "Stop! Let's assume that your group has now gone through to Mrs Claus's kitchen. You have thirty seconds to reset the room."

The three of them stood, uncertain.

"Now twenty five seconds; to sweep for litter, gather lost property, clean up any bodily fluids and put the snowballs back in this box!" hollered Daffyd.

They scrambled to gather the snowballs. Anika was hopeful that litter and bodily fluids wouldn't be a problem, but she scanned the benches anyway and spotted a small pool of liquid. Her eyes widened and she wondered what she was supposed to use. A spool of blue paper sat in the corner, by the box of snowballs. She ran forward, ripped off a length and used it to clean the bench.

"Time!" yelled Daffyd. "It is time for the next group to come in." He looked around, peering critically at the floor between the benches. "Good job. Of course you won't always have that much time, but I'm sure you can speed up. You passed the little test I set for you too." He nodded at the blue paper in Anika's hand. "Don't worry, it's lemonade, not urine. This time."

22

CHARLOTTE

Charlotte stood in Cameron Clasp's office. Inside her shoes, her feet were still wet. "You wanted an update on the Nick Bellingham situation," she said. "Um. Well right now, we've had this small setback, but—"

"Small setback?" Cameron exploded. "He was talking about ringing his journalist friends about our access issues."

"I think," Charlotte nodded, "I *think* I've convinced him not to do that now."

Cameron pulled a face and leaned back in his chair and steepled his fingers in the manner he'd probably seen some yuppie twat do on a movie once. "He's returned all of the lights that he bought here though?"

"Yes. He'd come here to do that anyway. Listen, I need you to understand that Bloomers are behind all of this."

"What? Really? Bloomers parked your car in a disabled

spot and then rammed it into another car while you were trying to avoid being noticed?"

"Not that part, no."

"I'm surprised the other owner isn't suing us or something."

"Actually, it's Joseph Gallagher's car."

"The plant guy?" Cameron stuck out his bottom lip. "Never imagined him as capable of driving."

"But Cameron, the point is, Bloomers have actively poached Nick Bellingham. They gave him some sort of massive discount and sold him all these fancy controllers. Not just for him but his neighbours as well."

Cameron pulled a face. "Those are all things we could have done, surely?"

"I mean, yes..."

"What you're telling me is that now his whole street will be lit up, pulling in journalists for miles around? And all we've managed to do is make him angry? Jesus Christ on a twenty-one gear mountain bike, Charlotte!"

"It's going to be fine," said Charlotte. "I've worked out a new strategy and I can win this back for us. We'll get Nick Bellingham back on board with Team Hedgelord and then we'll find a way to crush Bloomers too."

Cameron Clasp shook his head as he walked over to the window to grimace at Bloomers. He clasped his hands behind his back like a military leader. "Do it, Charlotte. Do whatever it takes. And don't let me down."

23

ANIKA

Daffyd led Anika, Sophie and Gillespie through the door into the next area of the grotto.

"When the grotto is in full swing, Mrs Claus will control this entrance, so you can knock and ask if she's ready. Make a game of it, but she won't unlock until she has reset the kitchen. Now, welcome to the messiest room in the grotto."

They all walked in and looked around. It had the aesthetic of a Swiss chalet interior crossed with the set of *The Great British Bake Off*. Warm wooden boards lined the room, Christmas trees sat in the corners (but now that Anika had started to peer harder at the inner workings, she could see that they hid the bins), and there was a long line of cupboards, topped with old fashioned kitchenalia.

Huge wooden tables with bench seating had individual stations for making reindeer food.

"You can all have a go at making reindeer food now," said Daffyd. "Take a seat."

They all sat at the tables. Anika noticed that everything she touched was sticky. The benches, the tables, everything. She looked at the recipes which were written out in old-style lettering and framed on the wall. They called for different combinations of the ingredients set out in the centre of the tables. Jars were filled with lurid coloured sugar and what looked like bird seed.

"Do reindeer eat this?" said Gillespie.

"No, it's actually bird food," said Anika. "You know, you put it out the night before Christmas for the 'reindeer' and it's all gone by morning."

"I think I'll make Super Booster Reindeer Power Food!" said Sophie, excited. "Can you pass me the blue please?"

Anika reached for the blue sugar, and realised the jars were the source of all the stickiness. She scooped some into her own little bag, and it oozed slightly, soaked through with colouring. She mixed in the seed and fastened the top.

"Now, it's important that we deliver value to customers at all times, so this might be a good time to talk about the elves' code of conduct," said Daffyd. "Who can tell me some things that elves would never do?"

"Er, hit a child?" said Gillespie.

"Snowballs alive! This is not a run through of the ten commandments. I'm talking about things that you might *think* are acceptable but are not. I will give you an important one: elves are never to be seen looking at their phones. As far as customers are concerned you do not possess a phone, got it?"

They all nodded.

"Any other things that an elf would never do?" Daffyd demanded.

Anika was starting to get the measure of this. "Be still?"

"Well, look who just shot to the top of the class! You are quite correct, an elf is never still. An elf is also never...?"

"Unhappy?" Sophie said.

"Good! Very good. So, here in the kitchen I want you all now to assume the role of elf. Assume Mrs Claus is currently distracted by a family who want some pictures with her. You are ensuring that everyone has a lovely festive time."

They all stood up. Anika plastered a huge grin onto her face and did some energetic capering.

Sophie looked crestfallen. "I mean, we can't do capering all day, can we? Some of us don't have the knees for it."

"If you have a full repertoire of jokes and Christmas songs then you could tone down the capering. Use the props in the room!"

Anika watched as Gillespie took this to heart and ran full-tilt at the Christmas tree. "Look at me, I'm a Christmas tree decoration!" He leaped into it, and screamed in pain.

"Holy shit!" yelled Anika.

"Elves do not swear!" snapped Daffyd automatically, but they all ran over to where Gillespie and the tree were now strewn across the floor, baubles smashed all around.

"My eye!" yelled Gillespie, his hand over his eyes. "I think I stabbed it on a tree branch."

"They're made of wire," said Anika, horrified. "What were you thinking?"

"I was trying to be entertaining," said Gillespie. "I can't lose an eye! I'll look stupid with only one eye!"

Daffyd spoke into his radio. "Do we have a first aider on call? Needed in the grotto."

"Yeah, it's Sophie. She should be over there somewhere," came the voice of Karen on tills.

"Oh yes, I'm on call!" Sophie knelt by Gillespie.

A few minutes later, Sophie's gentle questioning and assurances had calmed Gillespie down and he removed his hand from over his eye.

"See?" said Daffyd. "Not making fun of health and safety now, are we?"

To Anika's relief Gillespie's eye was intact, although it looked very red.

"Can I please sit up now?" Gillespie made his way to a bench seat, blinking and weeping. "I think I'll be fine in a minute."

There was a pause, while Sophie continued to peer at his face and fuss over the accident book.

"Good, well we can move on in a few minutes," said Daffyd. "I wonder what we might have learned from this incident?"

"Elves can get carried away," said Gillespie.

"Elves should pull together," said Sophie, giving his hand a squeeze.

"Maybe we will find better ways to be entertaining when there are actual customers here," said Anika. "Like, 'Oh hello young person, let's pull silly faces'."

Daffyd nodded. "Good. Or cracker jokes. You will all need to learn at least three cracker jokes. They will keep a group engaged if Santa hasn't yet finished with the previous groups."

"Cracker jokes," said Anika. "Got it.

"Reindeer facts are good too. Pass round those antlers over there if you want to do some show and tell."

They all looked over at a shelf, where there was a display of spruce boughs, fairy lights and reindeer antlers.

"They're real?" Sophie asked, sounding a bit nervous.

"They shed them naturally," said Anika, hoping she was correct. She'd have to look up more details about reindeer.

"If we're all ready to proceed," said Daffyd, "I need to get you acquainted with the clean-up in this room. It's time-critical, and the mess can be quite extraordinary. I will simulate the mess for you now and give you thirty seconds to clear up. You'll find the things you need over there behind the screen."

Daffyd upended one of the jars of coloured sugar and used his hands to hurl it around the room. He dipped a hand into his pocket and pulled out crayons and pieces of ripped up paper, scattering them across the tables and benches. Finally he picked up a half cup of cold tea from a side table and slopped it into the sugary, crayony mess.

"So, thirty seconds to clear the tables and set each place with a placemat and a bag for the reindeer food. Go!"

Anika didn't hesitate this time. She ran for the corner. There was a dustpan and brush and a roll of the blue paper, as well as a huge bin. She dragged them all out.

"Sophie! Brush up the dry stuff from that table!" She pushed the dustpan at Sophie. "Gillespie, help me get the wet stuff in the bin with blue paper." She ripped off armfuls of blue paper and used it to soak and sweep the mess into the open bin. She now understood why everything had that awful layer of stickiness. She threw the bin back into the corner and looked around for supplies of the reindeer food bags.

"Under the tree," said Daffyd.

Anika grabbed the bags and was about to run back to the tables when Daffyd held up a hand.

"And that's time," he said. "Well that was interesting. Probably one of the best efforts I've seen from a new group."

Anika's grin almost split her face in half.

Daffyd eyed her. "Are you one of life's overachievers, by any chance?"

Anika gave the question some serious thought. "I'm not sure. I can underachieve with the best of them. I do like it when someone notices I've done a good job though, and they tell me."

"You're a gold star seeker."

Anika looked up at him, eyes wide. "There are gold stars? Seriously? How do I get them?" She had always had a semi-mystical reverence for gold stars. They combined her general love of fancy stationery with the dopamine hit which came from receiving praise for something she'd done. Obviously, she could just go to the shops and buy some gold stars for herself, but earning one for real was what life was all about. She was a gold star junkie and she knew it. She hoped she hadn't looked too needy just then.

Daffyd smiled widely. "Let's see. I'll talk about homework in a few minutes. There will be stretch goals and maybe gold stars for anyone who can attain those."

"Are we talking about gold stars that are little stickers?" asked Gillespie. "Or is there a monetary value to them?"

"The sticker kind," said Daffyd.

Anika had not expected elf work to be this interesting. Her very being thrummed with the idea of being able to go after a gold star, even though she could see Gillespie thought it was stupid.

24

GALLAGHER

Charlotte stopped Gallagher and Luka as they were walking out of the store. "Where are you two off to?" she said.

Luka gave her a serious look. "Why? Is this routine stop? You want to check our identification papers too?"

"I mean, I need the bear."

"The bear is done," said Luka.

"And I need it delivering."

"Good. Good."

"Only we're done for the day," said Gallagher. "Early finish today."

"Oh—"

"And some of us have to go to the garage because *somehow* someone managed to smash into the back of my car."

Charlotte bowed her head momentarily, her cheeks

flushed with shame. "The bear's not going to fit in the back of my car, is it?" she said.

"I do not think so," said Luka.

"So I need someone to take it in the van."

"You can drive van. I believe in you."

"Yeah, but loading it up..."

Luka nodded solemnly. "Yes. It is tricky." He put his hands on Gallagher's shoulders and turned him towards the exit. "Thorny problem. We will be thinking of you as we drive to garage."

They walked out into the car park and to Gallagher's little car.

"Canon's Ashby," said Luka as he got in. "You know the way?"

"I do." There was a crunching sound from the bits of plastic brake light cover as he reversed out of the spot. "This is punishment, you know."

"What is?" said Luka.

"We agree to go move some weed for your friend—"

"Sonia Patterson is not exactly a friend."

"—and the moment I have the sniff of some money, the universe swoops in and smashes into my car."

"I thought it was Charlotte Mitchell."

"You know what I mean."

"Her insurance will pay for it."

"Oh, you don't believe that," said Gallagher. "The universe never gives you anything for free."

Luka tutted disapprovingly. "You are so cynical, Gallagher. Too cynical for a young man."

Gallagher scoffed. "You seem to forget how life works. If

the world was fair, I would have an unbroken car and I'd be driving home now so I could spend the evening in front of the PlayStation or having a few jars down at the Brewer's Arms."

"Instead, you get to spend an hour—"

"Two minimum."

"—with a good friend and the open road. I did my singing today. You want to hear some?"

"I do not."

Luka pointed to the right. "Canon's Ashby is that way," he said and began to sing.

25

ANIKA

The elf training continued. Anika had not realised there might be so much of it.

"So how might you speed up your cleaning of the kitchen?" Daffyd asked.

They all looked at the scale of the problem in the messy grotto kitchen. It wasn't obvious how they might have tackled it better.

"I'll tell you the main secret, and that is to sweep all the mess onto the floor," said Daffyd. "Clear up at the end of the day, but until then onto the floor it goes. There will be three times during the day when you get a slightly longer turnaround time. You can use wipes on the table at that point and refill the jars. All clear?"

They nodded and followed Daffyd into the next room, which contained Santa's throne, flanked by fuzzy plastic reindeer and a pair of Christmas trees.

"Families come from the kitchen through the door you've

just used. Sometimes we might open the side door, for example when we do Santa Paws."

"Santa Paws?" said Anika.

"For pets," said Sophie. "Very popular."

"If you're on Santa Paws duty," continued Daffyd, "please remember to roll out the plastic floor covering at the start of the session. Now, we will practise taking pictures and also posing in them. Roleplay time. Sophie, you're the customer. Anika and Gillespie, you are two cheeky elves. Strike a pose!"

"Again!"

"Again!"

Anika ran through a series of funny faces, and sassy poses. Hands on hips, knees high, tongue out. She could hear Gillespie grunting as he tried to do the same.

They switched roles, and Daffyd took more pictures.

"Not bad. Now come here and take the pictures. I will assume the Santa role. Don't touch anything to do with the setup, it's all in the right place, you just need to hit the button and take lots of pictures."

Daffyd sat in the throne and assumed a moody faraway look. Anika thought he looked as if he was dreaming of being able to grow a beard one day.

Anika took pictures. It was a camera phone clamped into a stand, so it wasn't very challenging. Gillespie and Sophie took some too.

"Now pretend I have a dog here for Santa Paws. Make it look at the camera!"

"Who can whistle?" said Gillespie, making small farting noises with his lips. "Never been able to do it."

"There's a squeaker toy," said Anika, picking it up. "Here boy! Good boy!"

"Now I have a baby! It's about to scream the place down, so we need to get a good picture really quickly. How you going to do that?"

Sophie sprang into action. "Happy birthday to you, Happy birthday to you!" she sang in a high quavering voice.

Everyone turned to stare at her.

"Blimey. I think that would actually work," said Daffyd eventually, blinking. "But maybe learn some Christmassy songs, just to keep the mood right, eh? There's a rattle there too, for those who want to save their voices for the other rooms. Now—!" Daffyd sprang up from his seat. "An important thing to remember is that we want to *sell* these pictures. Customers are not to take their own pictures in here, but we don't want to be negative elves. Tell me how we manage to do this? How can we be bright and cheery while stopping them doing something they all want to do?"

Anika looked at Sophie and Gillespie. This was a toughie.

"Do we playfully caper in front of their camera and spoil the money shot?" Gillespie tried.

Daffyd nodded. "Might work."

Sophie frowned. "I don't like to be a bossy boots. I would much rather ask them nicely before we come in here."

"Good!" said Daffyd. "Get them to fill their boots with pictures in the other rooms. Definitely the best approach. Now follow me to the toy room and the photo processing lab."

The toy room consisted of shelving stacked with cheap toys.

"No real rules about giving out toys, apart from one each, obviously. Don't be drawn into conversations about gendered toys. Customers will come in with their own ideas, it's our job to get them through with no dramas. Nod, smile, and don't say anything they can quote in the *Daily Mail*. Now, last room is where they can pick up their photos."

They walked through into a room lined with monitors where customers could see their photos from the Santa room. Each monitor was accompanied by a till where orders were be processed. "We can run through the training for that separately, but those who want to go for the stretch goal will want to remember the various formats that customers can purchase."

Anika thought Daffyd glanced at her, but she was too busy committing the list to memory from the posters on the wall. "Mugs, keychains, fridge magnets, baubles," she chanted to herself. "Digital copies, small print, medium print, large-framed print."

They filed out through the grotto exit into the outdoor world. The sun had set while they'd been in the grotto.

"You are now inducted. I can officially christen you with your elf names to show that—"

"Ah! There you are!" called Charlotte Mitchell, coming towards them. "Just the people!"

Daffyd turned testily to her. "Charlotte! You've just interrupted a very important elf ritual!"

Charlotte looked shocked.

"It's okay," Sophie reassured her. "We weren't going to sacrifice anyone or anything like that."

"I didn't... I didn't think you were."

Sophie turned to Anika. "It's the word 'ritual'. It's all..." She gave a pretend shiver. "Isn't it?"

Charlotte frowned at her, then shook her head. "Look. I do apologise. I had no idea you were doing an elf ... thing. I'm big on respecting other beliefs. But I've got a bear to move."

"Oh, the bear," said Sophie.

"I need to get it in the van. I'm sure..."

Daffyd sighed and gave her a dramatic eye-roll. "Fine. Fine. Elves ho!"

Together, they went across the floodlit plant section to the summer house where the bear was stored. Anika could see Charlotte had half managed to get it onto a pallet truck and that was all.

"Elves together!" said Daffyd.

As one they shuffled the bear onto the low trolley, then Gillespie and Anika did most of the pulling while Charlotte kept the bear steady as they made their way to the loading dock and the green Hedgelord transit van parked there.

Charlotte opened the doors, and with a wobbly and uncoordinated effort the bear was inserted headfirst into the back of the van.

"And down," said Daffyd, even though the bear was already in place. "Job done."

Charlotte looked at them. "Actually, I might need help at the other end."

Daffyd plainly wasn't happy with that.

"I can help," said Anika. "I don't mind."

Charlotte gave her a grateful look, although it was

possibly tempered by the fact Charlotte was angling for a bigger, stronger helper.

"I can help," Anika repeated, turning to Daffyd. "Worth a gold star?"

Daffyd scowled. "Fine, fine. Go help. But first—" he waved his hands about majestically "your elf induction!" He glared at Charlotte. "This is a private ceremony."

"Oh," said Charlotte. She quickly shut the van's rear doors. "I'll just go sit in..." She pointed vaguely and disappeared round the side of the van.

Daffyd arranged his three elves in a row. "So, *now*, I can officially christen you with your elf names to show that you belong," he said in a most grandiose voice. "I want you each to present yourself to me. Whisper your elf name and I will declare you to be a newborn elf. Ready?"

Anika nodded.

Daffyd beckoned her forward. "Elf name?" he whispered.

"Smartypants."

He nodded and tapped her shoulders with a candy cane which had somehow appeared in his hand. "Smartypants the elf is now ready for grotto duties."

It was an exam and she had passed it!

"Elf name?" Gillespie was asked.

It looked as though Daffyd gave a small frown at the answer. "Nunchuck the elf is now ready for grotto duties."

Sophie was last and she looked panicked, as if she hadn't yet thought of her elf name. She whispered to Daffyd.

His shook his head in mild consternation. "Babydoll the elf is now ready for grotto duties."

Sophie curtseyed to an imaginary audience.

"Homework for tomorrow. Who remembers what you need to learn?" asked Daffyd

"Cracker jokes and Christmas songs," said Anika promptly. "Juggling, British sign language, and the list of photo products as stretch goals."

Daffyd looked slightly taken aback that she'd remembered all of the stretch goals. "Yes. Excellent. Now go!" He wiped a pretend tear from his eye. "Go and be good elves!"

Grinning more than she'd ever done when she'd received her A-level results, Anika practically skipped to the passenger door of the van and climbed inside. Charlotte was behind the wheel, seemingly trying to work out what all the controls were.

"I'm an elf!" Anika declared.

"Good for you," said Charlotte, a smile flickering for a millisecond, then she started the engine.

26

GALLAGHER

Canon's Ashby was a village in name only and was really just a bunch of houses and farm buildings that had clustered together by accident. There was no pub, no shop, not even a church. It was the kind of place that Gallagher couldn't believe any person would come to on purpose.

He stopped at a T-junction. "Where we picking up from?"

"Hollybush Farm," said Luka and pointed right.

At least Luka had stopped singing. Luka had treated Gallagher to a rendition of several popular Christmas songs, and where he had not known the lyrics he'd replaced them with words from his homeland and some general expletives.

"Why are we doing this anyway?" said Gallagher, thinking it was a question he should have asked much earlier.

"We are being paid," said Luka.

"No. I mean why are *we* doing this? Doesn't your drug dealer friend have other people drive for her."

"Sure, but Squirrel let her down."

"A squirrel let her down?"

"No. A man, Squirrel. He let her down."

"Ah, he couldn't make it?"

Luka shook his head. "Let her down. Took cut for himself, I heard. So she made a few cuts herself." He waggled his fingers at Gallagher. "Now, Squirrel can't drive so much."

"Jesus Christ! We're delivering drugs for a woman who chops off fingers?!"

"Only when people let her down," said Luka calmly.

When they arrived at their destination, Gallagher saw that Hollybush Farm was a mess of agricultural outbuildings surrounded by dense thickets of holly. There was no sign of any actual farming activity. It looked as if the buildings were used for small businesses and storage.

"That one there, the florist."

One of the buildings had a sign for Candlewick Florist, with a row of pastel tulips painted on a board the colour of putty.

"You'll need to go in, mate," said Gallagher. "I need to keep the engine running."

Luka knocked at the door and disappeared inside. There wasn't much for Gallagher to look at. All of the other units were in darkness. Candlewick Florists had signs up urging people to order their Christmas flowers in good time, or perhaps sign up for a workshop to make a door wreath. Free prosecco was promised for attendees. Gallagher fantasised briefly about a world in which he might need a door wreath.

First of all he'd need an actual door, one that could be seen from outside. Then he'd need the sort of life where he welcomed people to his home, perhaps with a partner by his side. It seemed ridiculously unattainable, so he pushed it aside as Luka emerged from the building.

"Boot is unlocked?"

Gallagher nodded.

Luka opened the boot and swung a huge bag inside. It was the sort favoured by market traders: cheap woven plastic and very large. He slammed the boot. It bounced back. He tried again.

"Boot mechanism isn't working," said Luka.

"It works for me!" Gallagher shouted back.

"Think it might have been damaged in ding with Charlotte."

Gallagher growled in his throat.

Luka pushed the boot down and leaned heavily on it until something went click. He got back in the car. "Floristry supplies loaded up! All we have to do is take them to Clopton Howes. Easy money, my friend."

Gallagher gave a tentative nod. It was pretty easy so far, but that didn't mean he had to be happy about it. "Let's go."

27

CHARLOTTE

Charlotte felt it was important that she should personally deliver the polar bear to Nick Bellingham. She needed this visit to be the start of the healing process between Hedgelord and this valued customer. A small, calm success story was what it needed to be, which was why it was just going to be a one-to-one between her and Nick. A one-to-one – apart from the teenage elf in the passenger seat.

Nick Bellingham's house was a medium-sized detached house in one of the middling housing estates on the outskirts of town. All the roads had names like The Avenue, The Grove, The Croft. Nick had a large front garden open to the pavement. An inflatable snowman and Santa stood on the lawn. A light-up deer stood on top of the porch roof.

"The famous house," said Charlotte.

"Famous?" said Anika.

"World record-breaker for the most elaborate Christmas lights."

"Oh. Cool," said Anika, mustering absolutely the worst amount of enthusiasm.

"It's a big deal. Trust me."

Charlotte parked the van out front and rang the doorbell, eyeing the display on his house. It was impressive, there was no doubt about that, even though it was still a work in progress. Nick had the benefit of a large house, sitting behind an expansive front lawn, so it was like a blank canvas. He lived on a street of similar houses, and all of them had lights that framed the outlines of their main structural parts.

Nick opened the door. He looked deeply unimpressed to see Charlotte. "Oh, hello."

"Mr Bellingham. I wanted to deliver your polar bear in person so you can see that I am serious about apologising for the situation I created today. You are a valued Hedgelord customer, and I want to make sure my actions don't damage that moving forward."

He raised his eyebrows, grunted in assent and put on the barest amount of polite civility. "Yes, yes. Okay." He rolled outside on his wheelchair. "So have you seen the display?"

"I did," said Charlotte. She still didn't understand what it was, exactly. She felt sure there was a missing element, but she would keep her comments neutral just in case. "I love that you've got all the neighbours to join in."

He smiled. "The functionality of the LumaGrid controller has made so much possible for us this year. It's really exciting. I don't know if you can see, but each of us has a big lighting array on the front lawn, and once we've got everything connected up to the controllers, we will synchronise them so that we can have the words to Christmas songs, or maybe a letter to Santa. Jingle Bells is first up. My lawn will say *Dashing through the snow* and next door will say *on a one horse open sleigh.* It will continue down the street for eight houses, which is enough for the whole first verse."

"Wow. Really?"

"Cool, huh? It means that people who take a slow drive down have a different thing to see every day!"

"Amazing," said Charlotte, even though she fumed at the publicity this would give Bloomers.

"Have you got the polar bear in the van? It should be just the thing to go next to the array on the lawn."

Charlotte was slightly mollified by this. There would be a Hedgelord offering out there in that premium position. Just a shame it was old, broken stock that had been hastily retrieved from a skip.

"I'll just get it down, shall I?" she said.

Anika waited obediently by the rear of the van. She opened the doors and then climbed inside to feed the massive bear out to her.

Nick manoeuvred his chair around it, to take a better look. "I don't remember it looking over its shoulder when I saw it."

"We had a focus group session that agreed it was more Christmassy like that," said Charlotte as they levered it upright. "Less threatening. We paid to have it realigned. It's our gift to you. That's also why it's now wearing a scarf. All part of its redesign."

Nick nodded, apparently satisfied with her whopping great lies. Charlotte had long ago made peace with the idea of white lies being allowable because they made people happy.

"What's more, this is a programmable singing bear. Brand new. Only one in the country. Hedgelord is honoured to let you have this prototype." She handed Nick a small remote controller, then she and Anika began to rock, wheel and walk the polar bear down the wide pathway into the garden.

Nick regarded the device and pressed the power button. A green light could be seen inside the polar bear's body. "So I just press play?"

Charlotte grunted as she moved Bruin further on. "There's an extensive Christmas playlist built in."

He pressed the button and Charlotte gave up a tiny prayer for success. She had been assured it would work but she hadn't tested it herself.

"Oh, this sounds like *Little Drummer Boy*," said Nick with a smile.

He was right. The primary singer was unmistakeably Luka Sibersky from the plant area. Gallagher was in there as well. Luka had a pleasing voice, but the thing Charlotte most associated with him was his frequent and fluent swearing. He had an almost poetic way with profanity. The musicality of his accent made her smile at the most outrageous outbursts, even when he triggered her app if he swore nearby. She had no idea whether he was capable of speaking an entire sentence without swearing, never mind an entire song.

"It's a pleasant vibe," said Nick Bellingham. "Who's the singer? He's got a tinge of the Mickey Bubbles about him."

"My mum loves Mickey Bubbles," said Anika.

"He is," said Nick in a knowing tone, "by far the most accomplished singer of Christmas tunes and the Great American Songbook working in the country today. I am in awe of him. He lives not far from here at Denton-on-the-Marsh. You haven't actually got Mickey Bubbles to record this for me, have you?"

Charlotte bluffed. "I couldn't say. We reach out to many people to create our bespoke items. I can check."

Nick gave an absent nod as he played with the remote. "Looks as though I can relay the sound through the LumaGrid too."

"Oh good," said Charlotte, although she wasn't sure why he might do that.

A moment later she realised what he was trying to do as the sound increased to a bone-juddering volume that was coming from hidden speakers somewhere.

"Oh yeah!" said Nick. "Let's see how the bass pops on *Little Drummer Boy*, shall we?"

Charlotte smiled politely as he replayed Luka and Gallagher's song loud enough for passing cars to hear.

"Don't the neighbours mind?" she tried to ask, but Nick Bellingham could not hear her. He was lost in some sort of Christmas reverie. He had another controller in his hands and she saw that some of its lights were pulsing in time to the song.

"Fucking LumaGrid," she muttered. She might as well take advantage of not being heard.

"What was that?" Nick said, raising his voice.

"I said it sounds really great!" Charlotte shouted.

Filled with the satisfaction of a valued customer well-served, she took out her phone and scrolled through her contacts to *J Hartigan (Bloomers)*. She hit dial.

Jack Hartigan picked up with unseemly speed.

"Charlotte!" he said. He sounded somewhere crowded, somewhere fun. *"How very nice to hear from you! – Yes! Kathryn! Get one for me too, darling! – Yes, sorry, Charlotte."*

"Nick Bellingham is ours," she said simply. "He is a Hedgelord customer. Always has been, always will be. Your trash is coming down from his house."

"Really?" said Jack. *"Are you sure? I think Nick is delighted with our offering. I've potentially got reporters from a couple of the nationals coming over to take a look."*

"Yeah? Well, he's changed his mind," she said, knowing that really wasn't true. "You can't compete with Hedgelord's bespoke personal service."

"I'm all about bespoke and personal service, Charlotte."

"With a real focus on serving the community."

"Thank you for noticing."

"I meant *us*. I meant Hedgelord. We're all that stands between this town and a soulless commercial Christmas."

"Wow. Really? Is that on one of your natty corporate vision cards. Don't think I haven't noticed them. They're cute. Laminated."

Charlotte was momentarily stunned that he'd been inside Hedgelord *and* had even seen her homemade mission statement posters *and* she'd not known about it.

"You're going down, Bloomers," she hissed.

.

.

"I thought you'd enjoy some friendly competition," he replied. *"But if you want to go to war..."*

"You want to say that to me, face to face?" she said.

"You mean the Rumble Yard?"

She nodded viciously. "The Rumble Yard. Tomorrow. Dawn!"

"Okay. Er, and by dawn, we mean ... you know, I think it's probably best if we pick an actual time. It's easier."

"Eight o'clock!"

"Can we make it eight fifteen? I'm walking my girlfriend's dog most mornings at the moment and—"

"Eight fifteen," she said. "The Rumble Yard. Only cowards are late." She killed the call and started the van engine.

28

GALLAGHER

They were halfway to Clopton Howes, on that quiet stretch of the B912 which dawdles through the fields just beyond the ring road round the town, when Gallagher noticed a car flashing him from behind.

"There's a car flashing me."

"So? He's flashing," said Luka, licking the paper of a roll up he was making. "Drive on."

The car behind flicked on its blue lights and sirens and continued to flash its high beams.

"Oh fuck," said Gallagher.

Luka tried to swivel round in his seat but there wasn't much room for the big guy. "Oh, fuck," he whispered.

"I'm gonna have to stop."

"You don't think you can outrun them, eh?"

"Mate, they all have fancy fast cars that won't stall at the lights. There's no way this crate's outrunning anyone. And they can see my registration number."

"Okay, okay."

"Now let's just keep our mouths shut and play dumb."

"Oh, I will follow your lead," said Luka.

Gallagher slipped over to the side of the road at a farm gateway. The police car pulled up just beyond. No one got out for ages. Gallagher had a sudden nervous urge to pee.

He glanced at Luka and the cannabis construction still in his fingers. "Joint!" Gallagher hissed.

Luka put it behind his ear.

"Not there!"

A big bloke of a police officer got out of his car.

Luka stuffed the joint in his overall pocket.

The police officer made a window winding down motion. Gallagher did as he was told.

"Evenin' officer," he said, sure his voice cracked halfway through the sentence.

"Care to turn the engine off, sir?" said the copper.

"I'm keeping the hot air blowers going," said Gallagher. "Cold evening."

"Hello, Mr Policeman Sir," said Luka, leaning over to give the policeman a warm grin.

"Engine please, sir," said the policeman. "I need to show you something."

With a sigh, Gallagher turned the ignition off and got out. The policeman sniffed and beckoned him towards the boot. Gallagher decided he was probably just going to piss himself there and there.

The policeman gestured to the rear of the car and the damaged corner specifically. "Your lights aren't working here. Did you know?"

"Oh, right. Yeah. Sorry about that. Some crazy bint backed into me at the garden centre. I'm going to go straight to the garage to get it fixed."

"Which garden centre?"

Gallagher felt an irrational desire to lie even though there was really no reason. "Hedgelord," he forced himself to say.

The policeman turned around to regard the nearby countryside and looked out across the fields.

"Which garage are you possibly going to that involves coming out this way?"

Gallagher blinked. "Oh! I had to pick up my friend here first from, um, Canon's Ashby. And now we're going to go to the garage. Maybe the Kwik Fit on the Bedford Road."

"Do Kwik Fit do lights?" said the cop.

"I don't know. Do they?"

The police pointed a long arm along the road. "Might I suggest Stephenson's garage on Monkthorn Way. Get it booked in. Defective lights cause fatal accidents, especially this time of year. You don't want to ruin your family's Christmas."

Gallagher wanted to point out that any family he had were miles away from here, and if he died in a crash he was sure at least half of them would just nod as though that was a perfectly reasonable and justified thing to happen to him.

"I'll get it along to the garage right away," he said. Gallagher concentrated on looking deferential and sorrowful, but he knew that a decent performance was compromised by his neck tattoos and his unsubtle bearded friend who had now emerged from the car and looked across the roof at them.

"Shall we just take a look inside the boot, sir?"

Gallagher's heart banged in his chest. "In the boot?"

"Sometimes on these older models you can see if there's a loose connection," said the police officer. "Might be able to get that brake bulb working for the time being."

Was this how they did stop and search now? By pretending to be really helpful? If Gallagher said no, he'd be legally sound, he was sure of it. And the guy had already indicated he just wanted him to go along to the garage to get it fixed.

"I don't think—"

"Sure, we can look in the boot," said Luka who was suddenly beside them at the rear of the car.

"Can we?" said Gallagher.

"Old car like this there's a knack." Luka grinned, pressed the boot button and hauled it open.

The officer leaned into the corner behind the lights, playing a torch across the interior. He sniffed. "What's that you're carrying?"

"Floristry supplies." Gallagher could see sprigs of some twiggy stuff sticking out of the big bag. "Doing wreath making at the garden centre."

"Ah, Hedgelord. Right, right. You work there, huh?"

Luka gave Gallagher a look.

"Um..." said Gallagher.

The policeman straightened up. "No. I'd say your lights are jiggered, mate. Get to the garage as soon as possible, yeah?"

"Yes indeedy," said Gallagher.

The policeman sauntered back to the patrol car and got in.

"Fuck me, I thought we were properly shagged there," breathed Gallagher.

Luka's stare was penetrating. "Just 'picked up from Canon's Ashby' did you? Thought you'd tell the cops where we worked too, huh?"

"I was playing it cool!"

"You nearly told him everything."

"He's going now, isn't he?"

The police car was pulling away.

Luka hit Gallagher's arm. "Come on! Twenty miles to Clopton Howes."

Gallagher sighed peevishly and got in. He turned the ignition. The car made a pathetic noise like someone trying to throw up but without much effort or conviction. He tried again. The car retched again.

"Fuck. Engine won't start."

"Try it again," said Luka.

"I did try it again. You heard me."

"Try it again."

"I know this, mate, I know exactly how it goes. It needs to sit for a good couple of hours and then it might start."

"Couple of hours?"

"Unless it's too hot or too cold or too damp."

"Fucking hell, Gallagher. Why do you not have a car that works properly?"

"Says the man whose car doesn't work at all."

"Mine is a classic. Yours is a piece of shit." Luka turned to look behind. "This is not good. Do you know how much weed is in the back there?"

"I did notice, yeah. The weed you showed to the cops."

"I was playing it cool, like Steve McQueen. We cannot sit here."

"This car is going nowhere."

Luka's tone became firmer. "We cannot sit here. The weed cannot sit here."

Gallagher got out his phone. "Uber?"

"Fucking taxi the drugs to Clopton Howes?"

"I bet lots of taxi drivers do weed deliveries."

Luka was getting agitated. "We will be late with delivery. Sonia Patterson will not be happy. Especially if we turn up in fucking Uber."

"Finger-slicing unhappy?"

Luka shrugged.

Gallagher peered out of the window. "Where are we, anyway?"

Luka shrugged. "Fucking nowhere."

"We carry the weed."

"Twenty miles to Clopton Howes!"

"To your house then and rethink."

"Is still four miles and I am not having drugs in my house."

"You always have drugs in your house!"

"For recreational use only!"

Gallagher tapped at his phone to find a map. The way that copper had mentioned Hedgelord it sounded as if—

"Yes!"

Luka looked up.

Gallagher turned in his chair. "Hedgelord is only just over there!"

"What do you mean? Where?"

Gallagher held out his phone. "We're here and the garden centre is there. We could walk round the roads, which looks like about three miles, but it's much shorter if we cross the – uh – whatever that is."

Luka patted the phone with a pudgy finger and peered outside into the darkness beyond the gate next to them. "We can't tell what it is on here. Could be field, could be woods."

"Worth a look though, eh?"

"We carry the weed while we go on a fucking hike?"

Gallagher paused. "Yes. Yes we do, because it's better than sitting here and freezing to death. We get it into Hedgelord and hide it until the morning. Then we can get back on track."

Luka huffed, but it was a huff of acceptance.

It took them a few minutes to climb over the fence near the road, passing the bag across.

"See? This is going to be easy," said Gallagher.

"We are ten feet away from car," said Luka.

"But now it's an open field. We can do this. A handle each and off we go."

They both picked up a handle. The bag hung heavily between them as they walked into the field.

"You know the thing about these piece-of-shit bags?" Luka asked conversationally five minutes later.

"No? What's that?"

"They are piece of shit. I can feel handle coming off."

Gallagher had felt it too but failed to recognise it. A

muted twanging loose of something under tension. "Put it down."

Gallagher shone the light from his phone and saw that the low quality stitching had almost come away from the handle.

"Bollocks. Can we find something else to carry it with?

Luka's face was cast in an eerie half shadow which made his scowl even more grotesque than usual. "Finding stuff in the dark is not so easy. We drag it maybe?"

"Yeah! We can do that. Each grab a corner."

They crabbed across the field, pulling the huge bag along the damp grass. Gallagher had to use one arm to pull the bag and the other to shine a light ahead of them.

29

ANIKA

Anika sat quietly in the passenger seat as Charlotte drove her home in the Hedgelord van. She knew she was probably meant to make small talk. She was a clever person and sociable too, but making small talk with proper adults – like proper old adults, thirty plus – was not necessarily an easy thing to do.

"I think the bear looked good," she offered.

"You think?" said Charlotte with sudden flushing relief. "Really? I thought it might have been a bit..."

"A bit rubbish? No. No, I think it's good."

"Thank God for that," said Charlotte. "The stress this thing has caused me!"

It was said with such earnest passion that Charlotte clearly realised she'd slipped into a moment of vulnerable informality with an employee. She cleared her throat. "I mean, good. Yes. It will absolutely serve its purpose."

They drove on silently across town. Silence brewed between them.

They stopped at the lights in the town centre. Charlotte pointed at the big brightly lit nativity scene outside the church. "See that wise man there? I made his robe. Stitched it myself."

"Oh!" said Anika and wasn't sure what the appropriate comment should be. "Looks nice."

Charlotte nodded and the traffic moved once more.

"You're a ... a church person?" said Anika.

"I try to be." Charlotte glanced at her. "Your family...?"

Anika wrinkled her nose. "Hindu. Sort of."

"So, you don't do Christmas?"

"Not enough. We have a rubbish little Christmas tree. The same plastic one each year. The one my mum puts up at the clinic is way better."

"What does she do?"

"Dentist," said Anika. "A whole family of dentists and doctors and chiropodists. Oh, we keep the Indian stereotypes going in our family. Nah, I'd like a bit more Christmas glitz at home. I try to convince my parents to get a real one, but my mum moans about the needles going everywhere."

"Sure, the regular Norway spruces do," said Charlotte, "but there are some we stock that don't drop needles at all."

"Is that so? Oh ... in here."

Charlotte swung the van into the turning and Anika had her drop her off a good distance from the house.

"See you tomorrow," said Charlotte and drove off.

Anika walked up to their house. It wasn't the only house

on their street without Christmas decorations, but that didn't make it seem any less gloomy.

She unlocked the front door and went in. She was hit by the smell of cooking dinner. Anika realised she was starving. It was a mixture of the nervous energy from learning her new elf role and the simple fact that she'd neglected to eat while doing the induction training.

"Ah! Finally she comes home!" called her mum, which was as common a greeting as any.

At the evening dinner table, she piled her plate high and ate at a ferocious pace while her mother talked long and loud about a new air fryer that someone in the clinic had been talking about.

"Pakoras with less oil, imagine that eh, Sunil?"

Her dad gave a forlorn smile. "But will they still taste good?"

"On the one hand we have the yummy taste of fatty foods, and on the other hand we have your healthy heart," said her mum, using her knife to point at the offending organ. It was a gesture that looked more threatening than caring, but that was her mum all over. "Your cholesterol is what I'm thinking of. Why are you eating like a ravenous dog, Anika?"

"Sorry," said Anika, resting her cutlery in an effort to force herself to slow down. "It's very tasty, that's all."

Her mother pulled a face. "Did you not eat at Asha's?"

Anika adjusted her face while her brain scrambled to elaborate on her claim to have been out all day with a friend. "Oh yeah. We went to the library. She's researching something and we lost track of time."

"Research, huh? Chip off the old block, eh, Sunil?"

"What was the subject?" asked her father. He clearly felt obliged to get involved.

Anika needed something that they wouldn't dig into. "Family history stuff. Pretty boring."

Her mother pulled a face. "I thought Asha's family came from Mumbai? How is it possible that she can research this from an English library?"

"There's this cousin apparently," said Anika, enigmatically, "although it might be a dead end. We'll keep looking. Mainly we've been helping another friend with research. Daffyd."

Anika needed to shape her lies so that they adhered more closely to the truth. That way she'd have a chance of being consistent.

"Interesting name, Daffyd," said her father.

"Can we get a real Christmas tree this year?" asked Anika.

She wasn't certain where that had come from. It was partly an effort to distract her parents from probing her lies too closely, but also because she'd been immersed in Christmas so fully that she wanted to wallow in it at home too. The interior of the Chowdrys' house felt as if it was lacking the festive jollity of Hedgelord.

"A real Christmas tree?" her mother asked. "Well."

'Well' was a holding statement. It meant that her mother was processing something unfamiliar and hadn't yet decided how she felt about it.

"They smell so nice," said Anika.

"You think this house is not Christmassy enough?"

"Old decorations and a pathetic Christmas tree and you

putting on Mickey Bubbles records does not make a Christmas."

"But real trees drop a lot of needles onto the floor," said her mum. "Someone will have to clear up all of that mess."

"Ah no that's just the regular Norway spruce, there are varieties that don't drop their needles," said Anika.

Her father looked closely at her. "I can see that spending time in the library is doing you some good."

30

GALLAGHER

Gallagher's lungs were starting to burn with the effort of dragging a heavy bag across a dark field. He'd also twisted his ankle a couple of times on uneven patches of earth.

He was starting to think – thoughts made all the more serious by the encompassing winter darkness around them – that if they were set upon by a wild creature, like a rabid badger or a really angry cow, then he simply wouldn't have the energy to run away.

But they were close to the end.

"Fence coming up," he said.

"Is there?" puffed Luka.

"Yeah, see where that tree is?"

"I look forward to it," said Luka. "How far from the garden centre now?"

"Not far," said Gallagher without checking. "Come on now, let's do the fence."

They repeated their earlier process with the fence. Luka climbed over, while helping Gallagher balance the bag on top. Then he would take the weight on the other side.

An unearthly screaming sound came from behind them.

"Fuck!" Gallagher didn't wait for Luka to help, he propelled himself over the fence and onto the ground, taking the bag with him. He landed awkwardly on his shoulder and the bag was upended.

The screaming came again, but this time it faded into a *chok-chok-chok* sound.

"Was that a fucking bird?" Luka said.

As if in answer, a frenzied flapping noise came from the tree.

"I think it might have been a pheasant," said Gallagher.

"You know pheasants?"

"I've been a beater on hunts a couple of times, yeah." He stood up, clutching his shoulder. "I've buggered my shoulder."

"Never mind that, you tipped up the bag, there is spray everywhere," said Luka.

"Spray?"

"Little white flower. You know. She added a pile of it on top of the weed bale and said it was to make it look like floristry supplies."

"We still have the bale though?"

"Yeah, we just have no disguise anymore."

"Fuck the disguise." Gallagher felt that his injured shoulder deserved more attention than this, but he shook his head. "We'll need to switch sides. I'll use my other shoulder to pull."

They started off again.

"Why can't we see now?" asked Luka.

"Because my shoulder's buggered and I'm not holding my phone any longer. Feel free to take over," said Gallagher.

Luka huffed and fetched out his own phone. He peered at the screen for a long time. "I have a torch app on here somewhere."

"A torch app?"

"Yeah, I downloaded it because I am boy fucking scout."

"No! You don't need an app, it's just there. Look." Gallagher tapped Luka's phone and the torch lit up.

"Huh. Why they sell app?" Luka asked.

Gallagher didn't trust himself to answer, so the two of them trudged on in silence until eventually they could see a high fence that – yes, Gallagher was quite certain now – led into the plant and shed section of the garden centre. The whole place was shut up and deserted for the night.

"Thank Christ!" he whispered.

When they made it to the fence, Gallagher slapped a hand against the high wooden boards.

"We need to get over."

"I am not built for acrobatics," said Luka. "Also I do not have time or energy to fuck about."

"Your suggestion?"

"We take down fence."

Gallagher looked at the dense, lapped vertical planks. "I'm not sure how—"

"Hnyaa!" Luka grabbed the bottom of a plank with two hands and pulled it away from the rail it was nailed to. He levered it upwards so that he could remove it from the upper rail.

"Nice!" said Gallagher.

There was now a hole a few inches wide. They could see through it, but even Gallagher, skinny as he was, could not squeeze through. Luka had to repeat his strongman party trick several more times before they had a gap Gallagher could get through. From the other side, he tried to help enlarge the hole by kicking the fence, but all he did was hurt his foot.

A few minutes later they were able to squeeze the bale through the fence, with Luka shoving from the far side, and Gallagher heaving it towards him.

Luka came through the hole after it, and Gallagher pretended not to watch as Luka had to manipulate his belly to get through the gap.

"We split up for few minutes. I will hide the bale and you fix fence," said Luka.

"Fine." Gallagher rolled his eyes. If there was ever donkey work to be done, it was guaranteed he would be the one doing it. He went off to find some replacement boards and the tools he'd need.

He was crossing the plant area with some boards when a pair of headlights swung into the car park. Gallagher threw himself flat on the ground behind a raised plant display. The vehicle stopped, engine rumbling, lights still shining through the wire fence into the outdoor section.

Luka came along the path, crawling with elbows and knees like a commando.

"What is it?" he said.

"It's the fucking police," Gallagher hissed.

Luka peered out at the lights. "It is a van."

"The police have vans! Or is it your friend, Sonia?"

"Why would she be here?"

"Probably wondering where her sodding drugs are. Oh, God, she's going to do a Squirrel on us and chop off our fingers. I can't lose my fingers. All my favourite activities involve my fingers."

The van engine stopped. The lights went out. Gallagher heard a door creak and someone step out. The pathway was chill against his chest and groin. He could feel his balls shrinking as he lay there.

"For fuck's sake," a woman's voice said.

Gallagher crept forward and tried to see what was happening.

The woman was inspecting the car next to the parked van.

"Bloody moron," she muttered. "Just reverse out and move it somewhere else. Not a fucking lot to ask!"

Gallagher rolled on his side to look back at Luka. "It's Charlotte, I think."

"You sure?"

"She's swearing her tits off, so yeah."

They waited, cold and still, until Charlotte got into her own car and drove away. Luka got up and brushed dirt off his front. "Good. And now we make camp and guard weed."

"We're guarding the weed?"

"For sure," said Luka. "Like your fingers depend on it. Which they do."

An hour later they met in one of their sheds, and Luka

brought out the bottle of Slivovitz that he kept for emergencies.

"Fence is all fixed up, it's like we were never there," said Gallagher. "Where did you put the bale?"

"Hidden amongst bales of straw in warehouse. Inside big bale with red twine. Even if someone sees it, nothing remarkable. Clever, eh?"

Gallagher nodded. "We gonna try the car again tonight?"

Luka grunted. "Would be like three in the morning before we get to Clopton Howes. Let's get some sleep and fetch it in the morning."

"Oh man. The reindeer are coming in the morning," said Gallagher. "I need to be here for that. I'm the main contact." Gallagher was proud to be the person in charge of the reindeer while they were at Hedgelord. He was like the reindeer whisperer.

Luka shrugged. "Get car after that. We will take the bale in the evening, one day late. It cannot be helped."

"Will Sonia be all right with that?"

"She'll have to be."

They both pulled out sleeping bags and made themselves comfy. If Gallagher could ignore Luka's snoring, he decided this was not a terrible place to sleep. He drifted off into muddled dreams about making a cannabis wreath for the door of their shed.

31

GALLAGHER

Gallagher yawned and rubbed his eyes as he waited by the deliveries entrance to Hedgelord. He made it a big yawn, as if it could expel all the tiredness from his system. This morning he'd got up, trudged round unnecessarily long country lanes to find his car once more, driven home to wash and change, and had just made it back five minutes ago.

"Late night?"

Anika, dressed in the patchwork dungarees and pointy hat of a garden centre elf, was suddenly beside him.

"Jesus!" he said with a start. "How'd you sneak up on me. Frickin' elf powers!"

Anika lifted a curly-toed felt boot. "These make no sound. I'm like an elf ninja."

"Do elves have ninjas?"

She shrugged. "Assassinate Santa's enemies with, um, candy cane throwing stars."

"They're call shuriken."

"Nerd." She looked up at him. "Are you wearing a clean shirt?"

He avoided meeting her eyes. "I do change my shirt from time to time."

Anika leaned closer and sniffed. "Have you had a shower, too?"

"Again, I do have a—" He turned to her irritably. "Did you actually want something?"

Anika shrugged happily. "Not really. Grotto's not open yet."

A Range Rover pulling a long horse box slowed at the entrance and began to reverse in.

"What's this?" said Anika.

"Reindeer."

Anika let out a small laugh. "God, this place goes overboard for Christmas."

"Says the elf. Are your parents proud of what you do?"

She grunted. "Haven't told them. They think I'm on an extended work project because of a measles outbreak at uni."

Gallagher grunted and offered nothing. The horse box inched back towards them.

"Christmas star shuriken," he said.

"What?" said Anika.

"Elf ninja would have Christmas star shuriken and candy cane nunchucks. You know, like Bruce Lee."

"Glad to see you're putting some thought into it."

The Range Rover door opened and Amy Williams jumped out, her long brown hair bouncing on the shoulders of her thick knitted jumper.

"Amy!" called Gallagher and went to meet her.

Amy smiled. She had a gorgeous smile, like sunshine over wheatfields. "Mr Gallagher."

"Ah, just Gallagher," he said and waved her formality away. "Or Mr Gallagher. Whatever. I'll call you Amy. Amy's good, right? How long has it been?"

She gave him an amused and shrewd look. Just the way she looked at him, he could tell she was a billion times smarter than him. He found it intimidating and thrilling.

"About twelve months, I'd reckon. Wouldn't you? Seasonal business and all."

"Right, right," he said and grinned at her joke. Was it a joke? He was smiling like it was a joke? He hoped it was a joke. He was still smiling. He forced himself to stop.

Amy opened the doors to the rear of the trailer and folded down the ramp. Inside were eight reindeer, hitched to the walls next to hanging hay bags. Amy stepped inside to check on them.

"Oh, I see," said Anika. Gallagher gave another start at her sudden appearance right next to him. "You fancy her," she whispered.

"What? What, no. Me?" Gallagher flicked a finger between his chest and the trailer. "Me. I'm nice to everyone."

"Including me?"

"Elves don't count. They're not real."

"She's very ... wholesome. Country girl. Reckon she fancies a bit of council estate rough?"

"Piss off, Legolas," he hissed. "Or I'll tell your mummy and daddy."

Anika backed off silently and scuttled away.

"Fuckin' ninjas," he muttered.

"Are you going to give me a hand, Mr Gallagher?" Amy called.

"Right away, Amy!" he replied with joyful enthusiasm and went to join her in the animal funk warmth of the trailer.

"Same girls as last year," said Amy. "Apart from Comet there."

"We had Comet last year."

"Same name on the muzzle, different reindeer. Old Comet was fifteen years old. Good age. Died of liver flukes in the end."

"What's a liver fluke?"

"Dangerous. The rest are good and healthy. The secret is giving them large spaces to roam in." She passed the reins in her hand to Gallagher and went to untie the others. "Let's see what your enclosure looks like."

32

CHARLOTTE

Charlotte pulled up her car at one end of the Rumble Yard and waited. It was a cool morning, the last of the night mist curling among the rough grass which had forced its way through the broken concrete and compacted stone aggregate.

Charlotte didn't know what the Rumble Yard had once been. Probably a piece of hard standing for the local arable fields: a place to park tractors and combine harvesters. Maybe there had been sheds and out-houses here once upon a time. All it was now was a piece of wasteland, neither here nor there, halfway between Bloomers and Hedgelord.

Similarly, Charlotte didn't know where the name Rumble Yard had come from. She didn't know if she had invented it, or Jack Hartigan had, or if the name pre-dated the pair of them. But they both knew it as the Rumble Yard. It was neutral territory.

Jack's car appeared at the far end and slowly drew up onto the yard.

She paused her Curse Count app. "Jack fucking Hartigan," Charlotte muttered. "Fucking Jack fucking Hartigan."

She turned the app back on and got out of her car. If she been a smoker, this would have been the point where she ground her cigarette under the sole of her shoe.

They walked slowly towards one another.

"Jack mmm-mmm Hartigan," she said, coldly.

He grinned. "Charlotte. Lovely to see you. Breakfast bagel?" He held two wrapped sandwiches in his hand.

"I'm not here for bagels," she said.

"It's turkey bacon and cranberry," he said.

The man clearly didn't understand the professional sanctity of this neutral space. This was a place for cold hard deals.

"Did you say cranberry?" she said.

"Cranberry sauce. And brie, if I recall."

She huffed irritably, held back a swear and snatched one of them from him. "Fine! We're here to talk business."

"Nick Bellingham," said Jack.

"Nick Bellingham business. He's ours. He's a Hedgelord customer and has been for years."

"Exactly," said Jack. "He's been a Hedgelord customer for years. I think this year it's our turn."

She shook her head. "I think he's our customer because we're the best."

"Best?" He put his lip out a little. "If you're having to

source his decorations from our store then I think that technically makes us the best."

"We have the better ethos. The vision."

"It's a garden centre, Charlotte. We sell things. We're a place to go when it's rainy and you don't know what to do with yourself. We sell Christmas trees, barbecues and tropical fish. You're just a garden centre like us."

"That's what the pawn for a soulless corporate shop *would* say."

He smiled and looked away. He had a short stripey scarf around his neck. It gave him a handsome academic air, like a grown-up Harry Potter.

He unwrapped his bagel and bit into it. "Yours will be getting cold. Look – we all know Nick Bellingham has award-winning decorations. It's always in the local paper. I've got a contact at local BBC news who might come down if Bloomers is the official provider of decorations. The brie is nice." He chewed and swallowed.

"Tell you what. We have Nick Bellingham this year. You can have someone else. I hear that chap, Keegan, over in Swaddlethorpe is going for the record. He's willing to spend big, I know. We'll have Nick Bellingham. You have Keegan."

Charlotte was expecting this one. She made a sour face. "Keegan's a racist. It's not a good look."

"He's not a racist."

"You seen his house?"

"A lot of St George England flags outside your house does not make you a racist. He's a proud patriot."

She tilted her head. "Yeah. And a racist."

"He's got a lot of black friends."

She smirked. "Did he tell you? Did he use the phrase, 'I'm not a racist, I've got a lot of black friends'?"

Jack looked uncomfortable. "Actually he referred to them as 'our brown-skinned neighbours'. Look, okay, maybe Keegan is not the way to go, but we can't both be the official supplier of Christmas decorations to Nick. He's the big fish we both hope to catch. He raises money for charity; him and his house are very photogenic. Him being in a wheelchair. The optics of that. It ticks a lot of boxes."

Charlotte laughed. "Oh, ho! Ticks boxes. Fuck, what I wouldn't give for a recording of you saying that. It would be game over. Him being disabled ticks your boxes, huh? You don't deserve Nick Bellingham."

"But we're going to have him."

"Over my dead body, sunshine."

He waved his bagel around as he spoke. "I do have a solution. A sensible solution."

"I'm listening."

"We compete for him."

"Hundred yards sprint?"

"We do the hard sell. I'll let you start this morning. Give it your best shot. I'll go visit him later, after you've spent your ammo. I won't set a foot inside his door until later today. We alternate. End of the week or whenever, we ask him to pick, and whoever he picks, the other one gives in graciously."

"I can be gracious," she said.

He nodded. An agreement made. Smiling, he pointed at his bagel. "The brilliant thing about brie is you'd think it'd be full of calories, but actually the soft creamy cheeses are less fattening than the hard cheeses like cheddar and parmesan."

He raised his bagel in cheers. "Let the competition commence," he said and turned away, back towards her car.

"We're gonna pound you into the fucking ground!" she shouted after him. Her watch buzzed at the profanity.

"That's the spirit!" he called back.

Charlotte stomped back to her car and drove to work.

The turkey, cranberry and brie bagel was delicious, which was more bloody irritating than anything else.

33

GALLAGHER

The beautiful and wonderful Amy Williams offered a handful of nibbles to Blitzen and then brushed the remainder from her fingerless gloves.

The reindeer enclosure had both an inside area for shelter and an outside area where they could be viewed by garden centre customers. Gallagher had hung some bales for them to nibble on along the fence in order to entice them outside.

"You have the routine," Amy said to Gallagher. "Any problems, the e-mail address is on the card." She passed him a business card, their hands almost brushing.

"Maybe I should take your number as well," suggested Gallagher. "You know, just in case…"

She gave him a look. "Just in case?"

He tried to shrug casually. "I don't know. Reindeer emergencies."

"Such as?"

"That's the nature of emergencies. You don't know what they might be. Them liver flukes. What if I see signs of them. Whatever a fluke is."

"Ha! Ha!" declared Cameron Clasp with a massive clap of his hands as he approached the enclosure. It was not common to see the garden centre owner walking round his domain. He was wearing a long camel hair coat, with a scarf laid neatly around his shoulders. He looked like a premier league football manager or a chilled out mafioso. "This! This is Christmas!" He looked at Amy. "You the delivery girl?"

"They are my reindeer," said Amy.

"And she is a *woman*, not a girl," said Gallagher gallantly. He felt an unfamiliar moment of self-doubt and looked at Amy. "Woman. That's...?"

"Last time I checked," said Amy. "I mean, I don't need to check..."

Gallagher could see Cameron's eyes roving over Amy's chest. Her cable-knit jumper formed a beautiful curve over her boobs. Gallagher wasn't going to lie to himself and pretend he hadn't given them a good look, but there was a difference between surreptitiously admiring natural beauty and giving tits a solid ogle.

Gallagher tried to insert himself between those eyes and those boobs, natural like, as though he was just moving in that direction anyway, and not trying to deflect pervy laser beams. But Cameron's gaze moved on of its own accord.

He crouched to inspect the underside of the nearest reindeer. "Which one's Rudolph?"

"Sorry?"

"Don't boy reindeer have...?" He made a wavy floppy motion with his hand. "In the undercarriage."

"These are all female reindeer," said Amy.

Cameron's face creased in a mighty frown. "Oh, no, no. That won't do. We want boy reindeer. Big strapping man-deer. We don't want second rate."

Amy was frowning too now. "Females are second rate? All Christmas reindeer are female."

"It's the antlers," said Gallagher, keen to show knowledge.

"Eh?" said Cameron.

"Male reindeer lose their antlers at the end of autumn," said Amy. "It's less ... Christmassy."

"Huh." Cameron stared off into the distance as though trying to assimilate this. "Thought they'd be team players. Good stuff, though."

Gallagher watched him move away.

"Parasitic worm," said Amy.

Gallagher looked at her.

She smiled. "Flukes: sexless parasitic worms. Their mouths and their arseholes are the same hole." She took the business card from his hand and wrote a number on it. "For reindeer emergencies."

"Gotcha," he said.

He walked her back to her vehicle and waved her off. He almost skipped back through the garden centre. He bumped into Anika next to the tropical fish section.

"Someone's happy," she said.

"Got her number," said Gallagher, flicking the business card.

"So you do fancy her."

"I've got taste and so has she."

"Kim was looking for you."

"Where?"

"Café, I think."

34

ANIKA

Anika had walked to Hedgelord that morning for her first shift as an elf. It hadn't occurred to her that she would be making the trip in the dark, which was a lot less fun than walking there during the daytime. It had been bitterly cold and the ground was frosty.

She'd clocked in, enjoyed a few vital minutes poking gentle fun at Gallagher for fancying the posh country girl in the tight jumper, then went into the grotto. Sophie was already there, wearing a tall pointy elf hat that had ears on the side.

"Did I see you walking in this morning?" were Sophie's opening words.

"Yes."

"You didn't drive? You weren't dropped off?"

"No. I don't. I can't."

Sophie was horrified. "Give me your address. If we're working the same shift I can come and get you."

"Oh. Right."

Anika couldn't give Sophie her actual address. If Sophie came and knocked the door it would result in a new strand of things she'd need to explain to her parents. She imagined Sophie's kindly face, with those elf ears, in her parents' doorway.

"Haven't you got those ears the wrong way round?" said Anika.

Sophie felt them. "Pointy end up."

"Yes, but ... you've got the flat bit at the front and the curvy bit at the back. It looks like you're listening backwards."

"I don't think so..."

Together they walked through the grotto spaces into Mrs Claus's kitchen. "I've put on all the heaters," said Sophie. "It will be toasty in a couple of hours."

Anika pulled a face. "Are you sure? It's freezing in here!"

Sophie nodded. "Well at least we've got half an hour or so before the grotto opens. We can revise jokes and songs while we wait."

Anika needed no revision. She'd done her homework. "Okay, let's—"

She was interrupted by Daffyd bursting in from the next section, a big box in his hands. "Elves! Elves! Small emergency. All hands on deck!"

A gaggle of elves from other sections followed him in. A gaggle of elves? Anika wondered what the correct collective noun for elves was.

"Right, as we all know, the children do some colouring here in the kitchen when they have made their reindeer food. This would normally be in the form of a cardboard decoration they can hang on their Christmas tree. When we unpacked the boxes, it turned out they contained Easter decorations." He held up a packet with an Easter egg in it. The packet was emblazoned with yellow chicks.

"Oh goodness," said Sophie.

"What we have as an alternative are these photocopied Santa colouring pictures," said Daffyd, holding one up. "I will need you to punch holes in the top of each piece of paper and add some sparkly string, so that they become tree decorations."

They all nodded dutifully.

"How many?" asked Sophie. Daffyd had a bulging carrier bag.

Daffyd looked up as he ran through some numbers. "It's not a fully-booked day so we should get away with four hundred. We're hoping the correct stock will arrive by tomorrow."

Anika looked at everyone's faces. "Four hundred? Don't we open in twenty-five minutes?"

"Yes, but you have an extra fifteen minutes before they will be in here," said Daffyd. "They will be busy travelling to Lapland next door."

There was a subdued silence as they all processed the nonsense idea that fifteen extra minutes would be enough.

Sophie reached for the hole punch and made a hole in a sheet of paper. It was very off-centre. "Oops. Practice makes perfect I guess."

"Hang on though," said Anika. "What if we said these

Easter eggs were baubles? Rip off the packaging and they almost *could* be?"

There was a collective intake of breath. Everyone turned to look at Daffyd. He stalked right up to her and held out one of the decorations. "Do it!" he hissed in her face.

Anika knew that she should be intimidated by the task, as Daffyd obviously intended, but brightly coloured stationery awoke something in her. It was partly the enjoyment she'd felt as a neat primary school kid, partly the need to be correct and appreciated for being smart. She plucked red and green felt tips from the jar in the centre of the table and got to work while everyone watched. She made the egg into a dazzling Christmas bauble, with some yellow stripes around its plump middle. When she had finished she held it up by a string which was already threaded through its top.

"What do you think?" she asked.

There was a ripple of half-hearted appreciation from the room. Her colouring skills were not in doubt.

"Very good, Smartypants," said Daffyd, without much enthusiasm. "Gold star for you."

To her surprise and delight, he produced an actual packet of gold stars from a pocket and stuck one onto her colouring. Then he hung it from the Christmas tree in the corner.

"That is what we will do."

Anika had led the way and received a gold star for her efforts. She beamed around the room, delighted that she'd started her first real job and was doing well at it.

Mrs Claus swept into the room. It had to be Mrs Claus.

Either that or a mad woman in a Victorian cook's outfit and frilly mop cap who had decided to hang a hundred Christmassy trinkets from her outfit. She was as impractically dressed and as gaudy as any pantomime dame.

"What a wonderful team!" she shrilled and fist pumped the air. "Oh, the energy in my little kitchen! What a great way to start the day!"

The manic zeal on the woman's face was a stunning sight. Anika realised her jaw was hanging open.

"That's Miranda Colbourne," Sophie whispered in Anika's ear. "She's been Mrs Claus for years."

Mrs Claus – Miranda – swept round the room, eliciting high-fives off elves, even those who really didn't want to.

"Is she on something?" Anika asked.

"On something?"

"Ecstasy? Speed? Scientology?"

"I think she's just a really happy person," Sophie whispered. "She lives in a big house with four dogs. They say her husband up and left her in the night, never seen again. Four dogs and a husband. That's too much for anyone. I'm simply glad I've got my Douglas." Sophie managed to catch Anika's eye. "They *say* her husband left her, but no one's ever seen him since so..."

On that sinister note, Daffyd ushered the other elves back to their grotto spaces and Anika and Sophie were left in the kitchen with the grinning, maniac Miranda.

"Welcome, welcome!" she said. "I hope you're as excited as I am!"

"We are, yes," said Sophie in a tone that was several rungs down the excitement ladder from Miranda's.

"Tell me your names!" demanded Miranda. "Your elf names, I mean of course."

"Smartypants," said Anika, pointing to herself.

"Babydoll," said Sophie.

"Babydoll? Rarr!" Miranda made a clawing motion. "I used to have you in nightdress form, back in my more slender days."

Anika pulled a questioning face at Sophie, trying to get her to explain, but Sophie's face was as open and oblivious as ever.

"What do you want us to do, er, Miranda?" asked Anika.

"Address me as Mrs Claus while we're in here."

"Sorry Mrs Claus. What would you like us to do?"

"Timing and doors!" she pointed at Anika. "Dustpan and re-stock!" at Sophie. "Obviously the cleaning is for everyone. Singing is for everyone. Don't ever let it get quiet in here."

Anika jumped as there was a knock at the door.

"It's the first group ready to come in," said Miranda. "Look lively!"

At Miranda's instruction, Anika opened the door and customers streamed in.

35

GALLAGHER

Gallagher had gone to look for Luka in the cafe, with every intention of telling him he now had the mobile number of the fair lady Amy. He might also casually mention how he'd tried to take a perv bullet by leaping in front of her boobs.

The Pagoda Restaurant was already busy with the pensioner breakfast crowd. Luka hurried over to him.

"Guess what..." said Gallagher, already raising the business card.

"No, you guess what," said Luka seriously. He held up a hand as his phone started ringing. "I ignored this twice already. Sonia Patterson."

"Drug dealer Sonia Patterson?"

"How many Sonia Pattersons do you think I know?" He answered the phone. "Sonia. Sorry, was in the shower."

Gallagher watched Luka. It was rare to see concern of any kind on the older guy's face. It was like someone had told him he'd get worry lines when he was young and abstained ever since. His face was old, but smooth. It creased more naturally along the lines of a smile than anything else. Gallagher's hand went to his own face, which he knew was the exact opposite. Lines of worry were etched into it, even though he was half Luka's age.

"I can explain this to you, Sonia. Give me one moment. There was some car trouble last night. We are smart adaptable people though, so we made alternative arrangements."

Luka looked up at Gallagher. Something clouded his eyes. Was Sonia shouting at him? Gallagher thought he could hear the sound of a raised voice.

"No. No, I heard about Squirrel. Yes. The package has not left my sight. It will be there this morning, very soon. Yes. Will call you." Luka disconnected the call. "Sonia is unhappy with the delay."

"I gathered. Is she going to cut off our fingers? I did mention how attached to them I am, didn't I?"

"We will need to take that bale over to Clopton Howes as soon as we can."

"We can see if there's any deliveries going out, maybe swap with whoever's doing them?" Gallagher suggested.

Luka put a hand on his arm. "Tread carefully if you start asking if you can help out. I heard that the grotto is understaffed today. If they think we have free time there will be an elf hat on your head before you know it."

"Fuck off!" said Gallagher, recoiling in horror. A passing pensioner scowled at him.

"Consider yourself warned," said Luka. "Daffyd is already

on a knife edge because one of his Santas hasn't turned up yet."

"How many does he need?" Gallagher grinned, even though he knew the answer. One was for the regular grotto, while another was doing Santa Paws in one of the larger summerhouses set up as a mini grotto. "You not tempted yourself?"

Luka had the beard and the round face for Santa. What he lacked was any enthusiasm for engaging with people on matters unrelated to plants. "I think they know better now than to ask imbecile question like that," he said.

"Not even for Santa Paws? Dogs are way better than people," said Gallagher.

"It is true, but no." Luka gripped Gallagher's arm. "We get delivery in your car this morning and take to Clopton Howes."

"The car needs time to cool down again."

"Piece of useless shit."

"Says the man whose car doesn't even go."

"Fine. We lay low this morning. Avoid getting roped into anything else. We will devise reason for going out, yes? We need to move fast in order to save your finger, I think."

CHARLOTTE DROVE to Nick Bellingham's house before lunch. Weapon number one in her arsenal was on the passenger seat next to her. She had wanted to use the journey to mentally rehearse what she was going to say, but Cameron Clasp chose that time to call her.

"*You got this Nick Bellingham thing all sewn up?*"

"Doing it now," she said, taking a turning alongside the river.

"*I don't like it. You've got to bring this ship into port, Charlotte. There's more than kudos riding on this.*"

"I know."

A pause. A sigh. "*You know, you should step back. After the parking fiasco, this is clearly too big for you. I should be the one who's there.*"

She wrinkled her nose. "Do you know Nick Bellingham? Do you have any kind of relationship with him?"

"*I can speak to him man-to-man over a round of golf.*"

"He doesn't play golf."

"*Every man plays golf. It's what makes him a man. Along with the, um...*"

"Testicles?"

"*Trousers. This is high stakes stuff, Charlotte, and I can't sit idly by while you roll over and show your tummy to Bloomers. I need to be in the cockpit. I need to have my hands on the joystick.*"

"Is this a ship or an aeroplane?" she asked.

"*It's bloody serious. What's your gambit?*"

"My gambit?"

"*Gambit, Gamba, Gambini. Your ploy! Your strategy!*"

"I'm taking him a tasty gift."

"*Ah, a bottle of Macallan whisky. Good. Good.*"

She glanced at the stacked trays next to her. "Actually, I'm taking over some gourmet deli snacks and cakes."

"*Cakes? Fuck a duck, Charlotte. You can't win a man with cake!*"

"I believe you can."

"No. No. This is wrong. Abort! We need to strategize."

"Sorry. I'm going into a tunnel. Going to lose you."

"There are no tunnels round—"

She stabbed her car console to end the call. He tried calling her back. She didn't pick up.

36

ANIKA

Anika's first proper customers of the day, her first true encounter with the grotto-visiting public, was not what she had expected.

The group was not a tidy group of fresh-faced and eager children, as she had pictured, but a straggling line of chaotic humans. Some middle-sized children ran full-pelt to grab a seat and start pawing through the things on the table. Adults were either fussing over their children, scrolling through their phones while they ignored everything, or fighting their way in with a pushchair, a basket from the shop and a huge pile of coats. Quite a few of the smaller children were screaming loudly.

"Welcome!" boomed Miranda. "Welcome to Mrs Claus's kitchen. Take a seat, there's room for everyone. Pushchairs to the side where they won't block the doors."

Anika helped someone park a pushchair and find a seat.

She wondered how long it would take a person to go deaf simply from the noise of children. It was instantly overwhelming.

"Baking is what we do in here," roared Miranda, striding to the front, and casting her arms around the kitchen. "What do you think we've been baking?"

"Cookies," said one girl.

The noise level had dropped slightly.

"Mince pies!"

"Cakes!"

"Yes! One job we haven't done yet is reindeer food. Is there anyone here that can help?"

Miranda was merely shouting now, as the room had quietened right down. Lots of hands shot up. There was wailing, but it was a single child who looked half asleep in the arms of a woman who didn't seem to notice the noise.

Miranda gave out some basic instructions for the reindeer food and there was a flurry of activity as the children all grabbed for plastic spoons and started to spray the ingredients everywhere. Anika had assumed Daffyd was being overdramatic when he had demonstrated the mess they would make, but apparently not.

"One rule we insist upon in this kitchen is that we must sing!" Miranda yelled. "Who has a favourite Christmas song?"

"Rudolph the Red Nosed Reindeer!"

"Good choice. Let's sing that."

Miranda's voice wasn't a sweet and melodious thing, but it was strident. To Anika's surprise, most of the people in the room joined in. Not all of them were loud, but they were all keen to at least mouth along while they worked, as if it was a part of the cooking task they'd taken on.

Anika sang too, but when it came to the line about all of the other reindeer, there was a sibilant hiss at the end. Her head shot up. Had everyone just said 'reindeers'? Surely they knew that the plural of reindeer was *reindeer*? Was it part of her job to correct them? She glanced at Miranda who looked unconcerned and at the end of the song moved on to mention more about the practicalities of reindeer food.

When everyone moved on to some colouring and they'd sung more songs, Miranda pointed at the clock.

"Need to keep an eye on the time, Smartypants. See if Santa's ready for this group, and if so we can move them on."

Anika went through the door to find Santa was sort of ready. He was settling down into his seat and checking his mobile phone while an elf picked errant bits of fluff off his costume.

"Kids are coming through, Santa," she said.

Santa looked at her over his half-moon glasses. "Call me Raymond, love," he said in a rich and plummy tone. "You're new here, aren't you?"

"I am. Smartypants."

"Thought so." He brushed his lap with his white gloves. "I make a note to get to know all the new elves."

"Right. Can I let them through?"

"Number one thing you need to know in this gig is that Santa is the headlining act, whether it's me or someone else. Everyone can wait five minutes for Santa. You can entertain them with free drinks and vouchers and something until I'm ready, yes?"

"Er, we don't have vouchers or—"

"Once saw T-Rex in concert. Two hours late they were. These good people will cut me five minutes slack if we could tolerate Marc Bolan being two hours late."

"I don't know who that is." She put on a bright smile. "Punters coming through in one minute, Santa Raymond."

She ducked back through the door and helped orchestrate the exodus of paying customers from one space to the next. A few minutes later the room was empty.

"Oh my goodness, what a rush!" said Sophie. "It's enough to make your head spin. Now, how long do we have before the next group comes in?"

There was a thunderous knocking at the door.

"That's them now. We need to clean the room first though, so dustpan and brush – chop-chop!" said Miranda.

"But—" Sophie looked as if she just wasn't ready to accept the pace.

Anika dashed forward and grabbed the dustpan and brush. She whirled between the tables, sweeping the mess onto the floor in a messy spray, leaving something that might resemble a clean surface if you didn't look closely.

"Re-stock this table, Sophie, I'll do the rest!" she yelled.

"Great team work!" shouted Miranda.

Anika was almost ready to do it all again. She realised the entire day was going to be at this pace, back to back. She grinned in anticipation at the upcoming challenge.

Just one little fix was needed. While Miranda was getting the new group settled Anika walked over to the blackboard displaying the reindeer food recipes and picked up some chalk to add a note of her own.

The plural of reindeer is reindeer.

There. Now she had something to point at if people got it wrong. She could tolerate the crazy pace, the incessant noise and the sticky surfaces, but she wasn't going to tolerate abuse of the English language.

37

CHARLOTTE

Charlotte parked on the road outside Nick Bellingham's house, then walked up to the front door with the trays balanced in her hands, admiring the rebuilt polar bear as she passed. A video doorbell winked at her. The door opened before she could even press it.

Nick was wearing an eye-blistering knitted Christmas jumper. It featured baubles that stood out in a 3D display.

"Looking festive, Mr Bellingham," she grinned.

"Feelin' festive, Ms Mitchell," he replied. "Come on through. I'm just feeding the birds in the garden. What have you got there?"

He backed up the hallway and turned round to lead her through a large and spacious kitchen. A man's voice was softly crooning some sort of chestnuts, log fires and mulled wine jazz Christmas number. That would be the sound of Mickey Bubbles then. Clearly the internet rumours about the famous Christmas crooner having a penchant for Christmas-themed erotica hadn't damped Nick's love for him.

"These are just some little treats," she said. "A thank you for a valued customer."

He laughed. There was even a bit of a Santa 'ho-ho-ho' in there. "I am a lucky chap."

"Caprese skewers, spanakopita bites, macrons, truffles, petit fours."

"I don't even know what some of them are," he said happily as he led her on through a spacious conservatory utility area that led out onto a patio and the back garden. "It's been a day for food gifts." He gestured to a square tray on the side in the utility. On it rested twenty or more glistening white balls, dotted with what looked like crushed biscuit. "From Bloomers."

"Bloomers?" So much for holding off until tomorrow!

"Put your things there. I hope you'll help me eat them."

Charlotte put her own trays down and picked up one of the shiny morsels from the Bloomers tray.

She followed him out onto the patio. The rear garden was more expansive than the front. Trees broke up the long lawn. A bird house and a range of bird feeders dotted the grass.

"Love the birds," he said. "Bit of an amateur nature photographer. Love the tech. I'm lucky that I have the geese fly over going to and from Clopton Reservoir. Magnificent creatures."

She bit into the white ball. What she thought might have been white chocolate or melted cheese was neither. The texture was soft and slimy, the taste unpleasantly bland, only greasy. She tried chewing. The crushed biscuits were little tiny bits of grit against her teeth. She tried not to gag and chewed on.

Nick turned to look at her. "That's a fat ball," he said.

"It's..." She reached for any means of describing it and failed.

"For the bird feeder," he said, pointing.

She chewed on miserably. "Yes."

"It's just lard and seeds, really."

She forced herself to swallow and tried not to cry. "My mum always did say I ate like a bird," she managed to say. "But lard is underappreciated, don't you think? Yum."

"Well do save some for the birds, won't you? Oh, I think there might have been mealworms in them too."

Charlotte knew about breathing exercises to calm the mind. She had investigated many techniques that might work in her constant battle against the demons of her anger.

She fought the rising gorge with some deep, slow breaths. She could not afford to vomit in Nick Bellingham's presence. She was here to build bridges and charm him, not puke on his patio.

"Goodness me, I bet the birds go mad for these, what a powerhouse of much-needed nutrition they must be. I'm a firm believer in testing products as thoroughly as possible. It's part of Hedgelord's ethos of taking great care of our community."

"Your community extends to wild birds?"

"It certainly does."

Nick Bellingham nodded. "I respect that. Jack Hartigan said something similar."

Charlotte wanted to pour scorn on the empty claims made by her nemesis, but she couldn't afford to appear ungracious. She smiled and nodded. "I'm sure, yes."

"He made those fat balls himself, apparently. Wanted to make sure there was no compromise when it came to the ingredients."

Charlotte's mind was leaping ahead. Was he about to wax lyrical about plump juicy mealworms? She might not be able to deal with that, so she jumped in to change the subject.

"I hope you realise that Hedgelord is serious about our ongoing relationship. Your custom is important to us, and I think there have been a couple of instances recently where our enthusiasm has got the better of us."

He looked up at her. "Are you talking about when you lied about having the LumaGrid? Or maybe you mean that time you parked in your own disabled parking space and crashed your car trying to sneak away?"

Charlotte's hands started some kind of terrible mime where they patted an imaginary football, trying to somehow own the awfulness, but squish it into a smaller ball of awfulness.

"Yes. Those things. All of those things. Like I said, it all came of us trying too hard. I want to make amends. Hedgelord would like to start off by making a donation to your favourite charity. How would that be?"

"Honestly? That would be really lovely." Nick beamed at her.

Charlotte grinned widely. This was it! This was where she was going to recover the situation and get everything back on track.

"I'll need to think about which charity," said Nick Bellingham. "My go-to charity at this time of year tends to be the homeless shelter, but Jack Hartigan made a donation to that on behalf of Bloomers, so I'll think of another one."

Charlotte froze. Sometimes she pictured herself as if she was an outside observer. She saw the grimace of shock and horror on her own face. She saw Nick Bellingham, oblivious to the impact of his words, musing on the correct charity. The soundtrack would be one of those effects where the cheerful music was interrupted by the sound of a needle being dragged across a vinyl record.

"Yes. Do think about it." Charlotte would need to think of something bigger to top the desperate scheming of Jack Hartigan.

"Oh, there is one other thing you can help with," said Nick.

"Yes?"

"Your singing bear."

"It's beautiful, isn't it?"

"It's certainly majestic. Although there appears to be an issue with the sound quality."

"Oh. Really? I thought it sounded wonderful last night."

"Generally, it's fine. Come."

Nick set off around the side of the house, his wheelchair riding over the smooth, trimmed lawn. Back round to the front they went, and to Bruin the bear. Nick had the little remote control in his hand. "Now, listen to this," he said.

He pressed a button and the choir of elves began to sing *The First Noel*, soon joined in by the bassy vocals of Luka Sibersky.

"Lovely sound," said Charlotte.

Nick brandished his other remote and the sound came through the LumaGrid's speaker system.

It was all truly rather magical until the song ended and the volume faded, and there was a small but audible *"Thank fuck"* of relief from Luka.

"Hear that?" said Nick.

"Hear what?" said Charlotte.

"Don't worry. It comes again," said Nick.

The next track was elves from the grotto singing *Silent Night* in their sweet young voices.

Nick held up a finger for silence and Charlotte listened with growing trepidation. Right in the middle of the song, beneath the other voices but clear enough, was a muttering.

"Who the fuck do they think they are? Making me do this?"

It was as if the bear himself was objecting to his own performance.

The swearing was clearly audible. Nick Bellingham clicked the sound off. "What on earth do you think that was?"

Charlotte waited for inspiration to strike. Some plausible lie that would make this alright. "I ... I'm not at all sure what that was."

"Maybe I phrased the question incorrectly," said Nick. "What it *was* is not in doubt. It was the sound of someone swearing on a recording of Christmas songs that should be family friendly. My question should probably have been, why do Hedgelord think that such a thing is acceptable?"

"A quality control issue has definitely occurred here,"

said Charlotte. "I will fix that if you leave it with me. The smallest of edits is needed and—"

"Thank you." He drew in a heavy breath, as though he was deeply disappointed more than anything else. "Perhaps you could go away now, take your bear with you and come back when he doesn't have a potty mouth."

"Right," she said. Keen to comply, she went to the bear and began to lean it over. But what was she doing? She'd only come in her car. There was no taking the bear. Awkwardly, she righted it, patted it gently and said, "I'll have it repaired on site for you, Mr Bellingham, sir."

"See that you do," he said and went inside his own house.

Charlotte stomped back up to her car, hands shaking with fury and she got out her phone.

"Fucking Luka, fucking fuck fuck, fucking fucker," she fumed, feeling a bitter serotonin hit with every buzz her watch made.

38

GALLAGHER

Gallagher was contemplating moving the pallets of compost from outside the landscaping office when Luka tapped him on the shoulder.

"I have idea for a way we can disappear for an hour to do delivery of Sonia's gear and nobody will argue."

"Brilliant," said Gallagher, "What do we need to do?"

"I just need you to collect some reindeer shit."

"Excuse me? You what?"

"Reindeer shit. Droppings. They must have produced some."

Luka explained to Gallagher what he had in mind. Gallagher shook his head both at the lunacy of the idea and at what his role in it was going to be.

Ten minutes later he scrabbled in the straw beneath the reindeer in their outside pen. The reindeer were happily munching on the bales of straw and standing around like the dopey ruminants they were. The first of the child visitors to the grotto that day, clutching gifts from Santa and probably looking no happier than when they'd gone in, watched him over the fence.

"Mummy! He's touching poo!"

"Shush, Tiana. It's the man's job."

Gallagher wasn't sure he wanted to be viewed as the man whose job it was to touch poo.

"Excuse me, girl," said Gallagher as he gently manoeuvred a reindeer aside. The silly creature actually stumbled a bit and only stayed upright because it collided with the girl next to her.

Quickly enough, Gallagher had picked up enough of the dried turds and put them in a plastic box that had once held screws. It looked weirdly like a chocolate brownie, now it was set against the pale blue of the plastic. Gallagher very often suspected he was teetering on the edge of some sort of breakdown, but now, as he looked at reindeer shit in its presentation box and decided that it looked ... delicious he fucking *knew* he was.

"Here we are," he said as he presented it to Luka. Gallagher was determined that if he had to muck about with reindeer shit then Luka would have his fair share too.

"Very good," said Luka, unperturbed. "Now you must make it look the part in case anyone wants to see."

In another ten minutes Gallagher held the box and shook his head sorrowfully in front of Tom Eccles inside the shop.

"Liver Flukes?" Tom asked.

"It was a risk that Amy mentioned. She said to look out

for them. I need to drop this sample round so she can decide if a vet's visit is needed. Want to see?" Gallagher lifted the plastic box, ready to lift the lid.

"God no!"

Gallagher was slightly disappointed. He'd spent ten minutes sticking dried mealworms from the bird food department into the reindeer poo in an effort to make it look as if it was infested with parasites. He had no idea if they looked like liver flukes, but they did look truly horrible. He didn't want his effort to be in vain.

"Are you saying there's diseases in the shop?" said Karen Woodbine from tills, overhearing.

"Does this involve you?" said Tom.

She puffed herself up. "I am the health and safety representative for the shop," she said. "Those posters don't put themselves up and I do not want to see further accidents occurring this week."

"*Further* accidents?"

"Elf got stabbed in the eye yesterday. Surprised he didn't sue."

Tom huffed. Gallagher waggled his box hopefully.

"Fine. Just be quick, eh?" said Tom. "You said you were busy."

"Very busy," said Gallagher.

"You moved that compost from outside the landscaping office?"

"Top of my list," he said.

Gallagher went to find Luka.

Luka was deep in conversation on his phone. "I do not

see how this is my problem!" he said hotly. "You asked, I did. This was not in my job description!"

"Sonia?" mouthed Gallagher.

Luka covered the phone with his hand to talk to him. "Charlotte Mitchell. Says there is problem with mechanical bear and it is my fault." He returned to the call. "I did all the singing you ask. Why did you not ask elves to edit out swearing. Swearing in singing is normal." Luka rolled his eyes as Charlotte went on and on. "He *did* have a fucking shiny nose," said Luka. "It scans. I ad libbed. All is good. I do not know what you want from me, Miss Mitchell."

Luka ended the call irritably and looked at Gallagher.

"Operation Liver Fluke was a success!" Gallagher said to Luka with a brisk clap of his hands. "We've got a pass out from Tom, so we should have plenty of time to drop the you-know-what over to Clopton Howes."

"Was a good plan," said Luka proudly. "Let's go get package."

They strolled over to the warehouse and went inside.

"Okay, where did you hide it?" said Gallagher.

"In bales," said Luka and gestured at the small mountain of straw bales next to the stocks of animal feed and wild bird food.

Gallagher pawed through.

"Bale with red twine," said Luka.

Gallagher looked. "There are no bales with red twine."

"Sure."

Luka looked. Gallagher looked. Gallagher stepped back, tried to process, mimed lifting a bale and...

"Oh, shit."

"What?" said Luka.

Gallagher turned on his heel and ran.

He nearly bowled over a sticky child in his haste and vaulted clean over the reindeer enclosure fence, drawing some surprised bellows from the creatures. There was a bale of straw with red twine leaned up against the inside of the fence. A reindeer had her face buried in it.

Gallagher nudged the reindeer out of the way, although it seemed reluctant to move. When it was out of the way, he saw the plastic that had been wrapped around the cannabis package. It was nothing but shreds. Flakes of dried marijuana were few and far between. The package had been almost entirely cleaned out by probing tongues.

Trembling, he stood straight and looked around at the reindeer in the enclosure, all nine of them. "Jesus." He met Luka's eye. "This is not good," he squeaked.

Luka remained on the other side of the fence. He coughed. "Are we absolutely sure that this is the bale?"

Gallagher pulled out a bit of wrapper and the tiniest crumb of cannabis. An inquisitive reindeer nosed forward, seeking it out.

"Get off it you daft twat!" said Gallagher, pushing it away. He came close to Luka. "They've eaten the fucking lot!" he hissed.

There was a theatrical tutting, and Gallagher whirled around to see a man and a woman holding up a small child to see the reindeer. Gallagher was too frazzled to care.

He eyed the reindeer. They had eaten the entire bale in less than three hours. Had they all eaten some, or were there a couple of stoner reindeer who'd had more than the others?

If a reindeer was about twice the weight of a man, then it was like him chomping his way through a Christmas dinner made entirely of cannabis. Several times.

"Oh, this is bad," he said.

Luka nodded solemnly and stared at his hands. "I used to like having fingers," he said.

39

ANIKA

By the end of her first morning on serious elf duties, Anika was coming to grips with how knackering being a Christmas elf could be.

She had now been introduced to the other grottos. It was never overtly stated that there were different grottos, because that brought with it the implication there was more than one Santa, which was not on-brand. The way it was sold to customers was as silver and gold experiences. The gold experience was the full hour process, where Anika had worked in Mrs Claus's kitchen. The silver experience was cheaper and quicker, but the elves were still expected to deliver the best customer experience they could possibly manage in their separate conveyor belt of rooms.

Anika could not recall ever once being taken to a Santa's grotto as a child and had assumed it amounted to a queue, a "Ho ho ho, what would you like for Christmas, little girl?" from a sinister bearded man, and a wrapped gift to go home with. Either her assumptions were wrong, or the grotto business had moved on considerably since her own childhood.

Anika had spent some time at the colouring-in stop with two other elves whose elf names were Fairydust and Laughs-a-Lot. Everyone had an elf name, which they had to use exclusively when in character.

Being in character all the time in 'customer zones' was one of the things Daffyd had continuously drilled into them the day before. When they were in the customer zones they were elves. They were literal elves. They had to be bright and cheerful. They had to be cheeky and naughty – in an acceptable way. Daffyd had run through a list of cheeky things elves could do. Sticking out tongues and giving kids bunny ears in pictures were acceptable forms of cheekiness. Exposing your genitals was highlighted as a specific form of unacceptable cheekiness. It was *very* specifically highlighted.

In the training, Sophie had seen Anika's confused look. "Ashley," she whispered.

"Ashley?" Anika whispered back.

"We don't talk about Ashley."

The colouring-in stop in the silver grotto was described to Anika as an easy place for novice elves. There were no animals to deal with, no sharp implements to manage, and parents were at liberty to take as many photos as they wished. Deeper in, things became wilder, sharper, and only official Hedgelord photos were allowed to be taken.

Nonetheless, a full morning of "Hello! I'm Smartypants the elf!" and singing Christmas songs at full volume while managing a different swarm of children every fifteen minutes was exhausting. There was supposed to be a five minute gap between each group: a five-minute cleaning up session including any loo breaks the elves might need. But the groups kept on coming, not always strictly to time, and it soon became clear that cleaning up just meant shoving all the rubbish on the floor behind the trestle tables for someone to clear up later. Anika feared that someone was going to be her future self. By noon she didn't give a shit about her future self. Future Anika deserved all the punishment she could receive for having ever thought this job was a fine alternative to uni.

"It's tougher at the start of December," said Laughs-a-Lot the elf as they swept aside another set of abandoned drawings. Both had already given up trying to get lids back on top of all the felt tips. They were among the abandoned detritus on the floor.

"Is it?" said Anika.

"Sure. Parents who think ahead have booked slots in the final week before Christmas, especially the last weekend before the big day. They're the organised ones. The ones who've got their shit together. This time ... this is people who have taken whatever slot they can get. You see a big up-tick of divorced weekend dads around now."

"And that's tougher to deal with?"

Laughs-a-Lot gave a thoughtful headshake. The bell on the tip of her hat tinkled. "December twenty-third, twenty-fourth, you'll see parents who run their family like the Third Reich. Kids obedient to the point of creepy."

"Mentioning the Third Reich in the customer zones,"

said Daffyd, marching into the room. "Again." He put a mark on his clipboard.

"Sorry, head elf," said Laughs-a-Lot.

Daffyd was in his full elf costume, even though he wasn't elfing anywhere that day. It seemed to be part of his routine and role. He was in charge of elves both in character and in reality. His costume was a plush and expensive looking thing, unlike the flimsy felt get-ups the regular elves were given. Although the buttons did seem to be straining to hold the costume together around his belly. Anika suspected the costume had seen slimmer days.

Daffyd flicked his pencil at Anika. "Smartypants. With me." He walked away, expecting her to automatically follow.

"We've got the next lot in two minutes," said Fairydust.

"And you'll cope admirably without Smartypants," said Daffyd.

They slipped out through a gap in the snowy grotto scenery and into a back space that Anika had no idea existed. She followed him through a narrow passageway between the backs of other festive spaces. Christmas music reverberated through the scenery walls.

"Am I...? Am I in trouble?" Anika asked. "I've been smiling all the time I think. And I learned all the verses of the *Twelve Days of Christmas*. Is this because I didn't know about the life cycle of a reindeer?"

Daffyd turned round on her. She came up short in front of him. His glittering eyes stared at her.

"I have a mission for you."

"Mission."

There was suddenly an SD card in his hand, one of the

wider ones for cameras or laptops. "There has been a hiccup with the animatronic bear Charlotte delivered to our valued customer yesterday."

"Oh?"

"I've had to do an emergency re-edit on the Christmas songs."

"Oh."

"I am entrusting you to take this to the customer's house, where Charlotte will install it. You've been there before."

"I remember where it is," she said, trying to draw a mental walking map between Hedgelord and the estate he lived on.

Daffyd solemnly placed the SD card in her hand, the ponderous entrusting of a great treasure.

"It's more than just songs," he said, trying to imbue his voice with a gravitas it couldn't quite summon. "It is the hopes and dreams of this sacred space."

"I ... I'll take care of it," said Anika and was tempted to give him a salute before departing.

40

CHARLOTTE

Charlotte sat in her car across the road from Nick Bellingham's house as she had done for the last two hours. She had deep reserves of bitter resentment to keep her going during her watchful vigil. During that time, she'd seen Jack Hartigan's car draw up into the driveway and the smug git get out and head towards the house.

Oh, the lies he'd be telling Nick now, she thought.

Twenty minutes after arrival, Jack Hartigan sent her a text message, along with a photo of him sipping tea from china cups with Nick Bellingham. The text message read:

Sealing the deal on a lifetime Bloomers discount.

She recognised the background as being Nick Bellingham's kitchen. She assumed he was still in there, being all matey and false. Her mind flitted back to the sticker on Cameron Clasp's window. She gave a small nod of appreciation and wished she had something similar.

She gave a small grunt of satisfaction as she realised she could improvise. She fished in her handbag and pulled out a lipstick. She tried to imagine that she had x-ray eyes and could see through the walls to where Jack Hartigan was sitting. She made a small lipstick rectangle on the window to frame him and added the label below.

TWAT

That felt better.

Five minutes later, a Just Eat delivery guy on a moped pulled up outside her car and rapped on her window with his gloved hand. She wound it down.

"'Parked car outside the number 6 The Crescent'?" he asked.

"That's me," she said and he passed her through a hot chocolate and *pain au chocolat*.

A woman on a stakeout needed provisions.

She was also waiting for another delivery, this one for Nick himself. One that was much larger and would blow Jack's efforts out of the water.

She had scoffed the pastry (making sure she caught all the crumbs on the paper bag as she did so) and was taking the lid off her hot chocolate when there was another knock at the window. Charlotte nearly slopped hot liquid on herself in surprise.

It was one of the Christmas elves from the store, still dressed in full elf regalia. The new girl, Anika. Charlotte put down the window.

"Daffyd sent me," said Anika.

"I imagined as much," said Charlotte. "Get in. People shouldn't see you."

Anika looked around. "Right. Because it looks like I'm a sex worker soliciting for tricks."

"You're dressed as an elf."

"A festive sex worker?"

"Get in!"

Anika slipped inside and sat down. "Oh, it's warm in here. These elf outfits aren't very thermal, are they? I brought you this." She passed Charlotte an SD card.

"Do you know how to install this?" said Charlotte.

"Daffyd said you did."

"I'm sure we'll work it out," said Charlotte, because it was better than the alternative.

She saw a lorry and trailer appeared in her wing mirror. "Ah, here it is."

Anika swivelled round to look. "What is it?"

"A gift from Hedgelord to Mr Nick Bellingham. A rental, actually. But a rental for the whole Christmas period."

The huge trailer swung past, then backed up towards Nick Bellingham's drive. The driver climbed down and went to knock on the door.

"It's the ultimate piece of equipment to help someone work safely at height installing Christmas displays," said Charlotte.

She'd thought long and hard about what could be the most useful piece of equipment for the keen installer of Christmas displays and when she'd hit upon this idea, she'd given herself a metaphorical pat on the back.

The door opened, but from this angle Charlotte couldn't see Nick's face.

"What is it?" said Anika.

"A scissor lift," said Charlotte. "You know, one of those…" She made a mime of a flat hand rising up above the other. "It's wide enough for Nick's wheelchair so he can use it to work on his displays wherever he needs to."

Anika nodded slowly. "Will a man in a wheelchair want to go up in scissor lift?" she said.

"Anika. You should have a more positive outlook than that."

There seemed to be some sort of altercation at the door, but after a while the driver came back to the vehicle and began to roll out the big yellow scissor platform from the back of the trailer.

"Good, good," said Charlotte.

"Why does it say 'twat' on your window?" asked Anika. "Did you write that in lipstick?"

"Shush!"

Nick and Jack had gone inside. Charlotte's phone pinged with another text from Jack Hartigan.

Oh dearie me Charlotte. I'm just going to quote this verbatim 'Does she think I am some sort of circus act? How could I possibly be stable leaning over from a wheelchair up in that thing?'. Looks like it hasn't got the wow factor you were after. Soz :-(

"Fuck," she whispered. Her watch buzzed. "I mean 'gosh darn'."

"Everything okay?" said Anika.

"I was certain that lift was going to bring Nick Bellingham straight back to Hedgelord."

"Ah."

"It's only because that bastard Jack Hartigan is in there, trash-talking our offering as soon as it turned up. We would have been received with open arms if not for..." She growled. "The man is making it personal now."

Anika pointed at the window. "Is Jack Hartigan the twat?"

"He really is," said Charlotte.

No sooner had the trailer left than a delivery van pulled up outside the house. Charlotte stared through the window, curious to know what was arriving now. Nick Bellingham took some large boxes from the driver, Jack Hartigan nipping forward to help him carry them inside. Charlotte was taken aback when Jack turned and waved cheerily in her direction.

"He's seen us," said Anika and began to wave back before Charlotte reached out and stopped her.

"Don't wave at the enemy!" Charlotte hissed.

Anika shrugged. "He looks kind of nice in a dad sort of way."

"He's evil incarnate," Charlotte assured her.

A text came through a few minutes later from Jack.

Oho! I think this might be a hit. You should get a live demo very shortly.

Charlotte re-read the text but could make no sense of it. There was no picture with it, but maybe it was still stuck in the aether. She chalked it up to an excess of smugness which had gone to the man's head.

A tiny electrical whirring sound like a high-pitched wasp came from somewhere nearby and Charlotte twisted in her seat. She gasped when she saw a little drone hovering directly outside the car window.

"Drone!" said Anika with childish surprise. Charlotte lowered the window to get a better look.

"*Why does it say TAWT on your window?*" came Nick Bellingham's voice over a speaker.

There was the broken sound of a conversation and then, "Oh, yes. Twat. Right. Who's the twat, Charlotte?"

"I ... er."

"*This drone is a gift from Bloomers so I can inspect my decorations while staying safely on the ground. What do you think of it?*"

Charlotte turned and looked directly at where she assumed the camera was. "It's a lovely idea, Nick. I'm so happy that it suits your needs." She smiled to show that she was sincere, although she had her fingers crossed underneath the steering wheel. "I can see you have company so I won't come visiting just now, but I'll pop in tomorrow to discuss Hedgelord's big new idea." She gave a little wave, just to show that she wasn't weird or anything.

"*I would love to hear about Hedgelord's big new idea. You're very welcome to pop inside and join us, save you a wasted journey.*"

"No, I couldn't impose while the two of you are discussing business."

Jack Hartigan's voice came through the drone. "*Please come inside, Charlotte. We're eating the most exquisite shortbread biscuits from the Bloomers hamper I brought along. You'd be saving us from ourselves.*"

Charlotte kept her brittle smile plastered on her face. "Well then, how could I refuse?"

"*And bring your elf!*" said Jack.

The drone buzzed away.

Anika turned to her. "What's your brilliant big idea?"

"Not a fucking clue," Charlotte muttered. She slapped the SD card back into Anika's hand. "You sort the bear while I step into the lion's den."

She arrived at the door to the two smiling faces of Nick and Jack.

"Elf not coming in?" said Nick, nodding at Anika, who was investigating the flaps of fur around the bear's neck.

"Important maintenance work," said Charlotte.

"Ah, the sweary bear," said Jack, grinning in the hallway. "We shouldn't blame the bear. It was probably just the way he was raised."

Nick wheeled through into the kitchen. "This is all just lovely. The two of you must have a lot in common, even though you're competitors."

"We certainly do," said Jack. "Honestly there's nobody I'd rather share a cup of tea with. I'm sure Charlotte feels the same way."

She studied his face. There was no trace of guile or sarcasm. He was so good at lying with maximum sincerity.

"It's true," she said, certain she could give as good as she got. "If I really want to check in on whether I think I'm doing a good job, I ask myself 'What would Jack Hartigan think?' He's such a useful *tool*."

Jack's face faltered as he recognised the barb in what she said. She deducted points from herself for the cheap shot, but felt better anyway.

"What was the big idea you wanted to mention, Charlotte?" asked Nick as he passed her a cup of tea.

"Oh yeah, the big idea?" She thought quickly. It had to be

the germ of something good. "The, um, Winter Wonderland?"

The two of them stared at her, clearly expecting more.

"So what is that, exactly?" asked Nick.

"Well, I noticed that you've got some of your neighbours involved with the lights now," said Charlotte, playing for time while she formed the clay of her idea into something actionable. "You're likely to have a lot of people come by. What if we made it into more of an interactive trail?"

"Oh, for charity maybe?" asked Jack.

"Yes!" said Charlotte, "exactly!"

"I'm intrigued. I can see it now," said Nick, sketching it out with his hands. "An archway over the entrance to the road. A fireworks display at the same time every evening. Huge animatronics displays."

"Yep. Yep. All of that," squeaked Charlotte, a tiny glimpse of possible success overriding the many, many valid logistical and financial objections which her brain tried to raise. "Let's make it happen!"

Nick Bellingham raised his teacup in salute.

41

GALLAGHER

"Fucking eaten the lot!" Gallagher whispered.

It wasn't the first time he'd said it. It wouldn't be the last. He was stuck on getting to grips with the enormity of what had happened.

"We need to think fast," said Luka.

They stood by the low fence to the reindeer enclosure, where currently the reindeers were going about their business in a rather normal and indifferent manner.

"What if they die?" Gallagher waved a hand at the reindeer. "Amy already thinks I'm a fuckwit. She'll never speak to me again."

Luka gave a mirthless smile. "I am thinking more of me than reindeer. Sonia Patterson will want to know where her drugs went."

"Inside reindeers' stomachs."

"Yes. Not good. But let us deal with one thing at a time.

Drugged up reindeer. You are reindeer whisperer. Tell me what we should do."

Gallagher stared at the reindeer. They still looked normal. He had no idea what went on inside a reindeer. Maybe they ate stuff like cannabis in the wild and would be unaffected. Or maybe it was because cannabis edibles took longer to kick in anyway.

He glanced back over towards Luka and saw a high pointy elf hat next to him. It was Sophie, formerly from the café, now apparently a fully-fledged elf.

"Sophie, we need help," he said.

"What's up?"

"We have a bit of a situation." He sighed heavily and pointed at the reindeer. "The ladies have eaten something they shouldn't have."

"Oh dear. Did one of the kids give them the reindeer food? We always tell them not to in the grotto."

"No, not that. More like ten kilos of cannabis." Gallagher glanced across at the reindeer.

"I beg your pardon?"

"You heard. Weirdly enough, they seem to be all right at the moment."

As they watched the reindeer in the little paddock, one of them staggered to the side and bumped into another. Like dominoes they all toppled to the floor.

"Not all right any more," said Luka.

"Shit," muttered Gallagher.

"We must stop it getting worse," said Luka. "Gallagher. Make them vomit."

"How?"

"They have multi-chambered stomachs," said Sophie. "I learned about this in elf school."

"Right. So, you know about their anatomy," said Luka.

"I don't even know if vomiting works the same in ruminants," said Sophie. "Shouldn't you phone their owner and ask her advice?"

Gallagher had been putting that idea to the back of his mind. "No, no, no. I'm not doing that. I'm not calling Amy unless it's totally unavoidable."

Luka turned to Sophie. "He has the hots for this Amy," he explained. "Country girl. Jodhpurs and a tight woolly sweater."

"He doesn't want to disappoint his girlfriend," said Sophie, as though it made perfect sense.

"She's not my girlfriend!"

Sophie was looking on her phone. "It says here you should contact your veterinarian immediately. Do *not* induce vomiting unless directed to."

"What did you google?" asked Gallagher.

"What to do if my reindeer has eaten ten kilograms of cannabis," she said. "The internet's amazing, isn't it? Where did they find the stuff?"

Luka pointed.

"I mean, why is it here?" she said.

"Is long story," said Luka.

Gallagher really didn't want to call Amy and admit how stupid and careless he'd been. "Shit. I've got to call her, haven't I?"

"Yes," said Luka.

"I wonder if there's a version of this where I don't look like a twat?"

"I don't think so, friend," said Luka.

The high and giddy reindeer, Donner, tottered about. Cupid bellowed at Dasher. This in turn startled a third, Vixen, who in a wide-eyed shock – maybe the reindeer equivalent of drug-induced paranoia – bucked and kicked, and leapt over the enclosure fence.

"Mummy!" screamed a child in utter delight.

Gallagher, before he even knew what he was doing, was chasing after it. Vixen went straight through the automatic doors and into main body of the shop. She bounced off an aquarium display, knocked down a stacked display of jigsaws and wobbled on towards the tills.

"Gangway! Gangway!" Gallagher shouted. "Loose reindeer!"

People stepped aside as the panicked animal wobbled through. They seemed equally split between those who were rightfully fearful of a charging quadruped, and those who couldn't help but stare in wonder at the passing of this most Christmassy of animals.

Beyond the tills were the automatic doors to the car park. If the reindeer got through there then Gallagher had no way of knowing what would happen. Vixen might strike a car in the car park or, even worse, head out straight onto the ring road.

"Lock the doors! Lock the doors!" he yelled.

Karen on tills saw him, reached down and did something. A red light began flashing on the ceiling above. All the doors closed.

Ahead of Vixen, Tom Eccles cowered, his arms spread protectively in front of a delicate display of jars.

"Not the farmhouse kitchen jams!" he pleaded.

Vixen reared, spun about, appeared to consider running off into the display of men's and women's waxed jackets, giving Gallagher enough time to leap at the poor creature and grab her by the collar with one hand and the antlers with another.

"Whoa," he called in soothing tones.

She reared again, but Gallagher, acting more out of fear than expert animal handling, used his weight to keep her grounded, all the while making forceful shushing noises at her frightened face. Luka came huffing up seconds later and was round the far side, pinning her between them.

Vixen honked and rasped, but seemed to be calming down.

Tom Eccles was physically shaking as he approached. "What the hell is going on?" he managed to say hoarsely.

"She got spooked," said Gallagher.

"Some of the children here are very ugly," added Luka.

Together, Gallagher and Luka slowly but firmly led Vixen back outside.

"Someone needs to fill out the accident book," Karen shouted after them, but no one paid attention.

It took a matter of a few minutes getting the poorly reindeer back in the enclosure. Several others had that wide-eyed, paranoid look about them.

Sophie looked at Gallagher with a motherly seriousness. "Phone your girlfriend now, Gallagher."

"She's not my girlfriend."

"Whatever. I think you need to get over yourself, don't you? You can't let the reindeer die."

"You're right. Fuck." He dialled the number with a shake of his head. "Amy, hi, it's Gallagher at Hedgelord." He chewed his lip.

"Didn't expect to hear from you so soon," she said, with a lightly amused tone. *"You're not going to start abusing access to my number, are you?"*

"No, I'm not." He wished he had time to dissect her tone. Did she sound as if she'd be up for a non-reindeer conversation? Damn.

"What's going on?" she said.

"The reindeer. I think they might have eaten something bad."

Sophie tapped his arm and looked sternly at him.

"Sorry, Amy. I don't just think, I *know* they ate something bad," he said.

"I see. What is it that they ate?" asked Amy. Her tone was much cooler. He wondered what to make of that.

"Cannabis. A lot of cannabis. A massive bale of cannabis."

"Christ," she said quietly.

"I know," he said.

"I need to call the emergency vet. Right, we'll save the what-the-fuck-has-gone-on-here conversation for later. I need you to stay with my girls until the vet gets there, right? Even if it's past closing time. Especially if it's past closing time. See if you can get them to drink water. Have any of them shown any symptoms yet?"

"Yeah. They have kind of red eyes and they are roaring

and staggering. There might have been some light stampeding."

"Jesus, Gallagher. Right, water, get on it! I'll call you back."

Gallagher ended the call and relayed the essence of it to Luka and Sophie.

"I need to get back inside the grotto," said Sophie. "I can make sure we don't tell families to come over here like we normally do, but that doesn't mean people won't come."

"We can block path," said Luka.

"I'll see if I can make them drink." Now Gallagher was faced with the practicalities of the task he pulled at his face in confusion. "How on earth do I make a reindeer drink?"

He ran inside the building and went to the restaurant. It was in full flow, which meant that people were rammed into every last space. They were queuing to get in, they were queuing to get served, and they were hovering around tables as people finished so they could claim the space for themselves. Gallagher squeezed through the crowds, heading for the till.

"Afra!" he called as he got close. "Afra! I need a sippy cup. It's an emergency!"

"Young man, please wait your turn!" growled an angry senior as he shimmied past.

"A sippy cup?" Afra at the drinks counter asked.

Gallagher mimed a double handed sipping motion. "Yeah, like kiddies use when they're little. A sippy cup. I need one quick! It's really important." He turned to the angry senior. "A reindeer's life is on the line. Several reindeer in fact."

A few minutes later he had a sippy cup shaped like a

penguin. He filled a bucket with water and made his way back to the reindeer. He went round them all, trying to coax them to take sips of water from the penguin cup. Most of the reindeer lolled and wobbled, as if they were woozy and a little disorientated, but he got small drinks into them.

Blitzen however seemed as if she was in the grip of a psychotic episode. She charged at a fence post in a way that made Gallagher worried she'd hurt herself. He then moved on to worrying that Blitzen might decide to charge at him instead.

"Come on girl, it's going to be fine. You'll sip some water, lie down for a bit and the vet will be here. Trust someone who's been where you are right now. Going fucking mental probably feels as if it might be the way to go, but it never ends well."

"Is touching to see you found your spirit animal," said Luka, leaning over the gate. There was a violent noise from Blitzen. "If anyone's interested, it turns out reindeer definitely can vomit. Fun fact, huh?"

"Come on girl, let's get you another drink, shall we?" said Gallagher. He slipped on something and ended up on his back, winded.

"Like I said, reindeer vomit," said Luka. "Oh wait, maybe diarrhoea, based on smell."

42

CHARLOTTE

There was a small crowd outside the main doors of Hedgelord as Charlotte pulled into a parking space. Small crowds in unexpected places were rarely a good thing.

She had driven in sullen silence back to Hedgelord, with Anika the elf on her passenger seat looking out the window and trying not to make the uncomfortable silence any worse. There was too much to process from the stupid conversation with Jack Hartigan at Nick's house, too many impossible promises to fulfil to win Nick back to the Hedgelord camp.

All those things were dashed from her mind by the sight of the crowd. Charlotte parked hurriedly and got out. As she approached the closed shop doors were physically slid aside from within, and the pools of customers inside and out squeezed past one another to get through.

Tom Eccles and Karen from tills were there, apologising

to the customers as they exited the shop. Tom's tie was all skew-whiff and he looked like he'd just escaped a pub brawl.

Customers flowing in and out were grumbling and groaning, which possibly ranked among the worst noises she should be hearing at this time of year.

"What's happened here?" she said, unimpressed.

"Karen here hit the security alarm button," said Tom. "Shut down the doors and the tills."

"I was acting on instinct."

A serious looking woman with a hi-vis coat and a large medical bag approached from the car park. "Can anyone point me towards the reindeer?" she said.

Charlotte blinked and looked at Tom.

"We might have had a deranged reindeer incident," he said.

"It looked psychotic," said Karen.

"The reindeer," insisted the woman tersely. "If they've been poisoned..."

"Poisoned?" said Charlotte. "Oh, shit."

"This way," said Anika. "I'll take you straight to them."

The elf hurried away in a half-jog with the vet woman following closely.

Charlotte looked again at Tom and Karen. "Again. What the hell happened here?"

"Deranged reindeer," said Tom. "Poisoned, apparently."

"And I pressed the security alarm to stop it escaping," said Karen.

"We've only just got the doors open."

"Although the tills have gone into lockdown and don't want to reboot."

Charlotte could feel fury buzzing inside her. She saw a large plastic planter shaped like a Greek amphora, walked over to it, put her face inside, and screamed. It didn't help. It just made Tom and Karen and passing customers look at her like she was mad.

"Poisoned reindeer," she said faintly, hearing the crazy in her own voice. "Non-functioning tills in December. I thought sweary bears were the worst of it."

She walked away before she said anything else she'd regret. She walked up the stairs to Cameron Clasp's office to find Daffyd there with the boss. Daffyd was stepping unhappily from one elf foot to the other.

"Ah," said Cameron from behind his desk, "here's someone who'll know. Charlotte, tell us the latest sit rep."

"I've been working hard on winning Nick Bellingham back to our side," she said. "It's not helped that Bloomers have—"

"Not that, he scowled. "This business I'm hearing from Daffyd about the kiddiewinks being scared in the grotto by mad-eyed vomiting reindeer. Something to do with liver flukes."

"Poisoned, I hear," said Charlotte.

"What?"

Charlotte pursed her lips. "I'm concerned that something very underhand might be happening."

"Elaborate."

"Bloomers have gone all-out this year in trying to win Nick Bellingham over. Everywhere I look, I see Jack Hartigan sucking up to him. We might have a crack at a special bespoke installation over there, a winter wonderland, but I'm now starting to think that Bloomers are taking this thing to the next level."

"The reindeer thing?" said Cameron, disbelieving.

"I'm not sure," she said. "But we've got poorly reindeer and tills that I think are probably only going to be cash-only for the time being and—"

"Those bastards at Bloomers are trying to undermine us!"

"We need more information before we can start flinging accusations." She turned to Daffyd. "Do you still have contacts in Bloomers?"

"Contacts?"

"You used to be good friends with Nathan Carson?"

Daffyd lifted his chin and looked away as though in great pain. "Nathan and I are no longer on speaking terms."

"Oh, he's the elf we lost to Bloomers," said Cameron. "Charismatic little chap."

"We didn't lose him," said Daffyd through gritted teeth. "Losing him implies we were careless with him. I took great care of that elf. I trained him, nurtured him."

"So, he's not in a position to do a little spying for us?" said Charlotte.

"He's swallowed the Bloomers pill completely. Complete traitor."

"I was hoping we could get an inside eye on them. See what dirty tricks they're up to."

"We could take a closer look," said Daffyd, his gaze upon her once again, his eyes steely and cold.

"I tried going over there," said Charlotte. "They rumbled me straightaway, even though I sent Karen in," said Charlotte.

"I've got operatives," said Daffyd. "We can do a recce."

"And when I said whatever it takes I meant it," said Cameron. "Consider any and all action to be authorised by me."

"We're just going to see what they're up to," said Charlotte, not sure what Cameron meant.

"Good," said the boss. "Now, I'm already late for tee off with Patty Fufu but, just to be clear, if we need to break out the counter-espionage or the black ops missions, just say. I can also provide an alibi if needed."

"Er, okay."

43

ANIKA

It was distressing to see the reindeer looking so unwell, and Anika didn't hesitate leaping in to help Gallagher and Sophie, encouraging the reindeer to drink while the vet checked each of them individually and gave out injections. There were several discreet piles of reindeer vomit around the enclosure and Anika simply hoped that the more they yucked up, the sooner they would be well again.

Gallagher was utterly distraught. Anika might have guessed he was put out by what the reindeer lady would think of him now, but she soon saw that his love and sympathy for these animals trumped all. Nonetheless, when the reindeer's owner, Amy, turned up quarter of an hour later, Gallagher blushed with shame so deeply, his face turned red from his cheekbones down to his tattooed neck.

"Oh, my God," she said, stepping in. "What's happened to them?"

"Consistent with a form of poisoning," said the vet

crisply. "I've administered Naloxone, a toxicity reversal agent. Never used it in deer before, but it's worked on cows and sheep."

Amy turned to Gallagher, her attractive features drawn into a tight and vicious expression. "What did you give them?"

"I ... er..." Gallagher stammered.

"Whoa there, missy," said Daffyd, approaching the enclosure gate at speed.

Amy looked at the tubby elf chief.

"If I may," said Daffyd and stepped inside with a disgusted sneer at the vomit-dotted floor. He beckoned Amy closer with dainty hand gestures.

Amy, still looking furious, stepped over. Gallagher and Anika drew in.

"It looks like there may be nefarious forces at play," said Daffyd in a confidential whisper.

"There's what?" said Gallagher.

"Outside forces that wish the garden centre harm might have..." Daffyd did a little mime to indicate some general sprinkling, munching, then put his head on one side and stuck his tongue out as though dead.

"Someone's poisoned my reindeer?" said Amy loudly, not caring for Daffyd's attempts at confidentiality.

"Might be the case," nodded Daffyd.

Anika saw the complete surprise on Gallagher's face.

"Phone the police," insisted Amy.

"Investigations are on-going," said Daffyd. "And with that in mind—" he looked at Anika "—I need to have words with you."

A chill ran through Anika. Did Daffyd think she was responsible?

She mutely followed Daffyd out of the enclosure. Behind her, Amy began apologising to Gallagher for assuming he'd fed something to the reindeer.

Daffyd led the way into the grotto, which was still processing the seemingly endless queues of families. He stepped behind a wooden board painted to look like a snowy landscape and Anika followed through into what turned out to be a narrow corridor behind the scenery screens of the various parts of the grotto.

Partway along he stopped and turned to her. "I like you, kid," he said.

"Er, that's nice," said Anika.

It never crossed her mind that she should be worried about being alone in a secluded space with Daffyd while he told her he liked her. In her mind, she'd decided Daffyd was either gay, or some species of pansexual imp with tastes that would not include her.

"You've got moxie," he said. "Possibly chutzpah too. I've never known the difference. Spunk too, I'd warrant."

"A step too far," she said.

"For the record, you've shown real initiative as an elf and I've been watching. You did know all of the *Twelve Days of Christmas,* but you got stuck after the first verse of *Oh Christmas Tree.* For a first week, you weren't bad."

"Okay. Thanks."

"And I need you."

"Oh?"

He turned on his heel again and marched on. "Covert

mission," he said. "You're the ideal person."

"You sure? I'm new round here."

"You're the ideal person because you're new."

"I'm not the only new person. What about Gillespie?"

They emerged into a natural room made from the backs of the grotto huts and scenery, a secret hideout in the midst of the festive factory. There was a desk and rows of lever arch files. On the walls were pinned numerous childish diagrams and sketches with explanatory notes like *Elves on Skates?* and *Cost up price of real snow machine!.* There was also a dressing table and a mirror with lightbulbs round it, like this was a star's backstage dressing room.

"I don't believe that Gillespie, despite having the chiselled looks of a young Mickey Bubbles, is up to the task. I need someone with their wits about them for this mission."

"What kind of mission? An elf mission?"

"No," he said, with a sad weariness. "This is a human mission. I need you to revert to full human for me," said Daffyd, as though he was asking her to sacrifice her family for the cause. "We're going to Bloomers."

"The other garden centre?"

"The heart of darkness, my young apprentice. You need to see what happens when good elves go bad. I need you because your face is not known over there. We need to put our ears to the ground and see if we can work out what evil plots Bloomers is a-brewing."

"Er, okay."

"It's not something I ask lightly—"

"I still get paid though?"

"Yes."

She shrugged. "Sure. Let's do it."

"Good. Where are your street clothes?" asked Daffyd.

"Ah. Well there's a problem there. I like to travel light so I just put my coat on over the dungarees." Anika had worked out if she fastened her coat right up to her chin, it just looked as though she had chosen to wear brightly coloured trousers.

"Hm. Well let's see how you look."

When Anika had put on her coat, Daffyd made her parade up and down for inspection.

"Do you look too normal? That's the question."

"Too normal? I thought this was a covert mission?"

"Yes it is covert, but we have to cohere as a family unit. Attention to detail underpins good acting skills."

"Attention to detail, right. Well I will just come out and say it, then: we do not look as if we are related. My skin is brown and yours is white. Very white."

Daffyd was so white with his pudgy pale face that Anika couldn't even picture him with a suntan. He probably just went bright red. She refrained from saying so out loud.

"Obviously I know that," he said. "Have you never heard of blended families? Now I want you to put on some bright accessories. Let me see what might suit." He pulled open drawers and cupboards.

"There's another thing," said Anika. "Didn't you say that your face is known over there? If we're trying to make us look blended, why wouldn't we do it so that you look more normal, like me?"

Daffyd moved slowly, as if he might erupt with fury at any moment, but then he smiled. "Smartypants, you have a good point. I need to apply my acting skills here, and try to adapt my own appearance. What would you recommend?"

"A massive, boring hat," said Anika.

Daffyd pulled a face but went searching. He pulled out a knitted beanie hat and held it between his finger and thumb, as if it disgusted him. "This could work." He pulled it on over his head and stared at her.

His face still had that uncanny, baby-like quality. Anika pointed. "You need to cover your face. Maybe a scarf? It is cold outside."

Eventually, they transformed Daffyd into a well-wrapped sausage with no distinguishing features.

"We will walk over there. I don't know if they have ANPR, but we take no chances," said Daffyd, his voice muffled by the layers.

"ANPR?"

"Where they scan and identify a car's number plates. I don't even know if it's legal, but they are not to be trusted."

"No worries. The walk will warm us up."

44

ANIKA

The walk over to Bloomers did warm them up.

Anika was ready to shed her coat but she kept it on, as it was her outfit. She looked over at Daffyd: he was sweating profusely. "Are you alright?" she asked.

"I will be fine," he said. "Now, did I mention you are eleven years old? It is essential we present ourselves as a family that wants to visit the grotto."

"Eleven?" Anika didn't know whether to be pleased he had such faith in her acting ability, or annoyed that he thought she could pass as a kid.

"There's a very special award for elves who are able to transform themselves in this way, did I mention that?"

Anika knew where this was going, and was already annoyed with herself for buying into it. She licked her lips. "Is it a gold star?"

"It is! Rarely awarded, but I think you might have what it takes."

"Fine. Eleven years old. Excited to be visiting the grotto. Do I still believe in Santa?"

"I think you might know the truth, but you indulge your dad because he's such a sweet guy."

Anika rolled her eyes. "Yep. Sure. What's our actual goal here?"

"Reconnaissance is our primary goal," said Daffyd. "We want to understand what they are doing over here. We have reason to believe they might be indulging in unreasonable practices."

"Yeah? Like what?"

"That's what we're here to find out. Now, we will walk over to the houseplant display and take a tour around fish, pets and candles, so that we look like a normal family thinking about Christmas."

"Nothing says Christmas like fish, pets and candles."

Daffyd frowned. "I thought you wanted that gold star?"

"I'm just feeling my way into the character. I reckon I'm a quirky kid who jokes with her dad. He takes it well."

Daffyd narrowed his eyes. "Fine."

They entered the building and walked through a riot of Christmas ornaments that almost perfectly mirrored what Hedgelord had on offer. Ultimately, they emerged into a houseplant area. Daffyd stopped to consider a huge display of poinsettias. He pointed at them. "Two for the price of one. It's a good offer. As an elf, how would you pose with these?"

Anika glanced around. "I'm not an elf though, am I? I'm an eleven year old kid. Is this a trap?"

"Hypothetical question," said Daffyd.

Anika picked up a pair of plants, one in each hand. "I

would do this kind of open-armed, jazz-hands pose with them and grin widely at the camera. If I was an elf and not a normal everyday eleven year old kid."

"Yes. Good work. You are a natural." Daffyd looked lost in thought as Anika put the plants down.

"What's going on?" she said.

Daffyd sighed. There was an expression of genuine hurt in his eyes. He took out his phone, scrolled a moment, and showed her. It was a photo of an elf she'd never seen before. He was young, slender, and had a child-like face with what she'd have to say was perhaps the cheeriest and friendliest smile she'd ever seen.

"Nathan Carson lit up every scene he was in," said Daffyd sadly. "I taught him that." Daffyd flicked from a picture of Nathan, arms wide, welcoming people to the grotto to one of him peeking out from behind a Christmas tree. A third picture showed him with a gaudy poinsettia plant in each hand, eyes wide because they were two for the price of one.

"Ah," she said. "He works here now, doesn't he?"

"Broke my heart," sniffed Daffyd, tucking his phone away again.

They walked through to fish. It was quiet in there. Anika assumed they were not seen as especially Christmassy, so she was able to peer at all of the brightly coloured fish, big and small.

"Fish or fishes?" she asked Daffyd.

"Sorry?"

"Which is better to express the plural of fish? Fish or fishes?"

"I'm not sure why it matters."

"We're the sort of family that debates this stuff, dad! Surely you've got a favourite. Fish or fishes?"

"Fish. Definitely fish. Fishes just sounds weird."

"Yeah! I think so too. Do you know there are people who sing 'All of the other reindeers' when we do Rudolph?"

"I do, yes. And yet it is our job to continue smiling, always."

After trailing round several areas, Daffyd seemed to make up his mind. "Right, it's time to go and book a grotto slot."

"*This* is the secret mission?"

"I just need to see," he said. "Follow my lead. Act like a kid who's excited to see Santa."

They walked outside to the rear of the indoor space. Anika was struck by how functionally similar it was to Hedgelord, even though the spaces looked very different. She heard Daffyd gasp as they came to the queue for the grotto.

"It's him! It's Nathan." He turned to Anika and adjusted the scarf to further cover his face. "I'm going to need you to do the talking. Say I have a throat infection or something. We're looking to get a walk-in slot for the grotto."

Anika peered ahead and shuffled forward in the queue to listen in on the conversation Nathan Carson was having with another family. They looked like grandparents who weren't up to speed with how things worked. Nathan smiled down at the two children who were with them. In the flesh, it was an even more charming smile. Quite fanciable, really.

"The grotto is completely fully booked for today I'm afraid," said Nathan. "Can I book you in for another day?" His voice was light and unassuming, and he looked as if he really wanted these people to be happy. Anika tried on his smile for herself. Wide, but not weirdly wide. Crinkly round the eyes.

"All the way from Wales? Oh my goodness what a trip you've had!" he said. "No, you shouldn't feel silly for not booking ahead, how were you to know? If today's the only day you have available then let's have a think about options, shall we?" Nathan's fingers tapped the tablet as he scanned the booking system. "Hm, it's a tricky one. Have you considered Hedgelord at all? They are only just over the road and it's possible their grotto is not fully booked."

Anika gaped. Was he really suggesting to this family that they should go to the competition? Daffyd looked as if he might have something stern to say on the subject. It didn't matter anyway, as the family shook their heads firmly.

"Oh," said Nathan, "I might be able to do something. If you can wait for an hour, and let me assure you that an hour will *fly* past if you go and grab a cup of tea and a mince pie in the Lighthouse café, then I can squeeze you in with a little light jiggery pokery. How would that be?"

Daffyd looked as if he was filled with rage at the ease with which Nathan had accommodated the customers. His face suggested that rules had been bent or broken and he was unhappy about it.

Anika realised she was now at the head of the queue. She stepped forward and affected a slightly higher voice than her natural one. "Hi. Sorry my dad's lost his voice, we wanted to go in the grotto, please."

Nathan turned the full wattage of his smile onto her, and Anika basked in it for a few seconds before she realised he was waiting for her to respond.

"Spaces tomorrow?" she said. "I mean, I guess we could come back, dad, couldn't we?" She turned to look at Daffyd. Had she been a pushover? Possibly, but she wanted the golden, radiant smile of Nathan to appear for her once more. Daffyd shook his head and made a negative-sounding grunting sound.

"Sorry dad, are you asking me to double check?" asked Anika. She turned back to Nathan. "Is there nothing at all for today? Can't you squeeze us in? We are very, very small." She mimed smallness, hands over her head and drawing herself down like a hibernating dormouse. Daffyd nudged her in the ribs and she snapped out of it.

"I'm so very sorry, but today is completely full. I can get you in tomorrow though if you'd like to book?"

"Yes please!" said Anika. She studied Nathan's face, desperate to know how he managed to emit such a pleasing aura. He had smooth soft skin, but so did many young people. He had a good smile, but lots of people had that too. What was the secret ingredient?

"Card or cash?" Nathan asked.

Anika turned to Daffyd. He fished in a pocket and pulled out the cash.

"There we are, all booked in! Looking forward to seeing you tomorrow."

Anika had to drag herself away. She kept glancing back as they walked out of the store.

As they walked out of the car park, Daffyd pulled the scarf away from his face. "What on earth was that back there?" he huffed. "We wanted to get into the grotto today!"

"What's that got to do with poisoned reindeer, anyway?" she said. "I thought we were looking for information."

"We are, we are," snapped Daffyd. "I just…"

Anika gave him a sidelong look. "Did you just want to see Nathan?"

There was a moment of human weakness in Daffyd's eyes, then he harrumphed. "You didn't even try to make up a convincing sob story like that other family. Wales my foot. I mean, who has a fully booked grotto at the very start of December?"

"They do apparently. We nearly do."

Daffyd shook his head.

"Can I ask something?" Anika said. "Nathan, the elf. How is he so good? What makes him so … lovable?"

Daffyd emitted a low growling sound. "You do realise you're asking me to talk about one of the most painful episodes of my life, don't you?"

"Sorry."

He sighed. "He has a natural talent. Some people do." He glanced sideways at her. "You have it, I think. And that smile. He absorbed everything I ever taught him. He's an advanced caperer, an accomplished juggler, and he can bring forth a cracker joke based on any prompt you care to give him. But I think you're asking about that indefinable something else that he has. Some people would call it charisma, maybe; but it's more than that. If I knew what it was I would bottle it. And damn it, he's even better this year than I remember."

Daffyd fell into a sulk for the rest of the trip back, but that was fine because Anika was immersed in her own thoughts, pondering on what indefinable qualities made up charisma, and whether she might learn it herself.

45

GALLAGHER

Gallagher waved the vet off after she was satisfied that the reindeer were stable. She'd left him with very strict instructions about checking on each one every fifteen minutes throughout the night, and getting them to sip water if possible.

"Doing that every fifteen minutes means no breaks. It starts again each time I've done them all." He stated it out loud by way of confirmation, but nobody was dishing out sympathy – least of all the vet.

Amy stayed for a further hour. His mind immediately thought that, somehow, in some twisted way, an evening with her among high and nauseated reindeer might be the beginning of something beautiful; but as the sun set she informed him she had an unavoidable appointment and had to go.

He wanted to yell out to her that he had saved her boobs from Cameron Clasp's pervy laser beams, but wisely decided it would not improve the situation.

Even Sophie left him. Tom Eccles co-opted her to help transfer the afternoon's cash from the still defunct tills to the safe in Cameron's office.

"I am going to see if I can scrounge us some food from the café," said Luka, leaving Gallagher alone with his miserable ruminant patients.

"Fuck my life," he whispered.

"Do I hear the sound of someone filled with self-pity?" called Anika from outside.

"It's not self-pity if my life really is shit," said Gallagher.

Anika Chowdhry stepped inside the reindeer shed. "I'll stay and help if you like," she said.

"Why?"

"Because I care," she said. "For reindeer, obviously."

"Obviously."

"We can do shifts."

"You sure?" Gallagher said. "You don't need to go home? Your parents won't mind?"

She winked, and a few minutes later he heard her on the phone, telling her parents she was having a sleepover with someone called Asha. Well, it was an offer he couldn't refuse. It wasn't like he'd had an especially restful night's sleep for a couple of days.

Luka returned with portions of fish and chips he had somehow scrounged from the Pagoda Café for them all. "Reindeer emergencies mean we can invoke special privileges," he said with a wink as he plonked himself down with them at the edge of the pen.

"This is going to be an all-nighter," said Gallagher, munching on the steaming food.

"Fine by me," said Anika. "As long as we don't die of hypothermia."

They scrunched up their chip papers when they were done.

"Right, now we'll fetch you a sleeping bag and a roll mat," said Gallagher. "We do a shift, then get some kip in between, yeah?"

Anika grinned. "I did camping with the Brownies years ago, but it turned out to be bunk beds in dormitories. I've never done the proper outdoors kind."

"I need to go and make some phone calls," said Luka.

"Abandoning us?" said Gallagher.

"Maybe I need to speak to our friend Sonia about the fact we no longer have her product, eh?"

"Oh, God," Gallagher muttered. He flexed his hands and wondered if drug dealers cut your fingers off if it was your first offence.

Anika joined Gallagher in poking around in their equipment sheds. She selected a warm sleeping bag, also carrying a comfy reclining sunbed back to the pen as well.

"Actually, that's not a bad shout," he mused. "I reckon these dozy sods might piss on us in the night if we sleep on the floor." He fetched his own recliner. "Right, I'm going to go round and give them all a drink, then I'm putting the kettle on. Tea or cocoa?"

"Cocoa please," said Anika. "This is brilliant! I'm so glad the reindeer are all fine, by the way."

"Yeah. Blitzen might have a woolly head in the morning, but the vet seemed happy enough." He was getting the knack of the sippy cup now and he moved easily between the reindeer. "So, what have you told your parents about working here, then?"

Anika shuffled inside her sleeping bag. "I haven't told them yet. It's all wrapped up in the idea of quitting uni. They're going to be so mad at me. I don't even know how to have that conversation."

"Oh fuck, that's a toughie," said Gallagher. "What is it you want to do, then?"

"Honestly? I don't know. It might even be uni; but I feel like I haven't been able to breathe for the pressure, and I wanted to step away for a bit."

"Checking out is a temptation I understand," said Gallagher, "but not one I'd necessarily recommend."

"No, I get that. I suppose I mean it's more of a coping mechanism than an actual strategy. That must be alright, surely?"

Gallagher thought for a while before answering. "Yeah. A coping mechanism not a strategy. Good advice, thank you."

46

CHARLOTTE

Charlotte had set her alarm for three a.m. As she dressed and left the house, she had the lonely, hollow feeling that tended to come upon her in the small hours. Doubts crept into her mind and tried to challenge her resolve, but she had decided what to do, so she drove directly over to Nick Bellingham's road.

She could feel God's eyes on her as she drove. "I'm doing this for a good reason," she said to Him.

She parked some distance away, not wanting to be seen. The street lights were off along his road. She had no idea why some areas did this, but presumably it was cost savings dressed up as environmental concern. It made it easier to remain concealed, but it was less easy to see where she was going.

"Fuck!" She stumbled up a kerbstone as her smartwatch buzzed at her profanity. She should get a free pass for middle-of-the-night swearing.

None of Nick Bellingham's lighting displays were on. Presumably he had them on a timer so that he could get some sleep himself. She needed to locate the LumaGrid.

That was the plan. Cameron had authorised any action. Black ops, he'd said.

Bloomers had come along and tried to poach one of Hedgelord's most prized customers, and when Hedgelord stepped up their game, Bloomers had swooped in with crass presents and hollow promises. But the gits at Bloomers had not stopped there. They had brought the fight to Hedgelord. Trying to poison reindeer was a low even Bloomers had not stooped to before.

Oh, yes! The gloves were off now. Any and all actions against the enemy were acceptable.

Charlotte's eyes were gradually becoming accustomed to the low light and, through her cold breath misty in the night air, she could make out the dark shape of Nick's house.

The house helped her orientate herself in his garden so she knew roughly where she was headed. There! She had her hands on the LumaGrid central control box. She felt its edges, trying to understand what was where.

She pulled pliers and a screwdriver out of her pocket. She needed to figure out the swiftest way to disable the LumaGrid. She wished she had one of those tiny little pocket torches that spies in films had. She wasn't even sure if they existed in the real world, but she wanted something that would illuminate key parts of the LumaGrid but be barely noticeable from a short distance away.

A bit like the light she could see bobbing a few feet ahead.

She froze and watched. It was the tiniest light, but it was moving in a deliberate way, and she heard the tiny 'plink' of someone cutting something. Three times she heard it before she realised what it was. She pulled out her phone and shone the light ahead of her.

"Jack fucking Hartigan!" she said. He was standing on a box with a pair of cutters in his hand, poised to make another snip. He'd already removed several of the cable ties which fastened the polar bear's head in place.

"Charlotte! How lovely to see you!" His eyes fell to her hands. "With your pliers and your screwdriver." His own hands went to his sides and the cutters dropped into a pocket as if they were never there. His easy smile matched his nonchalant stance.

"What have you done to our polar bear?" Charlotte said. She stepped forward with her torch. Fortunately, the majority of the fastenings were still in place. She reached up and roughly pulled the scarf over the ugly seam. It somehow seemed important to protect the polar bear's dignity.

"What a funny coincidence, seeing you here at this hour," he said, with a laugh and a shake of his head.

"This is a new low," she spat. She thought about the reindeer. "A *new* new low."

"Me?" He gestured at the polar bear. "I'm just exposing this tawdry makeshift monstrosity for what it really is. What were you doing? Planning on sabotaging brand new and expensive seasonal display equipment that will once again secure Nick Bellingham national media coverage?"

"Oh, yes!" she said sarcastically. "Because you're all about doing things for the benefit of the customer, aren't you?"

"Er, yes!" he retorted. "I am! Genuinely focused on customer satisfaction. I'm not some petty point-scorer from the second best garden centre in the area!"

"You take that back!"

"Nothing to take back. It's true!"

A light came on in the upstairs of the house. Charlotte and Jack looked up. A shadowy shape moved behind frosted glass. Jack jumped down from his box and scarpered for the road. Charlotte was only a step behind him. He dropped to a crouch behind a parked car on the far side. Charlotte took cover beside him.

Jack tried to peer over the bonnet at the house and then dropped into a hiding position once more.

"I saw one of your minions this afternoon," he muttered.

"Who?" said Charlotte.

"The fat elf trainer. You know the one: got a bit of the Child Catcher about him. He was bundled up in a scarf and hat, but I knew you'd sent him."

"Just some basic surveillance. If you're going to try to actually sabotage our grotto experience—"

"Do I need to? You've always been playing catch up to us."

"You're frightened of us," said Charlotte. "We're bigger and better than you."

He seethed, a silver blast of frosted air gathering before his face. "This doesn't need to be a war, Charlotte."

"No, it doesn't."

"We had the better stock this year. I made astute purchases at the Xmas eXpo. Maybe you'll do the same for next year."

"Don't patronise me, Jack."

"What?" he laughed. "Nick wanted the LumaGrid. We decided to stock the LumaGrid. Maybe next year he'll want a sweary bear with a wonky neck."

She slapped him in the chest with a gloved hand. "You're fucking loving this!"

"I think you just need to see when you're beaten."

"Hedgelord is never beaten!"

He nodded slowly. "You have a real angry streak, don't you? I can see it. Even in the dark, I can see it."

"If I am, it's your fault."

He was still nodding. "I've heard the stories. Kicked out of every church in town, no?"

"Fuck off, Jack," she said and thumped a fist against the car they both leaned against.

The car alarm set up in a series of loud whoops and the hazard lights started flashing. On the near side of the road a couple of house lights came on.

Jack backed away, preparing to run off down the road.

"That temper of yours will be your undoing," he said to her as a parting shot, and was gone into the darkness.

Charlotte hurried away to her own car, black op aborted.

47

GALLAGHER

G allagher slowly stirred to find Anika was doing the rounds of the reindeer with the sippy cup. The reindeer shed had been a surprisingly warm place to sleep. The heat from a handful of stoned reindeer crowded inside made a little oven of the place, even if the air was pungent and thick.

"You know in the pictures of Baby Jesus ... where he's asleep in the hay..." Anika muttered.

"Yeah?" he croaked, sitting up.

"Why isn't he crying because of the damned prickles? It pokes right through my jeans every time I kneel down."

Gallagher made a single syllable response that he hoped conveyed both his understanding and agreement. He reached a hand across to the nearest reindeer and checked it for signs of life. It was warm and breathing. Alive. He sighed with relief.

The door opened, bring a cold breeze, morning light and Luka Sibersky. "You are awake," he said. "This is good. I have brought you coffee."

Anika clambered over a bale to get to the take-out cups.

"Americanos with extra shot of espresso," said Luka.

Anika took a sip and hissed at the heat, but continued drinking anyway. "You bring any food?"

"No."

"Could you get us a croissant or waffles or something?"

"I am not Deliveroo," said Luka, giving a coffee to Gallagher. "The beasts are alive?"

"They are," said Gallagher.

"Good. Then we only have half a problem," said Luka.

"Half?" said Anika.

Luka looked at Anika, and Gallagher could see him internally debating whether to tell her or not. He shrugged.

"There is drug dealer who is still probably wondering where her ten kilos of cannabis have gone."

"Fuck," whispered Gallagher.

Charlotte hadn't slept since her encounter with Jack Hartigan. She was filled with so much rage she thought she might never sleep again. She'd gone straight from Nick's house to Hedgelord, passing those dark hours until morning rage-baking. She'd put cookies in Mrs Claus's kitchen, both as a snack for the elves and an attempt to make the grotto smell appealing. She had also laid out a selection of cakes in

Cameron's office. The rage-baking had occupied her time, but done little to improve her mood. Her curse counter app had her at over fifty "Fucks!" before the sun came up.

At nine o'clock, she politely summoned Cameron, Tom and Daffyd for an emergency meeting.

"Early morning meetings are never my favourite, but I can always get behind a Chelsea bun," said Cameron Clasp, unravelling the outer part of the pastry's coil with his fingers and dropping it into his mouth from a height. "Tell us why we're here, Charlotte."

"I think we've all observed an escalation in Bloomers's nefarious activities in recent days," began Charlotte.

"Wow," said Tom.

"I know."

"I mean, did you just the word 'nefarious' in a normal sentence? What activities?"

Charlotte rolled her eyes and bit down on an expletive. "Who do you think poisoned the reindeer, Tom?"

Cameron slammed a hand onto his desk. "The reindeer are dead?"

"No, the vet came, and some of the staff have attended to them overnight," said Tom. "It seems they will be fine. You're saying Bloomers poisoned them?"

"It's an inescapable conclusion," she said.

"Those bastards!" said Cameron. He put the Chelsea bun down. "Very nearly put me off my snack."

"They are very good though," said Daffyd, taking another. He was the cake equivalent of a chain smoker.

"I am sorry to report that later on yesterday, things took a very serious turn." Charlotte searched for words which didn't cast her in a poor light, but nothing was forthcoming. "I caught Jack Hartigan sabotaging the polar bear Nick Bellingham bought from us."

"We gave it to him free, surely—" said Tom, but Cameron cut him off.

"Good grief! What did Mr Bellingham have to say on the matter?"

Charlotte inclined her head. "I wasn't in a position to alert him. It was in the middle of the night, and there might have been questions about what I was doing there."

Cameron and Daffyd nodded in understanding.

"Sorry, what *were* you doing there?" asked Tom. "Unless you were doing something wrong you could have just involved the poli— Wait—" he looked aghast "—were you there to sabotage *their* stuff?"

Nobody answered Tom, but understanding was starting to dawn. He turned to each of them in turn. "Are you all crazy? We can't behave like this!"

Cameron strode forward and clasped Charlotte's hands. "Charlotte, I want to thank you for going the extra mile. You check-mated their ruddy asses, and that's a beautiful thing. I'd love to have seen his face."

Tom looked as if he was going to say something, but he just shook his head and grabbed a mince pie.

"He didn't even look all that bothered," said Charlotte. "He always has that smug, superior expression, as if he was actually *expecting* me to swoop out of the darkness and stop him. He's an oily little twat."

There was a brief silence while they all digested the news.

"I went over there yesterday," said Daffyd. "I went to look at the grotto with Anika. You remember Nathan, the elf?"

"Of course," they all chorused. Nathan's elf powers were legendary.

"He was on grotto check-in. He did that thing of turning us away but somehow made us feel good about it."

Cameron smashed a fist into his palm. "How the hell did we let an elf like that slip through our fingers? What did they do to lure him over there?"

Daffyd sighed and shrugged. "I don't know. Anika and I have tickets for today, though. We were planning to go over and spy on the grotto."

"Spy? We need more than spying at this stage!" roared Cameron. "We need action. We need to make them wish they'd never been born."

Tom made an exasperated huffing sound. "You do all know that we ran an actual competitor analysis a few months ago? We profiled the local demographic and concluded that there's plenty of custom to support two garden centres. It's damaging for us to get caught up in the idea that we need to engage directly with Bloomers."

"Never had you down as a coward, Tom," said Cameron.

Tom persevered. "At best we lose focus on what we ought to be doing, and at worst I'd say we might end up liable for criminal charges, based on what I've just heard. I want to beg you all to take a moment; take a breath. Please."

Cameron pulled a face that belonged on a seven year old

who'd been told not to run indoors. "Your concerns are noted, Tom. Thanks. Now, you all know what to do, right?"

"What? No! I'm not sure we do," said Tom.

Everyone else filed out. Charlotte exchanged a look with Daffyd.

"Up our game?" he asked.

"Most definitely," said Charlotte. "Let's take the fight to them."

48

GALLAGHER

Gallagher was rearranging bags of wood chippings in the outdoor section and seriously contemplating maybe moving that compost outside the landscaping office, when his phone buzzed. Luka was calling.

Gallagher picked up. "Yeah?"

"I need to see you in the café. Now."

"I..."

"Now." Luka ended the call.

Gallagher worked his jaw as he thought. That was Luka, but not like Luka. The voice had been urgent and insistent, neither of which were qualities one normally associated with Luka. Gallagher tossed a bag high onto the stack, took off his gloves and went inside.

The Pagoda Café was busy. The bright cold day had triggered some instinct in the locals, an instinct to go potter around the out-of-town shops, buy some superfluous tat, and lunch at the Pagoda Café. Luka was sitting down at a table, with company. He saw Gallagher enter and simply looked at him: a dead and expressionless stare.

The dark-haired woman sitting opposite Luka had a kid, maybe six or seven years old, at her side. The kid had a colouring book open in front of him and the remains of a mince pie next to it. He was colouring in a jolly Santa scene, primarily in red.

Gallagher looked at Luka and the woman.

"This is my good friend, Sonia Patterson," said Luka. "Sonia, this is Gallagher."

Gallagher tried to think of something nice and friendly to say, but the fact that this was the drug dealer whose drugs they'd failed to deliver made nice words choke in his throat.

"Mrs Patterson..." Gallagher choked.

"Do I look like a missus?" she said.

In fact, she did look like a regular mum, married, single or otherwise; but there was something about her – in the sour set of her mouth, in the severe yet careless way in which her hair was tied back – that also made Gallagher think she was something tougher than a regular mum. She looked like the kind of woman who'd drag another woman out into the street by her hair. She looked like the kind of woman who'd willingly glass someone with a pint of lager, and probably had.

"Er, no, no..." said Gallagher.

"Sit down," she instructed. "Can't be arsed to look up at you."

Gallagher sat down next to Luka, tight together in the café seating.

"Where's my fucking gear?" said Sonia simply.

The kid switched crayons.

Gallagher looked at Luka.

"Don't look at him," said Sonia. "I didn't ask him. I already asked him. I'm asking fucking you."

"Mummy," said the kid.

Sonia looked over. The kid had drawn four wonky stars at the top of his colouring and was now adding a fifth.

"I've not done five," she said.

The kid nodded earnestly. "Five is another mince pie."

"You've not eaten that one."

"Ten is a new Bluey toy."

Sonia nostrils flared and she looked back to Gallagher. "My gear?"

"We've got it stored," said Gallagher. "It's fine."

A hand placed something on the table in front of Gallagher. The thing was a car wing mirror. A big man with cauliflower ears and a broccoli nose dragged over a chair and sat at the end of the table.

"Is this my wing mirror?" said Gallagher. "Is this off my car?"

"Don't make Vincent here go and get more parts," said Sonia. "He won't be happy."

"Sonia..." said Luka.

"I did not fucking ask you to speak," she growled.

The kid drew another star on the colouring book and returned to colouring in Santa. He'd apparently decided that Santa's eyes should be red.

The heavy, Vincent, produced a phone and scrolled through some photos which showed the plastic wrapping from the cannabis bale scraggy and empty in the reindeer paddock.

"Vincent's just taken these," said Sonia, "So I have to ask: what the actual—?" She paused and looked at the kid. She cleared her throat. "What the actual rubber duck is going on here?"

"We had an accident," said Gallagher.

"What the fuck?" said Sonia. The kid started to draw another star. "Shit." The kid picked up an extra crayon. "You don't get to draw two for that."

The child glared at her but only drew one additional star.

"Accident! Twat here says your reindeer ate it."

"Not all of it."

"That was twenty pounds of stuff. That's ten kilos if you're European. That's worth maybe forty grand to my business."

"Fuck," Gallagher whispered.

Sonia put her hand over the kid's as it moved. "You only do stars for mummy. Don't swear in front of my kid, Gallagher, or Vincent will get creative."

Vincent put a screwdriver on the table.

"Leave my car alone. Please."

Vincent gave him a look. "This is for teeth."

"Teeth? Teeth? It's a screwdriver! How do you even—?" Gallagher forced himself to shut up.

Luka put both hands on the table. It was a small gesture, but it drew everyone's attention. He looked Sonia Patterson in the eye. "We want to make this better. Give us three days to recover the situation."

"You're going to recover the situation, are you? No. You are not, because my supply chain is already disrupted.

People who want their gear are going to be disappointed, and that makes me look shit, doesn't it? Now, you can get me my money or my drugs. But make no mistake, that is not recovering the situation, that is stopping Vincent from having a party with his toolbox."

She dismissed them with a flick of her hand and a scowl. Gallagher tried to take his wing mirror back, but Vincent put his hand over it.

"Souvenir," he said. "Next time, I will take something else."

"Teeth?" said Gallagher, feeling a queasiness rise suddenly inside him.

Vincent shrugged. "Or maybe fingers."

Gallagher remembered what Luka had said about the last courier to disappoint Sonia.

"I like my fingers," he whispered.

"Good. I wouldn't want to take something you didn't want."

Luka hauled Gallagher upright.

"There will be no need," he said. "All will be well."

Gallagher couldn't help but notice the quiet happiness of the boy with his colouring as he was pulled away.

49

ANIKA

Anika tried to focus as Daffyd explain her latest top secret mission. She had had a disturbed night of fitful sleep in the reindeer shed and was, frankly, still finding bits of straw inside her clothing.

"Tell me again," she said.

"A honey trap," said Daffyd, his eyes glittering viciously.

"A what?"

"A honey trap."

"No. I heard the words. I'm just wondering what you mean."

"A honey trap. A sex trap. Like they used to do in the Cold War. Trying to catch someone in an incriminating situation with—"

"Yeah, yeah. I know what the *words* mean," she said. "What I don't understand is you just summoning me and saying the words 'honey trap.' You need to elaborate."

Daffyd gave her a focused look. "I think we should

capture Nathan Carson in a honey trap operation and take photos which utterly destroy him as an elf."

"Okay," said Anika. "And now the why. Nathan seems a perfectly nice guy."

Daffyd laughed bitterly. "Oh, if you only knew. The things he has done. The things Bloomers have done."

"What has he done?"

"I sometimes have this dream," said Daffyd. "It's a strange dream."

Anika wasn't totally sure she wanted to know about Daffyd's dreams. "Yeah?"

"I could have elved anywhere in the world. I did elfing duties all over the country. I was the recipient of the Elfie award, ninety-seven to ninety-nine."

"Yes. I know."

"And I washed up here. Is it the centre of the elfing world? Possibly not. Is it the grandest heights of elfdom? No. This is regional at best but, by Santa's beard, this is the finest regional grotto in the whole country. It is a beacon of festive cheer in a dark world."

"*That's* your dream?"

"No. My dream is that one day, the fripperies of civilisation will come crashing down out there. War, plague – the Wi-Fi going down. Civilisation will collapse and the world out there will become a wasteland of grey emptiness and numbing horrors. You know, Mad Max style. It's all going to go to shit out there, but here – right here! – there will still be a Hedgelord Santa's Grotto. People, the tired and huddled masses, will come in from the grim cold and they will find elves singing and dancing. They will find sugary festive snacks and delicious hot chocolate. They will meet with the big man himself and they—" he held out a trembling hand towards an invisible holy wonder "—they will sit upon his knee and know that there is still a kernel of goodness in this world. We will offer them succour and hope when there is none to be found elsewhere."

"And *that's* your dream?" said Anika, hoping the mad weirdo heard her utter disbelief.

"It's a strange dream, I know."

"You think?"

He chuckled and hugged himself. "It keeps me warm at night. Ooh, a little shiver went down my spine. It really did." His face became stony serious again. "But over *there*, less than a mile away, there is a hive of scum and villainy that threatens our dream. Bloomers isn't just another garden centre, it's a blot on the landscape. More than that, its insidious evil sends out its tendrils to infect us all."

"Um, okay."

"Trust me, Anika. This is all true. We cannot hope to make Hedgelord the shining beacon of hope and love and Christmas cheer in a fading world while Bloomers still stands. We must destroy Bloomers, and to do that, we must destroy Nathan Carson."

"With a honey trap?" she said.

"With a honey trap." He raised his eyebrows meaningfully.

With a plummeting stomach, she realised his meaning. "Me? Me! The honey trap? God, no."

"You're the perfect choice."

"In what world am I the perfect choice?"

"You're young. You believe in the cause. You have all the required—" he waved his hands generally towards her boobs "—equipment. I'm sure you've got feminine wiles to spare."

"Feminine...? Okay – listen up, mate. My equipment and my wiles are none of your concern. You want this job doing, why don't you do it? I'm fairly certain Nathan is gay anyway."

Daffyd scoffed. "Because he is in touch with his elfin spirit? Such naïveté. And a bit prejudiced, by the way."

"And because I think he's actually gay," she said. "You know, like..." She waved her hand at Daffyd.

Daffyd put a hand on his round chest. "I may present a certain patrician charm, a general cuddliness, but I'm not the man – or woman! – suited for this role. That person is you. Go to my dressing room and try to, you know, zhuzh this up. Sexy. Slutty. I've ordered you a costume."

"No. I'm not doing it."

Daffyd dipped inside his elf costume and pulled out a sheet of gold star stickers. "I have been authorised to offer you a gold star for your services in this matter," he said airily.

"I don't think a gold star sticker is going..."

They were very nice stars. There was twinkly edging on them.

"And there would be a certificate of commendation, signed by Mr Clasp, the head honcho." Daffyd added.

"A certificate..."

"With suitable wording that would look very good on a young woman's CV," he said.

She pressed her lips together, knowing she would regret everything that followed her next utterance. "Show me the costume."

He clapped his chubby hands together. "Follow me, my sexy volunteer."

They went through the back areas of the grotto until they reached Daffyd's secret space, his office cum dressing room. "Here," he said.

A plastic wrapped mail-order fancy dress costume had been laid out.

"Sexy elf?" she said.

"Sexy elf. Both the perfect disguise and the perfect weapon." He backed off and stepped outside.

Anika ripped open the packet. It was a cheaply made thing: a figure-hugging elf outfit with printed on buttons and collars. She held it up against herself. The jagged fringe barely came down over her hips.

"Where's the skirt with this thing?" she called out.

"It's a dress," Daffyd replied from just round the corner.

"For God's sake," she muttered.

There were stockings, striped like candy canes, and a tangled set of red stocking suspenders.

"There's a difference between sexy elf and slutty elf, you know!" she called to Daffyd.

"And what would that be?"

"About six inches of dress material for one. Am I supposed to be wearing this slutty outfit with my trainers?"

"Look in the wardrobe round the back. There's some heels. What size are you?"

"A six."

"Foot twins!" said Daffyd happily. "The red heels would be a good match."

There was a wardrobe containing many pairs of shoes.

"Are these all yours?" she said.

"I'm only an elf three months of the year," he replied.

Knowing that if she took the plunge and committed to this madness, there would be no going back, Anika stepped out of her clothes and wriggled into the sexy elf costume. She tugged it down, then tugged it down some more, but the hemline wasn't getting any lower. It took a full five minutes to get into the suspender belt and clip it onto the stockings.

"Is everything all right?" Daffyd called.

"I've not had to dress as a slutty elf before!"

"Sexy elf."

"Trust me. I'm right on this one."

The shoes however were the delightfully excessive things that Anika kind of loved – if she could ignore the fact that Daffyd had probably already worn them.

She regarded herself in Daffyd's dressing room mirror. Her first thoughts were not kind. She reminded herself she'd seen women on a night out wearing far less.

Her phone buzzed on the dressing table by her other clothes. It was a text from her mum asking how studying at Asha's had gone. Anika just looked at it. She didn't think she could even text her mum dressed like this.

50

CHARLOTTE

Charlotte was at Nick Bellingham's house, overseeing the construction of the promised winter wonderland display. She had been in touch with an events manager she'd met at a seminar in Bedford. He oversaw concerts and summer festivals that were held in the grounds of massive country houses, and she had secured the loan of a long plastic tunnel which would form the basis of the walkthrough display. It was being unloaded from a huge tour lorry, and a team of roadies were bolting it together and securing it with tensioned wires.

Nick Bellingham wheeled up the path to join her as she gazed at the scale of the operation. It was costing Hedgelord a lot of money, but it would be worth it when it appeared on the local TV news. There was a Hedgelord banner strategically placed where it would be visible if they interviewed Nick Bellingham from his driveway.

"This looks as if it will be rather impressive," he said with a smile and more genuine warmth than she'd heard from him in a while.

"I do hope so," said Charlotte. "They are building in a platform for the fireworks, and the snow machine will be up at the top. You'll have a remote control to turn it on and off."

"I am thrilled," he said. "So are all of my social media followers."

"You have many?"

"Three hundred thousand. People love Christmas."

She was quietly stunned. Hedgelord reaching out to an additional audience of hundreds of thousands, even if they were dotted all over the globe, was a level of publicity she'd do almost anything for.

"They have already pledged quite a sum of money for one of our chosen charities," said Nick.

"Have they? Well done you!" said Charlotte.

"Perhaps you'd do me the honour of presenting a cheque to one of our charities?" Nick said.

"Me?"

"Why not? You have made this happen. I think you should take some of the credit."

"No, I couldn't. That should come from you surely? You're the one who raised the money."

"I have raised some of the money, but Hedgelord will match what I raise, yes? I'm sure you said that?"

Charlotte reflected on the many claims, suggestions and offers she had thrown into the ring. Had she said that? Possibly. "Yes. Yes, of course."

"So the interim amount can be presented immediately I think. One of those big novelty cheques with lots of photos, and maybe the TV people in attendance, yeah?"

"I would be honoured. What's the charity?"

"St Stephen's church."

"St Stephen's church? The one in town?"

"Yes. That's the one. They do a huge amount of work for homeless families in the area, including refugees who've been kicked out of their current accommodation. A lot of mothers and children depend on them."

"You want me to deliver a big novelty cheque to St Stephen's church?"

"I think it's a good idea. It was Jack from Bloomers who suggested it."

"Did he now?"

"I know you're a person of the faith yourself, so I was sure you'd approve."

Charlotte could only clench her jaw and nod.

"I'll text Ralph and ask him when he's available for the presentation," said Nick, tapping at his phone.

She wanted to howl that this was the worst idea in the world and Reverend Ralph Robertson would be appalled if he knew she was involved. It might have been many months since she'd been given her marching orders from the church and burned her last bridge with the town's organised Christian community, but Reverend Ralph had not forgotten.

"Um, it will be pretty tough to align people's calendars at this time, I guess," she suggested. "They must be flat out over there."

"No he's just replied," said Nick. "Says he can do any day this week."

"Right. Good. I'm very much looking forward to it," said Charlotte, wondering if she could fake her own death if she played for time.

51

GALLAGHER

Back in the plant area, Luka and Gallagher retreated to their tea shed to discuss how to resolve their unresolvable situation.

"I am so tired," said Gallagher. "And at the same time I don't think I will ever sleep again. That Vincent is proper scary, and how is it possible that Sonia is all nice to her kid while she's threatening us at the same time? It's messed up."

"It is," said Luka. "Well, I guess this means we need to get onto that reindeer shit."

"The vet's with them, they should be fine," said Gallagher.

"No, you misunderstand. When I say 'reindeer shit' I mean actual reindeer shit. Is where the drugs are, no?"

Gallagher's mouth worked while his brain tried to process this new horror. "You what? Are you seriously saying we're going to gather up reindeer poo and try to pass it off to Sonia Patterson as her cannabis? It's going to look and smell like poo, isn't it? She will hang us out to dry."

"With that attitude we are already dead men. We will get the shit and see what can be done. Off you go."

"So when we say we will get the shit, what you mean is that I will get the shit?"

Luka shrugged. "It will look suspicious if we are both seen doing such a thing, no?"

Gallagher scraped the floor of the reindeer enclosure. To the casual observer he was giving the area a thorough deep clean to ensure the reindeer had the best possible environment. Nobody stopped to ask why he was separating faeces into a separate container. Which was just as well because he really didn't have the words to explain, or the will to invent a decent lie.

When he was done, he presented the product to Luka.

"Here we go." He held the box between them. "I have collected every last turd." He hefted the box in his hands. "Now I haven't weighed it, but I reckon we have somewhere between five and ten kilos here."

"Is good, no?" Luka offered

"It would be good if it was cannabis and not reindeer shit. I mean, what would Sonia think if we gave her this?"

Luka rolled his eyes. "We are not going to do that. Would be stupid. We will wash this, dry it, then we should have something a bit less … stinky."

"It's mad."

"It is not mad. Second World War, when fighting in great winter war in Scandinavian wilderness, my grandfather ate reindeer moss."

"What's that?"

"Moss, it grows on the rocks up there but is too fibrous for human digestive system."

"Right?"

"So what my grandfather's men did was kill the reindeer that had been eating the moss. Reindeer digestive system broke down the moss and made it something the soldiers could eat. Superior product."

"Are you fucking kidding me?"

"True story."

"You're trying to make some comparison between World War Two and our situation? You think passing through a reindeer's digestive system might have turned the weed into some super skunk?"

"It's possible. Like that coffee made from monkey poop."

"I don't believe you," said Gallagher.

"Is also true."

"And you think it might even be improved if I wash it? *Wash* it? How does that even work? You wash the fucking shit off shit and you're left with nothing!"

Luka put a hand on Gallagher's shoulder. "It is something to try. I will be exploring other avenues while you do this."

Gallagher wanted to make a joke about him always getting the shitty end of the stick, but he couldn't summon the energy to form the words.

52

ANIKA

Anika flopped into a seat in the Pagoda Café while she waited for Daffyd to be ready to go. He'd received a phone call from Charlotte that had distracted him, but assured Anika that he'd be ready any moment.

Sophie trotted over to Anika's table with a bottle of spray cleaner and a cloth. She somehow managed to switch effortlessly between the elfing and her café duties. "Let me wipe the table for you," she said. She sprayed the top and swept a sizeable pile of food onto the floor.

Anika looked at it and whispered. "You're not in the grotto now, Sophie. I think you're probably supposed to clean the food into a bin or something."

"Never mind that," said Sophie taking a seat opposite Anika. "We're worried about you."

"Who's 'we'?"

In answer to Anika's question, Karen Woodbine slid into the spare seat beside Sophie. "Hello love."

Anika was confused. She knew Karen by sight only. "It's nice to meet you properly, Karen." She turned to Sophie. "What do you mean, worried?"

Sophie waved a hand up and down Anika's outfit. "This?"

"I know," said Anika.

"Are you having some sort of crisis dear? I asked Karen to join me because she's a mum and she knows things."

Karen rolled her eyes. "I'm not just a mum. I do have other aspects to my personality you know."

Anika and Sophie waited politely for Karen to describe them.

On the back foot now, Karen looked as if she was casting about. "I *did* have other aspects to my personality. I'm bloody certain of it. Let me think and I'll get back to you. Anyways, let's talk about you, lovely. Why the change of outfit?"

Anika shrugged. "Daffyd asked me to wear this."

"I didn't think he was the sort," said Sophie.

"I'm to undermine Bloomers with a honey pot operation."

"Oh. My. God. This lot are so obsessed with Bloomers!" said Karen, slapping the table for emphasis. "Did you know that we now have to accept Bloomers vouchers on the tills? Frightened to death they might lose a sale! I wouldn't mind, but Bloomers are always doing those weird mixed promos where you get a hyacinth half price if you buy budgie food, or whatever. Different areas, different cost centres. It's a nightmare to put them through."

"Same in the cafe," said Sophie. "Bloomers started doing

dirty fries, so we had to put them on our menu too. It was a good couple of weeks before I realised dirty fries are actually chips with spices or sauce on them. I thought it was part of the reduce-reuse-recycle initiative."

Anika looked at Sophie with her mouth agape. "Tell me you didn't re-sell the chips off the plates people sent back?"

Sophie's doll-like eyes were wider than ever, and the prolonged silence told Anika all she needed to know.

"So you're a honey pot then?" said Karen, looking Anika up and down. "Well, it's something to put on your CV, I suppose."

"How would that look on a CV?" said Sophie. "It's a bit … rude, isn't it?"

"Nah. You'd dress it up in weasel words, wouldn't you, darling?" Karen said to Anika. "You seem smart. I bet you'd find a way to spin it."

Anika thought for a moment. "'Performed real-time study and stress-test on close competitor' maybe? Or perhaps something about disrupting the marketplace?"

"Oh, that's nice, that is," said Karen, laughing. "It makes me howl when I hear people saying stuff like that in real life. It's like they have to convince their robot overlords, who've never met any actual humans."

"Well I'm a bit worried that Daffyd is sending you into hostile territory," said Sophie.

"Trust me, I know the owners," said Karen. "Not nice people."

"We should equip you with some sort of self-defence," said Sophie.

"Elf defence," said Anika automatically, then frowned.

The grotto had done this to her, or more specifically Gillespie's insistence on elf puns throughout the day.

"We don't have weapons here," said Karen. "Unless you've got room to pack a pair of secateurs somewhere in that outfit. And I'm guessing that's a 'no'."

Sophie held out a hand triumphantly. "Pepper spray!"

Karen and Anika both looked at Sophie's hand.

"Not so much pepper spray as a sachet of pepper, is it Soph?" said Karen.

"We can make it into a spray," said Sophie, picking up the spray cleaner. "But if you don't want to carry this big bottle around then what you do is just sprinkle the pepper onto your hand and blow it in the face of your attacker. Poof!" Sophie mimed the coup de grace and gave a satisfied smile.

Anika didn't trust herself to look at Karen, so she took the sachet of pepper from Sophie. "Thanks for that. It could come in real handy."

Daffyd appeared beside the table. "Ready?"

She sighed. "Ready."

Karen gave Daffyd a firm stare. "Don't you hurt her."

Daffyd took a step back. His face twitched. He looked like he wanted to assert his authority – whatever the dynamic might be between his role and hers in the hierarchy of this place – but he balked before saying anything and simply nodded.

"She's one of my elves and I am going to look after her. Never leave an elf behind. That's my motto."

Karen made a doubtful noise.

Daffyd gestured for Anika to follow and scooted away from stern Karen.

"Let's get this over with," said Anika.

"Actually, we need to make a detour," said Daffyd. "Charlotte needs a photographer for a charity thing she's doing, so we're going to swing round to St Stephen's church in the town centre."

Anika wanted to complain, but in truth anything that postponed her having to use her 'feminine wiles' on Nathan Carson was a good thing.

53

CHARLOTTE

C harlotte parked her car near to the church. She'd asked Daffyd to come along and take some photos, because that was the minimum requirement. Daffyd and Anika were waiting in the car park. Daffyd had brought the large ironing board sized novelty cheque which Hedgelord used for charity events. There was something wrong with Anika's elf uniform. There was definitely a lot less of it than there had been before.

Daffyd gave Charlotte a snappy salute. "Ready for duty," he said and lifted his digital camera.

"Good," said Charlotte. "Let's do this." She looked Anika's skimpy dress up and down as the girl followed them. "Are you coming too? In that?"

"Daffyd won't let me sit in his car," said Anika.

"She might touch the knobs," said Daffyd.

"I'll just stand inside the church to keep warm."

Charlotte wasn't sure, but she had other pressing

thoughts on her mind. "Now, there might be some … hostility when we get in there," she explained to Daffyd.

"Hostility?"

"The reverend and I… We…. There was a differing of opinions. You know how people are sometimes."

Daffyd frowned, then understanding dawned. "Oh, this was one of *your* churches."

"They're not my churches per se."

"I've heard the stories," he said in a small, confidential voice.

"Ignore any stories you might have heard," she said, her own voice carefully controlled. "We just need to keep our eyes on the prize. We need a picture of me handing over the cheque, then we leave, as quickly as possible."

The front of St Stephen's overlooked a bulge of pavement in front of the town's key, three-way junction. In olden days it would have been a marketplace. St Stephen's must have held a truly commanding position: right in the heart of the town. Charlotte recognised the yearning within her to be accepted in this place again. Hedgelord was a wonderful and valued community, but she mourned the loss of Christian fellowship she once enjoyed here.

They walked past the nativity scene, and Charlotte forced herself not to look at it. She didn't want to be distracted by her previous life here. Today she would inhabit the shell of a different person. She would be someone brand new and unconnected to St Stephen's. She would maintain a respectful distance, and hope that previous events might go unmentioned.

They stepped through the dark doors into air which

pricked at her memory with its cool, distinctive smell of candles, dust and *Brasso* cleaner. There was also the tang of fresh greenery, suggesting there was a Christmas tree somewhere inside.

Reverend Ralph Robertson, dressed in a simple grey shirt and ecclesiastical dog collar, stood in the wide aisle near the altar. He regarded Charlotte coldly.

"Well I never," he said. "I saw the name Charlotte Mitchell on Mr Bellingham's text and assumed it must be someone different."

"The one and only," she said, attempting a smile.

"Because we all know full well that you are no longer welcome in this church."

"I don't want any fuss," she said. "I just brought you the cheque." She turned and clicked her fingers. "The cheque."

Daffyd had his camera out. Anika came forward with the big cheque. The elf dress was so low and the skirt so high that the big cheque pretty much covered up all of it.

"We'll get a quick photo and I'll be off," said Charlotte. "Daffyd will be doing the photography duties."

Daffyd offered Ralph a cheesy little grin and took a few photos of the priest as a sort of introduction.

"Daffyd," said Ralph, acknowledging him with a sombre nod. "I'm afraid you won't be taking any photo in which I appear with this woman."

Daffyd smiled widely at Ralph. Charlotte hoped that he wasn't about to try and charm him, because that was not going to work.

"Ralph!" said Daffyd, continuing to grin, "what a wonderful church you have here. A little dark in the corners, but it's really lovely. Now, this cheque comes to you from Hedgelord, where we hold our local community in high esteem. We bring it here with love in our hearts and we hope you can receive it in a similar spirit. Whatever you might have heard about Charlotte is likely to be—"

"Heard?" said Ralph. "What I have *heard* about her? Oh no. No – my experience of this woman is first hand, and deeply regrettable."

"No, but surely—"

"Her actions were monstrous!"

"Oh, come on," Charlotte snapped. "It was months ago! Over a year! You haven't got any Christian forgiveness in your heart?"

"Some of the children still have nightmares, I hear."

Anika edged closer. "Oh, God. What did you do?" she whispered, fascinated.

"That poor bird."

"The pigeon and the candlestick," said Daffyd, the words popping out of his mouth as though summoned without his volition.

"Yes," said Ralph darkly. "The pigeon and the candlestick."

"I don't think we should let one incident overshadow the importance of—"

"One incident?" demanded Ralph. "The business with Tufty Alan and the candlestick was the final indignity, the straw that broke the camel's back."

"Biblical," nodded Daffyd, approvingly.

"Charlotte was once a valued member of our congregation," said Ralph. "A trusted volunteer. As she had been at St Lucian's, and the United Reform Church, and the Eastfield Road Unitarians. I will not deny that she throws herself into things gladly at first."

"They really don't need to hear this," said Charlotte.

Out of the corner of her eye, she could see Daffyd making shooing motions at Anika. The girl sidled around the side of Ralph, cheque outheld. So be it, thought Charlotte. Distract him, get the shot, and get out.

"I'm glad though you recognise my good intentions," she said to Ralph, chin held high. If Ralph was determined to tell the tale then she'd let him, as long as they got their picture.

"But you had such a temper on you," said Ralph. "Something seething. Something wicked."

"I struggle with my temper sometimes," she admitted.

"Temper?" He looked at her reproachfully. "We all have a temper. Not all of us decide to treat the vestry as our own private rage room and take out our furies on the kneeler cushions."

"Just trying to channel my energies in a safe way."

Reverend Ralph scoffed. "Maybe you should try to exhibit a little more tolerance and patience before getting angry in the first place."

"It's just..."

Anika was almost beside Ralph, and Daffyd was casually taking picture after picture with camera held at waist height.

"I find it hard to bear when people thoughtlessly mess things up; when the hard work we put in to make this a better world is undone," said Charlotte with feeling.

"That's the world we live in," said Ralph. "Anger is the

emotion we feel when the world fails to meet our expectations."

"So wise," said Daffyd and raised the camera to take a better shot. Ralph whirled to see the sexy elf creeping up beside him, eyes boggling at the big cheque she was trying to insert in shot.

"Really?!" he exclaimed. "This is your ruse, is it?"

"Oh, no need to get angry, vicar," said Charlotte snidely.

"At least I limit my anger to selfish people who are thinking only of themselves. I don't kill defenceless pigeons."

"He wasn't defenceless! He'd been living in the church for three weeks, shitting on the congregation."

"Not a killing offence, Charlotte."

"The children's choir were performing."

"It was hardly a once-in-a-lifetime performance."

"No! It bloody wasn't!" she fumed. "The kids were shit. Mr Grail on the organ was shit. It was all a great big steaming pile of crap. I'd put weeks into preparing for that evening concert. A thing of beauty. That's what it should have been. No one bothered practising and hardly anyone bothered turning up to see it. This church is meant to be at the heart of the fucking community, Ralph! It should be a place people turn to. But what do we get? A bunch of shit kids performing to a handful of gormless and apathetic knobheads, checking their phones every ten seconds. And Tufty cocking Alan goes round and round overhead, going 'coo-coo' and crapping on people. What kind of fucking world is that, eh?"

"The best of all possible worlds, Charlotte," said the reverend.

"Really?" she spat. "Then the God Almighty did a fucking

shit job of it then, didn't he? Fuck me! If one of the employees at Hedgelord was so fucking incompetent they'd be out of the door before the end of the week, not put in charge of the whole twatting universe."

"You're angry with God."

"Of course, I'm angry with God!" she said. "I feel like ... I feel like I'm a supporter of the shittest football team in the league and I don't get to switch my allegiances. Yes! Of course I'm angry! And if you had any sense you'd have stood up during that concert and told everyone exactly how shit they all were!"

She stopped and she thought she could literally hear the echo of her own voice fading away into the high-vaulted ceiling. Anika was staring at her, agog. Daffyd had stopped taking photos and was just looking at her.

"I ... did shout at people a bit," she conceded in a much quieter voice. "And for reasons I don't rightly remember, I did have a large church candlestick in my hand. And ... the pigeon was flying close by." She focused on Ralph. "It was a lucky swing."

"Not for Tufty Alan it wasn't," he said.

He turned on Anika and with a degree of roughness, wrenched the cheque from her hands. "This money will go to a good cause, but there will be no pictures."

Charlotte nodded meekly and left with Daffyd and Anika following.

"Did you get any useable pictures?" she asked in a small voice once they were out on the pavement.

"Oh, yes," said Daffyd cheerily. "It doesn't matter, we can get the elves in the photo room to doctor them if needed."

IT DIDN'T TAKE Gallagher long to realise that trying to wash reindeer poo was even more disgusting and fruitless than he had imagined it might be. He would have given up after a few minutes, if it wasn't for the fact that he found some small fibrous fragments that were possibly weed and which he thought *might* be useable. That small glimmer of hope made him press on.

He was working outside in the plant area with a bucket of water on his left and his box of shit on the right. He smushed each turd between his fingers and swirled it in the freezing water as he rubbed. He wore nitrile gloves so that he could feel for any promising textures. The fruits of his labours lay on the paving slabs at his feet. There was a very small crop of what might possibly pass as weed, lying soggily in its own puddle. He needed a better way to dry it, so he stood up and fetched a handful of sphagnum moss from the little hut where they made up the hanging baskets in the spring. He laid out his tiny fibrous prizes on a bed of moss so they could dry.

He looked at the moss, with its stringy mottled greeny brown colour. He wondered if it might pass for cannabis in a pinch. He knew the truth, of course. It definitely wouldn't. What he really needed was something to pad out the tiny fragments he'd been able to recover. He wandered over to the compost heaps. He pulled back the covering and plunged his hand into the rich dark material. If he plucked some of the bits from round the edges, they had the right sort of colour and texture. Still not right of course, but maybe...

54

ANIKA

Anika had been so stunned by the episode in the church that she didn't speak again until she was back in Daffyd's car. "Is Charlotte insane?" she said eventually.

"Define insane," said Daffyd.

"Brutally bludgeoning a pigeon to death with a candlestick because the kids' choir wasn't good enough."

"A rather narrow definition."

"I mean ... are we safe around her?"

"She's not killed anyone," he said and started the car. "Yet," he added.

They were halfway to Bloomers before she felt the enormity of the task ahead of them truly sink in. "Okay. What's the plan?" she said.

"Plan?"

"Our, um, honey trap. The reason I'm wearing this ridiculous outfit."

"I'm going to cause a distraction, get all the kids out of the grotto. You're going to go in, make a beeline for Nathan, and – pow!"

She nodded slowly. "Okay. Let's unpackage that, er, 'pow' there. What am I actually doing?"

"You're seducing him," said Daffyd as though it was obvious.

"I mean, I'm obviously not going to do anything with him. This is my body. I'm not a sex worker. Not that I don't have respect for sex workers."

"You're not a sex worker," said Daffyd. "You don't need to actually do anything with him. The images are important. You find him, seduce him with sexy wiles, and get a selfie or two."

"Right. And you'll blur my face out."

"Yep, just like Google Street View, but hopefully a bit more raunchy."

"So..." Anika could feel her fingers tingling with nervous energy. "When you say 'seduce'."

"Hell's bells, Anika! Do I need to explain everything? Do you not know how to do sexy? You're not a ... you're not inexperienced?"

"Okay. You're being awfully calm about this operation when it's my body on the line. I should demand extra money for this."

"There's the sticker and the certificate,"

"And a letter of commendation from Mr Clasp."

"Okay. I think I can swing that..."

"Which obviously commends me in a general sense for my workplace skills without actually mentioning me seducing an enemy elf."

"Of course."

"For your information, I'm not inexperienced. I happen to enjoy a full range of... It's none of your business how much sex I've had. But I've never had to seduce anyone before."

"Oh, they just come flocking to you, huh?"

"I'm a uni student. I basically just drink three vodka and cokes, tell a bloke yes, I would like to shag him, and that's it. That's how it works. Nineteen year old lads do not need a complicated seduction routine."

Daffyd made a thoughtful noise and sniffed, momentarily lost in personal reverie. There was no further useful advice en route to Bloomers. He pulled into the car park of the rival garden centre. "You go in, do your alluring thing," he said. "It will all be fine. I will create a distraction to ensure you get some alone time in there."

She looked down at her lap and the tops of her candy cane suspenders. "Fuck me," she whispered.

"Whatever you do for the cause will be appreciated at the highest level," said Daffyd. "It's a noble sacrifice."

She had a ticket to the grotto, so getting in should be easy enough. She walked through the entrance and past the displays of baubles, tree trimmings and decorations. It really didn't look all that different to Hedgelord, if she squinted her eyes and ignored the signs carrying Bloomers's branding.

She was conscious that eyes were on her. What did she expect when she was walking around in an outfit that probably belonged in a nightclub? The customers in Bloomers were mostly pensioners, but that didn't mean they weren't capable of looking at her in a way which made her feel a little exposed. She decided the only way to deal with it was to hold her head high and stride through as if she ruled the place.

She presented her ticket at the grotto. To her disappointment, Nathan wasn't on check in. What if she'd come on his day off? She was now locked into the grotto experience anyway.

"Is it just you?" asked the elf on check in.

"Yes." Anika looked straight at him.

"Right. Good. In you go."

Anika entered with a large group who seemed to all be related somehow. They chattered amongst themselves, so she was able to concentrate on what she was doing. Until Daffyd provided the promised distraction, all she could do was enjoy the grotto. She appraised the quality of the elves and decided they weren't bad. She gave them a sound thrashing in a snowball fight, which felt good.

Bloomers didn't have a train ride like Hedgelord. Instead, there was an airport terminal where elves wearing little Santa Airline hats checked them onto their flight to the North Pole, and guests sat in seats where they could watch an aerial view of their own town as they flew over it, with reindeer dashing across the horizon. It was pretty slick.

"Ladies and gentlemen, boys and girls, you have now arrived at the North Pole!" said an elf. "Your captain would like to say a few words before you leave the aircraft."

There was a video showing Santa at the controls of a plane. He described the rest of the grotto and told them where they were allowed to take photographs.

"Cute!" said Anika, in spite of herself. She quite liked the uniform the airline elves wore.

Next stop was the Bloomers equivalent of Mrs Claus's kitchen. It was styled like a German Market, and Mrs Claus seemed more like a motherly innkeeper. The interior was decorated with shop frontages, with Christmas characters peeking out of the windows, and reindeer wandering through the gaps. Each table was like a stall, with an elf dishing out ingredients on request. Anika thought it was probably a lot tidier, although maybe she preferred the boisterous free for all of Hedgelord's offering.

She dutifully made some reindeer food, which was packaged in a green, white and red stripy cardboard packet, all the while wondering when Daffyd was going to create the distraction. More importantly: where was Nathan Carson?

Both of those concerns were swept away when the room started to sing *Rudolph the Red-Nosed Reindeer*. Now all that Anika cared about was whether they would sing 'reindeers'. She needed to know if this grotto was prepared to deal with the menace. She joined in, determined to at least set a good example. When it reached the part she'd been waiting for, she gave it everything she had to emphasise 'all of the other reindeer', but still she caught the sound of the extra 's' hissing around the room. She rolled her eyes and wondered if this was her opportunity to say something. She wasn't an employee here, so she wasn't answerable for her conduct.

As the song finished, she cleared her throat for the important announcement she was about to make – when the fire alarm went off.

"About time, Daffyd." Anika was confident in assuming

this was the fake distraction she'd been waiting for, so she ignored the staff who were asking everyone to please leave the way they'd come in.

She plunged through the next door into Santa's room. "Bingo!"

Nathan Carson was in there with Santa. There were no customers, which was good.

"Hello there!" said Anika. She smiled at Nathan.

"Hello miss. We are evacuating the grotto, so please make your way to the exit and my colleagues who will direct you from there."

She moved forward. "I have it on good authority that this is just a drill. It means we can have the place to ourselves for a while. I think you deserve a breather, don't you?" Anika tried to make her voice husky, but it just made her cough.

"Are you all right?" asked Nathan.

"Yes, yes," she said, dialling the husky voice back a bit. "You've been working so hard. Come with me and relax for a moment!" She pressed a hand to Nathan's chest and worked it in little circles.

"Sorry, do you work here?" asked Nathan, confused. "Your uniform is unusual."

"She's one of them strippergrams!" said Santa. "Let her do her thing, son! Make sure I can see."

Anika had been so focused on Nathan she had forgotten Santa. "I am not a stripper, and I am not here for you, Santa." She pointed at Nathan. "I've come for him."

"Did I reach a hidden tier in the rewards programme?" asked Nathan.

"Yes. Yes you did," murmured Anika, nuzzling close to his face. "Hey Santa, why not take a picture of the two of us?"

Santa looked confused. "But the camera only points at my throne."

"Well budge up then and let us sit down," said Anika. She nuzzled Nathan's face some more and steered him towards the throne.

Santa heaved himself out of his seat and wandered over to the camera. He seemed horribly up for what was about to occur. "Come on then, face the camera. Bit more thigh, young lady. That's it!"

She held back a disgusted comment. She had no more thigh left to show, it was only hip and waist from hereon up.

Anika thrust Nathan into the seat and sat on his lap.

"Er, I'm really confused as to what this is."

She pulled his head towards her chest. Anika rarely wished she had bigger boobs, but she did feel that alluringly thrusting a man's face into her tits would be more effective if she had more acreage for his face to thrust into.

While Nathan wasn't completely unwilling, this seemed to be out of sheer confusion. She needed to make him look more interested for the camera. This was meant to be a honeypot trap – not a recording of her sexually harassing an unwilling victim. She pulled out a candy cane and sucked on it while she stared deep into his eyes. He made a small sound. Anika couldn't decide whether it was a cry of encouragement or for help.

"Work it, baby!" cried Santa. The dirty old man clearly came from a time before human dignity had been invented. "Go deeper! Tip your head back."

Awkwardly, Anika did as Santa suggested.

"Are you alright?" said Nathan.

She looked at him. "What do you mean?"

He blinked at her. "I mean, you seem like a nice person."

"I am."

"Do you enjoy doing this?"

She paused. This wasn't how it was supposed to go. She was the all-powerful sex goddess and he was supposed to be in thrall to him. Now he looked at her with concern.

"What?"

His liquid brown eyes and soft smile showed nothing but kindness. "Do you enjoy this?" he said. "We can stop if you want."

Anika faltered. Whatever sexy confidence she'd managed to muster had been dispelled. "I ... I'm sorry," she said. "I didn't mean to embarrass you."

"Nothing to be embarrassed about," he said. He offered a hand to help her off his lap.

She slid off, meek and diminished. "I'm sorry."

"I can get you a drink at the café and find you someone to talk to, if you need it."

Oh, hell, she thought. He thought she was going through a mental health crisis or something. She'd gone at him with maximum sluttiness and he'd just assumed it was cry for help from a damaged woman. Maybe he wasn't far wrong.

"I'm so sorry. You are such a good elf," she said and literally ran off, stumbling in her heels as she fled.

Outside the grotto, she found Daffyd at the photo booth, scrolling through the pictures with the help of an elf.

"Ooh yes. One of those please! And that one. Digital copies, yes."

Anika approached him. "Are we sure this is what we want? Look at him."

Daffyd and Anika both gazed at the images on the screen. Anika looked every inch the naughty, alluring elf. She gave herself a mental pat on the back for that, it was a job well done.

Nathan though? What did his face say?

"Goddamnit! He looks like a saintly elf who feels sorry for you!" said Daffyd. "How the hell does he even do that?"

"I don't know. It's a shame we weren't targeting Santa. He was hot to trot," said Anika, but then she heard a terrible sound. It couldn't be...

"Well maybe you could—" started Daffyd.

"Shh! I need to hide!" hissed Anika. "I can hear my mother's voice!"

"Oh? Interesting." Daffyd craned his neck, curious.

She popped her head up by the crates of decorative stones, to check on where her mother was. What she saw made her blood run cold. Her parents stood near the open exit door to the grotto, pointing inside.

"Is that Anika?" she heard her mother say.

The pictures of Anika and Nathan Carson were still up on the screen.

55

CHARLOTTE

Orchestrating the delivery of a winter wonderland to the front garden of Nick Bellingham, while dealing with unreasonable vicars and the general demands of her job, was no mean feat, but Charlotte had achieved it.

Admittedly, she realised, she'd not sought planning permission from the council for a full scale Christmassy attraction which ran the length of his street, but that couldn't detract from the majesty of it all. The Sun had only just started to set. It wasn't even fully dark yet.

She stood and admired the scaffold tunnel that was to be switched on in a few minutes. It looked incredible! People would be able to walk through it, experiencing the wonderful lights and be gently showered with snow from the machine positioned overhead.

She put through a call to the contact who'd supplied it. "Hey, Thierry. I wanted to say thanks. This set up is perfect!"

"No worries. My team is red hot. They think on their feet, you know?"

"Great, great. A good team. They did well," said Charlotte. She could see Nick emerging from his house for the switch on.

"Yeah," continued Thierry. *"They had to find another snow machine at short notice, but it's a doozy. You'll love it. It's from a Canadian ski resort. You'll get loads of snow."*

"I can't wait to see it working," said Charlotte. "I need to go now. Many thanks."

Nick held out his hands in appreciation as he drew near. "I have to hand it to you, Charlotte. This looks amazing."

"Thank you." She beamed at the thought of her finally getting Hedgelord the upper hand in this rivalry. She glanced around, a part of her wishing Jack Hartigan could be here to see her moment of glory. And there he was! She smiled at him and gave a little wave, a tiny one, like Queen Camilla might offer from a passing carriage.

He seemed to take that as encouragement to come over, so the smile dropped from her face.

"Charlotte! Nick! What a superb display this is going to be. It feels so good for us all to be collaborating like this, don't you think?" Jack Hartigan grinned at them both.

Charlotte wanted to blast him into orbit with the venomous replies which rushed to her mind, but she didn't need to do that. The simple fact was that Hedgelord had banners in the right places, and Bloomers didn't. She'd won, and there was nothing he could do about it.

Her foot kicked something on the ground. She picked it up, not wanting Nick's wheelchair to become snagged on it.

"Wonder what this is?" It looked like flat sieve, but it was big, like a dustbin lid.

Jack Hartigan pointed at the branding. "*Snow Torrent.* They do industrial snow machines."

Charlotte looked at the scaffolding tunnel and shrugged. "Some sort of cover."

Nick Bellingham had a tablet on his lap. "So when I press this to begin the sequence, the LumaGrid controller will turn on all of the lighting displays, including the Hedgelord Winter Wonderland."

"Yes," said Charlotte, guessing he was right. "All this Christmassy magic at your fingertips."

"And it will also launch the drone display—"

Provided by Bloomers," put in Jack.

"And then the fireworks—"

"Provided by Hedgelord," said Charlotte.

"Yes, yes. You have total control."

She nodded. Jack could keep trying to insinuate that Bloomers was somehow equally involved, but as long as she made sure that Nick Bellingham was in the correct position when the TV people interviewed him, that was all that mattered.

In fact, they were here already: a van had pulled up across the road. She could see the newsreader who did the evening segment: former Cambridge United striker and sports commentator, Willy Sandford.

The news team came over. Willy Sandford was wrapped up in his trademark camel coat. The young woman on camera duties look thoroughly bored to be here. They pushed through the growing crowd of local residents.

"There he is!" said Willy, grinning, looking from Jack to Charlotte to Nick in his search for the man he needed. "Nick Bellingham! Willy Sandford. BBC News. This looks spectacular."

"Thank you."

"Now, we can go live at five, but we'd like to get some pre-recorded footage of the switch on. Now, the best place to interview you—" He cast about.

"It's here," said Charlotte firmly, pointing just off from where they stood, by the exit of the winter wonderland tunnel and beneath the snow machine. "You've got the snow, the lights, the beautiful animatronic bear..." And the Hedgelord signage, she added mentally.

Willy Sandford looked about. "Okay. Nikki. Let's set up here."

Charlotte saw a couple of familiar faces from the local newspapers across the road. She needed to make sure they got all the right pictures for their on-line and paper versions of the news. She wanted everyone in the town to know who was responsible for this sumptuous Christmas spectacular.

"Break a leg, Nick," said Charlotte before heading over to talk to the journos. No sooner had the words left her mouth, she feared it had been a tasteless and appalling thing to say to a man in a wheelchair. "Sorry," she said. "In a metaphorical theatre-referencing sense I mean."

Nick gave her a weird look. "What other meaning might I have taken?"

"Sorry. I mean, I just shouldn't have said it at all."

"Because...?"

Seeing this conversation could go nowhere good, she

simply gave him a thumbs up and went over to the reporters from the *Heart of England Sentinel* and the *Three Counties Echo*.

"Kitty. Joe. How's it going?"

Kitty lowered her camera. "This is all very nice. A step up from last year."

Joe gestured with the pen in his hand. "Who's paying for all this? You or Jack from Bloomers. Don't tell me you've collaborated."

Charlotte laughed. "Can you imagine someone like Jack Hartigan working with us? No. This is very much a Hedgelord production. Make sure you mention that. Our commitment to the community at this special time of year is unparalleled. You can quote me on that."

"You want me to put a word like unparalleled in the *Sentinel*?" laughed Joe. "Small words, Charlotte. Small words."

"Oh," she said, "and you'll want to know about Hedgelord's contributions to local charities – as picked by Nick Bellingham there. I've got some lovely photos of us presenting a cheque to Reverend Robertson at St Stephen's, who do such sterling work with the less fortunate."

"Yeah, send it over," said Kitty.

"Right away."

She woke her phone and sent Daffyd a message, asking for the photos from earlier to be sent over. She watched the TV crew interviewing Nick while she waited for a reply. An e-mail came through from Daffyd with a dozen links to photos embedded in it. She forwarded it onto Joe and Kitty.

"Lovely pictures, I think you'll find," she said.

The reporters nodded absently.

"If they're any good, we'll have them on the web version by the morning," said Joe.

Nick and Willy Sandford were wrapping up their on-screen banter. Jack Hartigan sidled up to Charlotte.

"You're really enjoying this, aren't you?" he said.

She gave him a superior look. "Bringing light and joy to this town at a religiously significant time of the year? Yes, Jack."

"I meant, trying to get one over on me," he said. "I'm sure we used to be friends, once upon a time."

"I'm friends with everyone, Jack. Even you."

Nick was waving his hands to get attention. "Right, everybody! I'm about to hit the button for the official launch of this year's festivities," he shouted. "Let's give a countdown! Ten! Nine!"

"He's really enjoying it too," Charlotte pointed out. Jack tilted his head, barely conceding the point.

When the crowd shouted zero, Nick stabbed at his computer tablet with a flourish.

Lights came on everywhere. It was unearthly to go from no lights to all of them. Charlotte felt as if she was immersed in light. She looked up at the Hedgelord tunnel and it was every bit as magnificent as she had imagined, although the banners along the sides were slightly overshadowed by the illuminations. Snow started to pour enthusiastically from the snow machine up there. Nick was right beneath it in the snowflake zone and seemed to be loving it. In truth, Charlotte noticed, the snow came out so thickly that she wondered what would happen if it was on for a few hours. It might cause a bit of a drift to form.

Nick brushed snow off his tablet.

"Oh look!" shouted someone.

There were gasps from the crowd as a slew of drones lifted up from the darkness of Nick's garden. Their own lights winked into life. The co-ordinated drone display lit up the sky. How many drones were there? It looked like a lot. They flew in formation, like a jet display team.

"Get a load of that!" Jack said to the reporters. "Drone display from Bloomers!"

There was a distressed honking sound from above. Charlotte searched the skies, but couldn't see where it was coming from.

"Geese?" said Kitty the reporter.

Nick had mentioned something about the geese flying over every night, from somewhere to somewhere. She'd not really been paying attention. A tiny gleeful part of her wanted Jack Hartigan's flashy drones to cause a minor drama, so she got ready to make a lot of fuss about harassing wildlife.

Suddenly visible in the light of the illuminations, the scattered flight of geese swooped into view. Some swerved high; some banked left and right.

One dropped at speed, attempting to fly low under the twinkling festive drone.

There was a horrific grinding noise from above the wonderland tunnel. The snow stopped falling for a moment, something grated horribly, mechanically, then the snow was spewing out in clumps: pink and red.

"Fuck," said Charlotte. She could not distinguish between the buzzing of her curse-counting smart watch and the fizzing terror coursing through her whole body.

Nick looked up in surprise. Splats of goosey red snow spattered on his face.

"Your drones," Charlotte heard herself say as the first child started crying. "They did it."

"Your snow machine should have had a guard, or a..." He looked at the circular sieve thing in her hands.

Charlotte instantly realised that Jack Hartigan was right. When she'd picked it up, the thing had reminded her of the cover that went over a room fan, but this was much, much bigger. Goose-mashing bigger.

"No, no, no," Nick began repeating over and over.

Charlotte yelped and skimmed the offensive guard piece away into the bushes. The crowd were shouting. Parents were hiding their children's faces. The TV camerawoman had suddenly come to life and was filming everything.

Nick was blinking bird blood out of his eyes. It pooled in his lap and on the tablet screen. He shook his head and swept the foul snow away.

Above the sound of the rattling and damaged snow machine, there was a tinny fanfare. On the scaffolding rig above the wonderland tunnel, Roman candle fireworks sparked into life. Despite the horror before them, at least one person in the crowd went "Oooh!" because some people just can't help themselves.

Nick must have set off the fireworks. He must have set everything off. The animatronic Bruin the bear was jigging in the garden and beginning his own rendition of *Have Yourself a Merry Little Christmas* in a Mickey Bubbles style.

The first of the fireworks rockets shot into the air. Which would have been fine enough if it hadn't struck one of the hovering drones. The rocket ricocheted, bounced off Nick's roof and then exploded far too low. The drone, fatally struck, wobbled and spun into the crowd. It was not the last rocket and it was not the last to strike a drone. Drones and rockets exploded on contact. At least one drone followed the poor dead goose into the snow machine's intake. Flames rained down on the wonderland canopy and the fire did not go out.

"Fire," said Jack, growing alarm in his voice. "There's fire."

There was a groaning, creaking sound. It was the sound of something broken, damaged, and possibly working itself loose.

Charlotte took one step forward. As struck drones spun in all directions, the giant snow machine pitched off its mountings and fell from the burning wonderland roof. Nick Bellingham, parked directly underneath, probably didn't know what hit him, or at least didn't get a chance to reflect on the situation, before he was clonked on the head and dashed from his wheelchair.

"Oh, fuck," Charlotte said.

Her watch buzzed.

56

GALLAGHER

"This is shit," said Luka.

"I know it's shit," said Gallagher. "Composed of one hundred percent pure reindeer shit."

Luka regarded Gallagher's bale of 'weed'. "No. I mean it is really shit," he said. "It's no good."

"It's a bale, innit?"

Gallagher was going to call it a bale of cannabis, whatever it truly was. He'd poured his heart and hours of effort into this creation and he was going to stand behind it, however crap it was. Reconstructing consumer quality cannabis from reindeer droppings hadn't been easy, and it was a terrible bale that nobody was going to accept, but he had one. He was, by now, so sleep-deprived that he took some semblance of pride in his bale. Where there had been nothing, there was now something. True, it was partly composed of fibres which had been through the digestive system of a reindeer, partly of sphagnum moss, and partly of stuff he'd pulled out of the compost heap. Instead of the mild, pleasant smell of cut grass he associated with cannabis, this smelled like shit and compost.

Luka sat with it on his lap on the drive over to the village of Clopton Howes. It might be a nowhere village, of zero consequence in a dull as ditchwater corner of England, but Gallagher felt like he was driving to a terrible and inescapable destiny. He also felt he was at a point beyond caring. Even though he could be driving into the jaws of hell itself, Gallagher was at peace with the idea of Sonia's people killing him. It would be nice to have a rest. He was physically and mentally so exhausted that a nice quick execution sounded pretty refreshing.

"This turning," said Luka in the voice of a man who truly wished this was not the turning; who wished they could take any other turning.

Gallagher steered his crappy car through the gateway. The building he drove up to was different to the desolate farm buildings from where they'd originally fetched the bale. This was some sort of swanky barn conversion, with a gravel-covered central courtyard and old farm equipment displayed as curios between doorways that were all painted in the same shade of green, like a postcard. He could imagine this place being used for weddings or fancy workshops in the summer.

Sonia's pet neanderthal, Vincent, emerged from one of the doorways. He walked over to Gallagher's car. He beckoned the car towards his position by a wall where a range of ancient farming implements were leaned artfully against the brickwork, as though their medieval owners had just left them there at the end of a long day.

Gallagher kept the motor running as he wound down the window. "Evening, Vincent," he said.

"Show me." Vincent wasn't the chit-chat type.

Gallagher reached over to take the reconstructed parcel from Luka.

"Get out and show me," said Vincent.

Reluctantly, Gallagher got out.

"I have to keep the engine running otherwise it won't start again," he began.

Vincent reached past him, through the open door, and turned the ignition off.

"Might take an hour or two to rest now," said Gallagher.

He reached into the car and Luka passed him the package. A powerful waft of that terrible smell emerged, but Gallagher pretended not to notice.

Vincent did not take it from him.

"What is this shit?" he asked.

"Your gear," said Gallagher.

"It's the best shit," said Luka.

Vincent thumbed his phone and spoke a few brief words.

"No. No. Not at all," he said and raised his eyes to Gallagher as he ended the call.

"Look, I appreciate it might have gone off a bit," said Gallagher. "The storage hasn't been ideal—"

He doubled over as Vincent brought a swinging fist round into his stomach. His hand was yanked up and Vincent pushed him against the wall and suddenly the sharp points of an ancient pitchfork were pressed against his throat.

"Hey, easy man," said Luka, getting out. "Let's not—"

Vincent's arm swung round so the pitchfork was pointing straight at Luka across the bonnet of the car.

"Now," said Vincent, "we're taking a walk round the back of this barn. All of us. Walk nice and calm and I won't have to stab you with a rusty trident."

"Pitchfork," said Luka.

"What?" Vincent growled.

"It's a pitchfork, not a trident."

Vincent slammed Gallagher back against the wall so his head knocked against the brickwork. "Same difference," said Vincent.

"Trident means three," said Luka. "Pitchfork has two."

Vincent pulled Gallagher forward and slammed him again.

"Ow! Luka! Will you stop educating him!" Clutching his head, Gallagher walked as directed in Vincent's clutches, Luka following close at hand. What else could he do? This was no place to be on the receiving end of cruel violence. It was a cutesy country home. Probably cost more money than Gallagher would earn in a lifetime. The whole place had a wholesome, rural look about it. Like a heavily manicured version of a farm.

At the rear of the barn was a flower bed with an even bigger piece of agricultural history as its centrepiece. It was a huge low barrel, wider than any beer barrel, with a plunger on a vice-like screw handle on its top.

"What the fuck is that?" said Gallagher.

"Cider press," said Luka.

"It's a cider press," said Vincent. "Apples go in, cider comes out. On your knees!"

"What, on the ground?"

"On the ground. Both of you."

"Kneeling here will damage soil structure," said Luka.

"Got to respect soil structure," said Gallagher.

Vincent jabbed Gallagher in the shoulder with the tip of his pitchfork, not quite enough to pierce the skin but enough to bloody hurt.

"Yes. Fucking now, on the ground, both of you."

Gallagher knelt down in front of the cider press. Reluctantly, Luka knelt beside him.

Gallagher couldn't help but look at the press mechanism more closely, hoping that it was really old, rotten and defunct, but it looked surprisingly sound. He saw there was plastic sheeting on the inner portion of the barrel. He wondered why that was there, afraid he already knew.

Vincent was at his side, hand pointing to the press. "See this gap here? That's where your head's going, so that you pay attention."

"Pay attention? I'm a captive audience. I'll do what you say."

"No need for heads to go in press."

"Oh, your heads are going in the press."

There was a crunch of gravel. Gallagher looked up to see Sonia Patterson approaching, wrapped up against the night in a warm cardigan. The movement was rewarded with a slap from Vincent.

"Heads in."

Gallagher reluctantly did as he was told, placing his head on the flat inner portion of the barrel. Vincent physically pushed Luka's head in next to him. Nothing good ever came from putting your head inside something that was designed to crush things, but it wasn't as if they had a choice.

"I'll take over from here, Vincent," said Sonia, approaching slowly. Gallagher saw she had a half-drunk glass of white wine in her hand. This was all just a small interlude in her evening.

"Now, gentlemen," she said. "Vincent tells me that you brought us some revolting crap instead of my weed."

"It got a bit messed up," said Gallagher.

Sonia walked forward and spun the big handle on top of the press. The huge slab of hard wood above Gallagher's head lowered so that it kissed his skull.

"Please do not do this," said Luka.

"Please," Gallagher echoed.

For all of the misery that his life entailed, this was fucking horrible. He tried hard not to imagine what it would be like to have his skull crushed like a watermelon, but the image was hard to dispel.

"Oh, this is fucking happening," she said. "How many turns of the handle before your skull gives way? Have you ever heard a skull pop before?"

"Course I fucking haven't," said Gallagher. He tried to pull out but the vice of the cider press had him now.

"We'll hear it go, Vincent and me. I suppose one of you will hear the other's head pop. Hmmm, better to be the first or the last?"

"Best if you don't have your head in a cider press, boss," said Vincent.

Sonia give the handle a quarter turn. The lip of the barrel

bit painfully into Gallagher's temple. Luka was hissing with pain.

"And what will it sound like?" she said, quite merrily. "Will it sound like a glass breaking, or a flowerpot?"

"Fucking flowerpot," said Vincent. "Look at him."

"Please! We can get you the money!" Gallagher yelled. "I promise you there'll be no more mistakes."

"I have never met a man who doesn't promise me the earth when he's in there," said Sonia. "Never."

"We can get it!" said Luka. "God's truth – ah! – we can!"

Sonia stepped back so that she was in Gallagher's eyeline.

"Christ, look at you. Your face is red and squished. You look like... What do they look like, Vincent."

"Like a cranberry," said Vincent. "Ready to pop."

"Pop!" said Sonia and giggled. She turned the handle again.

There was a colossal pain in Gallagher's head, but he was afraid to cry out, because any movement at all felt as if it could cause complete collapse. He was afraid to move his jaw or even breathe in case it was the final trigger for his skull to crack like an egg.

Sonia bent down close to his face and, randomly, licked his cheek. "I know you can't move or speak, so don't bother trying. You'll stay there for a few minutes, so you get a good clear picture of why you need to make this work. I've got accounts to look at, but Vincent will let you out if you haven't burst a blood vessel by then. You have twenty four hours to find my money."

"Twenty four hours," Luka gurgled, clearly in as much pain as Gallagher. "We can do that."

Gallagher could do literally nothing but watch as Sonia walked away back to the house. "They do it or they don't," she said to Vincent as she walked. "The Snowman's coming the week after next. I need my house in order."

"Yes, boss," said Vincent.

"Could have gone worse," Luka struggled to say.

"Worse how?" Gallagher grunted with painful effort.

"We still got all our fingers, haven't we, eh?"

57

ANIKA

Anika had not really slept that night.

She had fled home with only the thought of getting there before her parents, then hid herself away in her room, under the quilt of her single bed, headphones on, Nothing But Thieves turned up to maximum volume. If she could not hear or see the outside world then the outside world could not touch her. Not for now.

It was a short term solution, she knew, but she didn't have any others. Her parents – her parents! – had seen the pictures of her in that T-shirt-sized slutty elf dress. They'd seen her. They'd surely recognised her.

What the hell were they doing in Bloomers anyway? They weren't gardening types, and they sure weren't there for the Christmas decorations. Only a cruel and vengeful universe would have placed them there at that moment. Was this some holy sign that she must return to university? Screw that!

She burrowed down and buried herself in a miserable funk of duvet and music. In the middle of the night, she got up, stripped off the horrid, horrid elf outfit and screwed it up in a ball in the bottommost drawer of her bedside cabinet.

She must have fallen asleep at some point in the night. Her alarm for work went off, waking her. Feeling rotten and hungover, even though she'd had nothing to drink the night before, she got up and dressed. Her normal elf costume was at work. That was good. She just slipped into ordinary, anonymous top and trousers and made her way downstairs quietly, with every intention of popping on her trainers and going straight out the house.

Her mum and dad were sitting in the living room. Her mum was dressed. Her dad was in his dressing gown. Both had cups of tea with saucers in front of them like civilised people.

"Here she is," said her dad, as though such a thing needed saying.

Her mum sat stiffly on the edge of the sofa and looked at Anika. "So, I think we are owed an explanation," she said.

She was doing that restrained "I'm holding back the tears" voice she did when she tried to sound disappointed. Anika got enough guilt vibes from her mum without the need for that voice. It was a bad act anyway; her mum never cried in genuine sadness, only in outrage.

"Explanation," said Anika. She didn't make it a question. She didn't want to prolong the conversation.

"You've said you've been studying with Asha."

"I have," said Anika but lost confidence in the lie even before it was out of her mouth.

"You have university studies."

"We pay for those," said her father.

Anika almost blurted out, "I didn't ask for that!", but it would just sound petulant, like a teenager cliché.

"You need to tell us what you've been up to."

Fine, she thought. She'd tell them. She'd tell them a version of the truth. A true version of the truth, even if parts were omitted.

"I've got a job," she said, trying to inject some pride into the statement. "I have got a job with a local business doing customer-facing work. And I'm good at it."

"Is that so?"

"Yes. I deal with members of the public and sometimes handle money and I help organise the work of my colleagues."

Her mum was shaking her head. "We've seen the pictures."

Something snapped inside Anika. "What were you even doing at Bloomers anyway?" she demanded. "You never go there!"

Her dad pointed to the tree in the corner. Anika hadn't noticed it until that moment.

"Real Christmas tree," he said. "The kind that don't drop needles."

"Jesus," Anika hissed miserably.

"We don't understand what was going on in those photos," said her mum and there was perhaps genuine hurt in her voice now. "They looked a little … risqué. But at least the neighbours won't see that one."

Anika opened her mouth to speak, then her brain caught up with what she'd just heard. "What do you mean? 'That one'?"

Her mother reached for a folded newspaper. It was the morning copy of the *Three Counties Echo*. She held it up. "You're on page three!"

Anika was about to protest, but she couldn't, because her mum was quite correct.

She looked at the headline. She looked at the picture. It was her all right.

58

GALLAGHER

Gallagher sat on the steps of one of the display sheds, hands on his knees, and looked across the frosty plant area. Morning mist still clung to the gravel pathways. His temple hurt and there was a ringing in his ears which had not faded all night.

"When I was a kid I had this picture book," he said.

Luka took a final drag on his morning joint, stubbed out the end and put it in his overalls pocket. There were red bruises along both his temples from Sonia Patterson's cider press.

"You had a picture book?"

Gallagher nodded. Nodding made his head hurt. "It was about a man who couldn't sleep at night because of the wind outside, so the doctor told him to put a cow in his bedroom. Or a horse. Or a sheep. Maybe it was all of them. I don't remember. And the animals were noisy all night and the man couldn't understand the purpose of it all. But when he took them away and all he could hear was the wind at the window, he realised it wasn't so bad. The animals gave him perspective."

Luka nodded.

"That's me, that is," said Gallagher.

"You have a cow in your bedroom?"

Gallagher gave him a look. "I thought my life was shit. I'm up to my fucking eyeballs in debt. The black mould fills so much of my bedroom that I might as well be married to it. And I'm staring down the barrel of forty years of age with absolutely sod all to show for it. I was ready to kill myself."

"I remember," said Luka.

"But now – oh, now! – I have to find forty grand in cash for psycho drug dealer Sonia Patterson or else Vincent will be hosing my remains off that cider press."

Luka nodded with deep philosophical understanding. "It has given you deeper perspective about your own life. Things are not so bad."

"You kidding? You actually kidding me?" Gallagher felt a wild and giddy euphoria rush through him, except it wasn't euphoria. It was the same degree of energy, but it was all completely negative energy. Some sort of shitphoria. "No. Now, I've got a home I hate in a nowhere town, a car that's falling apart, no money, no life and some psycho drug dealer who wants to use my innards as Christmas decorations!"

"It's not so bad."

"Not so bad? Do you happen to have forty thousand pounds lying about, Luka? Cos I don't."

"No, I do not have this money. You could sell your car?"

"It's held together with duct tape. It's not worth five hundred, let alone forty thousand. We should sell your car."

"My car?"

"Your Mark Two Ford Capri—"

"Mark Three Ford Capri. You are joking surely."

"It's a return visit to the cider press we're talking about!"

Luka sighed. "No, it would need specialist buyer. And it has so many parts missing. It is a shell."

"Shit. You could get a loan? A credit card?"

"I have no credit rating. The banks would lend me nothing."

"Something else then. Something less official."

"A loan shark?"

"Do you know any?"

"And end up in a worse situation?"

"Fuck." Gallagher had started to load saplings into a trolley, but he whacked the top one down in a rage, and kept on whacking while it splintered in his hand.

Luka sniffed and looked through the wire fence leading to the car park. "Someone is angry."

Gallagher looked. Young Anika, not dressed in her elf gear today, was storming across the car park, her face a mask of outrage, a rolled up newspaper clenched in her fist.

"See, you do not have monopoly on bad times," said Luka. "Now, let us discuss getting our hands on forty k, eh?"

59

CHARLOTTE

Charlotte was not having a good a morning and suspected it could only get worse. There were already online versions of the *Echo* and *Sentinel* stories about Nick Bellingham's accident on her phone. The *Echo* had gone with Fireworks and drone display cause goose explosion horror. The *Sentinel* had chosen Garden Centres' Christmas decorations injure local man and start fire. Charlotte felt some small gratitude for the placement of that apostrophe, but it was negligible consolation in the face of the complete clusterfuck that had unfolded last night. She swiped them away, not up to reading whatever they'd written

She had been summoned into Cameron Clasp's office the moment she arrived.

Cameron stood in the centre of his office, angrily practising his golf swing with the club he kept by his desk. "What on earth went on with Nick Bellingham, Charlotte?" he said.

"There was an unfortunate accident."

"You blew up a goose!"

"Shredded it, Cameron. A very unfortunate sequence of events."

"Bellingham's not dead though, is he? Tell me we didn't kill our most treasured customer."

"He's in hospital."

"Good."

"I've arranged for flowers to be sent," said Charlotte.

"Surely you could take them yourself? The personal feminine touch might work there. You get a picture of you mopping his brow or whatever, no?"

Charlotte ignored the casual sexism. "No, it's possible he might not want to see people who were there at the scene of the accident." Charlotte forced herself to meet his gaze. "We were a contributing factor in what happened to him. So were Bloomers. We installed the snow machine that fell on him, but it was Bloomers's drones that sent the birds into its fan."

"Fucking Bloomers! Well, what else? Give me the details."

She nodded grimly. "The paramedics came. Nick was alive but they didn't say how badly injured. Our winter wonderland tunnel burned itself out, but it was ruined. Obviously, at the time, I was worried for Nick, but both Hedgelord and Bloomers were somewhat implicated in what happened. Jack Hartigan was keen to distance himself from the whole thing." She felt a twinge of guilt. "So was I. I tried to take down the Hedgelord banner on the scaffolding."

"Quick thinking."

"Those scissor lifts aren't as easy to control as you'd think, but yeah. It's a mess."

"You've screwed the pooch here, Charlotte. Whatever your job is, you're clearly doing the opposite."

"I'm currently working hard now, trying to remove our name from any mention of it in the press and commenting on all social media mentions. There are a lot."

"Make it so Bloomers get the blame, Charlotte. Make it so it looks like it's them and not us. Can you do that?"

Charlotte grimaced. "Quite honestly, at this point in time, we should be more focused on damage limitation. If we can get out of this without negative publicity that's probably the best result we can hope for."

"What? Really? I was hoping for more than that. Daffyd was telling me he has some compromising pictures from their grotto. The sort of thing that could bring them down. Can we use them at all?"

Charlotte sighed. "I'm not sure they're what we need right now. I think we just need to calm things down a bit."

Cameron blew out his lips scornfully. "Well, as long as nothing else terrible happens."

The door to Cameron's office banged open and elf-hire Anika stomped in. "What the hell is this?" she demanded shrilly.

"Who the hell is this?" said Cameron.

"Anika, you do not come barging into Mr Clasp's office," said Charlotte.

"I'm in the newspaper!" said Anika, waving a rolled up copy around savagely.

"Oh, the photographs," said Charlotte, wondering why Anika could be so angry at being pictured handing a cheque to Reverend Robertson.

"Did you actually look at them before you sent them to the paper? It looks like I'm wearing nothing while some bloke is ogling my tits!"

Charlotte frowned. No – that wasn't what she recalled. She'd spoken to Kitty and Joe from the papers, and Daffyd had sent her a bunch of photos, including the ones from the big cheque handover—

"No..." She hadn't? Had she forwarded Daffyd's weird sexy honey trap photos by accident? "Oh, please, no."

With vicious movements, Anika unrolled the paper and thrust it out for both of them to see.

It wasn't the grotto photos...

It was somehow worse...

It was on page three. Of course it was. The headline read HEDGELORD ELF GIVES LOCAL VICAR BIG SURPRISE.

The picture taken by Daffyd and chosen by the paper was ostensibly of a smiling Anika presenting a large novelty cheque for a large sum of money to Ralph Robertson. Except – and it was a big except – the light shining off the cheque almost obliterated all of the writing. And the large board came above the low top of Anika's slutty elf costume and below the bottom of her short, short skirt. So what the picture really showed was a young woman with apparently no clothes on, grinning – salaciously leering one might possibly say – at a vicar. And Ralph Roberston had been photographed, perhaps furiously saying something to Charlotte, while glancing in disgust at Anika, so he was caught with his mouth open and eyes bulging. Looking for all the world like he'd been accosted by this naked cheque-carrying youth.

Cameron tried to speak. "I... Do you..." He spluttered. "What ... what is going on here?"

"I'm the laughing stock of the town!" Anika yelled. "My parents are too embarrassed to even leave the house!"

"It's a feel-good story if people actually read the article," Charlotte tried to suggest.

"Who is going to read the article?" shouted Anika. "It's all there in the picture. Slutty whore, Anika Chowdhry, flashes her boobs at vicars! What more do people need?"

"It's certainly an arresting image," said Cameron, who couldn't take his eyes off it.

Anika made an incoherent noise of rage, threw the paper at Charlotte, and stormed out with as much stomping and door slamming force as when she'd entered.

Cameron and Charlotte stared at the door in silence.

"You don't get tarts and vicars parties anymore, do you?" said Cameron in a quiet, absent-minded voice. "Why is that?" He shook himself from his reverie and fixed Charlotte with a look. "Charlotte, I would have to say this situation has got worse. I'm almost impressed."

Charlotte swallowed the bitter spit in her mouth and nodded. She had no words. In her head there was only a high-pitched whine and acid flowing through her veins. She half-suspected she was going to have a heart attack. The sheer utter unfairness of everything that had happened to her was bubbling through her and threatening to explode.

She realised she needed to release it and fast. Otherwise, she would either kill someone or simply die. She snatched the golf club from Cameron's hand and marched out of the room.

"Hey, I need that," he said. "Got tee-off with Patty Fufu at quarter to three."

60

GALLAGHER

"We must steal the money," Luka said to Gallagher as they continued loading saplings into a trolley.

"What?" said Gallagher.

"We do not have the money. We need the money. No one will give us the money. We must steal the money."

Gallagher shook his head. "It's another cow in my bedroom, man."

Luka frowned. "You *do* have cows in your bedroom?"

"It's an allusion. Fuck, this is making the situation worse, not better. I'm not knocking off post offices or anything. I don't own a shotgun. Do you own a shotgun?" The expression on Luka's face made Gallagher do a double take. "Y-you do? You actually own a—" he made a pump action shotgun mime "—*chu-chunk*?"

"We do not need shotguns," said Luka. He turned

Gallagher bodily towards the main Hedgelord shop. "Items of high value. Low security."

"We're going to rob our own place of work? We gonna shit where we eat?"

"Says the man with cows in his bedroom."

"Who's robbing what?" said Anika, suddenly behind them.

Gallagher whirled. "Jesus! Always sneaking up on us. I'm going to put bells on you!"

He stopped. He could see there was something wrong with her face. Gallagher knew he was often wrapped up in his own problems, but he was still a human being and did not have a heart of stone. This was the face of a very unhappy young woman.

"What's going on?"

She shook her head viciously. She didn't want to talk about it. "You guys going to rob Hedgelord?"

"Um, no," said Luka.

"Why?" she said.

Gallagher had intended to deny it or offer some lame-ass excuse, but tiredness and depression made telling the truth easier. "We owe forty grand to a psychotic drug dealer. We need it today."

"Did he do that to your faces?" she said, pointing.

"She," said Luka. "And yes. She put our heads in a cider press."

"I thought she just chopped off fingers, but I was wrong," said Gallagher.

"I'm in," said Anika.

"What?"

"If you're robbing this fucking madhouse then I'm in."

Gallagher frowned, pulling back. "Why?"

"Does a girl need reasons?"

"Usually, yes."

"Well, I'm fucking furious right now. Fucking furious with the dickheads in charge." She pointed up to the roof of the shop and in the general direction of Cameron's rooftop panoramic office. "And, yeah, doing this place over will help reset my inner karma a bit."

Luka shrugged. This was good enough for him.

"Also," she said, seeming to calm a little, "you two are – and it shocks me to say this – contenders for the nicest people I've met while I've worked here."

"We do try," said Luka.

From across the outdoor section, there came a great incoherent scream of rage and, to Gallagher's ears, what sounded like a yell of "Shitting donkey mother-fucking cock wankers!"

"What the hell...?"

"I might not be the only one angry at the moment," said Anika.

61

CHARLOTTE

"Twatting bastard fucking shit-weasels!" screamed Charlotte as she whacked Cameron's golf club into a piece of discarded MDF leaned up against one of the skips in the waste area. The club head went through the weak damp board. She wrenched it free. "Shit arse pissing fuckballs!" she yelled.

As the boiling and limitless rage coursed through her, so did image after image of all the unfairness and indignity she'd suffered these past few days.

Cameron's attempts to re-steer her Christmas store design with his idiotic winter princess coach and horses.

"Dried up cock-infested pussy fuckers!" she yelled as she struck again.

Tom Eccles's over-concern for his mundane stock and his bloody farmhouse jams.

"Cunting bell-end tits and snatch!"

Nick bloody Bellingham (may he get better soon she

added in a quiet and easily dismissed afterthought) and his bloody affrontery in trying to defect to Bloomers.

She whacked hard. "Fucking fuck-fuckers!"

Jack 'the bastard' Hartigan then digging his claws into Nick Bellingham and doing all he could to humiliate her further and rubbish the name of Hedgelord.

"Saggy ball bum-fuckery!"

And the utter and galling unfairness of a series of events, totally out of her control, that led to diced goose, sweary bears, naked elf photos, wonderland fires, and a smorgasbord of bad press.

"Eye-fucking knob cheeses!"

And she'd bad-mouthed God. Her God. She'd compared him to the worst team in the football league. She'd spat in the face of the one constant, the one true rock in her life.

She froze, bent club raised high, panting for breath. Her watch was still buzzing, trying to keep up with her profanity.

She'd rejected God.

"Oh, fuck."

She let the club drop and, eyes closed, expelled all the energy from her lungs as she did so.

"Oh, God. I mean ... God, I'm sorry. You're not the worst football team. I don't even follow football. I'm the worst. It's me, isn't it?"

She took a deep breath. If she thought deep breathing was going to fix her mood and fucked up karma, then she knew she was well wrong, but there was nothing to be done other than get herself back up and put her feet on the right path in life.

She picked up the club again, pulled back her shoulders, and made her way back to the shop.

"Excuse me, dear," said an elderly customer as she neared the doors. "Can you tell me where you keep your bags of gravel."

"Wide is the gate and broad is the path that leads to destruction," she quoted at him. "But small is the gate and narrow is the road that leads to life."

"Right," nodded the customer. "So ... this way?"

"In the corner," she said, much more helpfully. "Past the large plastic pots, but if you get to the water features you've gone too far."

He smiled and moved on.

She went back inside to return the golf club to Cameron and to set herself on the narrow path to a restored Hedgelord.

62

GALLAGHER

Gallagher, Luka and Anika explored the outside area of the garden centre in search of anything that could be easily stolen and converted into the cash needed to pay off Sonia Patterson. The enraged screaming of Charlotte Mitchell seemed to have tailed off, although Anika's miserable mood did not seem to have improved.

"The garden office retails for fifteen thousand," Gallagher pointed out.

Luka sneered. "Loses half its value the moment you drive it out of showroom. Also, you have seen how big it is unconstructed. How will we get it out? And who will buy a used garden office? Too, er, too *niche*. We must pick something more generic."

Gallagher gestured to a stack of bags of compost. "Compost. Expensive stuff."

"Twelve pounds a bag. We'd need to steal hundreds of bags."

"More than three thousand," said Anika.

Gallagher looked at her. "We need to go smaller, right."

Luka spread his hands as though framing an ideal item to steal. "We need something that is of the highest value to weight. Highest dollar to kilo ratio."

"Light but expensive."

"But also something that we can sell."

"Unless Sonia wants paying in stolen goods."

"Let us not give her further reasons to kill us, Gallagher."

They walked inside. Gallagher assumed there would be many options here. Hedgelord, like so many garden centres, seemed to specialise in over-priced luxury items.

"Scented candles," said Gallagher, pointing.

Luka picked up two jar candles. They were Christmas scents. "Sparkling Cinnamon, I get. But what does Christmas Eve smell of?"

"Anticipation and sherry?" said Gallagher.

"Twenty pounds each. How many?" Luka asked Anika.

"Two thousand," said Anika promptly.

Gallagher tilted his head. "Maybe doable."

They walked on. Gallagher slapped Luka's arm with the back of his hand and pointed at the aquarium section of the pet shop area.

"Fish?" said Luka.

"Tropical fish. They've got to be worth a quid or two. Our best bet, if you ask me."

"Ask me," said Anika. There was still a hard, angry edge

to her voice, even when she was being pleasantly conversational.

Gallagher and Luka both turned to her.

"Ask you what?" said Luka.

"Ask me what my best bet is. Ask me where I would get that kind of money from."

Gallagher narrowed his eyes. "What do you know?"

Anika raised her eyebrows. "Maybe I know where there's at least forty grand in cash."

Luka ushered the two of them outside. "Some conversations should not take place inside" he muttered. "A lot of nosy bastards in this place."

Once they were safely behind the closed door of Luka and Gallagher's teamaking shed, Luka gestured to Anika. "Continue."

"I am a moral and ethical person," she said.

"Says the woman who said we should rob the shop," said Gallagher.

Luka nodded. "Please fast forward to the part where you say 'but'."

"You know Cameron Clasp's office?" said Anika.

"We do," said Luka.

"Well there's a safe in there."

"There is not forty grand in it."

"No, there's more than forty," she said.

"Impossible."

"The other day, when your reindeer friends went on a rampage, the tills went down and everything switched to cash for the afternoon."

Luka and Gallagher stared at each other.

"Fuck," said Gallagher quietly.

"It is still there?" asked Luka.

Anika nodded.

Gallagher laughed. "Imagine if we could actually pull it off and not die."

63

CHARLOTTE

Charlotte presented the golf club to Cameron in the manner of a Japanese soldier surrendering his sword. "I'm sorry, Cameron. I may have taken out my frustrations on your club."

Cameron considered it with a surprisingly philosophical air. "I always give Patty a thrashing on the back nine. This should even the odds a little." He put the club aside. "Has some aggression therapy given you any insights into how to fix our little shambles?"

"I'm going to focus on the social media, then do what I can to get Nick Bellingham back on side."

Cameron gave her a sceptical look. "Sending flowers to his bedside are not going to cut it, are they?"

She shook her head. "We've pretty much ruined his Christmas."

"And that man really likes Christmas! We have to restore his faith."

She eyed him critically. "You're not expecting us to engineer three ghosts to visit him in the night and reinvigorate his festive joy?"

"We need to pump him full of Christmas joy. *More* lights! *More* twinkle!"

"More lights might give him PTSD," she said.

"Well, what else does Nick Bellingham really, really love, eh?"

"Everything about Christmas. The food. The hideous jumpers. Mickey Bubbles. He loves Mickey Bubbles."

Cameron pulled a face. "Really? The singer? He's a pervert isn't he?"

"Alleged. Those rumours about his collection of Christmas porn are entirely unproven."

"Christmas porn?" said Cameron. "I heard he whips himself into a sexual frenzy with holly branches."

"Really? That just sounds unlikely. Point is, Nick Bellingham is a big fan. Do you want me to go hire Mickey Bubbles to serenade him?" she joked.

Cameron scoffed. "I heard he doesn't get out of bed for less than a hundred thousand. If hiring Mickey Bubbles is the platinum solution to us getting him back, you just have to work out what bronze or silver looks like."

"Right." She held a hand down low. "Flowers." She raised it above her head. "Hiring international singing sensation Mickey Bubbles." She placed her hand somewhere in the middle. "This. This is where we need to be."

Cameron picked up a pen and wrote on his whiteboard. *Buy Nick flowers. Hire Mickey Bubbles.* He put a question mark between them. "Exactly. Always happy to coach one of my team. Glad I can inspire."

Inspire us to go for the second-best option, Charlotte thought. That was the Cameron method.

She was more preoccupied with the realisation he'd written it with a permanent Sharpie pen rather than a dry-wipe marker, so it would stay up there until someone found whatever powerful chemicals were needed to remove it. She made a note to get a new whiteboard installed, as it would definitely be quicker.

With these thoughts in mind and no clear plan, Charlotte retreated to her office and set about doing what she could. She would start by trying to put a positive spin on the social media comments that both the Nick Bellingham accident and cheque-presenting incident had birthed. That alone would take her hours.

GALLAGHER, Luka and Anika sat in the tea shed and discussed the stealing of forty thousand pounds.

"Middle of night is the time for safe cracking," said Luka. "Everyone knows this."

Anika shook her head. "No, because then you have umpteen layers of security you need to overcome. Just getting into the building is quite tricky. Given that Cameron's the only person who uses his office, you just need *him* not to be there. He's going to play golf at two thirty."

"How do you know?" asked Gallagher.

"It's written on the whiteboard in his office. If that

whiteboard is his personal planner then his golfing schedule is his only fixture."

Gallagher dared to imagine the heist plan working. "What do we know about getting into the safe? Safecracking isn't a skill that I have." He turned to Luka with a raised eyebrow.

"What? You think just because I have this accent I should know all detail of criminal underworld? Is fucking presumptuous!"

Gallagher could see that he had a point, and was about to apologise, when Luka made a small noise.

"Depending on manufacturer, is possible I might have some resources," Luka said with a tiny shrug of dismissal.

"All I know is that there's a key that opens it and it's in the top drawer of Cameron's desk," said Anika.

Gallagher thought she was enjoying living up to her elf name, Smartypants.

Luka rolled his eyes. "Fuck. I think we can manage that."

Anika nodded. "So, I can't be directly involved in this—"

"Says the woman who's pretty much planned it all," said Gallagher.

"—but I think I've given you the bones of a plan, and I can be lookout for you, if that helps."

"It would help a lot," said Gallagher. "So we're on for two thirty today?"

They all nodded.

64

CHARLOTTE

Charlotte wore headphones while she sat at her office desk to work. She was listening to a playlist of Christmas holiday tunes. Wizzard's *I Wish It Could Be Christmas Every Day*, Shakin' Stevens' *Merry Christmas Everyone*, Mickey Bubbles' *The Very Heart of Christmas*, Kelly Clarkson's *Underneath the Tree*.

The actual tunes didn't matter. The headphones were primarily a signal to her colleagues that she didn't want to be disturbed, but they didn't always work. Tom Eccles would be hyper alert to her wishes and creep around in a way that was much more distracting than his usual pottering. He would make a massive pantomime around how he put his mug down on his own desk, softening any noise it might make by taking several seconds to ease it onto his coaster. Charlotte couldn't help watching because it was so absurd.

Once he was seated it became less troubling because the clicking of his mouse was the only sound she could hear.

The business of continuing to sort out the social media fallout from the Nick Bellingham incident (plus the elf/cheque debacle) was like fighting a multi-headed monster: an on-line hydra which seemed to sprout a new offensive head each time she successfully dealt with one.

A lot of her efforts were focused on the comments sections of the newspaper websites. Comments sections for any new article were usually filled with vitriol of the badly spelled and incoherent sort. Weak, shouty arguments were easily dealt with. Many of them sprawled off into tangents where they effectively killed themselves. For some keyboard warriors (she imagined many were angry and impotent men of a certain age) it was a short hop, skip and a jump from Christmas accidents to how everything was less good these days, to generalised complaints about the weak namby-pamby attitudes of young people today, then off into wild crazy person talk.

Trickier to deal with were those social media accounts where the stories were shared alongside damning comments about Hedgelord's actions. Were the fireworks fitted by a registered pyrotechnics specialist? Where had the plastic wonderland tunnel been sourced from? Did it pass legal safety standards? Hadn't several people heard the animatronic polar bear in the garden swearing during its musical routine?

A large number of comments targeted Hedgelord's contributions to the accident. The imbalance seemed unfair, especially since it was Bloomers's drones which had spooked the geese and sparked the accident itself. This unfairness needed redressing.

She swiftly cooked up a number of fake accounts on Twitter, Facebook and Instagram, and began flinging pertinent questions in the direction of Bloomers. Was it safe or even legal to fly that many drones in a residential area? How would the LumaGrid lights, across so many houses, affect nocturnal wildlife? Since Hedgelord had run safe light displays on Nick Bellingham's house for many years, was it a coincidence that Bloomers's involvement had come at the same time as this terrible accident?

The on-line trolls seemed to step up into high gear the more she deflected the blame.

HazyJane135, with a profile picture of a patterned carpet, started shouting the odds about exploiting a young Asian woman in a sleazy church publicity stunt.

WingManXXX, with a profile of a shiny horse brass, responded to the cheque story with some casually worded hearsay about the Hedgelord manager being kicked out of more than one local church for her anti-social behaviour.

SaltJuteSession41, with a profile image of an empty beer glass, posted a photo of Charlotte, on top of a scissor lift, frantically trying to cut down the Hedgelord banner with a knife too blunt for the job.

"Hang on," she muttered, taking off her headphones and turning to Tom. "What's the name of the pub on the A31, the one with all the horse brasses on the beams by the bar."

"The Colchester Arms," said Tom without hesitation. "They have that *Hazy Jane IPA* on draft."

"Little fuckers," said Charlotte and got up.

"Everything okay?" said Tom.

She grabbed her coat. "Everything is fine."

She was going to drive out to the Colchester Arms and, if she was right, she would find the source of several social media trolls there.

65

ANIKA

Anika watched Cameron leave the building and climb into his Jaguar at two thirty on the dot. She signalled to Luka and Gallagher that they had the green light, and followed them up the stairs into Cameron's office.

She tried to assure herself there were a dozen legitimate reasons why she might be there if she was challenged, but none occurred to her. She felt a tingle of fear in her stomach. She was creeping around where she didn't belong and, on top of that, she was helping two men steal a large quantity of cash. That was a major crime.

The buzz of doing something rebellious in retaliation for the embarrassment Hedgelord had inflicted upon her was fading. She was starting to realise that doing this stuff could not only get her fired, but also get her into real trouble. Law court style trouble.

"The safe is there," she said, needlessly pointing to the waist high safe under the window.

"Where is key?" said Luka.

"Top drawer."

Gallagher went to the desk and tried the drawer. "It's locked."

Luka stroked his bearded chin thoughtfully. "I could pick it or just break it open."

"Whatever," Anika said. "Just do it."

On the whiteboard by Cameron's desk, someone had scrawled *Buy Nick flowers. Hire Mickey Bubbles* and put a big question mark next to it. More stupid plans to 'win' Christmas, she thought.

"Look, I'm going to go downstairs and be the lookout," she said. "Do not hang about up here."

Luka rattled the desk drawer just in case Gallagher was somehow unable to operate drawers correctly. "Yes, yes. You have been very helpful," he said.

Anika went downstairs and positioned herself by the door. She'd need to have a convincing reason why she was loitering there, not even in her elf gear for the day's work. She didn't even have a moment to think about what that convincing reason might be when she saw Charlotte approaching.

"I'm just—" Anika began, with no idea where that sentence might be heading.

"I'm sorry, we'll have to talk later," said Charlotte and swept past in her coat, on the way to the door.

"Oh, okay," said Anika and watched her go.

This lookout business might be easier than she expected.

CHARLOTTE RECOGNISED she was driving a little too fast as she careered around the winding lanes, but she was in a dangerous mood. She had half-formed thoughts of scaring this annoying on-line troll a little so that they would back off, but mainly it felt good to be doing something rather than just looking at a screen.

It was a ten minute drive cross country to the section of the A31 that headed south. The Colchester Arms was a traditional country pub: a big, boxy building with white-washed walls and a steeply sloping tiled roof. Globes of mistletoe hung on brackets outside the pub door.

She walked into the bar and ordered a glass of wine. Dutch courage never hurt when it came to confrontation, and she wouldn't be over the limit with just one. Besides, she'd had a shitty twenty-four hours and a single drink in a pub with roaring open fires was a small piece of therapy that she deserved.

She took her drink and wandered through to the lounge area, wondering how she might spot the evil little troll who was making fun from Hedgelord's misery.

"Fuck."

Jack Hartigan sat at the table nearest the fire hearth.

She walked over and sat down on the other side of his table. "You are a twat," she said simply.

He held up his own glass of wine. "Charlotte! Gosh it's been a tough day, hasn't it?"

She shook her head. She should have known he was behind the onslaught of annoying and goading comments.

He frowned and pointed at her drink. "Tell me you're not ordering the wine by the glass?"

She glanced down and frowned. "What? Why?"

"Ah. You did. They have some terrible cheap stuff on tap. I bought a bottle – it's the only way to get hold of the good stuff here. Take a sip of yours and then compare and contrast with mine." He held out his glass.

Charlotte wanted to spit in it or throw it over his stupid smiling face, but she was also curious. She took a sip from his glass and then a sip from her own and pulled a face. "Fuck."

He grinned. "Hold on one second while I get a clean glass and I will pour you some. We deserve to kick back a little after the day we've both had, don't you think?"

"Wait, I've got things to say to you," she said, but he held up a finger to quieten her as he went to the bar. All she could do was wait until he returned with a fresh glass for her.

"Nick Bellingham is being discharged later on today," he said as he sat, "so I'm hoping the whole thing will just calm down a bit."

This was not how things were supposed to go! Charlotte had not entered the pub to drink socially with the person who had caused the frown lines she'd started to notice on her forehead.

He poured her a glass, pushing it across the table.

She sighed and pushed aside her drink. If she replaced her original glass with a better one then it was still only one glass. She took a sip and let it ride over her tongue because it was smooth and delicious.

"Fucking hell, that does taste better than the other stuff."

"Told you," he said.

"This does not mean I owe you anything though."

He raised his glass to her. "Absolutely not. Cheers."

"So are you Hazy Jane one-three-five?" she asked. Hazy Jane had been a thorn in her side all day long on social media.

"I am," he said, with more pride than Charlotte thought was appropriate. "I assume, while we're doing this, that you are DebsMumofTwins?"

She nodded.

"And if I had to guess, because it speaks of the same peculiar naming convention, Ron TopPlumber?"

"Well at least my names are less dull," she said, wishing she didn't sound so defensive.

"Hey, at least there's this." He held a finger in the air. "While we are sitting together here, sharing a decent bottle of wine, we can rest assured that no new social media trolling needs our attention. It's nice to take a break, isn't it?"

He had a point. Charlotte found it mildly depressing to think the bulk of her job wouldn't exist if she could incapacitate Jack Hartigan. She turned that thought over in her mind, enjoying the mental image of him in a full body cast, unable to operate his phone.

"Yes. Why not," she said cautiously. "A quiet drink can do no harm."

66

ANIKA

Anika had been on lookout duty for less than ten minutes when she saw Cameron Clasp approaching from the shop entrance. This was not right. He should be golfing right now.

"Hello Mr Clasp!" said Anika, as loudly as she could. She had no idea if Luka and Gallagher would hear her, but this was bad. This was really bad.

"Hello there, um—"

She could see him reaching for her name and failing to find it. "Anika," she prompted.

"Anika. Yes." He made to move past her.

She had to find a way to stop him going up to his office. "Can I ask you a question?"

"Is it about your rather explosive appearance in my office this morning? I think it's probably something we should all put behind us. Least said, soonest mended, what."

"Er, yes!" she said. "It was about that. I'm still very angry."

"About your picture in the newspaper? No, I understand. It must be surprising – although time was when a young woman would be very pleased to have a picture of herself, caught in the bloom of youth as it were, in the newspaper."

"Really?"

"I mean, page three, you know."

"Well," she said, striving to find some real anger in the face of her current anxiety over the burglary going on upstairs. "I don't expect to be used in this way."

"No, no," he agreed, chastised. "We do want to use our employees appropriately. And nurture them. You have such wonderful assets..." His mouth flapped shut and he swallowed hard. "I mean – you are a wonderful asset to the Hedgelord family."

"Well, maybe we should talk about that now. Perhaps over a coffee in the Pagoda Café. I'm sure you can spare ten minutes."

"I wish I did, Anita, but I'm already late for, er, an important business appointment. I just came back to grab a pair of gloves – business gloves – that I left up in my office." He moved towards the door that led upstairs.

"Let me fetch them for you!" shrilled Anika, inserting herself in front of him. "I have young legs. I can just whizz up there and back again, and maybe you can tell me about how you nurture employees as assets. I can still hear if you speak loudly."

Cameron shrugged. "Go on then! Gloves should be on my desk."

Anika trotted upstairs. "Keep going, I'm listening!" she called.

"Well, we like to think of employees as family..." he began.

As Cameron's voice resonated up the stairs, Anika sprinted into his office and made urgent hand signals to Luka and Gallagher. She pointed down the stairs and made throat-cutting gestures to indicate that the operation was compromised.

They both stared at her in confusion. She realised they probably should have ironed out these communication details in advance. Agreed a code or something.

"Cameron is here!" she hissed.

"Oh fuck!" said Gallagher.

Luka just grunted. He had his head in the safe, focused on the task in hand.

Anika felt as if time slowed down. Cameron entered the office. She could see the tableau presented to him. She was gesturing wildly, Gallagher near the safe, looking horrified, and Luka delving deep into the safe, unmistakeably retrieving bundles of cash wrapped with elastic bands.

Anika dashed to the desk and picked up Cameron's gloves, handing them to him. She wasn't sure why she felt it might help.

"What in the blue blazes is going on in here?" Cameron blustered.

Luka retreated out of the safe and looked up. He gave a rueful nod.

Anika channelled the energy of her elf performance in the grotto. Confident, loud, and a hefty dose of pantomime swagger. "Oh I think I understand!"

All faces turned to stare at her.

"You do?" Gallagher asked.

"Really?" Cameron said, eyebrows high.

Her eyes skated over the scribbles on the whiteboard. "You're getting the money for Mickey Bubbles!" Anika nearly slapped her thigh and chuckled, but decided that might be too much.

"Mickey Bubbles. Singer guy," said Luka.

"Christmas porn pervert," said Gallagher.

"So has Charlotte booked him?" said Cameron.

"Yes!" said Anika, throwing herself whole-heartedly into the lie.

"I know Nick Bellingham is a big fan, but Mickey doesn't get out of bed for less than a hundred grand, and we don't have that kind of money."

"Ah—" said Anika, hoping there were some other words to back up that exclamation "—she's got him for a knock down price."

"Really?"

Luka contemplated the cash in his hand. "Forty-two thousand pounds," he said. "Cash payment."

"Avoids tax bills," said Gallagher.

"Well I never!" said Cameron. "Well, that Charlotte's a bold one, I'll give her that."

Anika nodded. "Yep."

"Yes. Forty two thousand for Mickey Bubbles," said Luka. "Big hurry. Going to serenade Christmas hits to him tonight."

Cameron blew out his cheeks. "Well, that's a big chunk of cash. I guess she decided the bronze and silver just weren't going to cut it. Well, if Charlotte believes in this as an idea, I know she'll have worked out the sums."

"I bet she has," said Anika.

"Let's make sure you've got what you need there, then," said Cameron. He strode forward and squatted beside Luka, helping him sort bundles of cash.

Gallagher looked at Anika and pulled a face. She gave him a serene smile.

After a few minutes, Cameron straightened and slapped Luka on the back. "Good man. Make sure that gets where it needs to go. I'm off to my golfing – my business golfing meeting now, but I'm looking forward to seeing Mickey Bubbles perform. Make sure I get the details, won't you?"

They all nodded and trailed out of the office.

"Did we just walk out of there with forty grand?" whispered Gallagher. "Forty fucking grand?"

Luka nodded. "I believe we did. Forty-two in fact. Was an impressive performance you gave in there." He gave a small bow of acknowledgement to Anika. "Just one problem."

"What?" said Anika.

"Do we now have to make a Mickey Bubbles concert at this Bellingham guy's house?"

Anika could feel her heart pounding in her chest. "One thing at a time, please. I'm sure we'll figure it out. I think I need a cup of tea."

67

CHARLOTTE

Somehow – and truly Charlotte couldn't recall how – there was a second bottle of wine on the table because the first was empty. And somehow Charlotte thought she might also have accidentally drunk the first glass that she'd set aside as being undrinkable.

"The thing is," she said, "the only reason I hate you is because you're such an unconscionable bastard."

"A what?" he said.

"Unconscionabubble bastard."

"Ha!" he spat back. "The only reason I hate you is that you, Charlotte Mitchell, are such an – what was that word—?"

"Unconscionabubble."

"—unconscionable bitch."

She gasped theatrically and put a hand on her chest. "Me? I'm lovely."

"Are you sure?"

She thought, and thinking was hard. "Yes! I think I'm lovely."

"You might need to get a second opinion."

"You wouldn't know lovely if came right up to you and stared you in the eye!" she said.

She leaned over towards him and put her face right up against his, trying to give him an evil glare. Their eyes were less than a hand's breadth apart.

"I do know loveliness when I see it," he said softly.

"Do you?"

He took in a slow breath. "My girlfriend, Kathryn, is lovely."

Charlotte grunted and slumped back in her chair.

"She has the most adorable face," he said drunkenly. "This way of looking at you. An' she's smart. So smart! I'm a very lucky man. Did I tell you I'm taking her away to Paris later in the month?"

"You might have mentioned something," she pouted.

"A Christmas trip to the most romantic city in the world just before the Xmas Expo in Hull."

"It's all dogshit and graffiti."

"Christmas?"

"Paris." Charlotte sighed and topped up her glass. It was entirely possible that if she drank much more she'd be vomiting before nightfall. She looked out the window. The afternoon sky was already getting dark. "It's all dogshit anyway," she said.

"Paris, yeah. I get it."

"And Christmas," she said. "My Christmas at least."

"Is it really that bad?"

"Isn't it really that bad for you?" she threw back at him. "Our literal job is to make our respective garden centres the most successful and most loved Christmas venues in the area."

"And we did a shit job of it," he agreed.

"We *did* do a shit job if it," she said emphatically. "And we're going to get fired for it."

"Maybe," he said. "Maybe I'm just in denial right now. Maybe I'm giddy with dread and will have a big, long cry about it later." He took a breath. "You know what the stupidest thing about this is?"

"What?" she said. "There's a big, long list of stupid fucking things about this. Is it the slutty elf? It's the slutty elf, isn't it?"

He shook his head and waved his glass about, losing quite a bit of wine in the process. "The stupidest thing is that you and I have made this worse by competing with each other an' doing each other down. Publicly!"

"Yeah, well, you're a tit," she said.

"And you're a potty-mouthed Scrooge who generally gives Christians a bad name. Stupid thing is, we used to be friends."

She looked at him. "No, we didn't."

"We at least used to be nice to each other."

Her frowned deepened. "No, we weren't."

"Yeah, we were. Xmas Expo – what six, seven years ago? – we met properly for the first time. Went round the exhibition stands together. We could actually have been friends."

She drank deeply. "You remember it differently to me."

"I was certainly prepared to be your friend. Maybe you never considered me friend material."

"Don't think I did," she said. "Enemies to the bitter end. Maybe we'll both get fired on the same day and that will be the end of it."

"Nah, we can fix this."

"How?" she said. "Just how?"

"Dunno. We wait until Nick comes home later today and both give grovelling apologies."

"Apologies. No. Ain't gonna work."

"We give him the most Christmassy apology gift ever."

"Nope. Nothing left to give. We can't even—" She stopped, wondered if she might throw up, then remembered something. "You know a funny thing that we came up with in the office today?"

"What?"

"Mickey Bubbles!" She dissolved into giggles.

"What? What about Mickey Bubbles?" he said, not understanding.

"We thought about hiring Mickey Bubbles to do a little impromptu concert for Nick as an apology."

"Wait," said Jack. "Why is that funny? Mickey Bubbles is a legend! Apart from his holly fetish, anyway."

"It's funny because, A: Mickey Bubbles is a massive star. B: he doesn't get out of bed for less than a hundred grand and — Wait, what holly fetish?"

"His well-known sexual fetish for holly."

"No, no, no. Surely you're getting mixed up with his Christmas erot—" She paused, waiting for her mouth to catch up with her brain, or maybe it was the other way round. Either way she found it hard to form the words. "Chrishmash 'rotica. Fuck's sake, you know what I mean."

"Nah. 'S a holly fetish, everyone knows that," he said. "Whole room of it where he rolls round, stark bollock naked."

"Who's the fucking potty mouth now?" crowed Charlotte. She sighed, satisfied that she'd dragged him down to her level. "He is a legend though, Mickey Bubbles."

"He is."

"And Nick loves him."

"Really loves him."

They looked at each other.

"We should go and get him," said Jack.

"Yeah? Just pop round his house and ask nicely?"

"I know where he lives," said Jack.

"The fuck you do."

"I do. Least, Kathryn pointed out a house to me once and said, 'That's Mickey Bubbles' house'. It's in Denton-on-the-Marsh."

"You literally know where he lives?"

"I just said."

She gave him a long stare. "We *could* do that."

"We could."

"We have absolutely nothing left to lose, do we?"

"Good cop bad cop?" Jack suggested. "You do your schoolmistress thing and I'll turn up the charm."

"My what? Schoolmishtresh?"

"I only say schoolmistress because you look so prim and proper. It's brilliant, because then you pepper the conversation with profanities and catch people on the hop. That thing."

"I don't do that," she said, but that wasn't the point. "We should do it."

"We are drunk though," he said.

"Best way to do it."

Jack nodded. "We can get a cab."

Charlotte grabbed her bag. "Come on then. Let's go and get Mickey Bubbles."

68
GALLAGHER

The three thieves sat in Luka and Gallagher's tea shed and stared at the pile of cash on the table.

"I've never seen that much money in one big ... lump," said Gallagher.

Anika touched the pile of cash, not for the first time. "I could pay off my entire student loan and tuition fees with that."

"Fuck that," said Gallagher. "I could fix the black mould in my flat— No – get a new flat that isn't above a takeaway, pay off all my credit cards and..." He glanced at Luka who was slurping his tea. "Come on, tell me you're not blown away by the sheer sodding amount of money we have here."

Luka shrugged. "I have seen bigger."

"The fuck you have."

He shrugged again. "Palace of the Parliament in Bucharest. Nineteen eighty-nine. Big piles. That was a crazy Christmas." He drained his cup. "Thing is, we have two things we must remember. One, we owe that money to Sonia Patterson—"

"Well, yeah…"

"—and, two, Cameron Clasp thinks we are spending this money on Mr Mickey Bubbles, world-famous singer and well-known sex-addict."

"That's true…"

"Mr Clasp will want to see evidence of this appearance by world-famous singer. Pictures in newspaper, that sort of thing."

"So, we need Mickey Bubbles," said Gallagher.

"But we also need all this cash for Sonia Patterson," said Luka.

"I have an idea," said Anika.

"It better be a good one," said Luka.

She vanished, returning less than five minutes later, propelling one of the grotto elves before her. The man was complaining that he still had half an hour of his shift to go.

"Everyone, this is Gillespie," she said as she pushed him inside.

Gallagher handed him a cup of tea.

"Oh wow, this place is cool," said Gillespie, looking round.

"Is by invitation only," said Luka, waving a trowel at him in a mildly threatening manner. "You only come in here when we say. No taking liberties."

Anika positioned Gillespie in the middle of the floor and then stepped back. "Ta dah!"

Luka was nodding, but Gallagher couldn't work out what he was supposed to be seeing.

"Young man is spitting image of Mickey Bubbles," said Luka.

"Is he?" said Gallagher. "Honestly, I'm struggling to see past the elf costume."

"We put him in tuxedo and even old Mrs Bubbles wouldn't know he's not her son."

"That's our plan," said Anika. "We need to put on a concert at a customer's house. It's an important event and Cameron Clasp is sponsoring it. Mickey Bubbles is expected, but that's never going to happen, so we're going to create a tribute act. Something that is almost indistinguishable from the real thing."

"Must be *totally* indistinguishable from the real thing," said Luka.

Gallagher grinned. "Yeah, that would be great!"

"Wait, wait," said Gillespie. "Is this what you want me for? Do I not get a say in this?"

"Absolutely not, young man," said Luka.

"But I can't sing."

"Shh, Gillespie. It will be fine," said Anika. "You don't need to sing."

Gillespie pointed to the big heap of cash on the table. "And why is there a ton of money here?"

"Ignore that," said Luka. "That's, er, donation to charity we're giving after end of concert."

69

CHARLOTTE

Denton-on-the-Marsh was one of the more picturesque villages in the area, which basically meant there wasn't a major A road going through the middle of it and all the big farm sheds were hidden from sight.

"Here," said Jack, pointing.

The taxi driver pulled up at the end of the drive to what Jack claimed was Mickey Bubble's house. Charlotte had to admit it certainly looked the part. It was an enormous property, set back from the road, with grand chimneys visible above the trees screening it from the road. The sun had now set, so all they could make out was a silhouette which hinted at its size.

"Now, do we need to practise not sounding drunk?" asked Charlotte, conscious that she was slurring most of her words.

"I think," declared Jack, in the manner of someone

voicing a thought before forming it, "I think adrenalin will kick in and make us function. It'll be fine."

They walked up the drive, which was bordered by tasteful uplights.

"We knock on the door?" Jack said.

"Nah, look over there. I think he must be in the garage," said Charlotte.

There was a large garage building further along the drive, and its doors were open. They walked over and peered inside.

"Nice cars," said Jack. "I don't know what they all are, but they look expensive."

The interior was well lit by fluorescent strips, and very clean. The floor was red painted concrete, and the walls were lined with cabinets that looked as if they contained tools and accessories. Charlotte recognised a Porsche and a Maserati. There was a newish Jaguar, which looked as if it was the everyday runabout.

"Christmas crooning really pays the bills, huh?" said Jack.

"Mr Bubbles!" shouted Charlotte. "Hello!"

There was no reply, so they walked further inside. There was door.

Charlotte had expected extra garage space, but it looked as if it might be part of the house. They were in a corridor with several doors.

"We're in Mickey Bubbles house!" she whispered.

"He has a giant picture of himself on the wall!" Jack whispered back.

A more than life-size portrait of the man walking down a snowy New York street stood at the far end of the corridor.

New York Mickey Bubbles had a red scarf knotted around his neck and a cheesy but handsome grin on his face.

"Mr Bubbles!" she called again, looking around. "We're sorry to bother you..."

"Maybe he's upstairs," said Jack.

"We're not going to just wander upstairs!"

"But we could just wander around down here a bit."

Charlotte pushed open a door to the left and stopped dead. "Oh. My. Fucking. Life."

Jack leaned round to see what she had spotted. "Ooh. I might have to stand corrected," he said. "This is definitely erotica. Very Christmassy erotica."

They both stepped into a room that in any normal mansion might have been a library or study, but which was a – Charlotte went with the word 'gallery' – a gallery of what could only be described as Christmas erotica. It was arrayed on shelves of varying heights about the room. There were four huge Christmas tree cutouts made from plywood displaying ornaments. One tree was themed around penis ornaments, and Charlotte was wowed by the variety of shapes and styles. Some were two dimensional, and others were more sculptural. All were definitely erect.

"You know, I thought I knew a thing or two about the market for Christmas ornaments," said Jack, staring at the next tree along. "I had no idea that boob decorations were so very popular." He plucked one between his fingers before letting it drop back into place.

Charlotte had been thinking the exact same thing about the penises.

Some tall shelving held larger ornaments. Resin elves

frolicked in a nude orgy. A sex doll with red painted lips bent over a floor-standing chimney. It was labelled *Santa, are you coming?* Plushie reindeer with cartoonish genitals were a genuinely disturbing sight. There was a shelf of books and DVDs.

Charlotte bent to see some titles. *"Horny Shepherds Tend to their Flock,"* she read. *"Rudolph the Red-Knobbed Reindeer. The Mince Pie that Fucked.* I mean – that doesn't even make sense."

"We should get out of here," muttered Jack.

Charlotte nodded. "We're invading a man's private space."

"Totally."

Neither of them moved. Then Charlotte took out her phone and took half a dozen photos, mostly at random, in an attempt to capture the wild improbability of it all. Jack had taken equally as many before they silently agreed they'd really had enough and should actually go.

They retreated into the corridor and pulled the door softly closed behind them.

"So," she said, eventually. "We found the pervy porn room. Now to move onto the serious business of finding Mickey Bubbles."

"Got it," said Jack. "Sensible and professional business heads on."

He opened the door across the corridor. They both stood staring for a good long moment.

"I knew it! It's the holly dungeon!" exclaimed Jack. "See?"

It was undeniably the case. They walked in and saw that the floor contained a shallow pit, like a paddling pool, but it was filled with branches of holly.

Charlotte walked forward and picked up a branch. "It's all quite green and fresh," she whispered.

"Doesn't mean it hasn't been used," said Jack with a meaningful shift of his eyebrows.

"Urgh!" She dropped it hastily and stepped back. After wiping her hand on her coat she pulled out her phone and took more pictures.

"What in God's name is going on here?" demanded a voice behind them.

They turned. A man in a cotton dressing gown and boxer shorts stood in the doorway. Charlotte's mouth gaped.

"Mr Bubbles!" said Jack, extending a hand. "Can I just say I'm a massive fan!"

70

ANIKA

Six o'clock in the evening. The garden centre was closed, but the plants area was a hive of activity. Anika had commandeered a larger shed as their rehearsal space. Gillespie, Luka and Gallagher shuffled in and she showed them all where to stand.

"Gillespie at the front," she said. "You're the face, remember? Luka, right behind him. Gallagher, your job is backing vocals and moral support."

Anika put a Bluetooth speaker on an upturned plant pot and played a backing track from an album called *Christmas for Crooners* using her phone. "Who knows this one?" she asked.

Everyone nodded to indicate they did.

"Right. Luka, I need your voice singing."

"Really?" said Luka.

"You have a lovely singing voice. Gillespie, you're miming into this microphone." She handed him his mic. The garden centre sold karaoke kits that were end-of-line remnants from some other outlet. "Take it away – one, two, three, four!"

The first time round was clunky. The second time, they were able to co-ordinate Luka's voice with Gillespie's miming, and the third time through they started to add some vocal swagger, with Gillespie's hips bopping in time with the music. Gallagher had another mic and added some backing vocals that were not terrible. The karaoke microphones and PA were pretty decent on reflection.

"Fuck, man, we're killing it!" said Gallagher when Anika turned off the backing track.

"We're not done yet," said Anika. "We need to perfect four or five of these songs as a minimum. Let's move on to the next one."

71

CHARLOTTE

Mickey Bubbles glanced at the hand held out in front of him and ignored it. "What the hell are you two doing in my house? You can't just break in."

"Fuck. We did break in here, didn't we?" Jack said.

"No, we didn't break anything," whispered Charlotte. "I don't think it's illegal if you just walk in. Is it?" Nit-picking about the law probably wasn't going to win the day. She cleared her throat. "Mickey. Mr Bubbles. This looks bad, I think we can all see that, but the reason we're here...? It's actually a funny story."

Mickey's famously clean-cut jawline twitched with tension as he stood waiting for the explanation. His blue eyes were cold, which was a shame because Charlotte was hoping to see them twinkle in real life.

Jack stared at her too, and she remembered she had

promised a funny story. "Oh. Right. Well, we were in the pub – by the way, this is Jack and I'm Charlotte—"

"You're telling him our names?" hissed Jack.

Charlotte ignored him. "—and we decided to come and see you."

Mickey looked at her and waited.

"And that's funny because we just did it. Like that." It didn't sound as funny as she remembered, now she was saying it out loud. "And we came because we want you to sing some songs to someone we know." She looked at Jack, hoping he might chip in with something.

"He's coming out of hospital," offered Jack.

"*Yes!* Yes, he was in an accident, so we want to do something special for him," said Charlotte, grateful for the tiny hint this was all based on altruistic reasons. Was it enough?

Mickey Bubbles looked from one of them to the other and back again, as though there might be more. "And you think that's an acceptable thing to do?"

"We really wanted to cheer Nick up. He's gone through a tough time."

"Are we talking about a child?" asked Mickey Bubbles. "Jeez, I've known some desperate parents in my time, but you two broke into my goddamned house!"

For a long moment, Charlotte thought about the idea of committing to the enormous lie, where Nick Bellingham was a courageous, cancer-surviving child. It would provide the only acceptable excuse for their current predicament. However she simply couldn't see a way to make it work out in the long run. Even if they borrowed a kid it would— No.

She looked across and could see Jack going through the same mental gymnastics. "Not a child, no. Although he is disabled."

"He *has* a disability," said Jack.

"That's what I said."

"No, you said he was disabled. That's making his disability his defining characteristic."

"I don't think it is. And I think it's correct, isn't it? Disabled people called themselves disabled. I'm sure of it."

"I think not."

"Anyway," Charlotte said to Mickey, feeling they were getting off point. "Nick *is* disabled." Even as Charlotte said the words, she realised she sounded as if she had some sort of hideously cynical scoring system for worthiness: like a cancer kid scored ten, but a guy in wheelchair was maybe a seven. "Um, he's also a nice guy. Really nice guy."

"You two need to leave now," said Mickey Bubbles. "Walk out of the door and you can be away before the cops get here."

"It would be a terrible shame though," said Jack, with his wide smile. "Missing out on an opportunity like that."

"People who want me to do a charity gig go through my agent," shouted Mickey. Charlotte thought he was losing his cool a little.

"I'm calling the cops." Mickey patted his dressing gown pocket and took out a phone.

"This opportunity," continued Jack. "You don't want to pass it up."

Mickey Bubbles scoffed.

Jack swivelled with his own phone and took a random

photo of the room they were in. "An opportunity for us to not distribute photos of your 'special rooms'."

Charlotte gaped. "Jack, what are you doing?" she whispered.

"Improvising," he said in a panicked voice.

"You fucking dare?" said Mickey, his eyes bulging.

Jack clicked another random photo. "Apparently, so, Mr Bubbles, sir."

Mickey narrowed his eyes at them. "This is blackmail. This is invasion of privacy. This is at least five years in the slammer for you low-lifes."

Jack took a photo of the half-naked Mickey. As Mickey stepped forward to swipe the phone from him, Jack stepped out of the way.

"It's a hundred grand from the sleaziest tabloid paper in the country and everlasting fame for you, sir."

"This is blackmail! Plain and simple!"

"It's just a small appearance, and maybe a song or two, at the home of man who just wants a little Christmas magic when he gets home from hospital," Charlotte suggested.

Jack tilted his head slightly and gave Mickey his sunniest smile. It made him look like a psychopath, but Charlotte held her nerve and tried to join in.

Mickey Bubbles put his phone away and checked his watch. "How far away we talking?"

"What?" said Charlotte.

"This differently-abled guy. How far?"

Charlotte wanted to punch the air in excitement, but she held back. "It's just in town," she said. "Not far at all."

Mickey huffed again. "And if I do this, I need to know that those photos are not going anywhere."

"Scouts' honour," said Jack with a smooth (and inaccurate) boy scout salute.

Charlotte and Jack followed Mickey into the main part of his house.

"Now, I need to get changed, but I want the two of you where I can see you, right?" he said.

They nodded and followed him up a huge, sweeping staircase. It was lined with life-sized portraits depicting Mickey Bubbles on stage, relaxing on a chaise longue, and looking wholesome as he hugged a golden retriever.

Charlotte thought the style of the decor was Louis XIV as reimagined for readers of *Hello* magazine, with lots of pale colours, gilt highlights and carefully curated blank spaces.

"Mr Bubbles, can I please ask a question?" Jack Hartigan said. "It's for my own personal curiosity, and the answer will go with me to my grave."

"What?"

"What exactly do you do in the holly room?"

"Well, it's actually based on some solid scientific thinking." Mickey's tone was recognisably that of someone being asked about their favourite thing. The need to share overcame the impertinence of the question and the awkwardness of the situation. "You know how in Asia, the bed of nails has been used for many years?"

"I thought it was a cheap parlour trick," said Jack.

"No!" said Mickey. "It does have that showy element, but it's all about the acupressure. It's the same with the holly room. If I roll naked on compacted holly, it improves my circulation."

"Pardon?" said Charlotte.

"Improves circulation, relieves stress and increases my energy levels. I highly recommend it. You may have noticed that the floor is graded for different experiences?"

"Graded?" said Jack. "No I don't think I did."

"The fresh, green holly is at one end. It's where one begins a treatment session. It's much softer. At the other end is the older, more brittle, dried-out holly. And of course there's a gradual transition where we rotate the crop. It's possible to get a very rich experience if you choose where to roll – from the softer greenery over to the spiky brittle part and back again. I always attain a deep, meditative state."

Charlotte shook her head as she half-listened to the conversation. She was taking advantage of Mickey being distracted to get some social media messages out.

POP UP CONCERT *TONIGHT! MICKEY BUBBLES PERFORMING LIVE.*

THE COMMENTS and likes began to pour in immediately. Jack would certainly be doing the same in a moment, so they were guaranteed a good turnout.

They entered Mickey's bedroom. It was enormous, and naturally it featured a huge four-poster bed, painted and carved with cherubs who looked very focused on waking the person sleeping with a quick toot on their horns.

"Take a seat," he called to them as he disappeared behind a screen with a suit carrier. "And please don't touch anything."

Charlotte and Jack exchanged a glance. Charlotte didn't think she'd ever seen a bedroom with a built-in lounge area before.

"Started the socials?" asked Jack.

"Most definitely," said Charlotte, holding up her phone. "There will be a lot of eyes on this. The press are already on the case."

"Oh, the local rags are probably just wondering what horrors we're going to cook up next."

When Charlotte saw Mickey emerge from behind the screen she instantly saw why he was so successful. Gone was the peeved homeowner who had found them in his most private space. Here was Mickey Bubbles: a bundle of focused charm and enormous charisma. He strode out into his bedroom as if he was on an arena stage.

"Looking amazing, Mickey!"

Charlotte caught something in Jack's expression. It was somewhere between envy and awe. Charlotte suspected Jack got a long way on his own charming smile, but here he was overshadowed by someone who wowed millions when he appeared on television.

"You have a car waiting, I assume?" Mickey asked.

"Oh fuck!" Charlotte and Jack both scrambled to order a taxi.

72

GALLAGHER

Gallagher was impressed with Anika. Not only had she come up with this weird idea, she had also got everyone to buy into it. Even Luka seemed to be looking forward to performing.

They had four songs perfected, deciding that was enough to deliver a mini concert. Anika packed away the Bluetooth speaker, karaoke PA, and was talking to Gillespie about his clothing options.

Gallagher clutched Luka's arm and whispered in his ear. "You've still got the money, right?"

"Sure I have," Luka said. "Bagged up in lovely canvas holdall. Where would I have spent it?"

"We need to get it into Sonia Patterson's hands."

"This I know."

"Can we get it to her tonight? It's the only way I'm gonna sleep."

Luka gave a small, thoughtful nod. "Is good idea. I will call her and she will meet us tonight. She will not just kill us for fucking kicks. I will send her a message."

Gallagher dared to dream. His dreams were small things, but they currently involved not being killed in a cider press and getting some rest. He felt as if his life would be tolerable if he could achieve just those things.

Anika clapped her hands together. "Right gang, here's the plan. Gillespie has wheels. We all go in his car – but we need to go via his house because he can borrow a fancy suit that belongs to his dad. There are also some real microphones he can get. Everyone ready to go?"

"Ready," said Gallagher.

Luka now held the tan-coloured holdall with all the money.

Anika held out her phone for the rest of them to see. "And I don't know which of you guys started shouting about this on social media, but there already seems to be a bit of local buzz. We're going to get a crowd at Mr Bellingham's house."

"A crowd?" quavered Gillespie. "Like – real people?"

"It's going to be great," said Anika. "Let's go."

Gallagher looked at Luka as they headed out. "Did you put it on social media?"

"Like fuck I did," Luka said back to him.

MICKEY 'DROPPING in to do a little greet and sing' apparently involved a significant amount of equipment from the Mickey

HEIDE GOODY & IAIN GRANT

Bubbles mansion. A call came through from Cameron as Jack was helping the taxi driver wrestle a box of sound equipment into the poor man's car boot.

Charlotte would normally be happy to ignore a call from Cameron at this hour, but for once, she had very good news to share. "Evening, Cameron!" she said. "Good news!"

"I hear!" he said. *"Mickey Bubbles performing live at a little Hedgelord sponsored concert. Platinum-level response there, Charlotte."*

"Thank you."

"Obviously, I'd rather we didn't have to splash that kind of cash, but if it takes Mickey Bubbles to win the day for us, then – damn it! – Big Boy Dom needs to dig deep and pay up."

"Oh, right. No. It's not going to cost us."

"Oh? I mean I was prepared to shell out the forty thousand."

"Forty thousand pounds?" she said, confused.

Mickey Bubbles was now looking at her across his artistically-lit driveway.

"Mickey's fee, right?" said Cameron.

"Oh, no. Mickey – Mr Bubbles – is doing this for free. He was moved by the story of Nick's plight and is offering his services for free."

"What's this about forty thousand pounds?" said Mickey.

"Is that him? Is that Mickey?" said Cameron, excited. *"Put me on speaker!"*

"Um, we're really busy and..."

"For forty k, you can put me on speaker, Charlotte."

Puzzled beyond measure, Charlotte put the phone on speaker.

"Hello, Mickey Bubbles!" said Cameron, apparently shouting to be heard across the miles.

"Hello," said Mickey. "Who's this?"

"Mickey, this is Cameron Clasp, owner of Hedgelord. We're very pleased you're willing to do this for us and waive your fee."

Mickey Bubbles, the consummate entertainer, chuckled warmly. "A delight to speak to you, Cameron. Truly. I've heard nothing but good things about you. You mention my fee? My appearance fee?"

Charlotte really had no idea what Cameron had been on about and now this plan, this fragile thing, felt like it might crumble at any moment.

"We'd set forty grand aside for you," said Cameron.

"Had you?" said Mickey.

"But if you're doing it for free, well, that's just wonderful."

Mickey gave Charlotte a piercing look. Charlotte's mind was a blank.

"Of course, I'll do it for free," said Mickey. "And Charlotte and Jack here assure me that any money you've set aside you'll donate to my favourite charity, the children's ward at St Wulfram's hospital."

"Oh, yes. That's capital," said Cameron. *"A lovely gesture and will play well in the press. Wait – did you say Jack? Is that Jack Hartigan there—?"*

Charlotte ended the call. Mickey was still looking at her.

"You weren't going to mention the forty thousand pounds?" he said.

"I had no idea," she said, honestly. "But I can assure you, Mr Bubbles, that any money we have available at the end of the evening, we'll absolutely give directly to the kids at St Wulfram's."

The mega-watt superstar grin reappeared. "Wonderful! This evening just gets better and better!"

73

ANIKA

Anika was surprised how good Gillespie looked in his dad's formal suit. She hadn't fully bought into the idea that Gillespie could pass as Mickey Bubbles up until this point, but seeing him in costume for the first time made her realise that not only did Gillespie have a lot of the right physical features, but he'd also worked up some decent Mickey Bubbles moves.

As Gillespie climbed back into his car's driving seat, transformation complete, Gallagher nodded at Luka, who looked equally surprised.

"Everyone buckled in, ready to go?" Gillespie asked, turning to smile at them all. Even his voice and mannerisms were different. He was now fully inhabiting the Mickey Bubbles persona.

Anika was busy on her phone. "Daffyd is on point!" she said. "He's already shouting about this all over social media."

"How does he even know it's happening?" Gallagher asked with a frown.

"I guess Cameron must have told him," said Anika. "Either that or his elf powers are so highly attuned to Christmassy events that he detected it."

"Like a creepy spidey-sense for Christmas fun?"

Anika gave directions to Nick Bellingham's house. "Along the Avenue, past the Croft and— Oh."

Her surprise was well-justified. Gillespie braked to a shuddering stop. Down the end of the road, in front of a the brightly lit homes of Nick Bellingham and his neighbours, a crowd of people had gathered. It looked like the whole estate had put on their hats and scarfs against the cold evening and come out together.

"Are they here for Mickey Bubbles or for this Bellingham guy coming home?" said Gillespie.

Anika looked at a couple of the banners on display. "I'd say..."

Gillespie took some deep breaths. "Well, I suppose we'd best do this." He put the car into gear, but Luka but his hand over Gillespie's.

"No. We cannot do it like this."

"What?"

Luka tutted. "Mickey Bubbles is chart-topping singing sensation. He does not turn up to gig in his own car. Especially not in a Škoda hatchback that smells of cookies."

"He's right," said Anika. "We need a bigger entrance. Back up the road a bit so we can think of something. We don't want them to spot you."

Gillespie drove the car away from the crowd of happy well-wishers.

"We need ideas," said Anika.

"Skis?" said Luka. "Is a nice image, very cosy."

"Er, I agree," said Anika. "Where will we get skis from?"

Luka waved a hand airily at the well-heeled houses. "We rip some of the wooden palings off these fences. They would pass as skis."

Anika attempted to evaluate the idea (which was pretty good) against the possible consequences (which were pretty bad). "It could work, but I feel as though there's something better. Maybe we come back to that one."

"Holy shit, I know!" yelled Gallagher, pointing down the road. "The ambulance! It's got to be bringing Nick Bellingham back from the hospital. You get in there and emerge *with him*. Nobody will be expecting that, will they?"

"Actually, that's surprisingly good—" Anika started to say, but Gillespie was already leaping out of the car.

"He's just going for it," said Gallagher.

"This has gone to his head," said Luka. "He thinks he's James fucking Bond."

Anika jumped out of the car and ran after Gillespie, who was now waving his arms to flag down the approaching ambulance. It stopped and, giving a thumbs up, Gillespie circled round to the rear doors. Anika ran to catch up.

"What's your game, mate?" grumbled the ambulance attendant.

Inside, Nick Bellingham sat on a seat, his neck in a brace and a dressing on his forehead. "What's going on?"

Gillespie opened his mouth. He was actually going to speak. The man had forgotten he sounded nothing like Mickey Bubbles. Anika elbowed Gillespie in the ribs and stepped into the ambulance, past the startled attendant.

"Mr Bellingham, Mr Bellingham. I'm Anika Chowdhry. I'm here with Mickey Bubbles. He's come to welcome you home."

Nick struggled to turn with his head in the brace. "What?"

Gillespie stepped inside and approached. He grabbed Nick's hand and shook it. Nick gasped as though he'd been zapped with electricity.

"How...? What...?"

"Mickey here heard of what happened and he and the team of us from Hedgelord thought it would be great if Mickey welcomed you home. Maybe even sang a couple of songs outside your house."

Nick stared at his hand, touched by the wondrous 'Mickey', then looked up, blinking tears at Gillespie's handsome countenance. "How is this possible?"

Gillespie opened his mouth to speak but Anika elbowed him again.

"Mickey is going to rest his voice until he's had a chance to sing," she said. "But would it be okay if we drove with you to your house."

"This is not normal procedure," muttered the attendant.

"Oh, give over, Kenny," said the driver from up front. "It's bladdy Christmas. Let them have their fun." And without waiting for the attendant to fully shut the door, the driver started the ambulance down the road.

"I can't believe this is happening," whispered Nick Bellingham in stunned elation.

"Yes, it is all quite unbelievable, isn't it?" said Anika, maintaining a smile.

74

GALLAGHER

While the ambulance rolled down the road, Gallagher and Luka hurried to get ahead of them with all the gear. Pushing through a crowd of adults and children with a karaoke system, speakers, and a big holdall of cash (because neither of them were letting that out of their sight) was not particularly easy.

"We need to set up," said Luka. "We want 'Mickey' out, sing a few and – poof! – go away in the night."

Gallagher found the perfect natural performing area in the front garden: on a part of Nick's lawn that was slightly elevated. It was currently home to the big bear he and Luka had destroyed and then rebuilt in quick order.

"'Scuse me, mate, we're setting up here," said Gallagher, and with more energy than actual strength, gave the big brute of bear a solid tackle, shoving him off to roll away across the grass.

"Okay," said Luka, once he'd set down the karaoke

speakers and plugged them into one of the big outdoor extension blocks by the wall. "You and me, stand here. When 'Mickey' starts to perform, we'll need to get him just front of us."

"We're going to be seen?"

"We're backing singers," said Luka. "You and me will have the plugged in mikes. Gillespie. He'll be silent."

"Won't he need to talk to the crowd?"

Luka looked at Gallagher. "You think they gonna buy a Mickey Bubbles with a speaking voice like his?"

"Can you just not do the accent?"

"Fuck you say? This is my voice, Gallagher! I'm not multi-talented impressionist. You do the talky bits."

"Me?"

"Try sounding like a smooth talking singer that your granny loves."

"Oh fuck, I dunno."

Gallagher looked over to the ambulance. It was slowly negotiating the crowd, so that it could reverse up to Nick Bellingham's drive. Even the arrival of an ambulance was drawing cheers from a crowd, and when Luka put the microphone to his lips and did a 'one-two-one-two' into it, they even cheered that.

The ambulance doors opened and Anika stepped down ahead of the ramp they were lowering for Mr Bellingham. She came straight over to Luka and Gallagher and took a microphone from Luka's hand.

"Ladies and gentlemen," she said. "It's the moment we've all been waiting for. Welcome home Nick Bellingham!"

There was a polite round of applause, but the crowd had

been summoned by the name of Mickey Bubbles and there was palpable expectation in the air.

75

ANIKA

Anika remained stunned by the size of the crowd that had appeared. There must have been two or three hundred people there. One of the neighbours had dragged a table onto the pavement and was doing a roaring trade selling plastic cups of mulled wine from a row of slow cookers plugged into an extension block that trailed down their drive. They also had a huge pile of mince pies for sale.

It was a wonderful turn-out for a man's return home. It was a frighteningly large number of people to see a fake Mickey Bubbles potentially exposed on stage.

Nick took a few moments to descend down the ramp from the ambulance in his wheelchair. As he appeared, Anika made large gestures and whoops of encouragement to make sure the crowd continued to appreciate him.

"And with him, your favourite singer and mine – *Mickey Bubbles!*" cried Anika.

The noise was deafening. The crowd roared, clapped their hands and stamped their feet. Nick Bellingham made his way along the pavement, down towards the garden. The lights of a hundred filming smartphones dotted the pavement. Cameras flashed. Over to the side, was that—? Oh, God, she thought, it *was* a TV film crew.

And throughout it all, Nick Bellingham wore an expression that Anika recognised. It was the face of a child on Christmas morning, coming downstairs and finding all the shiny Christmas gifts under the tree. It was an expression of unbridled, true joy.

"Nick! This is all for you!" she called. She passed the microphone back to Luka and then placed an unplugged microphone into the hands of Gillespie, who was grinning and waving at the crowd. "Stay in time with the others," she said, more quietly. "Luka is singing. You follow his lead."

Anika turned and signalled Gallagher that he should start talking.

"Hi everyone!" Gallagher begun.

Anika saw Gillespie's hand had dropped, as he basked in the adulation of the crowd. She grabbed his elbow and pressed the microphone back up to his face so that it would appear that he was speaking.

Gillespie nodded, walked to his performance spot and kept his mouth covered while Gallagher continued. "What a treat this is, huh? You look like a fun crowd of pop pundits! Are you all ready to hear some toe-tapping classics harking back to the times you loved the best?"

Anika thought Gallagher was basing his persona on some sort of cheesy radio DJ with a tortured mid-Atlantic accent.

She gave him a little hand signal to suggest that he might dial it back a bit.

"You know this is the most wonderful time of the year, right?" he said. The tone was better. The weird voice remained, but that was fine.

As far as Anika could tell, nobody had noticed it wasn't Gillespie talking.

"Are you ready for the first song?" Gallagher yelled to the crowd. Gillespie threw up his hands, a little too late, but nobody cared because they all erupted in huge shouts of "*Yes!*".

Gallagher nodded to Luka as the two of them took their places behind Gillespie.

Anika started the backing track on the playback system, and the three performers slipped into their roles. They had decided on a jazzed-up version of *Rudolph the Red-Nosed Reindeer* as the first number. It had the advantage of not being a regular Mickey Bubbles song, so nobody would notice any vocal inconsistencies. It also practically guaranteed that the audience would join in, which was a bonus.

Anika backed away to the front of the crowd. Her work was done. It was up to the guys now, and it seemed to be going so well. Luka and Gallagher had a small co-ordinated stepping routine, and Gillespie made lingering eye contact with members of the crowd as his gaze swept over them.

Luka started to sing, and once again Anika was impressed with his rich vocals. He was actually a good singer. The crowd joined in with the words, as predicted, and everybody was having an amazing time.

Anika allowed herself a small smile of satisfaction at how well things were going, but then the smile fell away from her face as she realised they were coming up to the part about all of the other reindeer. She gritted her teeth, hoping this crowd would restore her faith in humanity and resist the urge to say 'reindeers'.

The line came, and there was that creeping hiss again.

Anika felt a strong urge to yell out they were doing it wrong – but she was interrupted by a hand grabbing her elbow. She nearly leapt out of her skin when she saw it was her mum! Her mum and dad were there, bunched up on the edge of the crowd with all the other townsfolk.

"What are you doing here?" she said.

"Big Mickey Bubbles fan," said her dad, pointing at her mum.

Her mum's grip on her elbow was vice-like. Anika wasn't ready for this conversation yet. She'd not yet tried to explain the slutty elf pictures to them, and she had no idea how she would ever do that. She could already feel the weight of their condemnation upon her.

"You never told me you knew Mickey Bubbles!" said her mum with a little squee of excitement.

"Er, yeah," said Anika. "Through work."

76

CHARLOTTE

Mickey Bubbles strolled along the suburban road from where the taxi had dropped them off. Charlotte and Jack trailed behind, struggling with his wheeled suitcase of equipment. Charlotte hadn't expected this job to be so physical, but that was mainly because she hadn't realised she and Jack would effectively be roadies. Worse the wear from drink roadies at that.

"Someone else is singing," Mickey observed as they drew closer to Nick Bellingham's house.

He was right. There was music and soft tuneful crooning coming from the Bellingham residence.

"You didn't mention a support act," he said.

"Uh huh." Charlotte gave a nod and tried to buy herself some time. "This is all very last minute, you understand."

Mickey raised his eyebrows as the voice became clearer. "Is that meant to be me?"

"There's only one Mickey Bubbles!" Jack assured him.

"That over there is the area's number one Mickey Bubbles impersonator," said Charlotte.

Jack looked at her. Was he going to help?

"Oh yeah!" said Jack. "This guy is super popular. Name's, er, Mic the Bub. We tried to book him for an event, but he's so hard to get hold of. A true professional."

Charlotte thought that he was overcooking it a bit, but she kept a smile pasted onto her face. "That's right."

A crowd of locals, dressed against the December night, many with mince pies and cups of mulled wine in hand, turned to watch them approaching. Whatever sort of Mickey Bubbles impersonator they were all looking at, none of them had expected to see the genuine article coming up behind them.

"Mickey Bubbles accepts no imitations," said Mickey. "We need to switch on the battery pack, get the amplifier set up and ready to go."

He said this firmly and clearly, but it still took Charlotte a moment to realise that it was her job to do. "Um. Battery, amplifier."

Jack was already opening the case and breaking out boxes and cables.

Mickey 'helped' by selecting a wireless microphone from the box and turning it on.

Jack and Charlotte did as instructed, plugging this into that, switching that on, and placing speakers where required.

Charlotte had no idea how they managed to do it so quickly, but Mickey was amplified to his satisfaction before the end of *Rudolph the Red-Nosed Reindeer*.

"Damned singer pretending to be me," muttered Mickey, affronted.

"As soon as you're ready, we can have you take over, or do a thing," said Charlotte.

"Do a thing?" said Mickey Bubbles. His tone was caustic.

"You know. A rap battle or duelling banjos – something like that," Charlotte said.

"Call and response?" said Jack.

"Yes?" Charlotte said, even though she had no idea what that would look like.

"I need a better platform," said Mickey. "A stage."

The imitator was beyond the crowd in Nick's garden. Mickey would need to be higher up.

"On that car?" suggested Jack, pointing at a parked Škoda hatchback.

"It'll do," he said, and with a decent show of athleticism stepped up onto the bonnet and climbed onto the roof.

Now that Charlotte had a moment to stand still, she took stock of the scene before her. If she wasn't mistaken, the support act appeared to be that elf-hire, Gillespie, out of the grotto. How could that be? She'd heard his contributions to the animatronic bear soundtrack. He had a voice like a pig in blender.

"Hello again all you fun-loving Christmas groovers!" said the support act in a smooth voice. "Are you all having a good time?"

The crowd roared.

Charlotte realised Gillespie wasn't actually the one speaking. Was the voice coming from the familiar looking backing singers. Her gaze fell upon another elf, Anika, who held up a hand, counting down on her fingers, directing them all.

"Huh."

And beside her was Nick Bellingham, watching the performance with wet-cheeked wonder on his face.

"I will need maximum volume," said Mickey from the roof. "Crank it up and let's go."

Jack shrugged as he fiddled with some likely-looking dials and Mickey started to warm up.

"A-bam-bam, ba-badum."

His voice was thunderously loud, drowning out the sound of Gillespie.

The group of people who were being directed by Anika all looked over as if their heads were joined.

Half the crowd turned.

"I said a-bam-bam, ba-badum." Mickey added a little more of the tune, and a hip wiggle. Charlotte recognised that it was starting to form the introduction to one of his big hits: *The Very Heart of Christmas.*

"Mickey?" said a voice in the crowd.

Anika seemed to catch on and she started some huge hand signals to Gillespie, Luka and Gallagher. She counted down and then pointed at them to go.

"Bam! Bam!" sang the trio, in a fairly convincing pantomime.

The real Mickey noodled through some more of the introductory chords, leaving space for the others to contribute, but then he led the crowd in a huge round of applause.

"Let's give a big hand to our warm-up act shall we?" he

said, with a warm smile. "How great was that? Almost as good as yours truly."

A ripple went around the crowd. Some had caught on at the beginning of the small sparring match, but now everyone was on the same page. The Mickey Bubbles that shimmied lightly on top of a parked car was the real deal.

"And where's our man of the hour?" called Mickey. "The reason we're all here at this charity fundraising celebration? Mr—"

"Nick Bellingham!" Charlotte hiss-whispered to him.

"Nick Bellingham! Get over here, man!"

Bewildered but elated, the injured Nick Bellingham wheeled down to the pavement and across the road to be at the feet of Mickey Bubbles.

"Oh, man, oh, man," grinned Mickey. "It's good to see you, Nick. I've heard so much about you."

"Me?"

"Oh, yes. You, my friend. With this beautiful house in this beautiful neighbourhood, doing so much to lift people's spirits at this time of year. You are *The Very Heart of Christmas.*"

And a beat later, he was singing the opening lines of his Christmas hit.

She might have been still drunk, but Charlotte thought it was possibly the most seamless piece of musical showmanship she had ever seen. Mickey sang and the crowd danced along in joy, their previous confusion forgotten, all eyes on the master crooner.

77

GALLAGHER

"Is that the real Mickey Bubbles?" said Luka as Anika took the microphone from him.

"I have no idea," she said.

The guy across the road sure had the moves and he really did look like Gillespie. Maybe Gillespie in fifteen years' time.

Gallagher felt the relief wash over him as he handed his microphone over. "Thank fuck that's over."

"I can't believe this is happening," said Gillespie. "Mickey Bubbles is dancing on top of my car."

"To be honest, I think I might be having some sort of stress-based hallucination," said Gallagher. "It's like every time I think that things can't get any more weird they fucking do. Oh, look, and here comes Sonia Patterson," he said with giddy indifference.

The drug dealer and her huge goon, Vincent, weaved their way through the crowd towards them. Just looking at the pair of them made the cider press bruise in Gallagher's head throb. Sonia wore a thick coat, fur-trimmed gloves, and utter indifference to her surroundings.

She did not speak until she was right up in front of Gallagher and Luka. "Is this your idea of a clandestine meeting?"

"It's where we are," said Luka.

"We have the money," said Gallagher.

Sonia looked at Anika. "Who the fuck is this?"

"I'm, um..." said Anika.

"She is no one. She is an elf," said Luka.

"Piss off, elf," said Sonia.

Anika glanced nervously at Luka and Gallagher.

"It's okay," Gallagher reassured her. "It's fine. Go get some mulled wine or something."

Anika reluctantly backed away.

Sonia sniffed and looked at the two men, then at the holdall in Luka's hand. "Is that it?"

"It is. And then some," said Luka.

Sonia nodded to Vincent. Vincent took the bag. He cradled it in his arms, unzipped it and looked inside.

"You can count it," said Gallagher.

"You think I should do that here?" she sneered.

"It is all there," said Luka.

"Of course it is," she said. "Cos if it isn't..."

"Shall I call the Snowman?" said Vincent.

Sonia shook her head. "I'll call him. Smooth things over personally." She looked at the two friends. "You two still here?"

"But we're square?" said Luka.

"What?"

"We're done? Finished? Resolved?"

Gallagher was only too happy to run away while he still retained a solid skull and all his fingers, but it seemed Luka needed a definitive answer.

"Yes. We're fucking square," said Sonia. "Now, get the fuck out of my sight."

Gallagher definitely didn't need telling twice. He pulled Luka away and didn't breathe easy again until they were halfway through the crowd.

78

CHARLOTTE

Mickey Bubbles finished up his short set with a rendition of *It's a Holly Jolly Christmas*. He belted out the last note and the crowded whooped and clapped in delight.

"Thank you, everyone! Welcome home, Nick! Goodnight!"

He didn't linger. He clean-jumped down from the roof of the little car while folks were still applauding wildly. He tossed his microphone to Charlotte.

"Get all the gear packed up. Neatly," he instructed crisply, then made a beeline straight for Nick Bellingham. He took Nick's hand in a firm shake. "Nick Bellingham – it's a total delight to meet you. Your home..." He took a deep emotional breath. "It's everything we love about Christmas, isn't it?"

Nick was speechless with delight and adoration. Mickey touched the fairy lights adorning his wheelchair.

"And you've really pimped your ride, festive-style, man."

"Thank you, sir," Nick whispered.

"And you get well soon, *sir*," said Mickey, treating him to a gigawatt grin of wholesome charm before turning back to Charlotte and Jack. "You not packed this up yet?"

Charlotte and Jack fumbled over each other to get the speaker and cables and other paraphernalia back in their case.

"Good. You're gonna delete those photos, show me you deleted them, and then we're collecting the charity money for the children at St Wulfram's Hospital."

"Er, yes. Yes, of course," said Charlotte.

Mickey turned to gladhand some of the nearest estate residents who wanted a chance to touch a bona fide Yuletide celebrity.

"So, this charity money?" said Jack.

"I know nothing about it," said Charlotte.

"Forty thousand pound, you said."

"It was Cameron who mentioned it."

"Well, Mickey's going to want to see it." Jack closed the case on the speaker. "I think I saw him here."

"Really?" She looked round. "If he's the one who stumped up the forty grand, he probably wants to see it handed over. And if there's forty grand of charity donations to give, I want TV and newspaper crews on it."

"Ah, the big win for Hedgelord," he said. She caught the tone.

For a few hours, they hadn't been enemies. Jack Hartigan had not been the smiling front man for the soulless corporate hellhole that was Bloomers. Charlotte found she'd actually forgotten there was a war for Christmas to be won here.

Nick Bellingham came up to the two of them. Mickey Bubbles had moved through the crowd, holding out his hands to touch the faithful like a wandering messiah.

"You two did this?" said Nick, stretching his neck in his brace. "You put this little show on?"

Charlotte looked at Jack, who shrugged.

"Yes, we did," she said. "I'll be honest – I'm surprised we managed it. But we wanted to get Mickey Bubbles to welcome you home because ... well..."

"Because we're really sorry for what happened," said Jack.

"Yeah, really, really sorry," said Charlotte. "The fireworks and the drones and the—"

Nick held up a calming hand. "Christmas excitement got the better of you, didn't it?"

"Yes," she said. It wasn't true, but it was a version of true.

"Happens to me all the time," said Nick.

"So we're forgiven?" said Jack.

Nick made an open handed gesture, a maybe. "Next year, maybe we should work together on what the big showpiece display should look like. I've got some big ideas, drawn them up on the computer. New Year, you should come round and we'll look at them together."

"We could do that," said Charlotte slowly, looking at Jack.

"We could," he said, equally wary.

79

ANIKA

Cameron Clasp was talking to Anika's parents and Anika didn't know what to do about that.

On the surface, Cameron was saying nice things about her. And that was good. Her parents had discovered she was elfing for a living at the expense of sensible, dull university studies, and anything that painted that decision in a good light was surely positive. And yet there was always something about the way Cameron said things that sounded, well...

"Oh, she's an absolute lightning bolt," enthused Cameron as he shook Mr Chowdhry's hand for the third time. "Shooting here, there and everywhere like a young Zola Budd. One minute she's singing with the adorable tots who've come to see Santa, the next she's dolling herself up to give our charitable donations."

"We saw," said Anika's mum, unconvinced. "She's meant to be focused on her university course."

"Pah! University never did me any good!" grinned Cameron. "I went to Eton and then Trinity and what bloody good did it do me? I might have worked in the Square Mile and made my first million before I was twenty-five, but it's only when I opened Hedgelord and, you know, really got my hands dirty with the true salt of the earth people—" he unhelpfully clapped his hand on Anika's shoulder as he said this "—that I understood what work and true effort could bring as a reward."

"She's not salt of the earth," said Anika's mum. "She's a straight A student who is going to get her degree and a proper job."

"And miss out on the learning experience of working in retail?" Cameron flung his arms wide. "What other eighteen year old—"

"Nineteen," said Anika.

"—nineteen year old could pull together a show like this in only a few hours?"

"She did all this?" said Anika's dad.

"She bloody did. Her and two of my most dedicated workers. Her and a tiny budget of forty thousand pounds secured an evening of high class performance and top notch PR for Hedgelord—"

"Forty thousand pounds," said Charlotte Mitchell, abruptly joining the circle. She gripped both Anika's and Cameron's arms. "Someone mentioned forty thousand pounds."

"Cheap at twice the price," grinned Cameron.

"Wh-where is the forty thousand pounds?" said Charlotte.

"Why?" said Anika, feeling her stomach flip.

"Because Mickey Bubbles is expecting a fee, or at least a donation to the kids at the local hospital."

"Oh, that is lovely," said Anika's mum. "Very noble."

"We're a very giving company," said Cameron.

"The money," said Charlotte.

Cameron waved a big finger at Anika. "Young Anita here had it. Her and those two plantsmen."

"Luka and Gallagher?" said Charlotte. Anika could see the unease on her face. "Where is it now?"

"Um," said Anika.

"They gave it to that woman to look after," said Gillespie, pointing across the way.

Anika could have punched him, but what good would that have done.

"Mickey Bubbles, delighted to meet you in person!" said Cameron, shaking Gillespie's hand.

"That is Gillespie, one of our elves," said Charlotte, peeved.

"Bloody hell! Really? What a talented bunch we have, eh?"

"Which woman?" Charlotte demanded.

"That one," said Gillespie, pointing to Sonia Patterson, standing by a car across the road and talking on her phone.

Cameron put his hand to his brow as he looked. "Patty? Patty Fufu?"

"That's Patty Fufu?" said Anika.

"Woman's a demon on the squash court, I tell you," he said. "Not so good a golfer."

The crowd parted and Mickey Bubbles swept through

with the local BBC news crew in tow. "Come on then, let's do this thing," he said.

"Who's this?" said Cameron.

"*This* is Mickey Bubbles," said Charlotte.

"And does he work at Hedgelord too?"

"Ah," said the singer. "You're the guy with the cheque for charity."

"Not on me," said Cameron. "But the cash is just over here."

Cameron led the way. Anika raced to keep up. She didn't know why, because the only thing that was going to happen was a total car crash in which the charity didn't get the money, Hedgelord's good PR vanished in a puff of smoke, and Luka and Gallagher would lose life or limb to a vengeful drug dealer.

"This way, this way," said Cameron. "You'll love Patty – Sonia Patterson I should say. Wonderful woman. Runs one of the most successful floristry businesses in England. Patty! Patty!"

Anika was there, two steps ahead of the others. Sonia Patterson had her back to the crowd, talking on the phone, totally unaware of what was about to descend on her.

"Yes, sir," she was saying. "All resolved. The books balance. No more logistics problems our end, I promise. Trust me, all's square."

"Patty!" called Cameron as he strode forward.

Sonia turned and her eyes widened. "Have to call you back, sir," she said quietly, ended the call, and plastered an unconvincing smile on her face. "Cameron! Hello! What a surprise to see you here!"

"My show," he said. "My team's big event. Glad you could come." He looked about. "Not brought your little scamp with you?"

"No. Just Vincent."

Vincent looked deeply uncomfortable to see himself and his boss surrounded by a small crowd of strangers and what clearly took him a moment to recognise as a TV camera crew.

"Fuck," he whispered.

Without hesitation, Cameron reached down, took hold of the handle of the holdall Vincent was carrying and lifted it up.

"Patty's been looking after this for us," he said to Mickey Bubbles and the TV people.

"What?" said Sonia, also putting a hand on the holdall strap.

"Willy Sandford, BBC," said the silver-haired reporter. "This is a wonderful good news story."

"Local businesses giving to charity at this special time of the year," said Cameron.

"What?" said Sonia again.

"Your generosity to the children at St Wulfram's Hospital is truly valued," said Mickey, reaching out and adding yet another hand to the bag handle.

"You rolling, June?" asked the reporter. "We get this segment recorded and it can go on the late news at ten thirty."

"What?" said Sonia, a third time.

"Oh, this will look great," said Cameron. "You and me and Mickey Bubbles. The real Mickey Bubbles, right?"

"Boss?" said Vincent.

Anika could see him bristling. She was in no doubt that if Sonia Patterson gave the word, this man would wallop everyone trying to take the bag of cash from them and make a run for it.

"Sonia Patterson, right?" said the reporter, Willy. "I think you did the flowers for my niece's wedding."

"Oh," she said.

"This is going to be really nice segment. Mickey ... Mr Bubbles: let's make sure we get you in shot."

And as Anika watched, the strangest and most disturbing transformation came over Sonia. From stern-faced confusion to bitter calculation to something that, if Anika was to put a name to it, she would describe as sickened resignation.

"A charity donation," she nodded.

"You chipping in too, Patty?" said Cameron, delighted.

"Oh, more than you know," she said. She glared at Vincent and he let go of the bag and retreated into the shadows. She invisibly swallowed her unhappiness. "Let's do this thing."

"That's great," said Willy. "Now, big smiles everyone. I'm going to chat to Mickey first and then move along to you two..."

80

GALLAGHER

Mickey Bubbles might have stopped singing, but now the owner of the over-decorated house had started to play Christmas music through his outdoor speaker system. People mingled in the street and chatted with their neighbours, while children, let out far after it was time to be indoors, ran round playfully through the people.

Luka passed Gallagher a cup of mulled wine from the stall. Steam curled up into the chilly air.

Gallagher sipped it. It was hot, spicy and aromatic. "Christ, it feels good to be alive," he said.

"Is that so?" said Luka. There was an undertone to his voice.

"Yes, it does," said Gallagher.

"Wasn't it only a few days ago that you said you would kill yourself if you had the guts?"

"Maybe."

Luka nodded sagely and sipped his hot wine. "Bear attack therapy worked on you."

"Yeah," said Gallagher sarcastically. "Or maybe it was having my head put in a fucking cider press and being forced to nick forty grand that has snapped my tiny little brain."

Luka made a thoughtful noise. "Or bear therapy. Maybe it is like your story and now the cows that were put in your bedroom have been taken away again, you can sleep easy."

"For now."

Through the crowd, Anika approached, bringing a middle-aged Asian couple with her. "Mum, dad," she said. "This is Luka and Gallagher. They helped me sort out this evening's entertainment."

Mr Chowdhry was all genial smiles, but Mrs Chowdhry looked the two men up and down with a critical eye.

"And what are you two?"

"Lapsed Jew," said Luka.

"Happy, I think," said Gallagher.

"These two are the hardest working people at Hedgelord," said Anika. "And they're very lucky men who pulled off tonight's ... whatever this thing is called."

"Easy as piss," said Luka.

"And Anika is your manager?" asked Mr Chowdhry.

Gallagher held back a smirk. "Oh. Oh, yeah. She's very good at giving orders."

"A real Smartypants," said Luka.

Anika gave them both a little waist-high thumbs up that her parents couldn't see.

81

CHARLOTTE

A taxi came to collect Mickey Bubbles. It parked a little distance down the road. Charlotte Mitchell and Jack Hartigan lugged Mickey's gear down the road and put it in the back of the taxi.

"Phones," said Mickey.

Charlotte knew exactly what he was talking about. She showed him her phone as she went into her images folder and deleted the pictures she'd taken in his house. She also showed him as she opened her phone's recycling bin and emptied it.

"All gone," she said.

Mickey watched as Jack did the same.

"And you ain't got any of them stashed anywhere online?" said Mickey. "Cos I tell you, if you do, I've got me some powerful friends. New York, Chicago, Vegas kind of friends – if you get my meaning."

"We do," said Charlotte.

"Serious men in hats," said Jack. "We understand."

"Good," said Mickey.

Jack shut the car boot. Mickey stood in the road and gave them one of his trademark grins. "I never want to see either of you again as long as I live," he said merrily and climbed in the taxi, which pulled away into the night.

Charlotte watched it go until it was out of sight. "I had hoped he'd grow to like us," she said.

"Like you give a fuck," said Jack.

"I give a fuck. I give lots of fucks."

Her smartwatch buzzed. She didn't bother to check today's profanity score.

They turned and slowly ambled back towards the impromptu street party.

"You really deleted all the photos off your phone?" said Jack.

"I did," she said. "You?"

"Uh-huh," he nodded.

She sniffed. "Of course, I didn't say anything about the videos I took."

Jack grinned. "Me neither."

He gestured at the houses ahead, with the garishly glowing centrepiece that was Nick Bellingham's house. "This looks nice," he said.

"In a really cheesy Christmassy kind of way," she agreed.

"The things we achieve when we team up," he said, lightly.

"Yeah," she said. "This was a one-time thing."

"Absolutely." He made a satisfied noise. "Of course, none of this would have happened if you'd put orders in for the

LumaGrid display system at last year's Xmas Expo. Nick wouldn't have even been tempted to come to us."

"Oh, I see. So it's my bad buying strategy at fault here, not your underhanded poaching of customers?"

He made a silent, 'it is what it is' gesture. "Better luck next year," he said.

"This Christmas isn't done yet."

"Oh, Hedgelord's still got some fight left in it, has it?"

"Going to pound Bloomers into the fucking ground," she said happily.

"That's the spirit," he said. "Now, let's get some mulled wine and a mince pie. I'm starting to get the horrible feeling I'm almost sober again."

"Can't have that," she agreed and they went off together in search of something warm and alcoholic.

ACKNOWLEDGMENTS

As always, there are numerous people who contribute to the writing of a book.

Heide and Iain would especially like to thank Kirsty Farnfield who gave them some valuable advice when it came to writing about wheelchairs.

Special thanks to Gerald, Beth, Josh and Lynn at Planters Garden Centre. Hedgelord is definitely not modelled on Planters, but they were kind enough to let Heide and Iain peek behind the curtain and see the potential for a fun setting.

ABOUT THE AUTHOR

Heide Goody lives in North Warwickshire with her family and pets.

Iain Grant lives in South Birmingham with his family and pets.

They are both married, but not to each other.

ALSO BY HEIDE GOODY AND IAIN GRANT

Runaway Santa

Christmas at Hedgelord Garden Centre should be simple—trees, tinsel, and a grotto full of jolly Santas. But when one of those Santas goes rogue and films an incriminating adult movie, with Hedgelord's grotto as the backdrop, sales manager Charlotte Mitchell finds herself in the middle of a festive disaster.

The only way to save Hedgelord's reputation is to track down the wayward Santa and secure the footage before it's released. Unfortunately, she's not the only one on the case — Jack Hartigan, her infuriatingly charming rival from Bloomers garden centre, is also in pursuit. Worse still, Santa has already fled to Lapland.

With time running out and disaster closing in, Charlotte abandons her responsibilities and embarks on a chaotic, high-stakes chase across Europe by sea, rail, and air — all while stuck with Jack at her side.

Runaway Santa delivers a tale of gangsters, gunmen, and unexpected corpses.

With Hedgelord's future hanging by a thread, can Charlotte outrun disaster, outwit her enemies, and save Christmas?

Runaway Santa

Clovenhoof

Getting fired can ruin a day...

...especially when you were the Prince of Hell.

Will Satan survive in English suburbia?

Corporate life can be a soul draining experience, especially when the industry is Hell, and you're Lucifer. It isn't all torture and brimstone, though, for the Prince of Darkness, he's got an unhappy Board of Directors.

The numbers look bad.

They want him out.

Then came the corporate coup.

Banished to mortal earth as Jeremy Clovenhoof, Lucifer is going through a mid-immortality crisis of biblical proportion. Maybe if he just tries to blend in, it won't be so bad.

He's wrong.

If it isn't the murder, cannibalism, and armed robbery of everyday life in Birmingham, it's the fact that his heavy metal band isn't getting the respect it deserves, that's dampening his mood.

And the archangel Michael constantly snooping on him, doesn't help.

If you enjoy clever writing, then you'll adore this satirical tour de force, because a good laugh can make you have sympathy for the devil.

Get it now.

Clovenhoof

Sealfinger

Meet Sam Applewhite, security consultant for DefCon4's east coast office. .

She's clever, inventive and adaptable. In her job she has to be.

Now, she's facing an impossible mystery.

A client has gone missing and no one else seems to care.

Who would want to kill an old and lonely woman whose only sins are having a sharp tongue and a belief in ghosts? Could her death be linked to the new building project out on the dunes?

Can Sam find out the truth, even if it puts her friends' and family's lives at risk?

Sealfinger

Printed in Dunstable, United Kingdom

74370114R10240